The Fence And Then The Trees

JF Smith

ISBN: 1495268942
ISBN-13: 978-1495268946

<010112>

Disclaimer

This novel is a work of fiction. All characters and events in this work are strictly fictional and any resemblance to actual persons (living or dead) or events is purely coincidental.

Contents

The
Fence
And Then
The
Trees

Day 1 – Thursday, March 23rd, 2000

Orange sherbet? How the hell is that supposed to help?

Jack shuffled as he was led down the long, concrete hallway. It was a hallway built of cinderblock with a bare concrete floor. And then painted the color of cinderblock. In spite of everything on his mind, his attention diverted just long enough to wonder why anyone would paint cinderblocks the color of cinderblock. To be fair, there *was* a stripe running down the hall the color of orange sherbet. Jack guessed it was supposed to cheer things up a little bit. It didn't work very well.

Jack listened for the noise. He was expecting a much worse noise. He had heard that the noise would be shocking and overwhelming, but it wasn't too bad here. Instead, it was the smell that hit him. It was a mixture of wet concrete, institutional cleaning supplies, body odor, and then a little acrid, but stale, vomit just to complete the feral aura. Something like a locker room in a warehouse. Actually, Jack knew too well what it reminded him of – his junior high school. Having those memories rekindled did nothing to ease his mind.

He dragged his feet along the bare concrete to try and slow time down before it was a done deal, but was shoved by the shoulder and told to keep it moving. He knew he was already here and had really lost it a while ago, but it still felt like the last few moments of freedom. Until he was in that cell, he was still free and anything could happen.

The month he had spent in jail prior to now entering prison had been but a brief blur to Jack. Waiting for trial and then the trial itself had hardly made any impression on him at all; it was like it was all something happening to someone else. He had given up at that point and any fuss society wanted to make over what he had done had been irrelevant. But now he was just angry. And scared. Angry about what had happened, and scared about what might happen now.

Once they got to the cell block proper, the guard directed Jack and the other guy upstairs and down the tier past a few cells. Jack looked at the guard, who had the name "Harper" on his badge. He was a little bit taller than Jack, and seemed to be in excellent shape. The other guy, another inmate, was a skinny black guy who he met on the bus ride to the prison; he looked to be about 25 or so with his hair braided into tight corn-rows. Jack had noticed on the bus that the guy had had some plastic beads tied at the end of each corn-row, but they were gone now, taken away during his intake processing, apparently. The guy had said on the bus that his name was T-Daddy and that he was going to be running this prison within a month. Jack had thought immediately that the only thing this guy knew how to run was his mouth, and was probably an expert at that particular skill. This was probably his first time in prison, just like Jack.

All the cell doors were open and the cells they passed were empty except for one. One cell had a guy on a bunk reading, who looked up as Jack was led past.

At the fourth cell down, the guard directed Jack into the cell.

The guard smiled a big, insincere smile with insincere white teeth and said "Home Sweet Home."

He looked at his watch, then at Jack, and said, "Most everyone's out in the yard for another 45 minutes. In about an hour you'll hear a bell sound letting you know it's chow time. You'll know where to go, just follow everyone else." The guy that had been in his cell reading had now cautiously poked his head out to see the two new guys.

The guard named Harper looked at the other prisoner and said, "Prisoner Clinton, follow me." And he turned and continued down the tier with T-Daddy Clinton.

Jack stood there for a second with his prison-issued supplies in his hand. He expected the cell door to clang loudly shut, sealing him in for the next three years, but it just sat there open. Jack assumed that prisoners were somewhat free to go during "yard time."

He turned to look at the cell. It was tiny, and there was someone else obviously assigned to it besides himself. Just like the hall, the walls were cinderblock, and painted the color of cinderblock. No feeble orange sherbet gesture in here, though. The cell was lit by one overhead light in a metal cage; even the light bulbs were imprisoned. On one side were bunk beds. The top one was obviously used. The bottom one still had the mattress rolled up and "clean" sheets next to it. In the center of the back wall was a sort of industrial, single-piece toilet and lavatory with a polished stainless steel "mirror" fixed into the wall above it. On the right hand wall was a row of simple, rounded pegs for hanging clothes and then a desk/shelf unit with a simple plastic chair. On the pegs were a couple of spare sets of prison-issued clothes. The desk unit was bare except for a clean, rolled-up towel on an upper shelf.

At the point when his trial had concluded and he had been convicted, Jack had finally awakened from his stupor and depression. That's when his anger had hardened, and the fear started to set in. It drove him into a survival mode, planning as much as possible how to live through three years in prison. He asked anyone that would answer him for as much information as possible on prison to start planning out how to survive. Almost universally, he was warned that how he handled his first day or two would define the rest of his prison term.

He looked out of the open cell door again. By some miracle, Jack had managed not to have to actually face any other inmates yet, but he knew he was on borrowed time in that respect. He was grateful for the additional time to steel himself for the troubles that were sure to come. He hung up his spare prison uniform up on a free peg and put his few prison-issued toiletries up on the shelf over the toilet. He looked at the other toiletries that were already on the shelf that belonged to whoever else was in this cell, but they were standard issue and didn't tell any secrets about the other person at all.

Whoever else was in the cell worried Jack tremendously. It was probably going to be trouble no matter what. It was the degree of trouble, and there was a wide range of unpredictable possibilities, that bothered him. He had made his career out of restricting outcomes to the narrowest set of predictable results possible. It was how a good con man got the results he wanted every time. But people were tricky. Jack had thought he had a good sense about people, that he could tell a fair amount just by observing them for a little while. But lately, he wondered about exactly how good he was at it given how he had wound up here.

He shook himself out of these thoughts, walked over to the door of the cell and looked out again. PattX, as people called it instead of Patterson Correctional Facility, didn't have cells on both sides of the wing. He looked across to a bank of large frosted windows, heavily barred. How enlightened of the Georgia Department of Corrections to have windows to let natural light in. But there were still big bars on them. It might be a "close" security prison, but there was no reason to tempt people into trying crazy things.

Jack stepped back over to the lower bunk and unrolled his mattress and set up his sheets. He realized there was no pillow on his bunk and looked around to see if he just didn't see it. Then he looked up and realized he had a tough decision to make. The top bunk had two pillows. He knew that in a place like this, taking a pillow, even one that was rightly his, could easily wind up getting him in the prison hospital damn quick. Normally, Jack would never take a chance like that without more information first. It was a con man's best friend – know and anticipate who you're dealing with.

But he also knew that if he didn't assert himself strongly and immediately, as soon as possible, he'd wind up a doormat in all kinds of demeaning ways faster than an insurance company could deny a claim. He took the spare pillow and put it on his bed. Jack had been in some scraps before and wasn't afraid to stand up for himself, but this place would be a world of different kinds of fighting.

Unconsciously at the thought of how physical this place would be, he stood before the mirror over the sink to assess his chances once again. He had always had rather unremarkable looks, the better to blend in and not be noticed given what he did for a living. His brown hair and brown eyes were like hundreds of others that people saw every day. His build was slim, but not particularly muscular. Not a good way to instill wariness in others here. Probably his best feature was his shut mouth. He reminded himself often that his shut mouth was one of the best things about him... as in, he knew when to keep his fat trap shut versus saying too much and digging himself in too deep. The counterpoint to that was knowing when to talk... when to be charming, flatter people, gain their trust by appearing open to them. All without saying too much.

He sat down on the bed to wait. If it hadn't been for the fucking gun and his reaction to it, he'd probably be in a minimum security prison, and hardly worried about his safety at all. At least PattX wasn't maximum security. He doubted he would last three days in one of those.

The noise level outside his cell rose and Jack knew the other inmates were starting to head back in. He was anxious at being around a bunch of prisoners he knew nothing about, and even more agitated thinking about who he might be stuck in the small cell with. He didn't have to wait long to meet his cellmate.

A hulking, dark haired man was being led roughly back by an equally huge black guard, who was yelling at the inmate. The guard pushed the inmate into the cell with Jack, half muttering and half yelling, "Pullin' that goddamn shit! You 'dis close to gettin' the hole!"

The inmate was huge, at least six foot five inches, with short, dark hair, and every bit of 260 pounds. The guy glared at the guard standing outside the cell. Details were important to him, and Jack noticed that even with the cell door open, the guard kept to the side to keep the bars there between him and the inmate. The guard glared for a second more at the prisoner, who never even turned around to see Jack there.

"Dumb fuck!" growled the guard through the bars.

And then, quicker than Jack could see, as fast as a snake strike, the inmate's hand shot out through the bars that separated him from the guard and punched the guard right in the eye, hard. The guard fell back against the railing behind him and his hand went to his eye, and then he doubled up a little. The guy then spat through the bars on the guard.

"Goddamn Adder! Lock down 205, 205, 205!!" shouted the guard into the radio on his lapel. Jack could now hear a lot of yells from below as other inmates he couldn't see realized what had happened. Almost immediately, the cell door slammed shut very hard and fast.

Jack hadn't made a sound during the entire thing, but it scared him bad to realize he was now locked in with this guy. The inmate named Adder had never looked at him, his gaze instead locked on the guard outside the cell, but then his hand shot out back towards Jack, warning "Don't even move."

Slowly, and while holding his finger out at Jack, Adder stopped watching the guard and slowly turned to face Jack. He dropped his hand and looked at Jack with piercing, deep set gray eyes for a second, but he otherwise had no expression on his face. Jack felt like his lungs had just swapped places in his chest, and he involuntarily took a small step back. The guy was huge and very cold. He turned back to the guard right as two other guards came running up, both with clubs out.

One of the guards said into his lapel, "Open it up."

The cell door clanged open again as one of the guards looked at Jack and yelled, "Against the wall!"

Jack immediately flattened himself against the back wall, and the two guards focused all their attention on the guy named Adder. Adder was standing there with both legs spread out a little and hands ready.

The guard yelled again, "Against the wall, Adder!!"

But Adder didn't seem to be in a cooperative mood. He stood his ground, clearly ready for a fight. The guards hesitated just a bit, deciding how to approach the situation. The older one grumbled, "Oh, fuck this shit," pulled out a Taser gun and shot the barbs right into Adder's midsection. Adder fell to the ground, writhing. The guards watched for a second to make sure, then the other guard came in, kept his eye on both inmates, and put cuffs on Adder's hands and shackles on his feet. Only then was the Taser finally turned off. Adder lay there for a second, before finally sitting up.

The older guard said into his lapel radio, "We got him under control."

He turned to look outside the cell at the guard that Adder had hit and said, "You ok, Jones?"

His hand was still on his eye, but the guard said, "Yeah. Sonofabitch!"

The older guard said, "Go on to the infirmary and have it checked."

Then he looked at Adder, who had not said a word the whole time, but was clearly still smoldering and watching the guards with hatred. The guard looked like he wanted to kick Adder, but he held back. He said to Adder, "Three days."

They yanked Adder up and pulled the barbs out of his abdomen, a little roughly, and led him out. As Adder passed the guard he had hit, the guard sucker punched him in the back of the head. This almost caused Adder to fall forward, but the other guards had yanked back on his arms. The guard looked over at Jack with a scowl and said, "What the fuck you lookin' at, fish?" and then walked away.

Jack heard someone outside the cell mock the guard and yell, "What you lookin' at, fish?"

Jack was still flattened against the wall. He finally relaxed a little and realized he was covered in a thin layer of sweat. He moved back towards the center of the cell, but didn't know what to do with himself. Several inmates wound up passing by his cell laughing. One of them, an effeminate black guy pointed at Jack and said to the others, "Got some new shit in there! Adder gonna spit that bitch out!" The others, fortunately, seemed more interested in what had happened to the guard than in Jack.

Right then, an alarm bell rang. Jack continued to stand there still taken aback by what had happened. Outside his cell, he saw T-Daddy strut past, ready for an appearance at dinner. The other inmates who had gone by a moment ago now passed back by again. They walked more slowly this time, checking out Jack a little more closely. One of them said to Jack, "You got some pussy for me, boy?" and they laughed. Jack just watched and the others moved on past.

Jack finally budged. He stepped outside his cell and saw them heading down the stairs at the end of the tier. Trailing behind them was the inmate he had seen alone in the cell earlier on his way up. He headed down to the stairs at the end of the tier walkway. He noticed for the first time that there was a glass observation and control enclosure over the stairway that had a clear birds-eye view up and down both the first and second tiers. A guard was sitting in it keeping an eye on things.

He got downstairs and saw the last of the inmates headed down the hall and past the TV room to the dining hall. Some were turning around to get a look at Jack and start sizing him up. He got in the line for dinner and looked around at the dining room filling up. The inmate in line in front of him, a skinny Hispanic guy, kept turning around and looking at him, but Jack just ignored him.

There was a half-height wall separating the chow line from the rest of the dining hall. The dining hall itself was just a large rectangular room with no windows. Just cinderblocks and bare lights in cages.

Jack looked out over the dining hall to check each table. There were about eight tables or so that held about ten people each. Jack was looking for a specific table for tonight. The first two tables were totally full already. The third table was all black, with everyone obviously gathered around the big black guy in the middle, who was talking to the guy next to him and pointing at someone farther up in line. The next table was also all black and seemed to be spillover from the third table. The fifth and sixth tables were a mixture of people, but again they seemed to be gathered around a smaller white guy at the fifth. The seventh and eighth tables also seemed to be a mixture, but as far as Jack could tell, no one was the "center" of those tables. He picked the table with the slightly more dangerous looking crowd and decided that's where he would head.

As he got a little farther in line, he finally paid a little attention to the food itself. He was hungry, but the food looked awful. He looked back up and saw T-Daddy heading out to a table. The guy from the third table that the head guy had spoken to got up and met T-Daddy before he got to the table. Everyone else in the room had turned to watch.

The guy said to T-Daddy, "Where you goin', punk?"

T-Daddy wasn't fazed and said, "Eat my grub up at that table."

"The only grub you'll get is eatin' my black ass later if you don't go sit your punk ass down in back."

T-Daddy moved to walk around the guy, who hauled off and punched T-Daddy right in the face and knocked him off his feet. There were all kinds of cheers and people laughing, and the guy that had punched him strolled back to his table and sat back down to eat. The guards up near the door just watched and did nothing. Jack's hands started to feel wet and he thought to himself, *great, my turn is coming up.*

As Jack got near the end of the line, he saw a Hispanic guy get up from another table and head up to near the front of the line to drop his tray off. But he was lingering just a little too long. Jack now knew who he'd be up against.

He took his tray and started to head over to the table he had picked out earlier, but sure enough, the Hispanic guy was waiting for him. Jack started to walk around him, but the guy reached out and flipped Jack's tray up and out of his hands, throwing the food everywhere.

Jack didn't hesitate. He immediately threw a high jab at the guy's face, who he knew would have to expect it. Jack pulled the punch, but the guy had already flinched and instinctively raised his arms to block it. Jack immediately punched again, but this time he jabbed directly at the guy's throat. The guy didn't expect this and Jack hit his throat as hard as he could. It wouldn't do much damage, and the guy would recover all too soon, but it bought Jack another brief opportunity. The guy's hands went immediately to clutch at his throat, so Jack kicked him in the nuts as hard as he could, and then pushed the guy over.

The Hispanic prisoner wheezed on the floor and held his crotch. Jack looked around quickly to see if anyone else was going to come after him. Every pair of eyes in the room were on him, but no one else looked like they wanted to challenge him. Jack turned back to the line and just grabbed an apple.

He sat down at the table he picked out earlier and didn't say a word to anyone there. No one went to stop him, though. He'd have to watch his back for that Hispanic guy from now on, but that's just the way it was going to be no matter what.

Jack looked a little bit at some of the guys at his table. Two at the far end were Hispanic. One was a black guy that looked out of place somehow. One was a white guy about Jack's age, and right next to Jack was a guy in his 50's that actually looked a little bit like Burt Reynolds.

The Burt Reynolds guy opened his mouth to say something, but Jack cut in before him. He said, through a mouthful of apple, "You know, you kinda look like Burt Reynolds."

The man stopped with his mouth open, then laughed a little bit and relaxed and said, "Yeah, I've heard that. You handled Fredo pretty well; he's tough, but a little stupid, too."

Jack shrugged. His heart was pounding like a racehorse, and he felt like he must have surely peed in his pants already, but he couldn't show fear and couldn't trust anyone yet.

The guy held out his hand to Jack and said, "Name's Sam Houlihan, but most everyone just calls me Hool."

Jack reached out and shook his hand. "I'm Jack Carber," he said.

Hool pointed at a few of the other guys at the table. The white guy about Jack's age was named Bickers and the black guy that looked out of place was Turner. Jack gave them a non-committal wave and finished the last bit of his apple.

Bickers leaned over and said, "Hey, we heard you got stuck with Adder. Did you see what happened earlier?"

Jack said, "Yeah, I was in there."

Turner, Hool, and Bickers all leaned in to see if Jack would tell them exactly what happened. Even the two Hispanic guys at the end of the table got quiet and were listening in.

So Jack told them the story. Hool laughed and said Adder must be getting soft in his old age. Bickers said that Jones should have known not to antagonize Adder like that without having his Taser out and backup near.

Of course, this type of talk got Jack more worried than ever on the inside. It was all he could do to hold it together as it was. But now, to make matters worse, he was getting the picture that this Adder guy was a dangerous psychopath. Jack felt lucky he hadn't thrown up the little bit of apple he had managed to eat.

So Jack asked casually, "So what's this Adder guy like? Why isn't he here at dinner?"

Hool said, "He got stuck in the tank for three days because of his little outburst, so you get a little more space until he gets out. Adder's an odd job. You're new, so a word of advice... what you pulled with Fredo would never work with Adder. He's smart, strong, extremely fast, and he can be vicious."

Jack chewed a bit of apple slowly and thought to himself, *shit.* "Vicious" wasn't a happy word for him to hear.

"What do you mean, he can be?" asked Jack. He was struggling hard to keep his voice steady and calm.

Bickers said, "He mostly keeps to himself. He doesn't really go looking for trouble, and he doesn't seem to pick on people just for the hell of it. He's not on a power trip like Quake or Troy. But he can be unpredictable. Some things can just set him off, and God help the person that sets him off. Dumb-fuck Jones better be thanking his lucky stars he didn't lose an eye today."

Jack thought to himself, *this is turning out just super.*

Then he said, "Adder was quick, that's for sure. And tough. He barely made a sound when they hit him with the Taser."

Hool said with a smirk, "Oh, yeah... he's quiet alright."

Jack gave him a curious look and Hool explained, "He's been in prison for well over ten years now and hasn't said a single word the entire time."

"Really?"

"Yeah, really."

Jack asked, "Is he a mute? Can he make sounds?"

"He's not a mute," said Hool "I've even heard him actually laugh on a rare couple of occasions. He grunts a lot in the gym when he's working out. He just doesn't talk."

Hool added gravely, "Seriously, though. If Adder wants something from you, he's going to get it. Don't try what you used on Fredo on Adder. It won't work at all, and you could easily wind up seriously injured. Probably permanently."

The dining room began to thin out, and Turner got up and left. But Bickers and Hool stayed a few minutes longer to give Jack a little more background information. The big black guy that was the center of the two all black tables was Quake, and his gang was the Brethren. Fredo, who had attempted the "chin check" on Jack as he left the line with his tray, belonged to the group called the Kennel. The Kennel was headed up by the wiry white guy at the two tables of whites, blacks, and Hispanics. The wiry white guy was named Troy and Jack's new best friend, Fredo, was the Kennel's second in charge.

Bickers commented to Hool, "Oh, now that you mention Troy... Talked to Norrison a little while ago, and it doesn't look like Pebbles is coming back."

"What all did they find out?" asked Hool.

"Collapsed lung, broken ribs, fractured skull, lost both kidneys. He's gonna need dialysis from now on so they're transferring him."

Jack was astonished. "This Troy guy did that to someone he hated? The guards let him get away with it?"

Hool frowned and said, "Not an enemy. Pebbles was Troy's bitch for a while now, but not anymore I guess. And Captain Marcus doesn't care what happens. He overlooks a lot of shit in here so he doesn't get burdened with the bureaucracy." He shrugged and added, "Just the way the world works."

As they were getting up, Hool told Jack not to worry too much. He had bought himself some leeway time tonight with what he did to Fredo.

Jack smiled, even if it was a fake one of calculated bravado, and asked Hool if it was that obvious that he'd never been in prison.

"Nah, it's not really how you act. If you had been in prison before, your rep would have gotten here before you," was Hool's reply.

~~~~~

Back in his cell, Jack was about to settle in when he heard a voice over a PA system call out "Line Up!" and he heard people shuffling around. He looked out his cell and saw everyone standing still outside their cell doors. Jack assumed it must be the inmate count for the night.

Harper, the guard that had brought Jack in earlier, went down the line on the second tier and checked off each prisoner's name and looked briefly in each cell.

When the count was done, everyone went back into their cells, and all the cell doors clanged shut at the same time. For the first time that day, Jack felt like he could relax a little bit. But at the same time, the weight of what he was facing hit him hard. The walls closed in around him with the enormity of his situation. Really, he wanted to cry. The cell door was definitely shut now. He was in for the toughest three years of his life – a daily fight for survival.

Jack still burned inside over what happened because of that asshole Stambeki. Sure, most of the things he had been convicted of were dead on. He was guilty of all of it, except for the stolen car and the gun. And that's why he was here at PattX instead of some other, cushier minimum security prison. He still burned over the fact that Stambeki and that bitch Kanya had gotten away with all of his money. He stewed over Stambeki in particular, though. That cocksucker had more than double-crossed Jack. But some of that anger Jack directed squarely at himself – he had let himself get suckered.

Well, Stambeki and Kanya had gotten away with *almost* all of his money. Jack had always kept a backup, a last line of support against everyone else that might try and screw him over. He had kept that account with some emergency money, laundered money, a complete secret. At least he still had that. He hadn't let himself get fucked out of that, thank God.

He had always been something of a loner. Con men rarely had close relationships. But even still, Jack never felt more alone than he did right then. The only person he could really count on was himself. But that was as it should be. He'd learned the hard way about getting too comfortable with anyone else.

He wished for his father, the one person in his life that he trusted implicitly. His father wouldn't have been happy to know where he was or how he got there, but he would have been there for Jack. He would have understood how scared and alone Jack felt, even if he couldn't do anything about it. He missed his dad more than any person in the world.

Jack stood up to clear all these thoughts and feelings out of his head. He knew moping about it wouldn't do any good. He walked up to the cell door and looked out and listened. He heard a couple of cellmates down below talking a little loudly and laughing some. Any laughter was good, especially in a place like this.

He looked around his own cell again. He walked over to the desk, which really didn't have anything on it other than the towel. No books or papers. No pens or pencils. It seemed to be another disturbing aspect of that Adder guy. He'd been in prison for over ten years now, probably in PattX since it opened a few years ago. And yet he had nothing personal. The other cells he had looked in all had an accumulated set of crap – things people had to define themselves, to tie them to other people or the world around them. Things to hold on to. But this Adder guy looked like he had just moved in here yesterday.

There was a small shelf under the desk, so Jack glanced at it to see if there was anything in there. This time, he hit a little paydirt. So Adder had some stuff after all. It was a few books and a pair of cheap reading glasses. One book was a worn *Computers For Dummies* book, the next was a book about the history of Rome, and the last one was the volume T from an old set of encyclopedias, all apparently from the prison library. So Adder didn't entirely waste his time in the big house. Given these books and what Hool had said earlier, Jack assumed that Adder probably was actually halfway decently educated, as well as being street smart.

Jack struggled to figure out how he should handle Adder when he got out of the tank. He could just stay out of Adder's way and hope that Adder would just ignore him. This thought was backed up by what Hool had said about Adder sticking to himself mostly. The downside to that was that it didn't get Jack a good association in prison that would help protect himself.

He could try to get on Adder's good side and see if Adder would look out for him at least a little bit. It was an option, but didn't seem very realistic. If everyone else's description of Adder was accurate, Adder didn't seem like the kind of guy that would really care about those kinds of deals. He could try that tactic at any point, though, and no harm done if it didn't work.

The third option was, of course, to beat the shit out of Adder and put him in his place, and thereby win the respect and fear of everyone in the prison and virtually guaranteeing his own safety. Jack actually laughed out loud at himself at this last option. He knew he had a better chance of eating his way through the cinderblock walls to the outside. But then, you never knew. Hool and Bickers and the others may have been mostly just setting Jack up as a fool, telling him how dangerous Adder was. Sure, he had seen Adder in action today with his own eyes, and he was quick, but he might not be anywhere near the level of vicious and dangerous that Hool and Bickers were playing out. He'd need to see more for himself first. He decided the best route was to just be friendly, but stay out of Adder's way until he could get a better sense of the guy.

Hool and Bickers, and even Turner, seemed decent enough. He knew that tomorrow, though, he'd need to take advantage of the little bit of respect he gained today and spread himself around some, either out in the yard or in the TV room.

Later on, after lights out and as he was starting to fall asleep, he heard someone crying softly in one of the other cells somewhere down the tier. He heard someone else yell at the crier to shut the fuck up. It just reminded him again how hard this was going to be. Jack wondered at what point he'd be the one crying in the middle of the night.

Day 2 – Friday, March 24th, 2000

The first thing the next morning was another inmate count, then showers. Jack watched and saw everyone headed down for their showers with their clothes on and no towels, so he grabbed his soap and headed that way, too. He was a little wary of the shower thing, given how everyone knew what supposedly happened in the stereotypical prison shower.

But it turned out to not be a big deal. It was crowded and people mostly waited their turn. There were a couple of guards watching, and no one really got that rowdy. Some of the inmates still kept an eye on Jack, but mostly people had moved on from the night before. Jack made an extreme point of not watching people too closely in the shower. That would be an easy way to get a reputation he absolutely didn't want in prison.

Jack did notice that the showers could easily be a problem if there weren't many people around, though. They were pretty well blinded, so getting caught in there at the wrong time could easily mean an ambush.

Breakfast turned out to be downright extraordinary. Jack wasn't certain what he expected from prison food, but it wasn't what he was served for breakfast. He was certain that the breakfast was as good as any he had ever been served, and he had eaten at some pretty swank places. There was scrambled eggs with some kind of herbs in them, thick sliced bacon, home fries with a little onion and garlic, and sweet corn muffins. He was blown away.

Jack had sat back down with Hool, Bickers, and Turner again, and he asked them with his mouth full of eggs, "Is it just me or is this food fantastic?"

Hool laughed and said, "Yeah, the breakfasts are way better than what we should be getting. But the lunch and dinners are pretty much the shitty prison food you expect. Louis, the cook that handles breakfast, is pure magic."

Bickers added, "Louis is probably the safest person in this prison. Nobody would risk messing up what we get for breakfast. If there was a riot here, Louis could walk out untouched. Hell, we'd hold the door open for him."

Another guy Jack didn't meet the night before was at the table, too, named Wilson. It was actually the same guy that Jack had seen reading on his bunk when Harper was first leading him to his cell. Wilson was a slim guy, about Jack's height, with wavy brown hair that was too finely textured and seemed to want to float off of his head. He seemed more nervous than the other guys, and kept looking around all the time. That and the haunted look in his eyes told Jack that Wilson was almost on the bottom of the heap at PattX. Wilson wanted to hear about Adder right from Jack, though, even though he had already heard some of it second- and third-hand. So Jack told him the story. Jack got the idea that the story on Adder would be a decent icebreaker with many people today, even if it did mean he'd get sick of telling it.

When Jack was done with the story, Wilson said, "Not as bad as he's been in the past." He paused and looked around a few more times, then said, "Adder freaks me out. I don't like being around him at all."

Jack decided to challenge them just a little bit on Adder to see if they'd stick with their stories. He pushed back from the table just a little and said, "Ok, what I saw yesterday was a lucky punch. That fat black guard doesn't seem too swift, either. Is Adder really the bad-ass shit-server you're claiming, or are you guys just talking out your asses?"

The four of them exchanged glances, then Hool said, "Look, Jack, you can listen or not listen. It's your life if you're not careful around him. You respect his space and it's possible he'll act like you're not even there. But the guy is, like I said last night, smart, strong, extremely fast, and vicious."

Turner finally really joined in and said, "Hool's right. Most of these other guys are stupid but strong. Dangerous when they get together in numbers." Turner looked to Hool, Bickers, and Wilson, and said, "You guys remember last year. You saw it. When that new guy thought he was going to teach Adder a lesson to get some juice in here. He snuck up behind him out in the yard. Three feet away from him, Adder spun around and kicked him in the gut and then broke the guy's nose, almost all in a split second. When he fell and tried to crawl away, Adder stomped down on him and cracked his hip in two. Adder went back to what he was doing just like nothing had happened."

Hool added, "Jack, that guy that Adder attacked lost his pancreas and can barely walk. They had to send him to a hospital prison."

"Ok, ok! I get it! The guy's totally wacko!" Jack didn't want to hear any more. He felt like he'd probably wind up lucky to make it a month in the cell with Adder without getting a permanent disability.

Jack changed the subject and learned a little more about PattX. Patterson was set up differently from most prisons. It was only a few years old, and was near Dallas, Georgia, just west of Atlanta where the locals weren't together enough to stop a prison from going in their backyard. The building itself was shaped like a large "X". Each arm of the "X" acted almost like an isolated, independent prison. So while it was one large prison, it worked more like four much smaller prisons. Each of the arms was almost totally isolated from the others, but some areas were shared. The prison yards, dining halls and some other areas were shared between two arms of the prisons. That's why there were specific times they had access to the chow hall and prison yards, and other times when they didn't. The hospital and administrative areas were shared among all four prison wings. Some areas, like the TV rooms, laundry areas, weight room, etc, were completely separate for each of the four wings. Even the guards were rarely shared between the wings.

~ ~ ~ ~ ~

Mornings were strictly inside time, and in the afternoons they'd get to go out in the yard. Jack spent the morning cautiously checking the place out. He spent some time in the TV room and met a black guy named Dugger, who turned out was a member of the Brethren. After what Jack had done to Fredo the night before, he apparently had a little juice with the Brethren guys, so he worked his charm with Dugger to extend it. Of course, the first thing Dugger wanted was to front Jack some cigarettes, but Jack knew better than to get into any kind of debt in prison under any circumstance. Dugger would want payment back in double, very quickly. Jack thanked him, but smiled really big and said, "My butt for a handful of your butts. Thanks, but I don't smoke." It had the effect Jack was hoping for – Dugger laughed, but also got the point that Jack knew what the offer was really about.

The TV room was plain, but with a good sized TV suspended from the ceiling. There was one crappy vinyl couch, and plenty of the cheap plastic chairs, just like the one in his cell. Some of the Brethren were in there, as were some of the Kennel guys. They seemed to keep some distance from each other, though. There were some others, too, but the Brethren guys seemed to be in charge of the TV room this morning.

Jack started to go into the library area, but caught a glimpse of Fredo and Troy in there, so he backed out before they saw him. He'd have to check that place out later. He didn't think he'd fare as well if he walked into the middle of the Kennel today.

He wandered over to the weight room next, but on the way in, he was stopped by one of the guards. The guard wanted to introduce himself to Jack, which Jack thought was really odd. He was a younger, blond guard, named Norrison. He told him that he had heard Jack had handled the chin check at dinner the night before well, and warned him that the other guards might ignore that kind of stuff, but he didn't. Jack immediately liked Norrison, not so much as a friend or anything, but Jack knew that he was one of those people you could immediately trust at face value. Norrison wouldn't say one thing and do another, and he wanted you to know where he stood on everything. Jack felt like this guy must be something of the young idealist guard, probably actually studied criminal justice in school and had to do guard duty to get his foot in the door of the system.

Jack hung out in the weight room for a while, but just watched. He wanted to understand the dynamic of how people used the weights. If people actually took turns, or if weaker people just got pushed out of the way of the more aggressive inmate.

One of the Hispanic guys that was at Jack's table the night before was there working out and came up to Jack. He was probably 5 foot 8, and he had a squarer jaw than you normally saw on Hispanics. His right arm was covered in a tattoo from the wrist up into the sleeve that seemed to involve lots of scorpions. He asked Jack if he was going to start working out while there.

"Probably, but for a day or two, I'm just strictly observing," was Jack's reply.

"Smart man. My third day here, I tried to push my way in on the wrong set of weights and wound up in the hospital for two days with a broken rib. I'm Hector, by the way." Hector smiled, flashed a gold-rimmed tooth, and held out his hand to Jack.

Jack shook the offered hand and introduced himself to him.

Hector noticed that the bench press he wanted to use had freed up and asked Jack to spot him on a set. Jack walked over and helped Hector load up the plates on the barbell, then stood over Hector's head as he lifted the weights.

As Hector was doing his reps, Jack suddenly got the slight feeling that Hector was staring at his crotch. He wondered if maybe Hector was gay and if this was a set up. Hector was being subtle enough to where even Jack wasn't sure that Hector was, in fact, checking him out. Jack shot a glance around to see if anyone else was watching. If Hector was gay, Jack didn't want to be labeled as gay also on his first day there. He noticed no one specifically watching them except Wilson, who he had met at breakfast, so he didn't worry too much about it. Jack excused himself after Hector finished his set, though, and left the weight area behind.

The guys in the weight area seemed to be playing nicely together, but then again, it might have been because Norrison was the guard around there that day.

Right before lunch, Jack swung by the library again to check and see if any of the Kennel guys were still there. They were gone, but among a few others, Jack saw the leader of the Brethren, Quake, in there, along with the nelly black guy, Chica. Since there were others in there, Jack decided it was safe to check the place out a little bit.

As he went in, though, Quake saw him and motioned him over. Jack would have preferred to fly a little more under the radar than this for a while, but he couldn't ignore this guy without causing trouble.

He went over and waited for Quake to speak to him first. Chica was draped over Quake's wide shoulder, and was watching Jack intensely. Quake had ripped the sleeves off his prison issues and Jack noticed a large branded omega on his bicep.

Quake studied him for a moment, then said, "I like the way you handled yourself last night. Anyone who tears up on a Kennel dog is all right by me. But I also know that you didn't know what scum Kennel dogs are. You were just standing up for yourself."

Jack immediately picked up on the Creole accent in Quake's voice. Quake paused and Jack waited, then Quake continued, "So, I'll give you, oh, three days where you are guaranteed safe around the Brethren. A free pass, to welcome you to PattX. After that, I cannot guarantee your safety."

Jack thought for a moment, then said, "Thank you."

And on a lark, Jack decided to take what he thought would be a small risk and see how a small joke would go over. He said, "Shit! Right! Well, three days is about all I'll need to come in, take over, and steal the Brethren away from you, so this works out great!" And then he smiled big to let Quake know for certain he was able to keep a sense of humor about him. Getting people to laugh was one of the fastest ways to get them to trust you.

Quake obviously wasn't threatened and smiled back at Jack. Chica saw that Jack was still in Quake's good graces, so he slinked over to Jack and purred, "Ooh, we got us a little smart ass, this one."

Chica moved behind Jack and put his fingertips on Jack's shoulders. He whispered into Jack's ear, "Maybe you'll get some of Chica's ass."

It was another test. Jack said, "If I took up that offer, Chica, I imagine my ass would be handed to me much faster than three days, despite Quake's offer. But my loss – Quake has obviously reserved the best piece of ass in the house for himself."

Chica moved back over to where Quake was and declared, "Oooh, he smooth, this one..."

And then Quake smiled again and actually laughed a little this time. He said, "Yes, he is smooth, this one..." and he walked out with Chica right by his side.

Jack looked around and saw that everyone else in the library had watched every moment of this transaction. He moved through the library and checked out the sad collection of hand-me-down books and magazines. He noticed that they did seem to get the Atlanta newspaper, which was good. He also noticed there was a PC in there for inmates' use. Jack thought, *excellent!* PCs were one of his favorite trade tools; they made stealing identities trivially easy.

He tried to bring up the browser to see if they restricted internet access, but got nowhere. The browser wouldn't bring up any pages at all. Jack checked the back of the PC and saw that it was indeed hooked into a network, so he assumed that the account left open on this PC for the inmates to use didn't allow any network access at all. But he also thought that if he could get into a different account, then maybe he could get to the internet. He filed that away as being a project for later.

~~~~~

That afternoon turned out to be a nice, early spring day. Everyone went out into the yard after lunch (which wasn't anywhere nearly as good as breakfast had been), and after another inmate count. Jack spent some time just watching everything going on, who hung out with who, who had hurried conversations with who, etc. A few people were jogging laps around the yard; some others were playing basketball, which was one of Jack's favorite games. Jack wished he could get in the game today, but knew it would be better to wait until he understood the politics of the yard better.

The yard itself wasn't much of a yard. It was the area between two of the wings of PattX. Mostly it was just trampled dirt. Out towards the fence, there were some forlorn patches of grass. Jack assumed most inmates didn't get too close to the fence for fear of being shot by the guards in the guard towers. There were some picnic-style tables with benches attached on either side, and a few bleachers next to the basketball court. There was something of a jogging route around the perimeter of the yard for inmates that wanted to run some.

Jack didn't see Bickers or Hool, but Wilson came up to him after a little bit and told him he had heard about Jack and Quake's meeting in the Library.

Jack asked him, "Was Quake's offer real, or is he setting me up?"

"Quake has double-crossed people before and set them up, but I think that's only when he really has a reason to. I think you can probably trust his offer. Did you really make Quake laugh?"

"Yeah, a little bit. What can I say? I'm a people person."

Wilson waited a minute, then asked another question. "You've been keeping to the side and watching everything closely. Are you getting ready to make a move?"

"What kind of move do you mean?" asked Jack.

"When Troy first came here, he laid low for a while, got the trust of a few key people. Then he consolidated all of a sudden. He betrayed some of the people's trust he gained, and expanded on the trust with some of the others. It was how he built the Kennel."

Jack got two things out of this. One, he got that Troy wasn't the dumb redneck he looked like and he shouldn't be underestimated. Second, Wilson was worried that Jack was trying to get his trust just long enough to use him, and then "betray" him.

Wilson needed a little help. He was trying to work Jack and was going about it entirely the wrong way. Jack felt a little sorry for him. No wonder the guy was low man on the pile here. He was adrift in a wild sea of violence, manipulation, and deceit, and he probably could barely keep his head above water.

Jack looked out over the yard and said, "No, I'm not planning any kind of take over."

Wilson looked a little relieved.

Then Jack said, stating what should have been obvious, "But if I was, wouldn't I answer that way anyway?"

And all of a sudden Wilson's face clouded over again.

Jack turned to face Wilson now and said, "Wilson, I read people pretty well, and I know when I'm being worked for information. If you want to know if you're about to get in the way of a violent situation by hanging around me, you're trying to find out the worst way."

Wilson turned a shade paler and now looked uncomfortable that Jack was obviously right on the mark. Jack said, "You gave me an opportunity to lie, and now there's no way to know if I'm telling the truth or not. If you had really wanted to get a better idea as to what I was up to, the approach you probably should have taken would be to let it gently drop that Troy was concerned that I was about to consolidate power the same way he did when he came in. My immediate reaction to that would have involuntarily been an honest one, and you could have read it. You never needed to ask a question at all."

Wilson's jaw dropped a little bit and he just said, "Jesus, Jack!"

Jack smiled and said, "Like I said, I'm a people person."

"If some of the population thinks that's what I'm trying to do, in particular the Kennel, then I *am* concerned. I don't want to get the shit beat out of me for something I'm not planning. Are people concerned that that's what I'm working on?" added Jack.

Wilson said, "Yeah. Then it got me scared."

Jack said, "You'll just have to trust me a little, Wilson. I'm not planning anything like that. I'm just using the skills I have to keep myself safe while I'm here. The same thing you want, really, just to be as safe as you can while you're here. For what it's worth, you're safe around me. I'm not a violent person."

Wilson seemed a little more at ease, but doubtful and unsure, too. Jack could smell it on Wilson as plain as cheap cologne and his trade skills picked up on it easily.

Jack moved on around the yard a little more. He was already a target of the Kennel, but if they really were concerned about him trying to pull a coup, then that made it worse. Jack was going to have to think of a way to defuse that quickly.

He picked out a few people to talk to. He obviously avoided the Kennel guys and kept an eye out behind him just in case they tried to pull something fast. He had seen Fredo and some of the others glaring at him a little bit earlier.

Two guys he talked to were in the Brethren, so he felt safe around them thanks to Quake's promise. But both of those guys were obviously hopped up on some drug they had gotten into the prison somehow, so he moved on from them quickly.

Dugger had just finished up with a basketball game and waved at him, so he went to talk to him a minute.

Dugger said, "I see that Wilson faggot's trying to make you his bone."

Jack was lost a little in the lingo on this one. "Huh?"

"His bone. Make you his daddy. The homos need protection and give up the hole to get it."

Jack was caught off guard on this one a little bit. Wilson was gay? That hadn't surfaced so far. Jack said, "Well, fuck me! I didn't even know he was gay. That's not what we talked about."

Dugger started laughing at this, laughing at Jack, but a pretty good-natured laugh, nonetheless.

Jack laughed himself and said, "No, I'm not planning on being anybody's bone."

Dugger then asked, "So, what were y'all talkin' 'bout?" He wasn't really laughing anymore. In prison, everyone wanted to know what everyone else was up to.

Jack thought fast and decided to take a calculated risk. He said, "I asked Wilson if he thought that I could really trust Quake's promise. He said that, sure, Quake was pretty honorable." Jack knew Quake would hear this and Quake would know that Jack didn't take much at face value. Second, it gave Wilson a tiny boost just because he vouched for Quake.

Dugger looked a little suspicious of Jack. Jack worried that questioning Quake's word could be interpreted as an insult. So Jack added, "I felt good about Quake's offer, but I've only been here a day. Never hurts to get a little independent verification, you know. Can't blame me for doing my homework."

Jack knew that every word he said to Dugger would get back to Quake. Dugger said, "True. True."

They talked a little longer, and Dugger gave him a little background on a few of the guards. Anthony Marcus was the captain. Jack guessed he was the one that Tasered Adder the day before. Clemson Jones was the big black guard that Adder hit in the eye. Dugger called him a "dumb nigger."

Jack also asked about what would happen to T-Daddy Clinton. Dugger wasn't sure who Jack meant until Jack mentioned it was the other guy that got a chin check the night before.

Dugger said, "Oh, you mean Prattle. He's been humpin' our legs like crazy tryin' to get in on the Brethren."

"I thought his name was T-Daddy Clinton."

Dugger laughed and said, "We don't give a shit what he says his name is. We call him Prattle because that's what he does. Mouth opens up... bullshit falls out."

Jack laughed out loud. The Brethren had T-Daddy pegged immediately. Jack said goodbye to Dugger and walked on around the yard some more.

That night, back in his cell after the final inmate count, Jack thought about the issues before him. The new one was the fact that Troy might see Jack as a threat and not just a matter of pride. He'd figure something out to eliminate this issue in the next day or so. His real issue was the one he'd had all along – Adder. He just wasn't comfortable that this wouldn't be a really dangerous situation. This

Adder guy was just too much of an unknown, too unpredictable. He decided again that the best thing to do was just stay out of Adder's way as much as possible. He just wished he had higher confidence in that path.

Day 3 – Saturday, March 25th, 2000

The next morning, Jack went back to the library and picked up a couple of magazines to have in his cell for the evenings when they were locked up before lights out.

He made his way back towards the cells so he could drop off the magazines and then head back to the TV lounge. Jack rounded the corner on the way to the stairwell and as he was passing the entrance to the shower area, he noticed Fredo coming his way. Jack realized immediately what was happening and turned around only to find another guy right behind him preventing him from going back.

Fredo and the other guy grabbed Jack and dragged him quickly into the shower area. Fredo snarled, "It's payback time."

In the shower area was Troy and two other members of the Kennel. One of them Jack thought was named Runnion. Jack thought about yelling out, but didn't remember seeing anyone close enough to hear him. One of the guys went to keep watch in case a guard came by, while Runnion and the other guy held onto Jack. Jack's blood ran cold thinking about what was probably about to happen to him.

Troy and Fredo watched him for a second. Finally, Troy spoke and said, "You made Fredo look bad the other night."

Jack knew he needed to stand up to them or it would be worse later. He said, "Fredo, Troy put you in that position. He made you come after me instead of doing it himself!"

And that lit Troy up in a furious rage. He walked quickly up to Jack and punched him hard in the stomach. Jack's legs gave out from under him, but the two guys held him up. Jack barely wheezed out a "Jesus Christ!" and immediately felt like he was going to throw up. Troy might not have been the biggest guy around, but he knew how to throw a punch. He looked like a mousy redneck, with light brown hair in an almost-mullet and a wispy moustache. He was pale, lean, and had shallow, cold, pitiless eyes. The eyes betrayed the kind of person that would punch his own mother in the stomach if she refused to give him her social security check.

Troy stepped back and considered Jack for a second more, almost like he was trying to decide something.

He told the two guys to let Jack go, and they did. Jack fell down on one knee.

Troy said, "Get up, boy."

Jack tried to catch his breath and stood up. He tried to prepare himself for a fight, but Troy had hit him hard. Troy walked back over towards Jack and Jack decided to strike first. His fist flew out at Troy's chin, but Troy ducked back and Jack missed by an embarrassing distance. Troy immediately landed a hard jab in Jack's upper midsection, which knocked all of the air out of him again. He wheezed and tried to pull the breath back into his lungs.

Troy struck again and hit Jack in the jaw this time, and Jack felt the concussion ring through his head. He fell on his side and just stayed there. He was dizzy and still trying to catch his breath. His vision was going dark at the edges, too.

Troy looked at Jack on the ground, and finally said with a note of indifference, "That's what I thought." He looked over at Fredo and said, "He's yours now." And with that, Troy walked out.

Jack was having trouble concentrating on what was happening, but didn't feel any reassurance now that Fredo was in charge. He walked over to Jack and kicked him in the stomach as he lay on the shower floor. This time Jack did throw up some, his eyes were watering from the pain, and every breath burned to take.

Fredo said to the other two, who had been standing by, "Pick him up and clean out his mouth."

Runnion and the other picked Jack up and took him over to a shower head. They turned it on and held Jack's face under the water. They forced his mouth open and under the water so it would clean it out. Runnion turned the shower off and they brought Jack back over to Fredo.

Fredo told the two, "Hold him down on all fours."

Jack was still a little dizzy, although the water had helped with that, and wheezing slightly. The pain in his midsection was agonizing. Runnion and the other guy forced him down on his hands and knees and held him that way. Jack looked up and saw Fredo undoing the front of his pants.

Fredo fished his dick out and started pulling on it. He said to Jack, "I'm about to feed you a little reminder of why you don't want to ever fuck up like that again. No teeth, now, or you'll carry every goddamn one of 'em back to your cell in your pocket. And if you got no teeth left in your head, *everyone* at PattX will want you on your knees in front of them. Be a good bitch and show me you know your place."

Jack could barely move, but he knew he needed to fight as much as possible. He struggled, but the flashes of pain and dizziness made the effort worthless.

He felt Fredo pressing up against his mouth, insistently, and for the next ten minutes, Jack was roughly forced to take Fredo's dick.

When Fredo finished, Jack didn't have the strength or breath to spit the rest of Fredo out. He stared at the shower floor, his eyes watering from what he had been through and his throat was burning raw. Runnion and the other stood him back up and Jack coughed a little bit. He was wondering if he could summon enough energy now to pull away from Runnion and the other guy and run out.

Fredo said as he pulled his pants back up, almost like he was trying to cheer Jack up, "Troy was right... you did bitch up pretty fast! Now we can finish up."

But right then, the lookout outside the shower area called in and said, "Floor's wet."

There was no discussion or glances. Runnion and the other guy immediately dropped Jack, and they and Fredo walked calmly and confidently out of the shower area.

Jack fell back to the shower floor and lay clutching his sides. His midsection was in so much pain still that he couldn't lift himself back up, and he felt like he might vomit again. So he just lay there.

Jack threw up again, but this one was just a dry heave. He felt hopeless and wished he could dissolve and wash away in the drain beneath him. This is what he had to look forward to for the next three years.

A moment later, a guard came running in and found Jack. The guard, Capt. Marcus as it turned out, called on the radio, "Inmate down in the shower! Downs, get in here!"

Capt. Marcus went to Jack and checked first to make sure his neck and back were ok. He asked Jack if he could sit up, and Jack nodded yes.

Capt. Marcus helped lift him up into a sitting position.

"Can you tell me what happened? Who did this?"

Jack knew better than to tell what actually happened. Under no circumstance did you ever squeal on a fellow inmate in prison. Jack just said, with lots of effort, "Just... fell in the shower."

Capt. Marcus was clearly used to this kind of response when someone had been assaulted. But right then, another guard came into the shower to help Capt. Marcus.

Capt. Marcus looked at Jack and complained, "We need to get you to the infirmary to be looked at. Do we need to bring a medical team, or can you walk?"

Jack wiped a little bit of blood from his nose and felt the extremely sore spot on his chin. He managed to whisper, "I can walk."

The other guard helped lift Jack up. Jack swayed a little, so the other guard put Jack's arm around his neck and helped him walk out.

As they were leaving, Capt. Marcus shouted at Jack, "You're making me do paperwork, Carber, and I fucking hate paperwork!"

In the infirmary, the nurse checked Jack out and said "No breaks. You'll be ok, just sore. What happened?"

Jack continued to lie back on the exam table with his eyes closed. By now, he was feeling a little more together and answered, "Mosquito bite."

"Oh, you're a regular comedian. Here's some pain medication, and some more to take tomorrow morning."

The guard that helped him to the infirmary came back in to take an official statement from Jack. Jack stuck with the story of falling in the shower. Downs wrote it down in the report even though he, Jack, and the nurse all knew it was a bunch of bullshit.

Downs took Jack back to his cell, and still had to help him along. They passed a number of people on the way. He tried to not make eye contact with any of them, but Jack noticed Hool and Wilson among those he saw. Jack was sure the story would get around pretty quickly.

Jack settled down onto his bunk with a groan. Downs explained to him, "We're going to lock you in so you can be safe and rest. If you feel better and want out, just wave your hand out the gate and the cage will open it for you."

Downs left and the cell door shut and locked. Jack lay still for a while because every little move caused a shooting pain somewhere. He only allowed himself a few minutes of this before he forced himself to get up and move around every once in a while.

So this was it. This was what it was like to be raped and beaten in prison. Jack breathed in and out in pain as he thought about it. It wasn't the sexual violation, not really. He kept his hand on the rib that hurt the most and he thought about the greasy, creepy banker man he had sucked off in Fort Lauderdale when he was down there. He'd never willingly have sex with a guy like that, either; he did it just to get paid a hundred bucks by the guy while he also stole the jerk's driver's license and a credit card. Having Fredo in his mouth wasn't a whole lot different in the end. What bothered him today was not being able to control what happened at all. To be totally at the mercy of someone else. Someone who had no mercy. To be used like a fucking rag and left on the floor.

Eventually, Jack got up and at least brushed his teeth. He saw a large bruise on his chin already. Moving around would help keep the soreness to a minimum and help keep him from being too stiff tomorrow, but God it hurt.

It all hurt so bad.

Saturday, February 19th, 2000

Jack rolled over on his stomach, trying to fall back asleep. It was difficult, though, with Chris biting on his earlobe. Chris also started rubbing around on his ass.

Jack mumbled, ignoring the fact that his face was buried in the pillow, "Lemmeehlone."

Chris popped him on the ass once and said, "What was that, sleepyhead? I couldn't quite catch that. Roll over and tell me what you said."

Jack rolled over in the bed and groused, "Lemmeehlone!!" It was just as unintelligible as it was with the pillow.

With Jack on his back now, Chris got up on his knees and straddled over him, grinding around on his waist playfully. "C'mon, sleepyhead! We'll never get this done if you don't get up."

Jack finally spoke clearly enough to be heard, but with eyes opened only by the tiniest of slits. "Quit it! Leave me alone. I'm still asleep." Chris had thrown the curtains in the bedroom open wide earlier and the winter sunlight was pouring into the room.

Chris leaned over and whispered in Jack's ear, "Well, well, you seemed to like this a lot last night. Now you don't care at all! I knew I was just a piece of ass to you all along. Jack the player!"

Jack finally grinned a tiny bit and wrapped his arms around Chris. Chris bit on his earlobe a little more before Jack pulled him down the rest of the way on top of him and started kissing him. Jack reached up and ran his fingers through Chris's light brown hair. It was short and felt like fine velvet on Jack's fingers.

Chris rubbed his entire body up and down Jack's as they kissed. Jack reached down and ran his hand down Chris' gym-tuned back and arms. Chris pulled away from the kiss and moved his mouth down Jack's neck, then chest. He kissed, licked, and bit Jack lightly.

Jack said, "I thought I had to get up right now."

Chris ignored him and continued to work his way further south down the body underneath him. Jack learned early on to let Chris do whatever he wanted to his body because it was always good.

They wound up spending another forty-five minutes repeating many of the things they had done the night before. When they finally finished and the heat between them subsided, Jack was ready to just lie back in bed and fall right back asleep again.

But Chris wasn't going to have any of that. Chris started pulling on Jack's arm to get him up. He said, "Come on! Time to shower! I'll even shower with you."

Jack finally sat up, then got up and stood next to the bed. His hair was all wadded up. Chris looked at his hair and said, "You look like Phyllis Diller, but not in the good way."

Jack turned slightly, scratching his rear indifferently at Chris. He said, playfully, "Kiss my ass!"

Chris jumped up and pulled Jack up against him, his hands grabbing Jack's backside. He said, "Oh, yeah? You just never get enough, do you?"

Jack laughed and kissed Chris on the forehead. "Alright, alright. Let me go before we get permanently glued together."

Jack shuffled over towards the bathroom, Chris pinching at him here and there the whole way to keep him in motion. Together, they got into the shower and began to wash each other in-between the gropes and bites. All told, they probably wound up taking as much time as if they had taken separate showers.

When they completed the showering and groping and rubbing, and they were finishing up in the bathroom, Jack asked, "What time did Kanya say she'd be ready to go?"

"12:30."

Jack looked at the mirror and said, "What time is it now?"

"Noon."

Jack looked over at Chris, his eyes huge, "Shit, Chris, I'll never have time to go get the rental car and meet her in time! How did it get this late?"

Chris said, spitting flecks of toothpaste as he did so, "Stop it! Kanya's getting the car this time. She told you that two days ago. And you know damn well how it got this late. You've got the fucking libido of a teenage Catholic schoolgirl."

Jack's face soured unhappily. "No, she's not getting the car. You know I don't like anyone else handling that. I want to get the car myself. I'm taking the point on this thing, and I want to make sure I do this myself so I know it's done right."

Chris spit out his toothpaste and looked over at Jack, exasperated from having to cover this again. "It's just a rental car, Jack. She's not getting an original Social for you. It's just a rental car. Besides, it gave us some extra time. I won't see you for another couple of weeks after you skip later today. I needed this time with you."

Chris moved over behind Jack and rubbed his shoulders some. He said to Jack, "You're the hottest con man I've ever seen. Shit, you're the hottest man I've ever seen. I needed what you gave me this morning. I love you, Jack, so much. I'd do anything to get more time with you like this."

Jack softened his stance a little bit and smiled. Chris was the best thing he'd ever had, and this morning had been great.

Chris said, "You've got your money safe, right? Ready to go?"

"Yep."

"I've got the neck and head x-rays copied and ready to go."

Jack asked, "How many times have you used these x-rays?"

Chris said, "This is a new set, never been used on any insurance claims before."

Jack said, "Good," as he put his clothes on, then headed into the living room to wait for Kanya.

Jack heard Kanya's key in the door a few minutes later, and she came busting in. Her dark caramel skin, bright pink lips, tight black pants and equally tight denim jacket with fur trim seemed to be smiling from everywhere at once.

"Hey, sweet baby!!" she said as she came through the door.

Jack smiled and said, "Hey, sugar!"

Chris met them in the den and the three of them went over the plans one last time, and everything seemed ready to go.

Chris headed off to his doctor's office, and Jack went out with Kanya to the rental car they were going to use. It was a relatively non-descript Sentra. Jack took the rental paperwork from Kanya and checked the identity information on it to make sure the stolen identity he was going to use matched exactly what was on the rental agreement as a second driver. Kanya had used a stolen identity of her own as the primary renter. Jack checked to make sure the VIN on the rental agreement matched what was on the car. Everything looked totally correct, so they left.

Jack took Kanya back over to her place to get her car so they could head over to the road where they were going to create the accident. They picked a busy road near Decatur known for a constant stream of aggressive drivers. There were a lot of shops along the road, and the road was especially busy on Saturdays.

Jack waited in the car while Kanya went inside to get one last thing. He noticed the Sentra he was driving smelled faintly of cigarettes. God, he hated cigarettes.

Jack thought about moving out west with Chris, to Texas. Jack would leave for the Lone Star state today after the accident. Chris would move out there in about three weeks after he put the insurance claims through and gotten the payment. Jack had been sitting on all of his money in cash from all the scams they had run in the last six months, over $90,000. He'd launder it in Texas and then it would be safe to use it however he wanted. Chris would do the same with his money when he came out a few weeks later.

Chris was the best thing to ever happen to Jack. The last ten months with Chris had been about the best in his life. They ran all kinds of grifts together, mostly against car and health insurance companies – Jack's favorite targets. Jack was totally in love with Chris, and Chris loved Jack just as much. They thought alike and Chris respected that Jack tended to focus his efforts on insurance companies after what they had done to both his parents.

Chris had been very sympathetic to what Jack had gone through in his life. Losing his mother to emphysema when he was nine, then his father dying of congestive heart failure when Jack was seventeen. Chris knew that the insurance companies could have and should have helped his parents way more than they did. And if they hadn't put every roadblock up in the meantime, Jack's parents could have lasted much longer. Chris knew that if an insurance company had any kind of choice between profit margin and actually helping someone desperately in need of it, they'd choose the profit margin every time. It meant so much to Jack to have someone that understood his anger and frustration, and shared it.

Jack even allowed himself a few thoughts about his father, who he missed very much. It had been so cruel to have his father taken away from him, even more so because of greedy, faceless, heartless insurance companies. Jack was glad to have had the time he did with his father, but felt cheated that he didn't have more. He wished his father could see him with Chris. Chris made him so happy, and that was all his father ever wanted for Jack.

Finally, Jack looked up and saw Kanya coming out of her apartment, waving and ready to go.

~ ~ ~ ~ ~

Jack sat with his head stiff against the back of the Sentra's seat. He had just gotten rear-ended, probably a little harder than he wanted, but the whole thing would be just that much more convincing this way. Kanya was in the car in front of him and had stopped when she saw he had gotten rear-ended.

The guy in the Volvo that had rear-ended him came running out and asked Jack if he was ok. Jack didn't move his head and said through the open window, "My neck. God, it hurts." He knew Kanya was already calling the police on her cell phone. Soon, she'd come running out to check on him.

Kanya didn't, but it didn't matter so much since a police cruiser was already pulling up behind them with lights flashing.

The Volvo driver kept trying to talk to the officer, telling him that Jack had slammed on brakes too soon and he couldn't avoid it. The officer told him to go wait over by his car.

The officer went to Jack's window and said, "Sir, are you able to move?"

Jack said, "I think I'm mostly ok. My neck hurts a little, but it'll be ok." Jack started to move it a little and winced at the pain, trying to be convincing.

He got out of the car slowly as the officer went to get his tag number. Kanya still hadn't gotten out of her car, and he waved at her. Then Kanya started her car up and drove off. She wasn't supposed to do that. Something was going wrong. Jack's heart went cold and he turned back around to the policeman. The policeman was talking into his radio and looking at Jack. Jack saw the policeman's hand reach down to his service revolver and Jack knew it had gone very, very wrong.

He turned to see the last of Kanya's taillights as she turned a corner. Jack had been had.

He heard the officer calling out at him. "Sir, put your hands on your head and stand against the car!"

Jack turned back around and the officer now had his gun pointed directly at him. He had been totally played.

Jack put his hands on his head and stood against the Sentra. The owner of the Volvo began backing slowly off from the whole scene, not understanding why a gun was needed all of a sudden. Cars were going very slowly to watch what was happening as they passed by. The officer came up carefully and put Jack in handcuffs and told him to stay put. The officer asked him, "Is this your car, sir?"

Jack was shaking, almost uncontrollably. "It's a rental car, officer. I'm listed as a driver on the agreement, which is on the front seat. What's the problem, officer?"

The officer kept an eye on Jack and opened the front door. Very carefully, and while watching Jack, he reached in and took the rental agreement and the keys to the car. He told Jack, "Sir, this car has been reported stolen. Did you steal this car?"

Jack flushed in fury and stammered, "No, no, no." Kanya had set him up. Jack knew he shouldn't have let anyone else get the fucking car.

Right then another cruiser came up and two more officers jumped out with guns drawn. The first officer went to open the trunk as the other officers were coming up to Jack.

The officer opened the trunk and looked around a second and said, "Weapon!" The other two immediately reacted. They jumped on Jack and threw him hard against the car and searched him.

The first officer asked Jack, "Is this your gun in the trunk?"

Jack went totally white, and he freaked out. He started struggling with the officers and screamed, "It's a rental car! I don't have any gun! If there's a gun back there, it's not mine!" The officers were caught unaware and tried to get Jack back under control. And that's when Jack kneed one of the officers while thrashing around. The stolen car wasn't enough. Kanya had put a gun in there, too. Jack wanted to kill the fucking bitch!

The officers threw Jack face-first onto the cold roadway, grinding his face on the asphalt. The officer almost crushed Jack's back, putting his full weight on Jack's spine with his knee. One of the officers screamed at him, "*Don't move!* Do it again, and you'll be Tasered."

Both officers stood up to see if Jack would behave. One of them yelled, "Just move, and we'll pump you so full of juice, you'll shit *batteries!* Sonofabitch!!"

They hauled Jack into the back of the cruiser. How could he have let this happen?

~~~~~

Jack sat in the holding cell. Three blank cinderblock walls, plus some bars. It smelled distinctly like piss in there. He had run over and over in his mind what had happened. How he had been set up. He knew why Kanya had done it. It was the cash. If she could get Jack out of the way for a while, she could get to his cash maybe. Jack had talked to both Chris and Kanya about where he had it until he would leave town. That's when Kanya had planned to get it for herself. She just needed Jack out of the way for a while so she could snatch and run. But at the last minute when he got all the cash together, Jack had changed his mind and put it in a different place. God, he was so glad he did that.

Hopefully, Chris would get there soon and be able to get him out quickly. Jack had made his call to Chris and told him what happened. Chris said he'd be there immediately and to not worry.

Jack couldn't do anything else but wait around for Chris to show up. The time just dragged on. He should have been on the road to Texas at this point. His mind kept playing over and over Kanya driving off and seeing the cop drawing his gun on Jack. He couldn't help but panic at the thought of actually going to prison. Christ, what would happen to him in prison?

Jack clung to the knowledge that Chris would be able to give an alibi as to where Jack was when the car was stolen. And Chris was a doctor, which meant he'd have that much more credibility. Kanya had said it was a rental and asked him to drive it back to her place for her. It would be hard, though, if they looked closely enough, they'd know Jack was using a stolen identity. It would stop there, though. Jack had gotten ready to leave town and had destroyed everything else he had used in previous jobs. All the identities, Social Security cards, birth certificates, driver licenses, hard drives, insurance paperwork, car titles, everything. But a stolen car and a gun were a whopping plenty bad enough.

A guard came to let Jack know that a Chris Stambeki was there to see him. He took Jack to a small, empty office where they could talk.

Jack walked in and Chris was there waiting. He still had his doctor's coat on from the office. Chris went over and hugged Jack, and Jack wanted to break down and cry. He wanted Chris to hold him and make this whole nightmare go away. Chris put his hand on his shoulder and said, "It's ok. I'm going to get you out of here soon. It'll be all right. We'll get a good lawyer on this and make all this go away in no time."

Jack couldn't stand it, "What the fuck is wrong with Kanya? Why would she do this to me?"

Chris looked around the room suspiciously and spoke softly, "I stopped by the apartment before coming here. I think she's looking for the cake you made." Chris looked Jack very seriously in the eye, and was very pointed with the word "cake."

Jack asked, "Someone's run through our apartment?"

"Yes. She's looking for the recipe to the cake. Is it safe, Jack? Will it stay fresh for an extended period? I don't know where you had the recipe, so I don't know if she found it or not."

Jack thought about this. Kanya realized the money wasn't where she thought, and she had gone to the apartment looking for anything that would tell her where it was while Chris was at the office. She had set this whole thing up, and now it was falling apart on her. Jack had put the money in a self-storage rental unit. He had only paid for one month, so that's how long the cake would stay fresh. But worse, Jack did have the unit number and padlock combination written down. He had that hidden, but Kanya could have found it if she had done a thorough enough search. It killed Jack not knowing whether it was safe or not. He grabbed desperately at the thought that maybe she might still be screwed out of the money.

Jack said back to Chris, "She might."

Chris said, a little panicky, "Shit. I just hope she's not back over there now looking again if she didn't find it the first time. We should never have given her a key to our place."

Jack blanched at the thought. He had been so careful to keep it safe, but this whole day threw a huge monkey wrench in all of those plans and it was falling apart fast.

Chris said, "Ok, I'm going to go get a lawyer so we can get you out of here fast. I just hope it's not a race between Kanya finding the cake and getting you out. She was desperate enough to set you up, and she knows she's on limited time to find it."

Jack's mind raced. He'd be out before long, but the money was at risk until then. He said to Chris, "I think I need to tell you where the recipe is so it'll be safe."

Chris shook his head, "No, no. Don't. You were smart enough to hide it the way you did. You don't need to risk any more."

Jack said, "No. I didn't work this hard for her to get her hands on my stuff. In my duffel bag is a pair of khaki pants with cuffs. In the cuff is a piece of rolled-up paper with the recipe. Make sure it's still there, and get me a lawyer as soon as you can."

Chris said, "Done! I love you, Jack. You know I'd do anything for you. I'm going to fix this for you. I know it's hard for you to sit tight and just wait, but give me two hours. I'll have the recipe safe and you'll be out of here." He reached out and rubbed his finger down Jack's chin affectionately, then turned and left.

~~~~~

Jack sat. Time had entirely stopped now. Jack had finally come to a cruel, terrible, crushing realization, and time had stopped on that moment to make it last forever.

Chris wasn't coming back. He had gotten what he had wanted from Jack, and he and Kanya were now off to who knew where. With all of Jack's money, except the secret, laundered set of money he kept separate.

Chris should have been back by around 6:00, but finally, at 10:00, Jack knew the truth. Jack had been blinded by his feelings for Chris. His heart felt like a walnut in a vise. Each minute passed and the vise cranked down harder, until it finally cracked. He had been robbed and left for dead by the person he cared for most in the world. The one person he had ever really connected with.

He thought back to the night he and Chris had connected. They had run across each other and started talking. They had gone out one night and sat drinking, talking about different cons and frauds they had worked. Successes, failures, and close calls. They got drunk and talked about all of it, two con men swapping war stories over scotch and sodas. And then Chris had laughed at something and put his hand on Jack's knee. And let it stay just a little too long. They didn't say anything, but Jack realized Chris was gay. And it just progressed from there. Even now, Jack had a hard time believing it was all just a set up.

The betrayal tore through Jack like his soul was a flimsy piece of tissue paper. Ten months they had been together since that night of drinking. It had worked so well for the both of them, why ruin it for a cheap money grab? Jack knew why. $90,000 in one easy swoop. It would tempt many people.

He also knew he stood no real chance of wiggling out of this.

Jack had put a lot of hopes on what he had with Chris. He had found what his father wanted for him, and it was the best thing in the world. But that person had now stabbed him in the back and twisted the knife brutally. The pain suffocated him, and Jack would never get close to anyone ever again. Trust wasn't a luxury he'd be able to afford any more. Chris had run off with all of that.

He wondered if all of it with Chris had been a set up from the very start. Chris would work with Jack, get close to him, then when a certain amount of equity had been built up, take that from him and run. Something about that didn't seem likely, though, even to Jack's paranoid mind. Sadly, the other alternative was what Jack believed, and it was crushing. What if Chris really *had* loved Jack? What if he had been happy with Jack, but still turned on him at the last minute anyway, just to grab a little cash? How could he get close to anyone, take another chance, love anyone, after knowing that they could turn on you that easily? How could you ever trust anyone again, under any circumstance?

Chris had ruined his chance to ever really be close to another person, to be intimate with them. Jack thought about the fact that, now, the only person he'd ever really be close to in his life was his father. He thought about the knife Stambeki had left deep in his back and how it would be there the rest of his miserable life. He wished he were dead instead of his father.

Day 4 – Sunday, March 26th, 2000

Jack woke up and almost couldn't move. He knew he would be stiff, but he forced himself up anyway to shake some of it off before the morning count. He was earlier than usual this morning getting up so he'd have a little extra time. He brushed his teeth again just to make sure the last of Fredo was gone. As he shaved, he noticed that his hand was still shaking a little from what had happened, and he could still feel it up and down his spine – he was still a little panicky over the assault. He decided to do a little gentle stretching to try and loosen up some, and to calm down some more.

As he stretched, he thought about what had happened the day before with a sad resignation. Well, he was only three days in and had officially been raped in prison. Jack might have enjoyed giving a guy like Fredo a blowjob under other circumstances. In prison, though, there were essentially three kinds of sexual contact – consensual sex, forced sex where the dominant was really just trying to get his rocks off, and then rape where the rapist was trying to hurt and dominate someone else. What happened to Jack yesterday was outright rape – there was no sexual gratification involved in it. It had been an assault, pure and simple. It made Jack's mouth run dry and his palms sweat thinking about it again.

He assumed that everyone would find out quickly enough about what happened. He didn't think that what had happened would get him a homo rep, though, and that was important to him. If there was a bright side to it, that would be it. He was being taught a lesson there, and that's all it had been. If people found out that he actually was gay, he'd become essentially what Wilson was – a piece of property used at will, passed around and pimped out. He was glad that no one would think of him as gay for what happened with Fredo, then.

The other thing Jack thanked his lucky stars for was that HIV was much less of a concern here than other prisons in the system. They had explained to Jack coming in that everyone in PattX was screened for HIV once a month, and anyone turning up positive was reassigned to the HIV wing of the prison, one of the four. The company that ran PattX had decided that prevention was cheaper in the end than dealing with a rampant spread, so the prison had specifically been designed to help minimize that risk.

The oral rape was unpleasant enough, but he felt really lucky to have gotten away with as little of a physical beating as he had. Had Capt. Marcus not come by when he did, the physical beating would have been far worse.

Jack finished his stretching and felt a little better than when he had first crawled out of his bunk. He laid back down for a few more minutes and started hearing others waking up and moving around.

He would have all kinds of people asking him about what happened yesterday, but he still wouldn't be able to talk about it. He had to keep his mouth shut or it would be very bad for him, and he didn't want to land right back on the top of Fredo's shit-list again. Besides, Fredo and the others would probably be bragging about it.

If anything good was to come out of it all, it was that Jack was evened up with Fredo now. They weren't going to be best friends all of a sudden, but Fredo had had the last word. Also, Troy got confirmation on something he had been concerned about. Troy now knew that Jack wasn't at all the threat he thought he might be. Jack had just gotten a little lucky the first night and was keeping a low profile since then. Troy had specifically set Jack up for a test to see what he was really made of, and he saw that Jack wasn't worth worrying about.

At breakfast, Hool and the others wanted to know what happened, but Jack just said he hadn't slept well the night before.

They all just laughed at this. Turner said that it must be some shit insomnia that gave him a bruise on the chin like that, and even Jack laughed at that one.

Jack watched throughout breakfast, and sure enough, the Kennel was now totally ignoring him, including Troy and Fredo. He thanked God that was behind him, except for the inevitable taunts for the next day or so.

Walking out of the dining room after breakfast, one guy at the Kennel's table yelled out at him, "Hey, Carber, you sure do have a purrrrty mouth!" The whole table erupted in laughter.

Jack wanted to yell back at the guy, "Well, that's because it doesn't have all the stretch marks like yours does." But Jack just ignored the guy and walked out, trying to keep the fear and anger that was roiling just under the surface from bubbling up too much.

~~~~~

The rest of the day, Jack got increasingly nervous about Adder. Today was the third full day, and his cellmate was going to get out of the tank at some point. He had been scared of Adder from the first day, but what happened yesterday made him dread it that much more. He had only gotten beat up like that one other time in his life, and the incident with Fredo and Troy was a little worse.

He spent some time with Wilson in the open lounge area playing checkers trying to take his mind off of everything. Wilson was especially sensitive about what had happened to Jack the day before. He admitted to Jack that that kind of stuff had happened to him more times than he cared to think of, and then added that he was sure Jack was already aware of that. Just from the look in Wilson's eyes, Jack felt sure it had all hurt him just as much as it had hurt himself.

Out on the yard that afternoon, Jack spent a little time talking to the earnest and idealistic guard, Norrison, who had yard duty that day. Out of everyone he had met so far, Norrison was the only guy he would normally have gone for. He was younger, blond, lean and in good shape, and he had great hazel eyes. Jack found out that he had started out as a street cop, but went to work for the private company running PattX about six months ago. The pay was a little better, and the bad attitude that was pervasive among most street cops had put him off on being on the force. Jack asked him if he thought it was much better here at PattX. Norrison just shrugged a little noncommittally. Jack thought to himself that Norrison was quickly finding out that the prison system probably wasn't a whole lot better.

Finally, about the middle of the afternoon, Jack decided to stop fretting about the Adder thing and to go back to his cell and wait for the guy to show up. He was going to have to deal with it sooner or later and the anticipation all day made him want to get it over with. He stopped by the library to pick up a book or magazine to pass the time, and went back to his cell. He was very careful and alert passing by the showers this time, though.

While he waited, it seemed like he jumped at every sound, expecting to see the hulking silhouette of his cellmate walking in the door. But it never was him. He thumbed through the magazine idly, and then, without even consciously thinking about it, he ripped a page out of the magazine and folded it up into a paper canoe. He put the canoe over on the desk. It looked a little odd to him that the canoe was the one and only thing sitting out on it. He rather regretted making it once he started staring at it... too many memories.

He was on the verge of crumpling the paper canoe up when it happened. He heard a few people loudly making their way back to their cells on the first tier, but he heard one of them call out loudly, "Hey hey, Adder's back! Did Jones fuck you with his big, black dick?"

Jack didn't know what to do. He jerked up and couldn't decide, so he just nervously stood up next to the wall between the bunks and the lavatory. He could feel the blood draining out of him, and he kept trying to get himself to man up a little more than this.

Adder strode into view and turned back into the cell. He was scratching absently at the dark shadow that had grown on his face over the last three days. He gave Jack a casual, unconcerned glance, then around the cell, but he kept walking right toward Jack and...

And all of a sudden Jack's head was swimming and he was so dizzy he couldn't see. His head was killing him. He realized, groggily, that he was lying on the ground. It took him a second to pull it together, and the dizziness started to clear a little. He sat up and felt a terrible throbbing on both his forehead and the back of his head. His hand went up to his forehead and it was really sore. He felt the back of his head and found a nice-sized knot there.

He shook his head to clear out some more of the dizziness and felt around to make sure nothing else was badly damaged.

Adder must have attacked him. Shit! All he had done was stand there! This guy was a total psycho! Jack hadn't even seen Adder go for him; it had happened faster than he could even see it. He shook his head again and went to stand up, but he had to hold onto the lavatory so he didn't fall back over. He looked in the mirror to see how bad his face was, and sure enough, there was a swollen bruise in the middle of his forehead, but that was all. Jack thought Adder must have head-butted him and then he cracked his head on the wall behind him from the force.

When he realized what had happened, the panic overflowed. Jack wheeled around quickly, and still dizzy, almost lost his balance in the process. It had hit him that what had happened might have been just the first taste and that Adder might still be waiting there to give him some more. He didn't see him, though, at first. His eyes finally found him; Adder was up on his bunk just lying there, arms behind his head and staring at the ceiling.

And then Jack noticed that Adder had two pillows piled up under his head. The pillow from Jack's bunk was gone. The head-butt was for taking one of Adder's pillows, even though it really was Jack's. So it wasn't a totally random attack, after all.

The dizziness had begun to clear off now, but his head was still sore in front and back. He gingerly touched the knot on the back of his head and wanted to run out and hide from this guy. He wanted to scream at a guard to move him to a different fucking cell so he could get away from Adder. But Jack steeled himself yet again, and with the tiny amount of bravery he could muster up, he said firmly, "Jesus! Adder, if you wanted the pillow back, you could have just asked!"

He watched Adder very closely to see what kind of reaction he gave. But there was none, Adder just lay there, completely ignoring Jack at this point. No turn of the head to look at Jack, no flinch at being yelled at, no roll of the eyes. Nothing.

Jack waited a second, then grumbled as he rubbed the back of his head, "I'm Jack Carber, by the way." Still nothing. Even if the guy never talked, Jack expected something, like being flipped off, or a glare, or a malicious smile. But he got nothing.

So Jack just left. He decided to go to the laundry area to ask for another pillow. On his way to the laundry, he passed Hector, who saw the fresh bruise on his forehead. Hector stopped and said, even as Jack ignored him and kept walking, "Shit, man! You already pissed off Adder, didn't you?"

Jack ignored everyone that he passed. He got to the laundry window and had to argue with the guy for a new pillow, but finally got the guy to give him one. On his way back to his cell, he suddenly wondered if this was going to turn into a game with Adder. Jack would go get a pillow, and Adder would just take it. It wouldn't be the first stupid mind-game played in prison purely out of boredom. Jack had this frustrating image of Adder up on the top bunk on this small mountain of pillows and Jack arguing with the laundry dude again and again. He almost lost the will to go back into the cell. The dread and helplessness was almost too much. But Jack shook his head a little bit and forced himself to pull it together.

When he got back to his cell, Adder was now at the lavatory shaving off the beard he had grown while in the tank. Jack looked at Adder's reflection in the mirror, but Adder didn't seem to be watching Jack at all.

He looked at Adder and didn't know what to do. The guy was huge, with broad shoulders, big arms and hands, and was obviously set to go off at almost anything.

Jack put his new pillow on his bed and laid down on it to wait for the dinner bell, which would be coming pretty quickly. He heard a few people headed back to their cells, some commenting that Adder was out of the tank.

Adder finished shaving, and in one quick, totally silent move, he put his foot on the edge of Jack's bunk (which scared him almost to death) and swung back up onto his top bunk. Jack held his breath for a second and then relaxed. Jack dreaded the thought of flinching like that every single time Adder moved for the next three years.

At the alarm bell, Jack stayed put. Adder swung down lightly off his bunk and headed calmly out the door to dinner. Jack sat up, but gave Adder a few more seconds' head start before he followed. He didn't want to be right in front of Adder, but coming up behind him now seemed like a bad idea, too.

On the way to dinner, Jack stayed plenty behind Adder, but close enough to observe a little bit. Chica was behind Jack and called out to him, "Jack, honey, I hear you been cheatin' on me!!" Jack ignored him.

In the chow hall, Jack sat down with Bickers, Hool, and the others. Hool looked at him and finally said, "So what'd you do to deserve that? Or was it for no reason at all?"

Jack gritted his teeth and said angrily, "I was using a pillow he wanted."

Hool laughed a little bit. Bickers was grinning, too, and said, "Man, you've had a bad couple of days."

Hool wasn't quite ready to let go. "Did you give him the pillow?"

Jack snarled at him, "Yes, I gave him the fucking pillow!"

Everyone laughed out loud this time. Jack looked up at Adder a couple of tables over. There were a few other inmates at the table with him, but Jack noticed they were as far away from him as possible. Adder wasn't looking around at anyone. He was quietly eating his dinner just like he was the only person in the chow hall.

Jack kept an eye on Adder since it was his first real opportunity to do so from a safe distance, but he kept the conversation on Adder as well.

"Has Adder ever fought with Quake or Troy?"

Hool said, "No, Quake respects Adder and is happy to leave that well enough alone. Troy hasn't fought with him directly, either. He's sent some of the Kennel after Adder once, five of 'em, just to firm up his juice here. Adder did get pretty beat up in that one but managed to escape. Four of Troy's guys went into the hospital for what Adder did to them, though. Adder went in to the hospital, too, but he got out way before the Kennel dogs did. The fifth guy chickened out. Troy beat the shit out of that guy personally for making the Kennel look bad. He wound up in the hospital longer than any of them."

Jack asked, "What's Adder in for?" He was kind of amazed he hadn't asked that already.

Hool said, "Armed robbery, aggravated assault, grand theft auto, abduction, carjacking, illegal weapons. I'm probably leaving some shit out."

"Quite a list," was Jack's only reply. It was a frightening list to Jack, but he didn't voice that out loud.

~~~~~

Back in the cell, after the inmate count, Jack sat on his bunk and leaned against the wall while reading the magazine he had brought back earlier, but he was really only halfway looking at it.

Adder had brushed his teeth while Jack watched him do so. Adder was a big guy, probably 6 foot 5, with short dark hair over a fairly high forehead. His hair had a sprinkling of gray to it, a little more so around the temples, so he wasn't a young guy. Even after shaving right before dinner, Adder still had a dark shadow on his face and strong chin, which had a hint of a dimple in it. He had dark, full eyebrows over deep set eyes, which were a bluish gray. His lips were a little thin, and there was a scar on his lower lip. And from the looks of it, his nose had probably been broken multiple times. From the face, Jack supposed Adder was in his early forties. The guy had wide shoulders that narrowed to a waist. His arms were thick, including the forearms, which led to big hands. The forearms had matching black hair on them that got denser towards his wrists. Jack had spied on his right arm the tip of a tattoo that looked like some kind of dagger pointing down from underneath Adder's t-shirt. The years he had been in prison were written over the guy's body pretty thoroughly.

When Adder finished with his teeth, he pulled the encyclopedia and his reading glasses out of the desk, leaned back in the desk chair, and started flipping through it.

Jack felt like if he stayed out of Adder's way, and Adder just ignored him the way he was now, then things might not be so bad. Adder didn't fit the mold of a super dominant inmate, though. He hadn't tried to establish his dominance over Jack, yet. He had head-butted Jack over the pillow, but that was more of just a corrective swat, the way a new owner pops a puppy on the nose when he does something bad. And it felt exactly that demeaning to think of it that way, too.

A few minutes before lights out, Adder put the book and glasses down, and turned and faced towards Jack. Jack started to worry slightly if the other shoe was about to drop. Jack watched nervously, but couldn't tell if Adder was actually looking at him or not. It was almost like Adder was looking at a point slightly past Jack.

But Adder merely stripped down for bed. He had a narrow jock strap under his pants that he left on. It was then that Jack saw the snake for the first time. All around Adder's waist was a large, expertly detailed tattoo of a snake. Right above Adder's pubic area, the snake's head was biting its own tail so that the snake totally encircled his body. He had a wide chest with a thin layer of black hair covering it, which got thicker right in the middle. Jack could see two small scabs on his abdomen where the Taser had hit the other day. Adder's body was very muscular, but not at all a gym body. It was the body of a seasoned street fighter, tense and powerful.

Adder stepped over to the bunk, which made Jack reflexively flinch once again. But Adder silently hopped up into his own bunk as he had done earlier that afternoon.

Jack went ahead and got up and brushed his teeth and stripped down to his boxers for the night. Jack had a decent body himself, visible pecs and a flat stomach, plus defined biceps. But Adder was in a class he hadn't seen yet on anyone else at the prison.

Before he had a chance to get back in his bunk, the lights went out on the tier. He waited for his eyes to adjust for a moment, then found his way to his bunk in the low night-lighting coming in from the walkways outside.

For the first time since he had gotten there, he was going to have to spend the night locked up in a room with someone that was genuinely dangerous. But after the multiple assaults he had already endured, his body needed the sleep, and he drifted off pretty quickly.

~~~~~

At some point during the night, Jack woke up to a huge weight pinning his arms and chest down, and something heavy being placed over his face. Jack panicked, sure that Adder was trying to suffocate him in his sleep. He thrashed a little bit trying to shake Adder off, but his efforts were totally worthless. There was no budging what was bearing down on him. In fact the pressure got worse and he heard Adder quietly say, "Shhhh..." It wasn't a request. So Jack stopped briefly, and as soon as he did, the pressure let up and he could breathe again.

That's when he realized that Adder was over him and the thing on his face suffocating him was actually Adder's ass. Adder rubbed it around a little bit, and Jack clued in to the agonizing truth. He wasn't being suffocated. Adder wanted his ass eaten out.

Jack started to thrash a little more and tried to push Adder off, but Adder sat back down on his face hard. Adder also took Jack's little finger on his left hand and started to bend it back painfully. Jack stopped thrashing immediately once again and screamed out in a yell that was muffled in the cheeks and crack covering his mouth, which came too close to giving Adder exactly what he wanted anyway. When Jack stopped fighting, Adder lifted up so he could breathe again and stopped bending Jack's finger back.

Jack sighed quietly as he realized that this wasn't going to go away and he was pretty helpless to stop it from happening. Adder was going to have his way or Jack would have his little finger broken in two in an incredibly painful way.

Jack lifted his head up a little bit to Adder's asshole and tentatively licked out at it. Thank God almighty, it was clean. Jack had eaten ass before, even some that he didn't care to, but he didn't do it very often and he'd certainly never been forced. But at least this one was clean.

When Jack's tongue made contact, Adder sat up just slightly and loosened up on Jack's finger even more, to let Jack know he was doing well.

Jack thought he really should continue to fight, to make it not worth Adder's time to try and get this from him, but he was pretty sure the price he would pay for not doing what Adder wanted far outweighed the benefit he'd get by fighting. Adder was going to get his way.

So Jack didn't try and fight it any more. He gave Adder the good rim job he was after.

Luckily, Adder didn't need a whole lot. After just a few minutes of this, Adder got up off of him, and Jack thought maybe he was done.

But he wasn't. Adder just got back on top of Jack and pinned his arms down. He faced towards Jack's head this time and leaned forward to feed his dick to him. Jack thought to himself he was being raped again as he was with Fredo. This was Adder exerting control over Jack. Jack was scared and beaten and just couldn't fight anymore, so he just let it happen.

Adder pushed his dick into Jack's mouth, and Jack didn't fight it. He sucked Adder off like Adder wanted. But it was different from what Fredo had done. Fredo specifically wanted to hurt Jack, but Adder wasn't particularly rough or violent. Jack decided that Adder wasn't really trying to prove a point to Jack or hurt him. Adder was just horny and Jack just happened to be the nearest hole.

When he was done, Adder got up off of Jack and silently lifted himself back up in his bunk to fall asleep again. There was no further violence or humiliation. Adder had just wanted to get his rocks off.

Jack slowly got up out of his bunk, trying hard not to appear threatening to Adder. He went over to the sink to rinse his mouth out and brush his teeth. When he was done, he turned back to the bunk and could see Adder up in his bunk on his side, watching Jack. Or, rather, looking in Jack's general direction; Adder didn't seem to be focusing on anything specific, but it was hard to tell in the dark. Jack finished wiping off his mouth, sighed, and got back in bed.

It was a long time before he fell asleep again. He was wondering if he was going to wind up being Adder's receptacle every single night, maybe even multiple times a night. He wondered if he'd ever be able to sleep again, constantly on edge that he was going to be attacked the instant he managed to nod off. It was depressing and frightening. And it was his daily life now.

Jack wanted to just go ahead and run up to the cell gate and wave out and yell for the guards, and when they came, just ask them to go ahead and shoot him then and there and end this. He couldn't take years of this. How could anyone? He started to understand why Wilson was constantly looking over his shoulder nervously. Jack wanted to curl up and go to sleep and never wake up. But he just lay there with his eyes open, and the minutes ticked by, agonizingly slow.

Day 5 – Monday, March 27th, 2000

Jack woke up with a start, panicked that he had allowed himself to fall asleep in the same room with Adder. It was still early, but the windows were beginning to show the faint light of dawn outside and he looked around the cell. He panicked even more when he saw that Adder was up already. The fear and resulting hatred reared up in Jack immediately and he tried to shrink under the thin sheet of his bunk as if that would do anything to protect him. The feeling of being completely helpless almost overwhelmed him. And the asshole over on the floor couldn't care less about what he had done to Jack. He probably took a great deal of pleasure in hurting and demeaning Jack.

But then, despite his bitterness, Jack started to notice what Adder was doing and couldn't help but be a little curious. Adder had spread out the towel from the desk unit on the floor of the cell and was kneeling on it. He was wearing pants, but no shirt. Adder was bent forward with his face all the way to the ground and arms stretched out in front of him. He stayed like this for a while, and Jack wondered if all this was some religious ceremony he was unfamiliar with.

But then Jack noticed a sort of rhythmic twitching and flexing in Adder's back and arm muscles. Adder sat up and crossed his legs. He extended his arms out straight and held them. Then the flexing and twitching started working its way across Adder's body again.

Jack's curiosity grew as Adder changed positions a few more times, always followed by the precise flexing of individual muscles while holding the pose. The best he could figure is that it was a sort of stretching or muscle control exercise that Adder did, working a single muscle at a time. Jack marveled at the level of skill and self-discipline it must take to be able to control individual muscles to that degree.

Jack couldn't help but watch. Adder totally ignored him and continued with his exercise. Adder went through a range of positions, holding in place and then firing the individual muscles in specific order.

Finally, Jack got up to brush his teeth. As he started, Adder finished his routine, stood up and rolled up the towel and put it back on the shelf over the desk. As Jack was brushing his teeth, he realized that Adder was standing there, hands clasped in front of him, watching Jack.

Jack panicked momentarily and said, muffled by the toothpaste, "Shit, you're waiting on me. I'm getting out of your way." He hated that he was cowed so completely and easily by this jackass. It embarrassed him to know how easy it was for Adder to control him.

But Adder's expression was totally blank, and Jack had that funny feeling that Adder wasn't even looking at him. Jack tried to stand out of Adder's way while he finished and watched him out of the corner of his eye, but Adder stood there patiently and waited his turn. Jack finished and sat down on his bunk, keeping an eye on Adder the whole time. Adder then moved up to brush his own teeth.

Jack thought about the blowjob he had been forced to give in the middle of the night. He tried to look on the bright side and thought that even if Adder wasn't really Jack's type, there were many, many people at PattX much more unpleasant than Adder to be blowing. He tried to console himself, too, with the fact that Adder wouldn't be bragging about it to everyone all day. The bright sides only went so far, though; Jack was absolutely powerless against this person he was locked up with and it scared him mightily.

Despite the minimal violence involved in Adder's attack during the night, it felt worse than what Fredo and Troy had done to him the day before. He thought through it, trying to understand what it was that made him feel that way, when he looked at Adder again. Then it hit him. With Fredo and Troy, Jack had been treated as another person in the room, even if that meant he was a person to be controlled, beaten, punished, and humiliated. Fredo and Troy had at least *some* kind of emotional reaction to Jack. Adder was precisely the opposite. To his cellmate, Jack was just an inanimate object in the room, worth no more consideration than the flimsy plastic chair at the desk. Jack wasn't worth rage or even some sadistic contempt. Adder had been less violent and less reactive, and it somehow made Jack far less than a human as a result. Why get mad at a flimsy plastic chair for being a flimsy plastic chair? The thought sent a shudder up Jack's back.

He looked at Adder, who was still brushing his teeth. A wave of depression hit him again. He wanted to crawl into some corner and just be totally forgotten.

That whole day, Jack hung out anywhere that Adder wasn't. His fear and depression dictated his day to him even more than the guards did.

~~~~~

Norrison had yard duty again that afternoon. Jack knew he needed to ask about it, and Norrison was the one to ask. Out of all the guards, Norrison was the one that would take him seriously and not see Jack as being a whiner or weak for asking. He spent a few minutes building up his nerve, then walked across the packed dirt of the yard and asked Norrison what he had to do to get moved to a different cell. Norrison shrugged, but seemed to be sympathetic to Jack's request. He replied that only Capt. Marcus could request a cell change, and he added that Marcus essentially never did that.

Jack put it all on the line. "What if it's really important?"

Norrison looked at him with just a touch of pity, but answered, "Capt. Marcus doesn't think that anything about an inmate is important."

Jack sat out in the yard by himself the rest of the afternoon and almost didn't move. If he could have just slept out in the chilly night air, away from everyone and his problems inside, he would have. At least then, he could have looked up at the stars.

Day 11 – Sunday, April 2nd, 2000

Jack sat down in a chair in the open lounge area along with a handful of other inmates that were waiting for the service to begin. He spotted Hector and Ramon among the inmates waiting. Jack had decided to attend the generic religious service the prison provided on Sunday mornings. Not so much that he was a religious person, but more out of a hope that maybe he could talk to the priest or preacher or rabbi or whoever it was they had running these things. This person would maybe have a more sympathetic ear about Jack's desire to move to a different cell than the guards did. Maybe the preacher or whoever could do a better job of convincing Capt. Marcus to move him than he could.

Jack still hoped he'd maybe be able to get away from Adder. The past days in the cell with Adder had shown Jack the chilling truth that the guy was a machine – Jack had never met anyone quite so cut off and emotionally empty. Adder never seemed to look directly at Jack, or anyone for that matter, never seemed to have any look on his face other than that of emptiness, never seemed to even realize Jack was in the room. Jack had made a life out of connecting with other people, out of false pretenses of course, but this guy was totally empty. No anger, curiosity, laughter, hatred, joy. Nothing.

At least things with Adder had settled down, and it wasn't quite as bad as Jack had originally feared. Jack had stayed out of Adder's way, barely even speaking to him, and Adder ignored Jack. Even the attack in the middle of the night was a one time thing. Adder had, so far, forced Jack into sex only one other time.

This last time was two nights previous. A few minutes before lights out, Jack was brushing his teeth and Adder had stripped down for bed. When Jack turned around, Adder was there totally naked this time. He pointed at Jack, then at his bunk, then he grabbed his dick. It was the strangest thing, because even though it was a direct command Adder was issuing Jack, it was still couched in utter disinterest.

Jack had gotten some of his fight back since the first time and said, "Hell no!"

That was the wrong answer and Adder was on Jack almost faster than he could see. He slammed Jack up on the wall, with his forearm underneath Jack's chin, supporting almost all of Jack's weight there, crushing into his trachea and choking him. Adder had pushed his right knee into Jack's balls. Jack couldn't speak and was already feeling dizzy from lack of air, so he thrashed at Adder with his hands and arms a little bit. Adder ignored him and pushed harder on Jack's balls with his knee. Adder's face was inches away from Jack's and it was the first time that Adder had looked directly into Jack's eyes. What Jack saw unnerved him. It wasn't fury, or effort, or hunger, or even amusement. It was just this emotionless intensity, but Adder communicated with Jack perfectly well, and Jack stopped and gave up.

Adder let him down to the ground and stood there, waiting.

Jack gasped for breath, rubbed his throat, and glared at the naked man in front of him.

And so Jack shuffled over to the bunk and wound up blowing Adder again. Like the time before, once Jack caved in and performed his function, Adder wasn't violent about it. And this time, it was just a blowjob. No rimming. Jack was glad of that small favor.

Jack hadn't said anything to anyone about Adder assaulting him this way, and Adder had been so quiet doing it that maybe no one else on the tier even knew it was even happening. He couldn't decide if it was better this way, or if it would be better to just be Adder's piece and maybe that would offer him a little protection from everyone else.

The whole situation might not be as bad as he originally suspected, but Jack still wanted to try and get away from this guy if he could.

Which is what led him to the Sunday morning service in the lounge area.

The priest came in and began the service (it turned out to be a Catholic priest, after all), but he kept the service pretty generic. Jack thought that maybe the priest route wouldn't be too bad. The priest was a younger guy, slim, blue-eyed and with dirty blond hair, fresh-faced and eager to make a difference in the lives of a bunch of convicts. He introduced himself to everyone gathered as Father Anthony.

After the service, Jack stepped up to speak to Father Anthony as he was gathering his briefcase to leave.

"Father, I'll be honest with you, I'm not a particularly religious man, but I've got something of a problem here that I was wondering if I could talk to you about," he said.

The Father was very pleased that Jack had come to him. "Certainly. Part of what I do is to advocate for the inmates. I'm Father Anthony." He smiled and held out his hand for Jack. Jack liked the guy's smile and he definitely liked his blue eyes.

"I'm Jack Carber."

"Jack, tell me about your problem."

The lounge area had cleared out, so Jack felt this was as good a place as any to talk to the priest. He still wasn't sure how much detail to give, so he kept it pretty general for now.

He said, "Well, my cellmate is a pretty rough guy, and I've been busted up a couple of times, and I want to know what it takes to move to a different cell."

Father Anthony nodded understandingly. "Have you talked to Capt. Marcus about this? I believe the procedure is that only Capt. Marcus can approve a cell transfer."

"Well, no. I asked one of the other guards and they said that Capt. Marcus wouldn't be likely to sign off on it. I, uh, was thinking that... maybe... if you talked to him, it would carry a little more weight than if I did."

Father Anthony said, "You realize that a cell transfer could easily mean you'd go from the situation you have to something far worse, right?"

Jack hadn't really thought about that. He assumed Adder would be the worst one to be around. But after the last few days, he probably would question that. He definitely would see Troy, maybe Quake, and several others as being much more arbitrarily cruel than Adder.

Jack said, "That's true."

"Do you feel like you're in immediate danger?"

"Well... no." Jack felt like he was in danger. He just wasn't sure how immediate it was. You never knew with Adder.

"Then I tell you what. Why don't you try talking to Capt. Marcus yourself first and see how that goes. Come back and talk to me next Sunday. If you don't get anywhere with the captain and you still feel like a move would be best, we'll talk about how to make that happen."

Jack said, "Ok."

Father Anthony put his hand on Jack's shoulder and smiled again. "Ok then. Take care, Jack!"

~~~~~

That afternoon, Jack was out in the yard running a few laps, when he saw trouble brewing out of the corner of his eye. He stopped to see what was happening.

A guy named Pelton, who was one of the Kennel dogs, had done or said something that had pissed off Chica. Chica went after the guy with fingernails and teeth and fury unleashed in a maelstrom.

They wound up near to where Adder had been working out with a jump rope. He was stretching some and not paying any attention to the commotion next to him.

All of a sudden, though, Chica pushed hard on Pelton, who fell back towards Adder, and got within about four or five feet of him. In the space of about two seconds, Adder had spun around and dislocated Pelton's shoulder and knocked the guy's knees out from under him. Pelton screamed out in pain from the shoulder while Adder shot Chica a dirty look to let him know not to come any closer.

A whole crowd from the yard came running up to see the fight, which was over before anybody could hardly even register it. Adder turned and walked away like it had never happened.

Watching it happen sent a wave of different emotions over Jack. He was glad Adder had never done that to him, but very scared to see how easily it could happen. Pelton wasn't a weak or stupid person, and look at what happened to him just for getting too close to Adder. He was amazed at the speed and skill that Adder could totally disable another person. But mostly, he was chilled to think how impersonal it was to Adder. Adder had given the whole thing no more thought or emotional weight than flicking a bug off of his arm in the springtime.

By the time the guards had noticed what was going on and had gotten over to Pelton, Adder was sitting up on top of a picnic table, indifferent and oblivious to the whole thing like it had nothing to do with him at all.

~~~~~

That night, as usual, Jack was waiting to see if Adder was going to leave him alone or if he'd be forced into service. He hated the waiting, dreading every minute that passed by, but unable to do anything about it other than wait for Adder.

Adder was sitting at the desk, reading a travel book about India. Jack was on his bunk and had a book as well – Catch 22 by Joseph Heller. But Jack wasn't really reading right now. He was looking at the back of Adder and thinking about what to do. He had never seen anyone so cut off or as cold as Adder. He didn't think a human could really survive like that, with no attachments or connections. When Adder hurt someone, there was no sick pleasure or anger involved, it merely happened. He seemed more like a machine than a person in too many ways. It made Jack want to crawl away from this *thing* called Adder and not be near it. It was times like this that even being roommates with Troy or Fredo seemed like the better option to Jack.

Jack thought how great it would be if he could actually fight back against Adder. He had started working out on a daily basis, with Hector and Ramon. It was good to have the workout partners, and the three of them together in the showers afterwards was much, much safer than Jack by himself. But he also knew that becoming stronger didn't make him that much better of a fighter. Plus, Jack had a suspicion that the only reason Adder hadn't permanently damaged him was because he was so little of a threat.

So, the more he thought about it, the more he thought that the solution to the problem wasn't to ignore Adder and stay out of his way. Nor was it to try and fight Adder. Rather, and much to his reluctant realization, it was to try and actually get close to him. To see if he could get Adder to respond in some human way, to see if he could form any kind of a connection with him. The others had heard Adder laugh in the past, although very infrequently. Jack had to figure out how to tap that in Adder. Finding that connection point was, after all, what Jack was good at. It was a con man's profession.

Adder turned around and looked at Jack (but kind of looked past Jack, the way he always did). Jack was startled and looked down at his book immediately so he wasn't looking at Adder. He realized he hadn't turned a page in his book in a while. Jack got up and put the book on one of the shelves over the desk next to the paper canoe, as Adder's eyes indistinctly followed him. Then Jack got back in bed, praying that Adder would leave him alone. He slept very poorly for the entire night.

Day 14 – Wednesday, April 5th, 2000

Jack watched Adder go through his morning routine. It was the strange set of muscle control exercises Adder went through every morning, without exception. And like usual, Adder behaved as if Jack didn't even exist. Jack wished Adder treated him like this all the time. But he wasn't that lucky. It was the combination of times Adder did, in his own way, acknowledge Jack's presence combined with the vacant unconcern the rest of the time that made his life hell.

The night before had marked a new low in prison for Jack. Adder had finally decided he wanted a little of Jack's ass. And Jack had given it up without a fight.

Jack had been suspicious of Adder because he seemed to be just standing there, waiting until Jack finished brushing his teeth. As soon as he was done, Adder pointed at Jack and then at the desk. Jack didn't quite understand what he wanted. Adder had the same face with no expression at all, and seemed to be looking at a point just to the side of Jack. Adder pointed at Jack again, this time indicating that Jack should take his clothes off and lean over the desk.

Jack tried to decide if it would be worth fighting, but knew it would end the same no matter what. He felt hopeless and helpless. He took his clothes off while Adder stood watching, pulling on his dick some, getting it hard. Jack sighed, turned around and leaned over and put his hands on the desk to brace himself against what was about to happen.

To make matters worse, there was no lube around and Adder wasn't exactly gentle when he pushed in. The pain of the entry caused Jack to cry out a little, and once Adder got going, he made more noise than usual, grunting and groaning. The other inmates were bound to hear this one.

From down along the tier somewhere, Jack heard a voice call out, "Carber's getting a big PattX welcome!!" followed by some laughs from a couple of different cells. Now Jack would have to deal with the humiliation from everyone else as well as Adder's attacks.

And sure enough, even as they got in the showers that morning, Troy had a big smile on his face and yelled for everyone to hear, "Hey Carber, are you going to clean your shit off Adder's cock this morning, or did he make you suck it off last night?" This caused all the Kennel dogs in the shower to burst out laughing at Jack.

At breakfast, Jack was lucky that Hool, Bickers, Wilson, and Turner all kept their mouths shut about the night before, and they mostly talked about other topics and gossip among themselves, topics and gossip that involved people not sitting at the table with them at the time. Jack saw Adder eating his breakfast like he was the only person in a big, empty room. He hardly said a word to the others at breakfast and finished as fast as he could.

~~~~~

Jack had been assigned a job working in the prison laundry for about three hours a day. It mostly consisted of doing whatever the manager, a guy named Charlie Campbell, told him to do. There was an upstairs area with sets of big washers and dryers for the inmate's prison-issued clothes, but the towels, sheets, and blankets were all boxed up and sent off to a contracted service.

Jack didn't mind this job so much. It wasn't hard and it put a little money in his scratch account so he could buy small items at the commissary. The downside was that he had to work side by side with Shimmey – a big, fat, incredibly stupid, black guy who was part of the Kennel. Shimmey liked to bad mouth Jack and try to push him around a lot. Jack was able to handle Shimmey relatively well, though, and gave him plenty right back.

One thing Jack liked the most about this job was when he was running clothes through the wash in the upstairs area, especially while Shimmey was dealing with the contracted laundry service. The area was a sealed-off part of the second floor accessed by a service stair in the main laundry area. It offered, though, one of the greatest luxuries Jack had experienced at prison so far – privacy. Jack could stay upstairs with the wash going and no one would be watching or bothering him. He would have given almost anything just to set up a cot up there and live there instead of his cell.

Charlie Campbell was a red-headed guy with an ugly, beat-up looking face, big nose, and a pronounced beer belly. He had been running laundry for the prison system for years and wasn't intimidated about being around prisoners at all. He seemed to like making Shimmey feel stupid, in fact, something that Shimmey was too slow to ever pick up on. But other than that, Jack couldn't figure out why Charlie kept Shimmey around.

While Jack was upstairs running some clothes through their cycles, he thought about what to do. Adder was going to use Jack for sex, and nothing was going to abruptly stop that, unless he could convince Capt. Marcus to move him. Getting a transfer was unlikely, but he still needed to ask about that, though, just in case. What Father Anthony had said did make Jack think twice about asking, though – if he got moved, he could go from bad to worse. Currently, Troy and Runnion were in cells by themselves, as was Jelly, a member of the Brethren. Jack had become familiar enough with all of them to know that all of these guys could easily wind up being worse than Adder.

But, barring a cell move, Jack was more and more convinced that avoiding and ignoring Adder was the wrong tactic, and as much as he hated the idea, maybe it was time to try and warm up to him instead. Just a little. Maybe that would help Jack be more than just a hole in the cell for Adder's use. It wouldn't be easy, though.

Communication was essential to forming a bond between two people, but it would have to be all one-sided with Adder.

~~~~~

      Out in the yard later that afternoon, the basketball court was free, so Jack, Hector, Ramon, and Turner played a little two-on-two. They played for a while, but Jack kept looking over at Adder, who was sitting cross-legged up on top of a picnic table that was out in the yard, one of his constant spots when he was outside. He seemed to be meditating or something. In the thirty minutes they played, Adder didn't move at all – it was a regular routine of his.

      When done with their game, Jack ran a couple of laps around the yard. He intentionally ended up close to Adder, so he went over to the table that he was sitting on, but not too close to risk Adder reacting suddenly. He started stretching a little bit. As he stretched, he said to Adder, "You know, you're just like a Buddha sitting over there."

      No response from Adder; he kept his eyes closed. Jack would have wondered if Adder maybe hadn't heard him except he had said it loud enough to know that Adder must have.

      Jack said, "I could probably start charging people a dollar to come up and rub your belly for luck." Jack hoped he didn't say exactly the wrong thing and set Adder off, and he braced himself to run fast if Adder lunged for him.

      Adder did open his eyes this time, but looked only directly ahead. There wasn't even a trace of a smile.

      Jack couldn't tell if Adder had even heard him or not. He said hopefully, "It's a joke. You know, like kidding around? You know?"

      Adder continued to stare blankly for a moment more, then sighed a little bit, and closed his eyes again.

"Oh, I get it! You're laughing on the inside!" With that, Jack walked off before his luck ran out.

Capt. Marcus was out walking the yard, so Jack decided now was as good a time as any to ask about a cell transfer.

He walked up to him and said, "Hey, Capt. Marcus. I've got a question for you."

Capt. Marcus just kept looking out over the yard in case there was trouble, but not that he'd be in any big rush to go break it up. He said, "What do you want?"

"What's the process for transferring to a different cell?"

Still Capt. Marcus didn't look at him when he said, "The process? What's the process? The process is that if I want you in a different cell, you'll go to a different cell."

Capt. Marcus looked over at Jack and said with an evil grin on his face, "What's the matter, Carber? Got something up your butt about a new cell?" Then he said harshly, "Maybe I should fuck you up the ass so you'll know what a real fucking is."

Jack wasn't going to play this stupid game with Marcus. He said, "Whatever. Adder's dangerous and arbitrary and you know it."

Capt. Marcus looked away and said, "Fuck off, Carber, I'm busy."

Jack gave up on Marcus and went inside in a bad mood.

Inside, Jack spent a few minutes glancing through the books that Adder had on the shelf under the desk, wondering if there was anything in there he could use to connect with him. He opened the encyclopedia to the dog-eared page Adder had left, on an article about the city of Toronto. There was no way Jack could work that into a one-sided conversation with Adder without being totally transparent, so Jack put the books back on the shelf.

That night, in the two-week old copy of the Atlanta paper Jack was browsing through, he spotted a random article about an abduction and was reading it as Adder reached for the encyclopedia to begin reading in it as he did most every night. Jack remembered that Adder was supposedly in for abduction, among other things, so he tried to decide if using that to open up a conversation with Adder would be productive or not. The risk was the same as always – that it would piss Adder off.

He was absorbed in his thoughts enough that he didn't see Adder push back from the desk, stand up and come over to where Jack was lying in his bunk. By the time Jack realized anything was happening, Adder had slammed his bare foot in Jack's face, cracking his nose and causing blood to start flowing freely from it. Jack rolled up into a ball and faced away from Adder in case there was more and felt pretty sure the guards were going to find his dead body in the morning. His nose had exploded in pain, and he had nothing to stop the bleeding with, but let it go in case there was more blows coming. He had to stifle the urge to cry out and beg for mercy.

As soon as it was done, Adder was back in his chair, his back to Jack, and was opening the encyclopedia volume again. At the sounds of the chair, Jack unfolded and peeked over his shoulder just enough to see. The blood was going everywhere but he was afraid to get out of his bunk just yet in case Adder saw it as a threat. What he did notice as he stayed put was the page Adder had opened the book to. Jack groaned when he realized he had forgotten to put the dog-ear back in place when he put the encyclopedia up earlier. He was paying for that mistake with a kick to the face and a bloody nose.

Eventually, Jack pulled himself from his bunk, always keeping a wary eye on his cellmate, and washed his face and then stuffing toilet paper up his nostril to stop the bleeding.

He had no choice that night but to fall asleep on a pillow that was sticky with his own blood.

Day 18 – Sunday, April 9th, 2000

Jack woke up a little early on Sunday, but lay in his bunk a while. He eventually heard Adder wake up and felt him step on his bunk as he got down silently.

He heard Adder take a piss, then he assumed Adder had grabbed the towel to start his morning routine. He rolled over quietly and watched his cellmate. He was already learning the pattern to this routine that Adder went through every morning. It was sort of like a cross between Tai-Chi and yoga, but then with the individual muscle movements thrown in. For someone Adder's age, he still had a very limber body. Some of the positions he put himself in and held for minutes at a time would cause a lot of other people agony. Jack watched a little bit, then got up to get ready for the morning count.

When the morning alarm bell sounded and their cell doors slid open noisily, Jack turned to Adder as they were headed out onto the walkway for the count and said, "Have you ever tried Jazzercise? I think you should try Jazzercise."

There was zero reaction from Adder, like Jack wasn't even there. Then Jack added, halfway to himself and halfway to Adder, "You just seem like a Jazzercise kinda guy."

~ ~ ~ ~ ~

Same as the previous week, Jack sat through the service that Father Anthony gave. He didn't really have a whole lot of use for organized religion. He saw it as being just another type of corporation, really. But he sat through Father Anthony's service nonetheless, tolerating it until he could talk to him man to man.

When the service concluded, Jack waited in the back for Father Anthony to speak briefly to one other inmate that needed some attention, before he made his way over to Jack. The handful of other inmates that had attended filtered out.

"Hello, Jack. I'm glad you came back for another service."

"Sure, Father."

Father Anthony said, "I'm sure you want to talk some more about your situation. But, may I suggest something? Let's go into the office so that we can have some privacy."

The office was a shared office located near the central security cage for the floor. It was a generic office shared by whoever needed it. Sometimes the police came there to follow up with inmates on information they might have, sometimes inmates met with their lawyers there. And Father Anthony got to use it too, since he served as a counselor for the inmates.

Father Anthony led Jack into the office, closed the door and locked it. Jack found this a little strange, and actually a little reckless, considering that Father Anthony didn't know him at all. Father Anthony settled into the chair behind the empty desk and Jack sat on the other side.

Jack asked, "Isn't it a little dangerous for you to lock yourself in here with inmates?"

Father Anthony smiled and said, "I have faith in you and trust you. The locked door is for your privacy so no one will barge in. Besides, showing a little trust in you will help you trust me in return."

Jack thought to himself, *a play directly out of the con man's handbook.*

Then Father Anthony added, "Besides, I did ask about you a little bit, and the guards assured me that you were a safe person to be around."

Father Anthony had done some homework as well.

Jack said, "Ahhhh. Yeah, I never managed to pick up a killer reputation around here." Then he added, "So, I asked Capt. Marcus about moving to a different cell. He said he'd have to think about it." That was a mammoth understatement. "So I thought maybe if you asked as well, he might agree to it."

Father Anthony was leaned back in his chair listening to Jack. When Jack finished, Father Anthony leaned forward, put his elbows on the desk and clasped his hands together while he studied Jack.

Jack watched him hopefully. He definitely didn't mind watching the Father. The blue eyes and blond hair and innocent face were hitting several of Jack's buttons. And the shape of the Father's jaw line and chin were very handsome. Nonetheless, Jack wondered cynically if Father Anthony had fucked a ten-year-old boy like every other Catholic priest.

Father Anthony finally said, "Tell me more about your situation. Who do you share a cell with?"

"This guy named Adder."

"Oh. Yes, I've heard him mentioned before. He's a very dangerous one, isn't he?"

"Yeah, he is."

"Has he hurt you before?"

"Well, he's pulled my finger back and almost broken it in two. He choked me one night, almost to the point of passing out. He's kneed me in the nuts. He almost suffocated me one night. And he's head-butted me. I don't know how long I was out for that one." Jack looked at the priest hopefully, and then remembered, "Oh, and I got kicked in the head one night, too. Got a bloody nose that time."

Father Anthony listened very carefully and watched Jack very intently.

"He has hurt you, then." Father Anthony paused for a second, and then asked, "Has he forced himself on you?"

Jack turned a little red at the question. He wondered, *isn't the violent behavior enough?* But he also caught that tiny bit of emphasis that the Father placed on the word "forced." Jack looked down and away from Father Anthony's gaze. He might have otherwise avoided talking about this and going through the humiliation, but the emphasis on "forced" caught his attention. Plus, Jack remembered depressingly, it wasn't like it was some huge secret that no one else knew.

Jack continued to look down and said softly, "Yeah."

Father Anthony said quietly, "How has he hurt you in this way?"

Jack paused. "Everything we talk about in here is completely confidential, right? You won't discuss it with anyone else under any circumstance, right?"

"Of course. I'll be the only one to ever hear your words."

Jack looked at Father Anthony; he watched him closely. He chose his words carefully. "Yes, Father, he has forced me to, umm... service him." His voice has sunk down very low as he spoke

Jack saw that Father Anthony was focused on every word he said like a laser. Father Anthony asked, "Sexually?"

"Yes."

Father Anthony said nothing, waiting on Jack.

Jack said, allowing his voice to crack just a little as he avoided the priest's gaze, "He's, uh... he's made me service him orally multiple times." Jack watched the Father to see at what point he might finally blink.

And on the next word out of Father Anthony's mouth, Jack totally confirmed what he thought was going on and knew exactly what he would eventually get out of the situation.

Father Anthony's lips were tight he was listening to Jack so closely. Then he asked Jack, "And?"

Jack put his face in his hands, but it was all relatively fake at this point. He replied, almost in a whisper, "And he's raped me anally as well."

Father Anthony slowly sat back in his seat and said, "I see."

"You have been placed in a bad situation, and my heart breaks for you, Jack."

Jack looked up at the Father. "Can you help me?" he asked.

Father Anthony said, "Of course I will do what I can. I'll speak to Capt. Marcus on your behalf. I'd like for you to come back next Sunday so we can see what progress we can make on your situation. Jack, you're a strong person, and you're going to be ok. If you feel like you're in danger again, you need to go to a guard immediately. God be with you, Jack." At this, Father Anthony had unlocked the office door so Jack could leave.

Jack said, "Thanks, Father," as he stood up and left.

As Jack walked out, he would have bet anyone a thousand dollars that Father Anthony would spend the next ten minutes locked in that office beating off to the thought of being raped by an inmate.

~~~~~

Later that afternoon, Jack went out into the yard. He walked past the picnic table that Adder was sitting up on, meditating again. Jack called out to him, "Yo, Buddha! Whassup?" but just walked on. He found a spot away from everyone and sat on the ground up against the wall of the prison.

He felt jaded and disappointed by Father Anthony. Not only was the guy gay, but he got off on the idea of being raped by a bunch of prison inmates. He had probably even specifically volunteered for this assignment just so he could be that much nearer his fantasy. It was sad that the priest was probably there just working an angle, waiting for the day some prisoner bent him over the desk in that locked room and plowed him. Jack had no doubt that Father Anthony took his priesthood seriously, and probably would truly help many of the inmates over time. But that didn't change the fact that the guy was specifically seeking out arousal after having taken a vow to turn away from that very thing.

Like so many organizations that were there to help people, Father Anthony really met his more fundamental, selfish needs first. And if he wound up helping other people along the way, well then, hallelujah and praise God! And the familiar hatred of the insurance companies flared up within Jack again. Fucking insurance companies!

But despite what Jack saw as the sad, true nature of Father Anthony's interest in the inmates, he knew it was a great opportunity for himself.

First of all, Jack would have that priest's legs in the air within the next couple of times that he saw him. Jack missed being the top since he had come to PattX, and Father Anthony would be a great one to get back in the saddle with. Jack didn't mind bottoming, but the circumstances he had been the bottom at PattX so far weren't really his preferred way.

It was a little bit dangerous to push down this road with Father Anthony. The priest could have a guilt fit at any point and make all kinds of claims to the guards about Jack. He didn't think it would happen, though. He knew people's natures well enough to know that Father Anthony's chance to start living out his fantasy would be too strong of a draw to resist.

And the second opportunity was a little more tantalizing for Jack. Father Anthony got off on this kind of stuff, and it would make him submissive to all kinds of requests. Jack knew that at some point, it might be nice to have a way to get things into the prison. Things that might ordinarily be prohibited.

As he thought through all this, Bickers came and sat down on the packed down ground next to him with a grunt.

"Is the priest going to do you any good?" asked Bickers as he lit up a cigarette.

"He might. He's going to try."

"I hope he does. But if you're trying to get a cell transfer, I've never seen Marcus give one to anybody since I've been here, just so you'll know. Shitty thing to tell you, but I don't want you getting your hopes up."

It flashed through his mind that Father Anthony might drag his feet on talking to Capt. Marcus just so he could keep Jack coming around, hoping for a little rough stuff. He appreciated Bickers trying to keep him from getting his hopes up, though. He asked Bickers, "How long have you been here?"

"Twenty months. I came here to Patterson right after it opened. And in another three years, I'll be out." Bickers blew a smoke ring and watched it float off.

"What are you in for?" asked Jack.

"My wife had been sleeping around with this trashy guy. He got drunk one night and beat the living shit out of her. When she came home, she called the cops and claimed I did it to her. She did it so she and this nut could be together. What the fuck is up with that, huh? There was all kinds of evidence to show it wasn't me, but the DA didn't care. It was an easy win for his office. So here I am. I hope the bitch and the dickwad beat each other senseless. Maybe they'll kill each other," Bickers exhaled a long stream of smoke from his lungs. "What about you?"

Jack answered, "Bunch of trumped up shit on identity theft and insurance fraud."

Bickers laughed and said, "Man, that kind of pussy shit doesn't land you in PattX. What else you got?"

Now it was Jack's turn to laugh. He confessed, "Weapons and aggravated assault."

"Now we're talking!"

Jack added, "And it was assault on a police officer, too."

Bickers lit up, "Sweet! I can't believe you only got, what is it, three years?"

Jack said, "Yeah, well it was only technically assault. The police found the gun in my trunk, and it wasn't mine. I started yelling at them and kneed one of them in the nuts accidentally. It was stupid of me."

Bickers said sarcastically, "Accidentally, of course. You poor, sweet, misunderstood thing!"

They both had a good chuckle at this, Bickers blowing out cigarette smoke as he laughed.

They sat for a second, then Bickers said, "For what it's worth, I know you're in a bad position with Adder. Not everyone thinks it's funny. I know I don't. Enough of us here have had to endure that kind of abuse at one time or another, and I don't wish it on anyone."

Jack immediately wanted to know who had plowed Bickers, but would never ask directly. So he asked, "Not anyone?"

Bickers flashed a look at Jack, then grinned and said, "Well, maybe Marcus."

Jack was surprised that Capt. Marcus might not have been making a hollow threat about fucking him.

It did make Jack feel a little better to know that a bigger number of people out on that yard right then than anyone realized had probably been forced into sex at one time or another. And that didn't count the consensual sex. That probably wound up including everyone at PattX.

They sat for a minute more and then Bickers said, "Wilson probably gets it worse than anybody. He got found out pretty quick that he was gay and has been passed around ever since. Troy's been focusing on him lately, though, which is bad for Wilson. At least he was a little bit used to that kind of sex before it was forced on him. Wilson didn't get his cherry busted by a sexually frustrated guard that bent him over and handcuffed his hands to his ankles." Bickers snuffed out his cigarette bitterly in the dirt at his side and looked out over the yard.

Jack was surprised at how open Bickers was. He liked him, though. He was glad Bickers trusted him. Jack nodded at him and said sincerely, "Thanks, Bickers. You helped."

Day 25 – Sunday, April 16th, 2000

Father Anthony sat down in the chair behind the empty desk and Jack sat down on the other side, just as he had done a week earlier. Father Anthony had already locked the door.

Jack didn't say anything; he instead waited to hear what Father Anthony said.

"Capt. Marcus is not going to move you to another cell," said Father Anthony with something of a regretful look on his face. "He seemed very adamant about it."

"Motherfucker!" Jack already knew what the answer was, but he said the word bitterly for Father Anthony's benefit. The cursing, the heightened emotions, it would all help get Father Anthony going.

Father Anthony said, "I know. I'm sorry. I know you must be disappointed."

Jack waited for the father's next step.

Father Anthony paused awkwardly for a second. "Capt. Marcus felt compelled to point out that you aren't completely blameless here at Patterson yourself."

"Yeah, well, who fuckin' could be? Prison drives people to do all kinds of things they might not otherwise do." Jack kept his emotional level up, feeding Father Anthony just what he wanted.

"Son, tell me what you have done to others."

Jack glared at the Father. "I beat the shit out of a guy my first night here, in front of the whole dining hall. The guards let me, too."

Father Anthony's eyes flashed just a little. He said, "That was wrong of you."

Jack jumped up out of his seat and seethed, "I don't give a shit! It was him or me! He got what he asked for!" Then Jack pretended to catch himself and sat back down. He cooled off the emotion and said, "Sorry, Father." This cool-down was Jack's way of giving Father Anthony an out, but it would be the only one he would get.

"It's ok, Jack. I'm sure you've been put in multiple survival situations."

Jack waited to see if Father Anthony took the out or not.

"How did it make you feel to hurt this person?"

Obviously, Father Anthony wanted more. Jack said, "It felt good! The asshole comes up to me wanting to start something, and he got it!"

Father Anthony watched Jack intently for a moment, his lips thin and tight. "Have you sexually attacked anyone?"

Jack was happy to make up stuff to keep Father Anthony going. He paused just a moment before answering to keep the priest baited.

"Yes."

"Why would you sexually attack another person in this prison?"

Jack leaned forward and let his emotions heighten again. "Because if I'm going to have some asshole use me for sex, I'm going to turn around and use someone else."

Jack notched it up a little more and actually stood up and leaned over the desk towards Father Anthony. He said, "Because that's how you stay a man in a place like this!"

He moved around to the side of the desk towards Father Anthony to let him have a good look. Jack grabbed his dick through his prison-issue pants and shook it at Father Anthony. "You get horny, and you want to shoot your load. And you find the nearest hole that you can take control of and you use it!"

Father Anthony was clearly wallowing in it all. He had a terrified look on his face, but his eyes hadn't moved from Jack's crotch since he had stood up. Jack had kept looking at Father Anthony – his handsome face and clear, blue eyes. The thought of actually screwing Father Anthony right there on the desk in the office got Jack's motor running and he had a hard-on that was clearly visible through his pants. Father Anthony's eyes couldn't have been pulled off Jack's dick with a tow-truck and a high-powered wench.

Jack moved around even closer and actually towered over the priest. He said menacingly, "And that's what I did. I found a hole, knocked it around a little bit, and then I fucked it."

And for the final touch, Jack said in a whisper while he was still practically on top of Father Anthony in his chair, "Just like I'm about to do now!"

Father Anthony looked up in horror and said desperately, "Please, no!"

And for a flash, Jack thought he'd have to back down, that maybe Father Anthony really didn't want the fantasy to become reality after all. But then Father Anthony leaned over in his chair just a little bit so that his shoulder touched Jack's hard-on through his pants. Jack thought, *well, that answers that!*

He stood up straight and pulled Father Anthony up by the back of his shirt and pushed him over the desk. Father Anthony didn't fight at all, mostly because his hands were already busy trying to undo his belt. Jack had to admit that the whole scene had definitely gotten him hot, even if it was just a bunch of role-playing on both sides.

Jack roughly pulled Father Anthony's pants down around his ankles and shoved him back down over the desk. He pulled his own pants down. The sight of Father Anthony's ass was definitely welcome. He had a great ass, and Jack was anxious to pop it.

Father Anthony whispered, "Please, no!" again.

Jack just hissed, "Shut up!" He paused just a second before going in because the thought of a dry entry made him wince a little before it even happened.

But then he just pushed it in. Father Anthony actually groaned in pleasure. Jack almost wanted to laugh out loud and had to genuinely stifle it. It wasn't a dry entry. Not by a long shot! The motherfucker's ass was already lubed up and ready to go! Father Anthony had given an entire service earlier, had extolled pure hearts and minds, with his ass lubed up, waiting and hoping for it to get plugged right after. Jack thought about people and the filthy, dirty little secrets they kept.

The last hesitation and doubts behind him, Jack plowed into Father Anthony's ass over and over. He had himself a great time and played his part well. He leaned over a couple of times so his face was next to Father Anthony's and whispered names like "Goddamn bitch" and "fucking cunt" into the his ear. He let the Father have it just a little rough to make it authentic.

When he was done, Jack would have actually liked to relax and hold Father Anthony for a while, maybe even kiss some. Just because Jack had managed to go his whole life without an extended relationship didn't mean he didn't have a romantic streak. But the role he was playing wouldn't allow any nonsense like that; it would have ruined it for Father Anthony. So, instead, he pulled out, spat on the Father's ass and stood up.

Jack pulled his pants back up and stood there waiting on Father Anthony with his arms crossed.

Father Anthony slowly stood up after a moment and put his clothes back together. He turned and faced Jack, but didn't directly meet Jack's gaze. He said, "I, uh, think that, uh..." Father Anthony stopped and cleared his throat, then continued, "I think that I should continue to monitor your situation in case it worsens for you. Please, come back if anything changes." Father Anthony started patting at his forehead to blot the sweat off, all without once looking at Jack.

Jack said nastily, "That's what I thought." He moved to the door and unlocked it. Before he stepped out, Jack sneered, "I think this counseling did me some actual good, for once. I'll probably take you up on that. See you 'round, Padre!" And he walked out and closed the door as he left.

Jack was exhilarated by what had just happened. Despite knowing that he was faking, it had been quite a rush to really have it play out like that. Jack decided to stop by the shower area and clean up. It was an odd time of day, and the showers would probably be deserted, which would make it a little risky. But Jack was hopped up on adrenaline and didn't care.

As he stepped under the showerhead, Adder came in, glanced at Jack and started taking his clothes off. Jack was immediately suspicious. He wondered if this was planned and Adder was going to force himself on Jack, or if it was just a coincidence.

Jack played it casual and continued what he was doing. He said, "Hey, man, what's happening?" Of course there was no response.

"I guess you caught me. I come in here sometimes when no one's here to turn on all the showers and practice my 'Singing In The Rain' routine."

Adder was scrubbing his hair under the showerhead next to Jack, but stopped and looked in Jack's direction for a second, at least sort of in Jack's direction. Still no emotion on Adder's face, though. Jack looked at the snake wrapped around Adder's waist, the dagger and skulls on one arm, and the thorn and flame tattoo on the other. Adder's size and tattoos were intimidating, but what made him really intimidating was his silence. Well, that and his utter indifference. There was always the strange sensation that Adder didn't see any other people in the prison. Just things to use, or hurt if they got too close. It made Adder seem sociopathic. Jack started getting nervous, but tried to stay cool. If he could just get even a tiny smile out of Adder, he would know he was on the right track.

He said, "You know... for the prison talent show."

Adder went back to showering, and so did Jack. After about another half minute, Jack stopped and asked, "We do have a prison talent show, right?"

Adder stopped again and looked off at the shower wall, then went back to washing the soap off. Jack thought for sure he would have gotten at least a smirk out of Adder with that one.

~~~~~

That evening after dinner, Jack was lying on his bunk and Adder was at the desk reading, same as every night.

Jack had been thinking about what happened with Father Anthony. Mostly, he wondered if Father Anthony would wind up having a guilt attack over the whole thing and cut him off entirely, or worse, accuse him of rape. Normally, Jack would have thought that either of these could easily be an outcome of what had happened. But Father Anthony had so completely anticipated the whole thing. He had shoved his shoulder into Jack's hard dick and had pre-greased himself for a good pounding, for shit's sake! Preacher man was a complete slut for this kind of stuff. Jack was so sure that Father Anthony was totally into it that he started to wonder if the Father was working more than one inmate this way.

Certainly, Jack would not go back to see Father Anthony for several weeks now. He had to let Father Anthony twist in the wind a little before going back to give it to him again.

The disappointing thing for Jack was that outside of this prison, he would have definitely thought Father Anthony was good-looking. Of course, outside of PattX, he probably wouldn't have known how sexually messed up Father Anthony was, either. Father Anthony probably would never be able to have a regular, healthy, intimate relationship with another man, which was a shame. But, God, he was good to look at.

Over in the chair, Adder was still reading, his back to Jack. Jack's attempts to get a smile or a laugh out of Adder for a while now and had gotten nowhere. He was definitely listening to Jack, but he never showed any sort of emotional response at all. The fucker was a real puzzle, all right. Jack wondered what had happened to Adder that he wound up the way he was. He wondered if maybe his cellmate was simply always like this, since childhood.

Adder leaned back in his chair, stretched his arms up over his head and yawned widely.

At any rate, Jack wasn't nearly done with the humor tactic. He could move on to other strategies, but he'd keep it up with the humor for now. He had nothing but time on his hands, anyway.

Far too much time, in fact.

Day 168 – Wednesday, September 6th, 2000

The heavy, solid metal door screeched open, letting a blinding light in on Jack. He blinked and saw what he thought was Norrison standing outside the door, but it was a little hard to tell squinting against the light. Jack looked out the door for a second, shielding his eyes with his hand. Yeah, it was Norrison.

Norrison said, "Come on, Carber, get a move on. Your pardon came through from the governor."

Jack stepped out through the door and said amiably, "Fuck you, Norrison."

Norrison smiled and clapped his hand on Jack's bare shoulder. He pushed Jack lightly to get him moving. Jack was completely naked and probably smelled like rancid compost. In fact, now that he was out in the light, even he noticed how bad the smell had been.

Norrison pointed him towards a showerhead just down from the door. Jack got under the shower and started to clean off. The hot water felt incredible and he was sure there had to be a couple of pounds of filth and grime rinsing off of him. His nose no longer hurt, but his right shoulder was still a little stiff and the hot water immediately made it feel better. Norrison stood by waiting for Jack.

Jack was soaping up with his back to Norrison. "You like the show, Norrison?" Jack asked him. "You want to get in here with me?"

If he wasn't still blinded by the light and still sore, Jack might have laughed to himself a little bit at this. Norrison was still the only one at PattX that he would have actually liked to have join him.

Norrison only snorted.

Just as Jack finished rinsing the soap off and was feeling good under the warm spray, Norrison reached over and turned the shower off. He said to Jack, "That's good enough, princess."

"I guess that makes you my fairy godmother. Not that I'm surprised, you know."

Norrison laughed out loud at this and said good-naturedly, "You're so full of shit."

Jack and Tommy Norrison had gotten to a point months ago where they went back and forth with each other all the time. The teasing was always fun, and Norrison was the only guard that Jack could horse around with, on top of the fact that he respected him. Tommy was as fair and impartial as they came, not on a power trip, and had a good sense of humor once you got to know him a little bit.

Jack rubbed on his shoulder where it was still a little stiff. Norrison threw Jack's pants to him, which had been hanging up next to the metal door and Jack started getting dressed so he could rejoin the rest of the prison population.

Norrison walked Jack from the Ad Seg section back to his wing of PattX, and then turned him loose. When Jack got back to his cell, Adder was sitting in the chair reading the encyclopedia.

Jack said, "Didja miss me?"

He walked right over to the mirror and looked at himself. His right eye still had a little bit of a bruise left underneath it.

"I can tell why you like getting thrown in the tank. No wonder you get yourself thrown in there all the time."

Jack wet his hair in the sink some more and combed it out, trying to get it under control.

"The daily massages were my favorite."

He looked at the week-old beard in the mirror and decided to leave it, for now.

"But I think I wound up liking the sports massages better than the Swedish ones."

Jack finally looked over at Adder. Adder was looking blankly at Jack over his reading glasses.

"What? Don't tell me you never got the massages! You just tip the concierge some and she'll do anything for you."

Jack grabbed a shirt, turned around and walked out of the cell. He wanted to go outside, but knew it had to be raining, or Adder wouldn't have been in the cell at this time of day. Either way, he wanted to get out and move around after being in a dark room for several days.

Nothing had really changed between Jack and Adder. Jack had gotten used to having Adder around him all the time, and they had both settled into something of a routine. Jack had long since given up on fighting Adder when Adder wanted to get off. He just gave Adder what he wanted, and in return there was no real need for any force. Even if he didn't fight back, he definitely wasn't enthusiastic about performing for Adder, and he didn't bother doing a good job. For one, he didn't care about being forced into anything with the guy, and secondly, he wanted Adder to know he definitely wasn't enjoying any of it even if he didn't fight it. Adder wasn't rough or violent with the sex, so it had become easy enough to accept as a part of life. Maybe that was Adder's intention all along.

Jack thought that Adder would make some woman a pretty decent partner if he ever got out of PattX and could keep from beating the everloving shit out of her. In fact, since he didn't talk at all, he might be perfect for most women. Other than getting horny occasionally, Adder was actually a good roommate. He didn't push Jack around, respected Jack's things, and helped keep the place clean. Once Jack had learned the boundaries with Adder, like not touching the books Adder was reading or taking his pillow back from him, he found Adder was content to ignore him.

Before Jack ever got to the door out to the pound, though, he knew the weather must be bad because of all the people he saw indoors. He got to the door and, sure enough, it was locked and he could see through the barred window that it was pouring down outside. He really wanted to run a few laps and get outside after being in the tank, but it wasn't going to happen today.

Jack decided to head over to the weight area instead. After being pinned up for a week, the weights would be a good Plan B since Plan A hadn't worked out. With the weather the way it was, though, he knew the weight room would be crowded too. He rounded the corner and, sure enough, saw that the weight room was packed. He looked to see if he could spot Hector or Ramon in there, but neither of them was around. He did see Devers standing off to the side with one of the other Kennel dogs. Devers and the other guy were looking back at Jack.

Jack pointed at him and yelled, "Hey Devers! You ready to eat my ass and tell me you're sorry?" A whole lot of the Brethren guys burst out laughing at this. Jack wheeled around and left before Devers or any of the other Kennel guys could start making trouble.

Jack thought about looking for Hool, Bickers, or Wilson in the lounge area, but then he just decided that he'd rather go back to the cell and stretch out on his bunk. That thin, flimsy mattress would actually feel pretty comfortable compared to the concrete floor in the hole.

Adder was still reading, just as Jack had left him. Jack sat down on his cot and rubbed his shoulder some; they had hit it pretty hard for it to still be sore a week later, but at least it was hardly noticeable now. He would have done just fine in the fight if it hadn't been for Marcus and Harper. They were the ones that worked him over and actually did the damage.

A week earlier, Jack had just gotten his lunch tray and was about to go sit down, when this redneck kid named Devers had gotten cute and tried to trip Jack. Devers was new and had only been at PattX about a month and was trying to join up with the Kennel, and this would be a way for him to score some points with them.

He didn't fall, but Jack did lose his tray. Jack wasn't about to let a snot-nosed, freckled punk like Devers have this for free. He threw himself on Devers and wound up punching him violently in the ribs a couple of times, giving him a bloody nose, and cock punched him before the guards showed up to pull him off. Marcus and Harper were the guards in the chow hall that day, and were all too happy to have a reason to use their clubs. Then they had immediately dragged him off to the hole for a week.

Jack finished rubbing on his shoulder and looked at Adder's back. He wondered if he'd be able to get as big in the shoulders as Adder, or if past a certain point, genetics were the only thing that would help you. Jack really admired the body that Adder had, and the shape he kept it in.

Jack had started working out and training hard pretty soon after arriving at PattX. Hector and Ramon were good workout partners, guys he could trust. Jack had also become a much better fighter by training with the two of them. They sparred a lot with gloves, and they all fought dirty occasionally to keep each other on their toes. They used the punching dummy for practicing with force, and they even fought each other bare-knuckled some to make sure they had a feel for it and to really toughen up. Part of it was for the self-defense in a place like this, and part of it was just the boredom. The limited options for things to do and the same exact routine every single day made you start looking for things to do to break the monotony. Stupid bullshit things like beating up on each other bare-fisted. Things that probably would never even enter your mind to do on the outside.

It had all done Jack a world of good, though. His body was now in the best shape it had ever been in. His chest, stomach and arms had a level of definition they had never had before. His increased skill at fighting had given him a lot more confidence around the prison. There were still plenty of people that could and would beat the shit out of him if they were given a half a chance of getting away with it. But at least now they'd think twice before kicking his ass. And that was better than kicking his ass with no thought at all.

~~~~~

After dinner, it was one of the evenings where the inmates were allowed additional time outside of their cells before the final count and lockdown for the night. Normally, Jack would have gone back to the library or the TV lounge, but he felt funny and didn't feel like being near anyone else. He wished he could get into the laundry area so he could be totally alone, but that wasn't an option except when he was working there.

In his cell, Jack had taken a page from an old magazine and had spent some time folding it up into a small paper giraffe. It was one of the things he did unconsciously that, even after all the years since his dad's death, made him feel closer to his father. It was one of the things his father had done with him while he was still alive, teaching him all sorts of origami tricks.

He would have thought that after being locked up naked in a small, dark room for a week that he'd be ready to move around and be with other people. But really, he felt empty. Jack wasn't sure why, but he felt like a ghost, a tissue-thin shell of the person that used to inhabit his body.

It had definitely given Jack something of a thrill to know he was being thrown into the hole for a week. But now he was back to the mechanical routine of his regular prison life. The worst part of prison was the boredom, the routine that made each day the same as every other. It affected everyone here. And everyone either gave in to it and let their years drain out of them, or they fought back. The ones that fought back found something to focus on, something to hold onto that was bigger than the bars and cinderblock walls with their cinderblock paint.

Jack finished with the giraffe and put it over on the desk, next to the butterfly he had done before he had gone into the tank. He stood there and looked at it blankly for a minute. He thought to himself with a heavy breath, *now what?* He got in his bunk and just lay there.

He looked up at the bottom of Adder's mattress above him. Adder had been in prison almost fourteen years now, he had found out a while ago. And his roommate had had no visitors, no contact with anyone, no things to tie him to a life beyond the cinderblock walls and iron bars of his cell at PattX. Jack looked at the bottom of Adder's bunk some more and wondered at Adder. How did he manage it?

Thoughts of Chris Stambeki crept into Jack's mind, as they still did far too often. Why did it have to turn out the way it did? For the first time in his life, Jack had felt a real connection with another person, something bigger than the con he was running at the moment. Was everything that he and Chris shared fake? Or did Chris just sabotage what they had out of his own fear of commitment and intimacy?

Jack caught himself daydreaming about what it would have been like if Chris had been true and shared Jack's feelings. How his life would be a polar opposite from what it was right now. He'd be in Texas with Chris. Chris would have set up some cheap and sleazy medical practice and they'd start running some scams, keeping it light until they got a better feel for Texas. They'd have an apartment together. Chris would have his collection of Fleetwood Mac, Steely Dan, and Pink Floyd CD's and Jack would have his Shawn Colvin, Bonnie Raitt, and Lyle Lovett discs. They'd argue over what movie to go see or TV show to watch. Chris would cook and start trying his hand at more southwestern dishes.

Jack pushed those thoughts out of his mind, though. They were poison and just made his reality worse, and the last thing he should be pining for was a life with the man that had betrayed him so badly. Trust, it turns out, was just a weakness exploited by others.

Day 298 – Sunday, January 14th, 2001

Father Anthony looked across the desk at Jack and smiled politely.

"I can't tell you how happy I am with the progress we've made over the last year. I think that this counseling has done you a lot of good."

Jack internally rolled his eyes. This whole charade with Father Anthony had become almost unbearable. The only reason that Jack continued with it was that it was Jack's only chance to be in control of the sex for a change. Jack wasn't even that attracted to Father Anthony like he had been originally and the whole thing was losing its luster. The guy was just too screwed up. But at least he could still be the one on top and not give a fuck-all if the priest got off or not.

The other reason that Jack was there this week was that there was, finally and hopefully, going to be a new kind of payoff.

Jack hauled out the ruthless convict face he wore for Father Anthony, the one that took increasing effort to put on. "Shut the fuck up, faggot! God help you if you didn't bring me what I told you to."

Father Anthony got an alarmed look in his face like he couldn't believe Jack had just spoken to him that way.

Then he looked scared and said timidly, "Please... don't hurt me. I did as you asked. It was awful. I was afraid for my life!"

Jack said slowly and menacingly, "Show me."

Father Anthony reached into his pocket and pulled out a small glass bottle. In it were six pinners. Pinners were small marijuana cigarettes, barely larger than toothpicks. They were easy to hide and relatively easy to smoke without being seen – perfect for prison.

Jack took the bottle, stood up, and bluntly barked, "Finally, you're worth something other than just being a cum hole."

Jack walked over to Father Anthony, hit him just hard enough against the head and walked out of the swing office.

Jack didn't like treating Father Anthony this way. Somebody like Troy could be this way without even thinking about it. But Jack wasn't like that at all. He had actually stayed away from Father Anthony for weeks and weeks at a time, but that just seemed to whet Father Anthony's appetite that much more. And the few times when Jack had tried to soften his approach with the Father had completely backfired; Father Anthony's disappointment was very visible when Jack didn't treat him like worthless trash.

Walking out on Father Anthony like this today instead of "raping" him was a little risky, but Jack thought the Father would probably like being treated like this, being denied what he secretly wanted so badly.

The previous week, Jack had gone to see Father Anthony, talked to him like he was slut trash, fucked him rough (in the priest's still greased up ass), and then he had taken it a step further. He told Father Anthony he wanted some joints to smoke. It was the first request (demand, really) he had made of Father Anthony to become a mule, to sneak contraband into prison. It was clear now that Father Anthony was willing and able to be used in this way, too.

He pocketed the small bottle and smiled to himself for not having to perform any more this week than he did. Jack really didn't care that much about having joints for himself to smoke, although getting high once might be a nice little diversion. He had specific plans for them other than personal use.

~~~~~

Wilson hadn't been at lunch, so Jack made his way around to him when he spotted him out in the yard afterwards. Wilson had a cut under his eye that wasn't there a day or so ago.

It was cold outside, and Jack pulled the cheap prison issue jacket closer around him as he stepped up to his friend. "The cut under your eye is new. Troy again?"

Wilson spoke, but just barely, "Yeah. Because of me and Runnion."

"Shit, you hooked up with Runnion and Troy found out?"

Wilson had become the exclusive property of Troy about the same time that Jack had come to PattX. Not that that position of distinction bought poor Wilson any particular benefits, though.

"Runnion had done some favor for Troy or something. Troy gave him a free ride on me and watched. But afterwards, Troy, uh... hit me for cheating on him and told me I'd have to make it up to him."

Troy was about the cruelest person Jack had ever encountered anywhere. Ruthless and completely ego-centric, he lived for finding mind games he could play and wounds he could rub salt in. Inmates tended to fear Adder, but it was Troy that was the really dangerous one. Troy could be charming when he wanted, and it gave people a false sense of security. Adder never spoke, which meant people never had a feel for where they stood with him, which meant they always were unsure and scared of him.

Jack genuinely felt bad for Wilson. Wilson had always had something of a defeated look about him, but ever since Troy had claimed Wilson for his own personal use, he had looked even paler and more run down. The idea of being raped by Runnion, though, almost made Jack want to throw up. Jack inwardly thanked his lucky stars he had kept himself in the closet this long, or he could easily wind up in the same situation as Wilson. He had resigned himself to being used by Adder, but he didn't want it to spread beyond that if he could help it.

It wasn't what he intended, but he had a few to spare, so Jack took two joints out of the small bottle. He gave them to Wilson and said, "Here, give these to Troy to make up for him being a fuckwad. Maybe it'll buy you a little peace and quiet for a while."

Wilson looked at Jack in awe. "God, Jack! I don't know what to say. Troy will be thrilled to see these! He loves getting high! I just wish they mellowed him out like they do everybody else. Shit, this is perfect!"

Jack said, "And when Troy asks where you got them, what are you going to say?"

Wilson's mouth dropped open and he said, "Uh..." stupidly.

"Yeah, and that's the answer that will get you beat up again."

Wilson looked down at his feet because he knew Jack was right.

"If he thinks you've been trading out to get these, or that you have some source he doesn't know about, Wilson, it's gonna hurt."

Wilson looked at Jack like he didn't know what to do and was totally lost.

"When he asks, tell him you found out Prattle had some, so you stole them from him. He'll appreciate you stole them from the Brethren."

Wilson lit up again. "Oh yeah, that's the perfect story."

Wilson looked at Jack and put his hand on Jack's chest. He said, "You've been really good to me, Jack. You've helped me a lot. And you've never asked for anything in return."

Jack smacked Wilson on his shoulder in a show of solidarity. "It's not that much. Glad to do it."

Jack was about to walk away but Wilson grabbed his arm. Wilson looked down at his feet, then back up at Jack. The slight flush in his face had nothing to do with the cool air. He told Jack, "You're the one person at PattX that could probably ask me for anything, and I'd be happy to give it to you, you know."

Jack didn't think it would be a wise move to accept the offer, but knew that Wilson was very sincere in saying it. "Thanks, Wilson. Really. But the last thing you need is yet some other asshole making demands of you. Besides, we'd both wind up just getting the stuffing beat out of us."

Wilson laughed a little, and Jack walked off. Jack had tried to help Wilson whenever he could, and today he had done Wilson a huge favor. He had gotten a whiff previously that Wilson may have had a little bit of a crush on him, but that was just because Jack was nice to him and didn't expect anything in return.

Jack found Adder sitting cross-legged up on his picnic table meditating. He climbed up on the picnic table and sat next to Adder. He looked over at him and saw that Adder's eyes were closed, but he knew that Adder knew it was him. If it had been anybody else, Adder probably would have already beat the crap out of them, or maybe not. It was hard to tell sometimes what Adder would do. But Jack had spent months and months getting to this point with Adder, where Adder felt no threat at all from Jack and therefore silently tolerated and ignored Jack's presence and occasional comments, even outside their cell.

He had been as nervous as a ten-year-old boy in a room full of pedophiles the first time he went to sit up next to Adder on the picnic table a month or so earlier, and somebody out in the yard had yelled at him that it had been nice knowing him. But Jack had forced himself to climb up and sit down on the table with Adder anyway. As far away as possible, of course, but it wasn't a huge picnic table. He still had no sense of where he stood with the guy, but decided he had to take the step at some point, no matter how much his guts told him to stay as far away as possible.

Jack didn't say anything to Adder while he was still meditating. Instead, he looked out. Away from the beat down yard, the inmates, and away from the prison. He looked past the fence, at the field and the woods beyond. He looked up over the bare, winter trees. There was a bird circling way up over them, not even having to beat its wings, just soaring. Jack watched the clouds in the cold, clear sky, slowly moving through the air, always a cloud, yet constantly shifting so that it wasn't the same as before. Jack wondered if Adder sat out there sometimes and saw these things as well. Time was passing and yet it felt like it was stopped, and it would be another year or two before he was allowed to start back up.

He looked over at Adder and saw that his eyes were now open and he was looking out past the fence as well. He wondered what Adder saw when he sat there.

Jack said, "Did you ever hear the one about the guy and the horse in the bar?"

Adder didn't even look over towards Jack, not even slightly.

"Ok, so here it is... A guy walks into a bar, and there's a horse standing there. The guy asks the bartender 'Why's the horse here?' The bartender says, 'Oh, he's part of our ongoing bar bet.' The guy asks, 'So what's the bet?' The bartender says, 'See that jar full of money, put $10 in and I'll tell you. Win the bet and get $100 out.'"

"So the guy takes $10 out of his wallet and puts it in the jar. The bartender says, 'If you can make the horse laugh, you get $100.' The guy thinks a minute and tells the horse, 'Come with me.' He leads the horse back down the hall where the bathrooms are. They come back a second later and the horse is just laughing himself silly. He's bent over double he's laughing so hard."

"The bartender is amazed. He takes $100 out of the jar and gives it to the guy, but he doesn't appreciate losing the money. He tells the guy, 'Ok smart-ass, if you can make the horse cry, you win the whole jar of money. Lose, and you give me my $100 back.' The guy immediately says, 'Done!' and leads the horse back to where the bathrooms are again."

"A few seconds later the guy and the horse come back and the horse is crying like a baby. Big tears coming out of his eyes. The bartender is completely bowled over. He gives the guy the whole jar of money and says, 'Ok, I can't stand it. You're the only one to ever win this. What's your secret? How'd you do it?'"

"The guy says, 'Easy. First time, I took him back there and told the horse that my dick was bigger than his!' The bartender just shook his head and said, 'Sonofabitch! That made him laugh. So how'd you make him cry?'"

"The guy said, 'Well, the second time, I just showed him!'"

Jack looked over at Adder to see if he would get even a tiny smirk. Adder just stared straight ahead at the trees, his usual stony self.

Jack groaned and said, "Aw, come on, man! That's a great joke!"

He waited a second and then tried again, "See, the joke is that the guy's dick really *was* bigger than the horse's. And it made the horse cry. 'Cause the horse may have a horse dick, but the guy's dick was even bigger."

"Get it? Horse dick? No?"

Adder didn't seem to be paying any attention at all because he was now staring at his hands. Jack sighed and sat there, next to Adder.

As he sat, Jack began to ignore Adder and started thinking about things he missed – music, swapping out cars often, being near the water, even the sushi he had just started liking before being arrested.

After a minute, Jack said to himself out loud, "I miss the stars." He leaned back on his elbows and looked at the clouds above and the blue sky they glided across.

"I wish I could be out here at night and just look at the stars."

Jack looked up, wishing they were there right now. A fear gripped him suddenly. What if he never did get to see the night sky again? The stars at night carried a tremendous amount of meaning to Jack, and it would be the loss of a precious thing to him to never see them again.

"Before my father died," said Jack to no one in particular as his mind pulled him back to days that were no more, "he would take me out sometimes and we'd look at the stars. He'd show me Orion and the Big Dipper, and point out Mars or Venus if they were out. He showed me how the stars shift north and south in the sky as the seasons change. He'd tell me how there were millions of stars up there, even millions more that we couldn't see. And that even some points of light that looked like stars were actually entire galaxies of their own. One little faint point of light that was really millions more stars. It was all so huge and immense and complicated and hanging right there over us."

Jack sat, lost in his thoughts about his long gone dad. Then he added, "Of course, this was mostly all because he had sold the TV set just to try and make ends meet for one more month."

Jack laughed at the thought, and let the emotions wash over him momentarily. He looked out past the prison yard again.

"I miss being able to see the stars. And my dad – I miss him, too." Jack said this so quietly, it was almost like he had completely forgotten Adder was there.

Adder was looking out past the prison fence. Jack, still caught up in his reminiscing and without really thinking about it, turned and gave Adder a friendly punch in the arm. Then he realized what he had done and inwardly cringed while his heart skipped a nervous beat. He waited a second with held breath to see if it pissed Adder off or not, but Adder continued to look straight ahead.

Jack got up and walked over somewhere else, anywhere else, before he pushed his luck too far. He thought maybe that had been a step forward with Adder. It was the first time that he had ever touched Adder like that, and it went ok. He was still alive, and with both kidneys intact, to tell the tale. Jack felt pretty good the rest of the afternoon.

~~~~~

In their cell later, after the night count, Jack walked over to Adder, who was reading at the desk. Adder looked over his reading glasses at Jack as he squatted down next to him.

Jack pulled out the pinners in the small glass bottle and said, "Look, I got these earlier. I don't know if you like to get high or not, but if you want 'em, you can have a couple of them." He held the bottle out for Adder to get a better look.

Adder looked at the bottle for a second, then looked at Jack. Adder had what Jack interpreted as maybe being a thoughtful look on his face, but then Adder shook his head "no." It was so slight that Jack would have missed it if he hadn't been watching closely. But Adder had definitely answered his question.

Jack said, "You're sure?"

Adder shook his head again.

"Ok, but if you change your mind, just say so."

Then he added, "And you have to promise not to tell mom and dad. They'll ground the hell out of me, and I'll have to kick your ass for being a fucking tattletale."

Adder looked at Jack one more time, and if Jack wasn't mistaken, there was a bare trace of a "you're so full of shit" expression on Adder's face.

Jack put the bottle back in his pocket. He went and sat down on his bunk and looked at Adder's back. He was a little disappointed because he had really expected Adder to go for the pinners. He'd gone to a fair amount of risk and effort to get them, and Adder didn't even seem the slightest bit tempted by them. He'd have to figure something else to try to use to get through to Adder. But even the tiniest reactions this evening were in reality a huge step forward. And plus he had been able to punch Adder in the arm today, so that was something.

Tomorrow, though, he'd take the pinners to the laundry area and hide them behind one of the washing machines where he had found a good spot for stuff like this. He'd probably smoke one up there, too, while running some loads through. After all, somebody needed to get some enjoyment out of them.

Day 359 – Friday, March 16th, 2001

Jack walked over across the yard to Tommy Norrison. It had turned out to be a relatively mild day outside, so maybe spring was finally going to arrive. The sky was overcast, but the air and sky felt like it had the promise of a spring shower instead of the threat of a winter rain in it. Jack thought someone not too far from the prison must be burning a fire, as he smelled smoke in the late winter air. Norrison nodded at Jack, and Jack waved back.

He reached Norrison and asked him, "How's Adder doing?"

"Doesn't matter. Capt. Marcus gives us strict orders to not even look in on him. I'm sure he's fine. He ate his lunch a little while ago."

"What about Shimmey?"

"They had to transfer him out to a real hospital. He's pretty messed up. Adder may get out of the hole before Shimmey gets out of the hospital."

"So how much damage did Adder wind up doing?" asked Jack.

"Broken nose and jaw, multiple fractures in his wrist and arm, broken rib and a lacerated liver, and a concussion. And they're hoping there's no internal bleeding."

Jack whistled, "Wow."

Jack hadn't seen it happen the day before, but Hool had seen it and told Jack what happened. He heard that Adder had been watching TV in the TV lounge, something Adder didn't do very often. Shimmey had come in, a little tweaked out on some drugs he had gotten his hands on, and walked towards the TV. He didn't change the channel, and might not have even wanted to, but Adder just went nuts. He jumped all over Shimmey in a second. Shimmey tried to fight back, more than a lot of people would be able to do given his size, but it still did him no good at all. Adder completely shattered the guy's nose, then his jaw, twisted and broke his arm at the same time Adder kneed him in the side, and then gave Shimmey a head-butt that knocked him out cold. It had made Jack shiver to hear about the head-butt, having been on the receiving end of one of those himself.

Norrison looked at Jack a second. He said, "I don't know how you hang out with him the way you do. Anyone else that gets near him like that is running a very serious risk."

Jack brushed it off. "Oh, well, we're roomies. He doesn't have much choice but to be used to being in close quarters with me."

"Yeah, but it's different. The way you sit up on the picnic table when he's out there. No one else has ever done that. Not even any of his old cellmates. What do you say to him when you're sitting up there?"

"Bullshit mostly," said Jack. "I try to crack some jokes, hoping to get a reaction out of him one of these days."

It was the truth, in a limited way. He still cracked jokes with Adder trying to get some kind of a positive reaction. But somewhere along the way, and Jack wasn't even sure when, he had simply started talking to Adder. About anything. About his life. Once he had gotten comfortable that Adder wasn't automatically going to send him to the hospital, he opened up to him in ways he'd not really ever opened up to anyone before. He had talked about some of the scams he had run, including insurance company executives whose identities he had stolen and run into the ground. He had even talked about his parents some. Jack had hardly ever shared that kind of stuff with anyone else, and absolutely not with anyone else at PattX. But since Adder never communicated with anyone, he felt pretty safe with putting it out there. Jack also had this idea that Adder was actually sort of interested. Of course, Jack assumed this was just his imagination running away with itself, but Adder had never shut him up when he talked about this stuff.

Jack said to Norrison, "Well, I notice you guys are too chicken shit to take him down like real men. You always use the Tasers. Adder's the only one you do that with."

Norrison nodded through his grin and said, "I wanna have kids one day, Jack, and I need my balls for that. Adder, Troy, and Quake are the only three here that we go directly to using the Tasers on. Of course, Troy and Quake don't ever get caught since they always use lookouts. Adder couldn't care less. He'd punch the Pope in the face with Jesus Christ watching. The stupid thing is that he'd already have his ass out of here if he'd just behave."

"Really? He could have already been paroled?"

"Yeah, probably at least a couple of years ago, for sure. All this bad behavior scares the parole board shitless, and they keep him here. He's almost maxed out, though, and in about a year, he's out and no longer my problem. Fifteen years was his max sentence, so he's out then whether the parole board likes it or not. But I bet it won't be hardly any time at all before he's right back in here. Guys like Adder... they can't function on the outside."

Jack almost started arguing this point with Norrison. He felt that Adder actually stood a decent chance outside. In a strange, twisted way, Adder was a decent person. Somebody like Troy was the one that would never make it outside. Too indiscriminately cruel.

Jack asked, "Does he have anybody outside? Any family? Has he ever had any visitors or calls from anyone at all?"

Norrison said, "He's never had a single visitor or letter even that I know of. I think his family's dead. Jones used to be a guard at the prison Adder was at before being transferred here. He told me one time that they had to give notice to Adder that his father had passed away. He said that Adder was totally indifferent to the news."

Jack left Norrison, and went over to the picnic table where Adder usually sat and meditated. Jack leaned up against it and looked back at the rest of the inmates spread across the yard. He was actually going to miss sitting out with Adder on the picnic table this week.

Jack had told Adder all kinds of things out on this picnic table and even in their cell at night. He had talked about all the times he had bought some piece of shit car, insured it as if it were in much better shape than it was, then burned it beyond recognition and reported it stolen to collect the insurance. The times he had gone in with other people to stage a mild accident, then use a crooked doctor to bill the insurance companies for all kinds of treatments and tests, treatments and tests that were never needed or performed. His favorite story was the time he had stolen the identity of the VP of the claims department at an insurance company. It was the company and claims department that was supposed to cover his mother; the very asshole, in fact, that had denied all of the claims for his mother's emphysema. He spent two weeks at the Ritz-Carlton in Naples, Florida on that guy's credit, running up every restaurant, spa, and golf bill he could. And Jack didn't even play golf. He had even hired four expensive male hustlers on the guy's stolen credit card number (instead of the accounts Jack had created under the guy's name) and then just talked to them all night.

But despite how much he had opened up and how many one-liners he had delivered, he had still gotten virtually nowhere with Adder. It got very aggravating to know how much he had poured into getting through to the guy, only to have Adder still ignore him or use him for sex the same as always. It must have been a little bit of the Stockholm syndrome thing – one minute fascinated by Adder and trying to get closer to him, the next hating him for being so un-human.

Jack figured that somewhere along the way something had happened to Adder. People didn't cut off the rest of the world like that for no reason. People walled themselves off out of fear or hurt. Jack wondered what in Adder's past had caused him to end almost all human connection.

He also wondered what would happen to Adder when he got turned out of the prison system in a year. Jack would potentially get out not too long after Adder, actually, if the parole board cooperated. Maybe he'd look the motherfucker up and give him a blowjob for old times' sake.

~~~~~

A little while before dinner, Jack had been in the library trying to hack into the network from the PC that was there. He still hadn't been able to guess any passwords for an account other than the inmate account, though.

Suddenly, Jack realized it had gotten too quiet in the room and he cursed himself for letting his guard down. He looked around and suddenly realized that Troy was standing there watching him. Everyone else was gone. Or had been sent away, more likely. Troy had no shirt on and Jack saw the creepy tattoo that Troy had on his chest. It looked like the skin had been peeled back and pinned down to his chest, exposing the bare muscle underneath. Jack felt himself going white and he realized he was in for some shit this time.

He stood up to leave and said, "I'll leave so you can have the place to yourself."

As he moved to leave, though, Troy shook his head and put his hand on Jack's chest to stop him. Jack hadn't thought he was going to get out of there that easily. Out of nowhere, Troy hit him hard with an uppercut to his chin. Jack fell back and over one of the desks.

Troy stood there and watched Jack as he tried to get back up and shake it off. Jack's chin and mouth were killing him, but he scrambled up and went behind the desk he had fallen over. He grabbed the chair behind the desk to use as a weapon, but it was the standard lightweight plastic chair used at the prison. It was useless as a weapon, but at least if he could keep the chair between himself and Troy, Troy wouldn't be able to do much.

Troy smirked at Jack holding the chair up like he was about to tame a lion. Troy laughed casually and then said to Jack, "C'mon Carber, that's not how a man fights. I've seen you fight better than this."

Troy shot his hand out and grabbed a leg of the chair. He pulled on it to force Jack to stay in place and Troy swung around the side of the desk. Jack tried to shake the chair loose from Troy's grasp, but Troy held tight.

With the desk no longer between them, Troy kicked out at Jack and caught him right in the crotch. Jack bent over from the kick at the same time that Troy pulled hard on the chair. This yanked it out from Jack's hold, and Troy threw it to one side.

Jack tried to run back around the desk to get away from Troy, but Troy grabbed the back of his shirt, pulled back, and then kneed him in the small of the back. He pushed Jack down face first on the floor, then sat down on him, pinning his arms so he couldn't move.

Troy pulled on Jack's hair to lift his head up to make Jack listen to him. He said, "I'm just trying to talk to you here, Carber, and you're just making it worse on yourself."

Troy smashed Jack's face down on the floor and then lifted it back up.

"I don't like you messing with my things, Carber."

Jack was dizzy and could taste blood in his mouth. But he couldn't think of what Troy was talking about. He'd never been near anything of Troy's. He could feel Troy's legs rapidly cutting off the circulation to his arms.

"If you want a punk to fuck, you'd better start sniffing around a different one. I can't tell you the amount of pain you'll experience if you if think you can plug my property."

Troy smashed Jack's head into the floor again sending a round of black spots spinning around in front of his eyes. But he got it that Troy was talking about Wilson.

Jack coughed and tried to get it out, "Never. I never..."

Troy shook Jack's head by his hair and sneered into his ear, "You keep your dick in your pants, Carber!"

Jack felt Troy get up and was hoping he'd just leave. Jack couldn't move his arms from the loss of circulation. But Troy wasn't done just yet. He kicked Jack in the side, which caused Jack to gasp for breath, but he still could hardly move.

Troy flipped Jack over and said as he started undoing Jack's pants and pulling them down, "But while we're here and while we've got a few minutes together. Maybe I should try out a little of what Adder's been getting."

Jack cringed at what was about to happen and tried to move his arms, but the circulation was slow coming back and he couldn't get them to do much of anything yet.

Troy said, "Where ya goin', Carber?" He stepped down on Jack's exposed dick, crushing it, causing Jack to really cry out in pain this time. Jack found that his hands could move after all as he clutched at Troy's foot, trying to move it.

Troy moved his foot and instead stepped on Jack's throat. He said, "I want you to beg me to fuck you. I know you want it, so it shouldn't be that hard to say it." Jack's hands were clawing at his throat, trying to get air. He couldn't breathe, much less say anything.

Troy let his foot up off of Jack's throat just a tiny amount, and Jack managed to barely whisper, "Fuck me."

Troy said, "That didn't have enough emotion in it to get my dick hard. You want my dick hard, don't you? Beg, Carber!" Troy let up on Jack's throat just a little more.

Jack croaked out, "Please fuck me!" His throat was a raging fire and every word burned him like someone had crammed a blowtorch in there.

Troy moved his foot and flipped Jack over onto his stomach. He kicked Jack in the side of the head and said, "Fredo said you gave pretty good head. Let's see if that hole is worth a damn."

Jack's head was spinning, his ears were ringing and he felt like he might lose consciousness, but he could feel Troy kneeling down over his legs. Troy leaned forward over Jack and said in his ear, "You don't even deserve this privilege."

Jack groaned in pain and could feel Troy just starting to push himself in, but right then, a voice outside the library said, "Man walking!"

Troy swore, "Goddammit!" and stood up. He pulled his pants up and said, "How sad, Carber. You don't get to have my baby." And Troy walked out.

Jack lay there on the floor, a bleeding, bruised, and despairing wreck. He knew he needed to get up in case Troy decided to come back for some reason. He hoped whatever guard was around saw Troy leaving and would come in to investigate.

Jack could still taste blood in his mouth and there was blood running down his face, but the ringing in his ears was going away and he was able to move his arms some. Jack forced himself to sit up and spat the blood out of his mouth. His head and side were killing him.

Jack's fear and hatred of Troy was now on a level equal to that of the insurance companies that had sat by and let his parents die.

~~~~~

Jack lay on his bunk after dinner (which he had skipped), very sore from the attack earlier. Moving anything hurt terribly, so he lay as still as possible, panting from the soreness.

After the attack, he had gotten up and found the guard Downs, who took him to the infirmary. As usual, they wanted to know what happened, but Jack had just said he stepped on a rake and it popped up and hit him in the face. They bandaged up where he had been kicked in the side and put a couple of stitches in his forehead where it had been banged into the floor. Otherwise, he'd be ok. Just tender and bruised for a while.

Jack lay flat, but looked over at the empty desk chair. He wished Adder was there. He could talk to Adder about it a little, which might make him feel better. He wondered if what happened to him today would make any difference to Adder. Probably not. But at least he'd listen. Or pretend to listen. Or not even pretend to listen. Who knew what the fuck made it into Adder's head and what didn't.

Every breath in and out shot ice hot streaks of pain through his chest. Jack thought how this place got to you over time, how it wore you down, how it turned you into something different than what you were when you came in. How it bruised you. How it broke you. Two years in here were two years in hell. He couldn't imagine being stuck in a place like this for fifteen years.

Jack looked back up at the bottom of Adder's bunk and started crying, and the sobs heaved out of his chest, despite the stabs of agony they sent through him. Someone down the tier yelled for him to shut the fuck up. He hated and feared every last detail in this place.

Wednesday, August 12th, 1981

Jack sat with Brian, a rerun of *Good Times* playing on TV and the sound crackling through the thoroughly shot speaker. It was blazing hot and humid outside in the middle of the afternoon, and neither of them had wanted to be out in the heat. It was hot inside, too, though. Jack's dad didn't like running the air except when totally necessary, and the heat and humidity left it musty smelling inside, even with the windows open.

They were arguing about the dare and the coin on the worn, brown sofa between them.

Jack said, "It doesn't mean anything if you touch it while I've still got my pants on."

Brian insisted loudly, "Yeah it does, too."

Jack said, "We've already seen each other hard, touching it isn't a big deal. Doctors do it all the time and they're not fags."

Brian finally said, defiantly, "If it's no big deal, then you go first."

"No way! You lost the toss fair and square."

Brian seemed a little embarrassed and frustrated by this, but finally said, "Ok, but then you have to touch mine, right?"

Jack said, "Duh! Sure I will! I wouldn't double-cross you like that."

Jack and Brian both pulled their pants down and sat on the sofa. This had been building up all summer and was now coming to a boil. They had talked about hard-ons and jacking off. They had talked about eating pussy, the missionary position and doggy-style. They had talked about blowjobs and getting head, which they finally decided was the same thing, even though they were both still guessing at that conclusion. They had talked about all the things they had been hearing about and getting curious about, but had never experienced themselves. And a few weeks ago, they had shown their erections to each other for the first time.

Brian's hand hovered over Jack's dick, which was raging hard. Brian's eyes were still locked onto Jack's face, trying to see if the whole thing was a trick or not. He hesitated a couple of times, but wound up touching Jack, almost smacking it he touched it so rapidly. And after a little back and forth, they finally both wound up touching each other's penises. The touching led to groping. Both of them agreed that it felt better than just having your own hand on it.

Brian seemed a little nervous about it and was glad to pull his pants back up. He said to Jack, "You know I'm not a faggot, right?"

Jack said, "I know that. Almost all guys do this to find out what it's like, they just don't talk about it. Besides, the only real way to tell if you're gay is to kiss another guy."

Brian said, "What happens if you are? How do you know?"

"I heard it's like feeling electricity or something," said Jack with a shrug. He really had no idea if that's what it was like or not, or if it meant anything or not.

Brian poked his lip out, hesitating, and then said, "Should we try it just to make sure?"

"Do we need to do the tongue thing? If we're going to make sure?" asked Jack, also unsure about all the details.

Brian said, "We'd better, to make sure. How long do we have to go before we know for sure?"

Jack said, "I dunno. A minute? Thirty seconds? Thirty minutes?"

Brian laughed and said, "Crap, it won't take that long, will it?"

"Let's just go and see what happens. No open eyes!"

JJ on *Good Times* droned in the background on the TV. Jack and Brian leaned forward awkwardly, trying to decide when to close their eyes versus not being able to see where they were aiming. Their lips finally met and sat flatly against one another for a second. Then Jack opened his mouth a tiny bit and slid his tongue out. Brian opened his just a little bit to let Jack go farther. Jack pushed his tongue into Brian's mouth just a little, and then Brian met Jack's tongue with his own. As they got more comfortable with the sensation, they pushed in a little closer and opened their mouths a little wider. Jack definitely felt the electricity and he hoped Brian did, too. They continued to kiss like this, sloppy but increasingly less cautious, getting more and more used to it, and a little more and more into it. Neither of them knew quite what to do with their hands, so they just kept them away from each other.

Suddenly, Jack heard a noise back over near the kitchen. He looked up and saw his father standing there, ashen-faced, watching him and Brian.

It felt like Jack's heart stopped beating and like all the air was instantly sucked out of the room. Jack went into shock at being caught by his father doing this. His father was supposed to have been at work for another three hours! Brian had turned around and saw Jack's dad there as well. Brian looked back at Jack, terrified and as pale as a ghost, and made a choking noise that sounded like he had swallowed his own tongue.

As soon as Jack stammered the word, "Dad..." his father turned and walked the other way, and Brian jumped up, muttering, "Oh, crap, crap, crap, crap! Oh, crap!!!" and ran out the front door as fast as he could, almost tripping down the front steps and planting his face in the broken up cement pavers.

Jack suddenly found himself sitting alone on the sofa. The TV was the only sound in the room, but it sounded like it was a mile away, and he was paralyzed. His dad had just seen him kissing his best friend. His dad was going to know he was gay now. He never wanted his dad to know about this. He barely understood it himself. After everything else his dad had been through, after everything he had done for Jack, now he had this to deal with. Jack wanted to run away to avoid having to see his father, to face up to what his dad now knew, to see the disgust in his father's face. He wanted to run away before his father just kicked him out. Kicked him out for being a queer. Jack felt like he had ruined everything now, for his father and for himself.

He was still paralyzed, frozen to the sofa, unable to move his legs or even blink. He finally forced himself to look around and saw he was still alone in the room. He unglued himself and jumped up off the sofa and ran out the front door, just as Brian had done. He needed to get away, way far away. He couldn't face his dad, and he needed time to think about what to do, but had no idea where to go. He ran back around behind the house, away from his dad's bedroom window and went behind the storage shed. He had a spot back there, private, hidden by the shed and some scrubby azalea bushes between his house and the neighbor's yard that he could hide in and think.

He sat down and leaned against the shed. The tears filled up his eyes and stung them. How could he have been so stupid? How could he have taken that kind of a risk? He had known for a long time that he was attracted to Brian in a way that didn't make sense. He knew it was the way he was supposed to be feeling about *girls*. It's just that he and Brian were so alike, and Brian seemed curious about Jack, too. But to do what they did today in a place that was so easy to get caught was just plain stupid and now he had messed everything up.

Jack didn't know what to do. When he had messed up before, he could always go three blocks over to Brian's place and hide out there. But Jack couldn't even do that this time. He had messed up with Brian, too. Brian would hate him now for getting both of them caught. Jack cried and beat his fist in the gritty dirt next to the shed. He was so mad at himself. He had been so stupid!

He started having visions of all the terrible ways his father might react. Jack saw his dad screaming "Faggot!" at him, hitting and kicking at him, and throwing him out, pushing him down the front steps and then locking the door behind him. Another version was where his dad just never spoke to him again, never acknowledged Jack again, other than to look at him with a burning hatred every so often. The most awful one was that he would eventually go back inside and find his father dead from a heart attack, killed by the shock of what he saw and his disappointment in Jack. He thought in horror, *what if he's dead inside right now?*

His dad was almost all Jack had. He didn't have a lot of friends other than Brian because he was so poor. Most kids just thought he was weird for being poor, but being poor wasn't his fault. Since his mom had died, his dad had become everything for Jack. His dad had worked so hard to keep it all going, keeping the rent paid up, working his job, paying the insurance premiums, paying the doctors and hospitals screaming for money, and trying to have time with Jack, too. He didn't have a mom any more, and now he had ruined it with his father, too. Jack was fucked.

And at that moment, Jack heard his dad calling from inside the house, "Jack!"

Jack froze and didn't answer. He stayed where he was, paralyzed with fear. He heard his dad call a few more times out front, then moving around towards the back of the house.

Finally, Jack heard in the back yard, on the other side of the shed, "Jackson Carber!!" The voice was harsher this time.

He knew he was in for it then. He started crying again at the thought of what he was about to face, and he couldn't stop it. He got up and walked around to the front of the shed.

His dad was looking down the side of the house, searching for him, but wheeled around and saw his son there. He had his hands on his hips and he looked at Jack, then said bluntly, "C'mon inside."

Jack still cried. He hated crying like this in front of his dad. He felt like such a baby, but he couldn't stop. He was scared to go in.

His dad nodded towards the house and said, "C'mon!" and went on in through the screen door to the kitchen.

Jack slowly followed and saw his dad head into the den. He stood outside the screen door and didn't want to go any farther.

His heard his dad in the other room calling at him loudly. "C'mon, Jack. Come on in here and sit down."

Jack slowly opened the screen door and went in, his breath shallow and raspy. He walked through the hot, still kitchen with its scuffed-up and cracked linoleum that had once upon a time been yellow and green. He saw on the kitchen table four camels made from folded up papers of different colors. Three were poorly folded and looked like mutants, but the fourth, the blue one, was just right. The sight of them brought fresh tears to Jack's eyes. He walked to the doorway into the den, and the instant his father's eyes were on him, it all came spilling out. "Dad, I'm sorry! Don't kick me out!! It won't happen again! I swear!"

Jack's dad was sitting on the sofa, waiting for him. He said calmly, "No one's kicking anyone out. Park it!" And his dad pointed to the spot next to him on the sofa.

Jack wiped at his eyes. His dad wasn't reacting as violently as he thought he would. He sat down next to him, and looked at him suspiciously with a wet face and hitching chest.

Jack's father eyed him seriously for a while, which made Jack squirm uncomfortably. His dad finally asked, "Did Brian make you do that?"

"No! I swear Dad, that's all it was! I'll never do that with anybody ever again, no matter what! Ever!" His voice was almost shrieking trying to make this all go away.

"Whoa, whoa, whoa. Just slow down a second."

His dad paused a moment, then asked, "Did you *want* to try that with Brian?"

Jack was terrified to answer truthfully, but didn't want to lie to his dad and make it worse, either.

Jack sniffled a little through his tears. "Yeah, a little bit."

"Do you know what it means when someone is gay?" asked his father.

Jack felt beaten. His dad knew. Jack's shoulders slumped and he gave up. He looked down at the stained carpet on the floor and snuffled. "Yeah, I know what it is."

"Jack, are you gay?"

Jack still just looked at the floor, fresh tears flooding from his eyes and down his cheeks in rivulets. He nodded a miserable "yes."

Jack and his father sat for a minute. Jack feeling totally hopeless and his dad clenching his teeth repeatedly and staring off at nothing.

Jack couldn't face his father, and without looking at him, started to get up. He said, "I'll go get some stuff and leave."

Jack's father finally broke out of his reverie and said, confused, "Huh? Wait... no, no, no."

Jack felt his dad grab his arm and pull back on him. Jack managed to face his dad and saw him smiling. His dad pulled him back over to him and said softly, "You're not going anywhere, buster." He put Jack in front of him, and held him there, his hands on both of Jack's shoulders.

Jack said, "You're not going to kick me out?"

His father smiled and Jack could see the tears in his dad's eyes. "Why would I kick out the best thing that ever happened to me?"

He pulled Jack back down onto the sofa, and pulled him over, up against him, and held his son tightly.

Jack realized this wasn't anything like what he expected to have happen. Maybe his father wouldn't kick him out.

His father said, "Jack, you're all I've got and I love you more than anything else in the world. I love you exactly the same as I did when I left for work this morning."

Everything flipped around for Jack at those words. Jack was fifteen and didn't normally like being hugged by his dad like this. But at this moment, and after feeling like his life was ruined, he needed this desperately. He held onto his dad's arms to keep them around him.

His father continued, "It's a little bit of a shock, but only just because I wasn't expecting it. That's all. I wonder if any parent ever would." He laughed a little bit at the thought.

Jack still felt ashamed, but was so relieved that his dad still loved him. He said, "I just don't want you to be grossed out by me or mad at me."

"I'm not mad and I'm not grossed out, either, so don't worry about that. You're still you. It's good to know this about you. I'd feel disappointed if you hid this from me for very long. I want you to know that there's never anything you need to hide from me. You're a good kid and I'd *never* be ashamed of you, ever. You're my son."

And he leaned over and kissed Jack on the top of his head. Jack didn't want the moment to end. He had heard other kids talk about their parents at school like they couldn't stand them, like they were the worst things in their lives. He knew what he had, though, and today just made it more so. His father loved him, and he loved his father. He might not have much else, but he had his dad.

His dad ran his fingers through Jack's hair. He said to him, "You know, after mom died, you were the one thing that kept me going, even through the hardest, darkest moments. You still do, Jacky. You keep me going, even five years later. Life's too short to not be with the person that makes you the happiest, that fills you up. You never know how much time you'll actually be given with them. It doesn't make any difference if it's a boy or a girl, just as long as you love them and they love you. If you find someone you love, your heart will tell you even before your head realizes it. Listen for that, Jack, and pay attention. Love doesn't come along often. Return that love. Cherish it. Protect it. It's everything in the world. It can be scary, and there's a million ways to get hurt. And only a tiny handful of ways to be happy, but it's worth the risk. If you find it, it's worth any risk in the world."

Jack thought about what his dad was saying. He asked him, "Was it like that for you?"

His dad laughed and said, "It absolutely was. I had to ask your mom out three times before she finally said yes. Each time got harder than the time before, I was so scared that she was going to say no each time, which she did the first two times. And then when we did go out, I knocked over a water glass all over her dress. She was so mad at me! She told me she never wanted to see me again! I was terrified, but I told her I was sorry and eventually asked her out again. The thought of what happened and having her hate me for what happened was terrible. But deep down, I knew I had to try. I just knew deep down she was the one I had to make the effort for."

Jack let it all sink in. It had all been less than an hour and so much had changed. And thankfully, very little had changed, too.

~~~~~

That night, after dinner, Jack's father decided it was a good night to sit outside and look at some stars. In the late summer, they might even see a shooting star. They sat out in the folding lawn chairs and found the stars they knew. Jack's dad said, "Brian seemed pretty scared about being caught. Is he going to be ok?"

Jack said, "I dunno. He'll be really mad at me for us getting caught. I'm sure he's freaking out that you're going to tell on him to his parents."

"Yeah, some parents might not be very happy to hear this kind of news. I really don't want to be the one to tell them what happened, especially if Brian was just experimenting a little. I tell you what, Brian probably is pretty mad, but you need to try and talk to him. Let him know that you're ok and he's ok, too, and that I'm not mad. Tell him I'm not going to tell his parents anything about today."

Jack said he would and looked up at the sky some more. Both he and his father sat in silence for a long while, then his dad said, "Maybe you could invent your own constellation."

Jack said, "Invent one? Can you invent a constellation?"

"Sure, you just pick a set of stars, and imagine a shape to go with them, then name it. You could invent the first gay constellation!"

Jack knew when his leg was being pulled. "Dad!"

"Sure, it could be like a flamingo, or something."

"Why a flamingo? Are flamingos gay?" asked Jack, unsure if his dad was still pulling his leg or not.

His dad laughed out loud and said, "I don't know. I guess kinda. They always seem to be associated with gay people."

"Why is that?"

His dad was stumped this time and chuckled, "I have absolutely no idea!"

Jack was sporting a huge smile now. To have his dad joke around about it made it all so much more casual and less serious. His father sat in thought a little more, and Jack studied him in the low light coming out of the kitchen door. The messy brown hair. The slightly worn-down look on his face from everything he had endured. The soft eyes that had seen too much. Jack hoped he would be as good and as strong as his father was when he grew up.

His dad put his hand on Jack's head and rubbed it. He finally spoke up again. "Jacky, I want you to promise me not to hide things from me. I know you weren't intentionally hiding anything from me today since you're still just figuring it all out for yourself. But I just want to make sure you know you never have any reason to hide anything from me. I can't be there for you if I don't know what's going on. I can't make you tell me, but I'll take your promise. Will you promise me?"

Jack already felt so much better that he knew he'd never want to hide anything from his father ever again, no matter how awful. He said, "I do. I promise, dad."

"Good," said his father. "Now there's one other thing I want you to know. You're fifteen now and that's the age where most kids would start to date. And I don't want to treat you any differently than any young man your age. So, if you find someone, another... uh, young man, and you think the interest is mutual, and the two of you want to explore it some, I'll be behind you. Like any parent of a fifteen year old would. So, if Brian finally trusts you, and me, again, and if he wants to, I'll let the two of you have a date. But here's what that means – it means... I'll drop the two of you off for dinner, then pick you up when you're done, then you can watch a movie back over here, with me supervising. The same type stuff any parent would let their fifteen year old kid do on a date. Is that a deal?"

Jack couldn't believe that his dad was this cool about the whole thing. He felt so very lucky to have his dad. He couldn't feel the contempt for his dad that other kids felt for their parents. Jack just couldn't feel that way. His dad had been through too much and had been treated too bad by the world around him, but he had never wavered in his love for Jack, even when most other parents would have completely broken down or taken it out on their kids.

Jack said, "It's a deal."

Jack stood up and hugged his dad hard. He said, "I'd rather have you for my father than anyone else in the world."

Jack felt his father reach up and wipe his eyes a little as they held each other tightly. His dad said, "I don't expect something like this from a teenager very much, but it just means that much more to me when I do get it."

Jack decided that maybe he needed to hug his dad a little more often.

Day 438 – Sunday, June 3rd, 2001

Jack waited for Father Anthony to finish his service. He had been going through this stupid farce with Father Anthony for way more than a year now, and wished it would just end. Lately, he would go six or eight weeks without going to see the Father. He really didn't even care about screwing around with him anymore. He preferred beating off up in the laundry area to dealing with this guy's sick trips.

The only reason he was here this time was that he wanted to get Father Anthony to bring him some more joints. He'd have to put on a good show for Father Anthony to get him to bring them, which really irritated him. Father Anthony and Adder were both just using Jack, and it was seriously getting under his skin.

But Wilson had asked for a few more joints a few days before, and Jack still wanted to help Wilson when he could. He also wanted to try again with Adder to see if he'd accept some joints this time. Not to mention that a couple for himself when he was doing laundry would be nice.

When the service was over, Jack waited for Father Anthony to come to him. The Father said hello to a few others, then came over to Jack with a large smile, which Jack returned with a scowl, a very sincere one. Father Anthony said, "Jack, I'm so glad to see you! It's been a while since I've been able to talk to you. I hope nothing bad has happened to you since we last spoke. Let's go to the office."

Father Anthony led Jack to the swing office and they sat down in their chairs. Father Anthony asked, "So how have you been doing in your life here at Patterson? I trust that the Lord has kept you safe since we last spoke?"

Jack said, "I need you to bring me some more weed next week."

Father Anthony frowned silently. Jack knew this wasn't how he should approach this kind of request, but he was in no mood for the protocol today.

Father Anthony eventually said, "Jack, I'm disappointed in you. You know I can't bring anything in to a prisoner, much less drugs. I wouldn't even know where to find that kind of stuff."

Father Anthony was going to force Jack to go through the routine.

Jack sighed. "Can we just cut the bullshit? You know where to get the stuff, you've gotten it before. Aren't you tired of this fucking game between us?"

Father Anthony looked shocked, "Jack Carber, I don't even know what you're talking about. If you're going to have wild delusions like this, I'll recommend that you be sent to a psychologist for evaluation."

Jack rubbed his forehead for a second in frustration. He wondered how Father Anthony would react if he got up, walked over to him, and punched him in the face. Really punched him this time. Not the fake, harmless "roughing up" he had always given him before. A punch that would knock his teeth loose and make him see spots. Maybe then he'd realize what had always happened was just a game.

Jack clenched his mouth and decided that the easiest way was just to go through the routine.

He jumped up and physically dragged Father Anthony up out of his chair and slammed him face-first up against the wall of the office.

Jack snarled in his ear, "Listen here, you shithead fuck! I didn't ask if you wanted to do this or not. Bring me the goddamn joints!"

Father Anthony shook like a leaf. His face was pressed up against the wall, and Jack was pressed up against him. He said, "Oh Jesus! Please don't hurt me. I'm at your mercy. I'll do anything."

Jack let the Father go and said, "Good, I'll see you next week to get the stuff."

Father Anthony turned around and looked a little puzzled. He looked at Jack like he was waiting for something else. The silence got uncomfortable. Once again, Jack wasn't going through the proper routine.

Finally, Father Anthony said, "You know I can't honor a request like that. I think you need to leave this office."

Jack was very close to actually hitting the Father again for real. The asshole was going to make him go through all of it.

Jack grabbed the Father by the collar and threw him against the desk, then bent him over it. Jack leaned over on top of the Father and said, "I'm not leaving till I get what I came for! And you'd better bring me the fucking weed or I'll fuck you so hard you'll be coughing up cum for a week, you filthy son of a bitch!"

Father Anthony groaned in fear, but was rubbing his butt up against Jack's crotch at the same time.

Jack then gave Father Anthony what he wanted. He gave it to him rougher than he ever had before, pushing the desk across the floor with each thrust until it was against the far wall. The way he could fuck only when he really hated someone.

When it was over, Jack thought Father Anthony would have had a hard time walking for a couple of days, if it weren't for the fact that the priest was such an accomplished pussy. Jack was sick of being a pawn in stupid sex games. Absolutely sick of it, and it was burning him up.

~~~~~

Jack spent a while in the weight room with Hector trying to work out some of the frustration of the morning. Even after all this time, Jack still had the suspicion that Hector was gay, but hiding it very well, much like himself. It was just tiny little things Hector would say or do that would register as a blip on Jack's radar. He always felt like Hector was trying to get Jack to open up about it or acknowledge it.

But even the physical activity in the weight room didn't seem to calm Jack down a whole lot, so he went out on the yard to spend some time outside.

Out in the yard, in the heat and humidity, Dugger and some of the others tried to get him in on a game of basketball, but Jack didn't feel like playing any ball with them, either.

He wandered and found himself at Adder's picnic table, so he sat up on the spot next to where Adder would typically be. Jack thought to himself that Adder should be getting out of Ad Seg any time, so maybe he'd see him out there.

It was a hot day outside, and Jack could feel the sweat forming on his brow and along his hairline at the back of his neck. He watched the birds flying around overhead and thought about how nothing had changed in all the time he had been at PattX. How everyone was out to get something out of you. And nothing changed. Day after day after day.

He caught a movement out of the corner of his eye and saw Adder coming up to the table. Jack was a little surprised to find he was actually relieved to see Adder. Adder looked no worse for the week in the tank, other than the dark beard he hadn't shaved off yet. The beard made him look a little older, a little dirtier. And psychopathic looking, too.

Adder sat down on the top of the table next to Jack and planted his feet down on the bench. He was squinting a lot in the light, but Jack knew what it was like to come out into daylight after being in the tank for a week.

Jack said, "I thought you had gotten parole. Did you already kill some innocent schmuck and get your ass thrown back in here?"

He looked over at Adder, who was staring out past the fence while resting his chin in the palm of his hand.

They sat in silence for a couple of minutes, and Jack asked, "Were you much into music? Before you came here? What kind of stuff did you listen to? Opera? You seem kinda like the opera type."

He paused before continuing. "I miss Bonnie Raitt."

Another pause. "She and I had a thing going before I got thrown in here. She's saving herself for me until I get out."

Jack sighed and scratched himself.

"Yeeeaahh, I'm just kidding. Bonnie Raitt wouldn't know me from a hole in the ground. I like her music, though. I miss it."

Adder continued to stare without moving. This kind of stuff wasn't going anywhere. Two seconds ago he was glad to see Adder, and now he was frustrated with him the same way he had been with Father Anthony that morning. He was starting to feel a little invisible to everyone around him, like he was of no consequence at all. It rankled him. All of it. Everyone.

"I don't know if it makes any difference to you or not, but I'm gay."

Jack suddenly realized what he had just said to Adder. It came out before he realized he was about to spout it. Nothing else seemed to work on Adder, so he had just blurted it out.

He looked sideways over at Adder, sort of hoping unrealistically that he hadn't heard him, but sort of hoping he had and that Adder would react in some way. *Any* way.

Adder didn't even look at him, though. He smoothed his whiskers down with a swipe of his hand and continued looking past the fence at the trees and clouds in the distance. Adder's eyes were almost shut he was squinting so hard.

Jack held his breath for a moment, waiting on something from Adder. Behind him, he could hear the guys on the basketball court yelling and ragging each other.

The lack of any reaction from Adder got Jack even more frustrated. He didn't know what kind of reaction he wanted from Adder, but no reaction at all wasn't it. He had spent over a year now trying to get Adder just to notice him, and it had all been a huge waste. Jack didn't know why he ever should have expected anything different from Adder, though.

He muttered, "Fuck this," under his breath and stomped inside.

And just to make his day totally complete, on the way inside, Troy passed him in the hallway. Just as they got equal, Troy stuck his foot out and tripped Jack, who went sprawling face first on the floor. He turned and looked at Troy, who had stopped long enough to laugh at Jack and grab his crotch for Jack's benefit. Troy had been on him like this ever since he had been interrupted while mauling him in the library.

~~~~~

Jack stewed over everything the rest of the day in his cell. He barely spoke to any of the guys at dinner and continued to simmer in his own bitter anger even past dinner. He had a year old magazine from the library that he was trying to look at while on his bunk, but he was still just fuming over everything. He was sick of feeling helpless. Feeling like everyone else was dictating everything. Tired of being marginalized.

All he had managed in his life was to hate insurance companies. All of his cons and crimes were just revenge against the system that had killed his parents. He had had a flash that there might be something more. Just that once. He had thought that Chris might help him find out that there was something to life other than petty revenge. But he had just been used then, too. Jack felt like a total failure. He felt like giving up.

Chris Stambeki could go to hell. Father Anthony could go to hell. Adder could go to hell. Troy could go to hell. Capt. Marcus could go to hell. Jack could go to hell, even. He was over it.

"WHAT?!" Jack barked at Adder. He was so caught up in his thoughts that he hadn't realized Adder was standing right next to him and until he had tapped him on the leg.

Jack looked over at Adder, who was wearing just his jock strap. Adder grabbed at his dick through the jock, which was his usual way of saying he wanted a blowjob. Scratch that... it was his way of saying he was going to get a blowjob.

Jack stood up and hissed, "Fuck you! I'm tired of just being the warm hole in the room you use whenever you get a tickle in your sack! I'm tired of playing stupid parts in other people's sick fantasies!" By now Jack was really going on a rip and was right up in Adder's face. If he had noticed that Adder's eyes had narrowed, he probably would have realized what he was doing, the deadly serious risk he was running, and stopped. But Jack wasn't really paying any attention to anything other than getting it out.

"I'm sick of assholes that use sex to hurt other people as much as possible! *I'm sick of this god-forsaken shithole!*"

Jack was still up in Adder's face and he was in a rage now. His face was red and balled-up up in anger. He focused back on Adder slightly, but the tirade continued in a boiling whisper.

"And YOU, dickwad, I've put up with you for over a goddamn year now! Put up with the way you treated me and the way you've used me! I've poured myself out to you to get some kind of reaction. I've tried to be on your side and gotten nothing. I've tried to get you to fucking *look* at me for a year, but you're always focused just past me!"

Jack actually poked Adder in the bare chest at this point. "Why should I even bother trying with you? Huh?"

"What happened to you? Huh?"

"Why are you like this?"

"What are you fucking hiding from, behind your silence and your god-damn distance?!"

Jack paused, fuming, his chest heaving in and out. His eye was twitching rapidly.

Then he poked Adder in the chest again and seethed, "At what point did you stop being a person and turn into a goddamn machine, huh?!"

Jack finally stopped and just burned. He watched Adder stand there, the same blank as always.

And with no thought whatsoever, Jack snapped. He hissed, "You *fucking* son of a bitch!!" and hauled off and slugged Adder in the chin as hard as he could.

Instantly, Jack came back to himself and realized what he had just done. Adder stumbled back a couple of steps, and looked genuinely surprised for a flash.

The blood drained out of Jack and he almost lost control of his bladder. He knew full well he would probably be permanently disabled within the next five seconds. He was frozen like a deer in headlights, though. Everything ground down so that it was moving in slow motion all of a sudden. Jack waited for his fate.

Adder stood there for a second, eyes wide, then reached up and rubbed his chin.

And then he smiled. Not an evil, "now I've got you" smile. It was a genuine smile. One of genuine amusement. And then Adder laughed a little bit – a deep, good-natured laugh. Adder continued to rub his chin as he laughed. He looked at Jack and his blue eyes sparkled. Then Adder reached out and gave Jack a friendly pat in the middle of his chest, which made Jack flinch with fear. But Adder continued smiling the whole time.

Jack slowly started to resume breathing. Adder backed up a step and made a comical expression and held up both his hands in surrender, the sparkle in his eye obviously trying to tell Jack, "Ok, tiger, I give up!"

Adder stepped past Jack over to the sink to look at his chin in the mirror for a second. He moved his bottom jaw back and forth to make sure it was ok. Jack just stood and watched dumbly.

With another grin towards Jack, Adder grabbed one of his books off the desk, then vaulted up onto his bunk and started reading.

Jack continued to stare. He wondered what the hell had just happened. He looked around in confusion, hoping maybe somebody else had seen everything and could explain it to him. Did he really just pop Adder in the chin? Was he really still standing up? Maybe he was really already in a hospital and this was some weird coma dream.

Jack walked over to the sink and looked in the mirror. He still seemed to be in one piece. He splashed a little water on his face, and then walked back over to the bars and looked out over the tier.

The next thought that went through Jack's mind wasn't what he expected at all... Adder had a really great smile. It was the first time he had ever seen Adder smile. He had been in this shithole with this sociopath for well over a year now and finally saw him smile.

Then Jack started to cloud back over some. As much as he wanted to think that everything would be different, he wasn't sure it would be. Had he finally cracked through Adder's wall some? Was the reprieve from Adder's "needs" just a one-time thing just because he had made Adder laugh? Would everything be back to normal tomorrow night? If things had really changed, would he like the way they had changed? He had told Adder earlier that he was gay. He had so studiously avoided letting anyone at PattX find out, and yet he had just thrown it out at Adder's feet for no reason. Why did he get reckless and say that?

Why did none of this make any goddamn sense?

What the fuck was he supposed to do now?

The knuckles on his hand were killing him.

Day 454 – Tuesday, June 19th, 2001

Jack took another pull on the pinner he was smoking. The things were tiny and only took the edge off, but that was all he really wanted anyway. He had just gotten a load of laundry going in the big machines and would wait for them to finish and then start them up in the dryers. There was a chair in the room, but Jack had sat down on the cold concrete floor on the other side of a table. If Charlie or someone else came in, he'd have enough warning to lose the joint before they could see him. Until then, he had some time to sit back and relax. Smoke a little. Unwind.

Jack had gotten just what he wanted now, finally, but it still didn't feel quite right. He wished he could nail it down better than that. It had been nagging away at him in the back of his mind for the last week.

Ever since the night a couple of weeks ago when he had punched Adder and Adder had backed down, things had changed some between the two of them. Jack wasn't stupid enough to think that he had intimidated Adder into backing down. For whatever reason, Adder had chosen to respect Jack's refusal of sex, and Adder could have gone back to the way things were before if he really wanted. But he hadn't.

After that night, most things felt just like they had been before. Adder still pretty much ignored Jack. Jack still tried to interact with

Adder some. Adder still wanted sex, but now he asked for it instead of just taking it. Twice now since that night, Adder had indicated to Jack that he wanted to get his rocks off, and Jack had flatly refused. Jack wasn't going to pass up a chance to actually be in control of his sex life for a change. Plus he wanted to see if the change would last, or if saying "no" was a one-time free-pass Adder had "allowed." So far, though, it seemed to be a real change.

Jack had thought it likely that as soon as Adder had found out he was gay, then Adder would be even less inclined to give Jack any say in the matter. He couldn't quite figure out why Adder had reacted the way he did and finally changed a little bit. Jack knew he must have made some kind of connection with Adder, he just wasn't sure what it was.

But the two times Jack had refused since that night, Adder had calmly honored his refusal.

Jack took another drag on the joint, letting the wispy smoke blow slowly out and he finished it off. He put the small bottle back in its hiding place and sat back down to wait for the laundry.

Father Anthony had brought the pot just has he had asked for, and Jack did his part to get Father Anthony to give them to him. Jack had given a couple more of the joints to Wilson, and he thought Wilson was going to hug him right in front of everyone, which scared him given his last run-in with Troy in the library. Jack had limited his time with Wilson a little bit, but he wouldn't cut Wilson off entirely, even with the risk. Troy *wanted* Jack to avoid Wilson. It showed he could control Jack, and it would hurt Wilson by cutting him off from one of the few people he felt safe around. It was a double-score from Troy's point of view. No wonder Troy liked the idea. But Jack wasn't going to roll over that easily.

Jack had also offered some of the marijuana to Adder, but same as the first time, Adder didn't seem interested at all. So he had brought all the rest of it up in the laundry area and hidden it.

He started moving some of the laundry from the washers to the dryers and thought some more about the small, nagging feeling, trying to get a clear fix on it. But it was like a reflection in a window that you could only see out of the corner of your eye; as soon as you went to look directly at it, though, it wasn't there anymore.

~ ~ ~ ~ ~

At lunch, Jack finally stopped looking at the refried beans on his tray that looked more like a bodily function and noticed that Wilson seemed even more jittery than usual. He barely ate anything and his hands were shaking. The food tasted worse than usual, though, and Jack really didn't want a whole lot either. Even Turner asked Wilson if he was feeling ok. Wilson just said he wasn't feeling great.

Jack tried to get Wilson to go out in the pound after lunch, but Wilson refused to go out in the yard. Instead, Jack led him over to the lounge area. Wilson insisted on sitting on one of the cheap, black vinyl couches with his back to the wall and he closely watched every person coming into the lounge area.

Jack said, "Wilson, I want you to tell me what's happened. You seem really shook up."

Wilson didn't say anything. He shrugged and picked at the bridge of his nose nervously.

"Was it Troy? Did Troy hurt you again?"

Wilson looked off to the side a little bit, shook his head a little, and could barely get the word "no" out.

Jack tried to give Wilson a little time to pull himself together to tell him what happened. Finally, Wilson said quietly, "All this time I've managed to avoid him. And now it's happening..."

"Who? Avoid who? What happened?"

Wilson looked down breathing heavily. He seemed terrified. Finally, almost so low that Jack missed it, he squeaked out, "Adder."

Jack immediately sat up and said, "Adder?" almost with the tone of why would anyone be worried about Adder? Then he caught himself and remembered that not everyone had the semi-charmed relationship with Adder that he seemed to have lately.

"Did Adder hurt you? What did he do to you?"

Wilson said softly, like he didn't want to think about it, "He, uh, forced me to, uh, you know... blow him this morning."

"Did he hit you?" asked Jack, a little more forcefully.

"He choked me until I understood what he wanted. Then he made me go down on him."

"So aside from getting your attention, did he do anything else to you?"

"No, I don't guess. How do you do it, Jack? How do you make him not bother you? The guy terrifies me. I'd do almost anything to have him never look at me again."

Jack tried to calm Wilson down. He said softly and smoothly, "I know he can be kind of intimidating. And he definitely can hurt people if he wants to. But I don't think he really wants to."

Jack waited for that to sink in a little bit. "You know, I don't talk about it much, but Adder's done the exact same thing to me that he did to you. But he's never been particularly violent about it. He just wants to get his rocks off."

This only seemed to run Wilson up again, though, "You've seen how he is, in front of everybody. People just come near him and pow! They lose a kidney, or an eye! Jesus, Jack, what do you do that you can get near him and not have him go off like that?"

"I think it's really mostly just that he has to be used to me being around him since I've been in the same cell with him for over year now. He doesn't see me as a threat, so I don't have to worry too much. I doubt you've really got much to worry about yourself, either."

Wilson looked at Jack, but he still seemed very skeptical of the whole thing. He looked like he was on the verge of crying, which is not what Jack wanted in the middle of the lounge. Jack tried again, "Wilson, I'm not trying to be nasty, but the choking was just to make sure he got your attention. After that, it was just a blowjob. You are gay, and you've given blowjobs before, right? In the end, he just wanted a blowjob. I bet Troy treats you way worse than Adder did."

Wilson said, "Troy doesn't scare me the way Adder does."

Jack wanted to say that he should be way more scared of Troy than Adder. But for Wilson, Troy was more of a known factor, and Troy could say all kinds of lies to make you feel just comfortable enough to get near him again. Troy was a master at that kind of manipulation.

But instead, Jack told him, "Look, the same thing that Adder did to you today, he's done to me, too, and I'm telling you, he's not trying to hurt you. You don't really have anything to worry about."

Jack thought about what the real risk was to Wilson after what happened. He asked, "Now think carefully... Did anyone see you and Adder together? Troy will go ballistic if he finds out Adder used you, and he'll mostly take it out on you."

Wilson considered for a minute when he realized what it would mean if Troy found out. He turned pale at the thought, but then he said, "No, I'm pretty sure no one did."

"Good, and obviously Adder is going to keep his mouth shut, so you don't have to worry about anything there. Try not to think about it anymore. Adder's not out to get you or hurt you, and chances are you'll never wind up in that situation again."

Jack stayed with Wilson a few more minutes just to make sure he didn't work himself back up into a rabid fright again. He remembered back to his first day at PattX and how terrified Wilson was of Adder even then.

~~~~~

Out in the pound later that afternoon, Jack decided to run a few laps around the yard and think it through. He saw Adder over on the picnic table, his shirt off and laying on the table next to him. He could see the dagger tattoo with dual skulls on Adder's right arm, and the top of the snake tattoo around his waist barely peeking up from the top of his pants.

So, Jack had gotten Adder to leave him alone, but now other people were having to fill the void. If it had been anybody else, Jack probably wouldn't have cared at all, but why did it have to be Wilson? Wilson simply wasn't prepared to handle Adder, and that probably actually did put him at a little bit of extra risk around Adder.

He shifted his eyes over and spotted Troy, who was playing basketball with some of the Kennel guys. Troy elbowed Fredo hard to clear a path for a lay up. Troy played just as dirty at basketball with his own buddies as he did with people he hated. Wilson was terrible at reading people and understanding them beyond just the baldest, shallowest perception. Troy was the one that Wilson should be afraid of.

Jack had been honest with Wilson about the fact that Adder probably wouldn't hurt him. Adder wouldn't need to in order to get what he wanted. But Jack had lied about one thing, and that's the idea that Adder would never do it again; if Adder wasn't getting what he wanted from Jack, he'd go get it from somewhere else. Jack knew that, in the end, the biggest risk was if Troy found out about it. Jack knew eventually Troy would find out if it started repeating, and then Wilson would be in extremely serious danger.

And then Jack faced up to the obvious, disturbing question. Was Adder doing this just because he was horny but wouldn't force Jack anymore, or was he trying to manipulate Jack back into being his outlet?

~~~~~

That night, Jack lay on his bunk thinking about the whole issue some more. Adder was sitting in the desk chair with his back to Jack like usual, but he wasn't reading – he was just sitting there, thinking. Or maybe dozing. Jack couldn't really tell.

The thought that Adder might be using Wilson to manipulate him had stirred up disturbing thoughts in Jack. If Adder was doing this, it meant there was a new aspect to Adder that Jack hadn't realized was there until now, a much darker aspect. Just based on his intuition, though, he didn't want to think Adder would be like that. Adder, despite his occasionally violent ways, and despite his distance from everyone around him, always seemed to have a certain amount of honor in his behavior. Adder didn't seem like the type to use guile to get what he wanted.

Using more of a basic logic, Jack still came to the same conclusion. If Adder wanted to use Jack for sex, why go through Wilson to get it? Up until recently, if Adder had wanted it, he would just take it. Adder had been a complete "what you see is what you get" kind of person.

Jack watched as Adder finally stood up and stripped down, then got up in his bunk for the night.

In the end, Jack decided it didn't matter what Adder's motivations were. Jack now had a choice of putting Wilson at a terrible risk, or distracting Adder so he'd leave Wilson alone.

The choice irritated Jack. It had just been a blowjob, for crying out loud. How many times had Wilson blown some guy, and only *now* was freaking out over this one lousy suck job? Jack had given plenty of blowjobs over the years, and Adder was no big deal. Hell, for the most part, Jack had decided that Adder was a better top than Stambeki had ever been.

The lights went out in the cells, except for the little bits of light coming in from outside on the walkways. Jack lay there looking up at Adder's bunk, and finally made his decision. But at least this time it was his decision and not someone else's.

He got up out of his bunk in the dark. He could tell faintly that Adder was aware of him, even if he wasn't directly watching him.

Jack stood up close to Adder's bunk. He spoke very softly so those in other cells wouldn't hear. "Hey Adder, I need to say something. I need to ask a favor."

"I know what you did to Wilson today. I know you were just trying to get your rocks off, but it really has him freaked out. I know I can't force you, so I'm just *asking* you to leave Wilson alone. You scare the guy so bad he's about to shit puppies outta his ass, and if Troy ever finds out that Wilson gave you a blowjob, he'll probably kill him."

Jack could hear Adder softly breathing in his bunk, and Adder was on his side looking at Jack.

"If you need to get off, come to me instead. You know I'm gay now, and I can handle it. I might occasionally still not feel like doing it, and I'd appreciate it if you didn't force me. The choking thing isn't much fun. But otherwise, I'm willing to help you out." Christ, those last few words left a bad taste in his mouth.

And Jack tentatively, very tentatively, reached out and patted Adder lightly on the leg through the blanket. Before he knew what was happening, Adder had grabbed Jack's wrist. He moved it down slowly until Jack's hand brushed into his crotch. He made Jack feel his hard-on through the cheap blanket and sheets.

Jack was resigned to doing what he had to and said softly, "Yeah, yeah, I get it. You're ready now." He sighed and said, "Ok, Adder, give me your best shot."

Jack backed up as Adder jumped out from under his sheets and stood in front of Jack with nothing but his jock strap on. Adder stood there a second, then reached out like he had done once before and gave Jack a friendly pat on the chest. Adder peeled his jock off and lay down on Jack's bunk with his hands behind his head.

Jack moved over to where Adder was on his bunk and went at it, for the first time consensually if not totally willingly. In reality, it was hardly different than the scores of other times he had been made to do the same thing for his cellmate. But the fact that Jack had chosen to do it this time made it feel very different. It was kind of like hating to eat broccoli just because your parents forced you, but as soon as you try it on your own, you find out that broccoli's not the big deal you thought it was. Jack felt like he'd be able to handle Adder's needs from then on with no problem.

When he was done, Adder stood up to get back up in his bunk. Jack stopped him and said, "Will you leave Wilson alone?"

In the dark, Jack could see Adder cock his head to one side and look curiously at Jack for a minute. But then Adder clapped him on the shoulder a couple of times to tell him, "No problem." Adder jumped silently back up on his bunk and rolled over to go to sleep.

Day 488 – Monday, July 23rd, 2001

Jack looked up from the book he was thumbing through in the library. He had been trying to decide if it would be worth reading or not when he saw Wilson walk in out of the corner of his eye. He was about to wave to Wilson when he saw Wilson's eyes get big and he immediately turned around and walked back out.

Jack already knew what the problem was. Adder was in there tapping at the computer a little bit. He had the *Computers For Dummies* book out next to it and was trying to learn some basic operation or other. Adder had finally taken it out of the desk drawer in their cell and actually started looking at it, and then progressed to trying a few things out on the machine in the library.

Jack ran after Wilson. When he caught up to him, he said, "You should come into the library. Adder's just messing around on the PC. He won't even notice you're there."

Wilson said, clutching for excuses, "No, I don't even know why I was going in there. I don't need anything in the library, anyway."

"You were going in there to show yourself you aren't completely paralyzed around Adder," said Jack. "Or you should. C'mon, I'll be there with you."

"Nope," said Wilson flatly as he started to back away from Jack.

"Adder hasn't bothered you except that one time, right? He's left you alone, right?" asked Jack.

"I've really avoided him."

"Look, sooner or later, you're going to accidentally get closer to him than you want. If you go ahead and do it on purpose now, it won't be so bad when it happens accidentally and you don't expect it."

Wilson seemed to think about this for a moment, but then he said, "Not ready yet. Thanks, though, for trying." Wilson walked off in the direction of the TV lounge instead.

As Jack was about to walk back into the library, the guard named Jones passed right by him coming from over near the Commissary. Jack asked him, "Aren't you on TV Lounge watch today?"

Jones stopped and said, "Leaving early. Got my little girl's twelfth birthday today."

Jack put on a big smile. He said, "Oh hey, that's great! What's April getting for her birthday?"

Jones looked at Jack like he was an idiot. "April? You mean Tanisha. My girl's name is Tanisha. Who's April?"

"Sorry. My mistake. I thought I heard you say her name was April at one point."

Jones looked like he was about to walk on, but Jack stopped him again and said, "Norrison said you've been guarding Adder since he first got thrown in."

"Yeah, I've had to fuck with that asshole from day one."

"Has he ever said even a single word? At all?" asked Jack.

Jones laughed, "Shit, no! That jackass is crazy."

Jack said, "Huh!"

Jones said, "He learned to fight in prison, though."

Jack said, "Really? There was a time when he wasn't very good?"

"Shoot, when he first came in over at Calhoun, he could fight a little bit, but not much. Just about anybody could whup his ass if they put a little mind to it. He trained, though. And he *picked* fights. He constantly got the shit beat out of him. He got into more fights than anybody else. I couldn't ever decide if he was fighting because he wanted to get better, or if he just wanted to get beat up all the time. He started doing these weird exercises like them Chinese people do. Like they's doing karate in slow motion. After a couple of years, nobody messed with him anymore because he got good. He was the one beating the shit out of everyone else by then. He still wanted to pick fights, though. He just wasn't a joke no more, and people started avoiding him just so he wouldn't pick on them. Even the guards if they could avoid it."

"No shit, huh? It's hard to imagine Adder getting his ass kicked," said Jack.

Jones laughed, "It's been a long time since he's gotten his ass kicked. I think he beats people just to stay in practice these days."

Jack asked, "And he's never had a visitor?"

"Not even his parents while they was alive. No visitors, no letters, no calls... nothin'."

Jones left to go to his daughter's birthday and Jack went back inside the library. Adder was still at the computer. Jack sat down and watched him from behind, thinking about his conversation with Jones.

Jack had just gotten two things from Jones he should never have gotten. Jack now knew his daughter's name and birthdate. He suddenly had a much better chance of getting into an account with net access on the PC. Although, at this point, he wasn't sure what he'd really go after. Naturally, he could steal identities right from inside the prison if he could get to the network, but sooner or later they'd track down the use of Jones' computer account, if the guy even had one. Noting the name and birthday was reflexive for Jack, the tool of the trade for a con man and identity thief, but Jack wasn't sure if he'd ever do any of that stuff again. Screwing companies, especially insurance companies, had been everything that drove him for a while, but after what happened with Stambeki, he wasn't sure he wanted to even do that anymore.

And if he was really honest with himself, it was more than Stambeki. Then the shadow of Jack's father crept into his mind. He thought about the times when his father would make him go out and rake leaves with him in the fall in the yard outside the crappy house they rented. His father had always made it more fun than work, and it always took probably twice as long to rake them than it should. He'd have Jack out there with him, though, so they could be together. Even after his dad started getting sick, too, and was almost too weak to do it. Jack almost started to tear up thinking about his dad. His dad would not be happy with him, with how he had chosen to live his life. And now, sure enough, Jack was ashamed of how he had lived it as well. It's just that his hatred of the insurance companies that killed his family always outweighed the fact that he knew the cons he ran were wrong. But now the balance was tipping and Jack felt lost. Dear God, what would he do to have his father back, to have his father hold him and run his fingers through Jack's hair the way he would and say it would be ok, that he wouldn't always feel lost like this.

Jack shook this off and watched Adder, who would look at the book and then try to figure out what to do on the screen.

He had learned a little bit more about Adder, too. Nothing earth-shattering, though. Jack figured there must have been a rift between Adder and his parents. They never communicated with him, and Adder hadn't been affected to find out they were dead. He wondered if maybe the rift between him and his parents, the fact that they ignored him in prison, was what caused him to wall himself off from everyone else. It was kind of funny to think of Adder as constantly picking fights and constantly getting kicked around, though. Hard to believe given how effortless his violent skills were now. The thought was funny, but it did impress on Jack the determination and iron will Adder must have had to put himself through that.

Suddenly, Jack didn't want to be around Adder, so he left the library to find somewhere he could be a little more alone. He thought maybe this was the time to enjoy the recent little bit of contraband he had gotten and saved up.

~~~~~

Jack ran by the laundry area to pick up a towel to take back to the cell. Charlie was there and tried to hand him one, but Jack said there was one upstairs that he wanted instead.

Charlie yelled at him as he ran up the stairs, "You better not be smoking more pot up there! At least not without sharing!"

Jack didn't mind Charlie, and Charlie didn't care that much about what Jack did. Charlie had caught Jack up there once smoking one of the joints, but Charlie just wanted to smoke one with him, so they sat and got high together one morning. Charlie had turned out to be a pretty cool guy.

Jack reached the upstairs where the washers and dryers were and went to his stash area. This time, though, it wasn't pinners that Jack had hidden away.

The day before, Jack had gotten Father Anthony to bring something else in. Father Anthony had brought it, but Jack had noticed a little bit of a change in his attitude. It seemed that even Father Anthony was getting bored with playing out his little fantasies with Jack, and was starting to just go through the motions. Getting raped by a prison inmate was becoming a little too run of the mill for the priest. *'Bout fucking time* was Jack's entire reaction to realizing the change in Father Anthony. It was the perfect time to be done with the priest once and for all.

He picked his item up from its hiding spot inside a loose mechanical access panel on one of the commercial dryers, rolled it up in a white towel, and strode out of the laundry area with it. Pinners were easy to conceal. This was much more difficult to hide and riskier to have in his possession, but the towel would work great to get it back to his cell. Jack was much more excited about this than the marijuana, that's for sure. He missed this way more than pot. He thought about sharing with Adder when he first got it, then decided he didn't want to, but now he thought he might try it after all, so he took it back to their cell to give it a try after dinner.

~ ~ ~ ~ ~

In the cell that evening, Jack bided his time, mostly listening to the faint conversations other cellmates usually had once the doors had been locked down for the night but before lights out. Adder was at the desk chair with no shirt on since it was pretty warm on the tier. He was flipping through the computer book a little more. Jack had stripped down to his boxers, too.

Adder definitely had the body to back up the threat he posed. The broad back, the short, dark hair that came to a widow's peak over a high forehead, and the deep-set gray eyes. Jack had watched Adder in the weight area many, many times. Adder had muscles, but not like a bodybuilder or steroid abuser. He was a naturally big, muscular guy and he sure could work a huge amount of weight. He tended to exclusively do the free weights and avoided the machines, and he used the punching bag a lot. Jack could see the speed that Adder was famous for in the punches and kicks he could land incredibly rapidly on the punching dummy. It made Jack feel much better that he had worked as hard as he did to get Adder to be comfortable with him. What Hool had said to Jack on his first day at PattX was true, Adder was incredibly quick and could be incredibly destructive when he wanted to.

Jack had never told another soul that he had punched Adder, or that he had gotten Adder to the point where the sex was consensual now. Not Hool or Turner or Bickers or even Wilson. For some reason, it was between him and Adder and wasn't for anyone else. He doubted anyone would easily believe him anyway. Jack felt it was only right to respect Adder this way since Adder had finally shown him some respect.

One thing that still nagged at him was whether or not Adder had used Wilson to get to him again. He couldn't figure out why Adder would go that route if that's how it was. But then, maybe that was just the manipulative con man in him suspecting something that wasn't there. Jack realized he had become much more suspicious of people trying to manipulate him, and with good reason, so he tried to account for that. He just didn't quite know what to think.

Adder leaned back in the chair and stretched his arms up over his head and yawned loudly. Jack could see the dagger and skulls tattoo on one arm, and the thorn and flame tattoo on the other.

He decided it was time to enjoy some of his bootleg before lights out. Downs had already made the last pass down along the tier for the night, and it would be pretty safe at this point. He got up and walked over to Adder, and squatted down next to the side of his chair.

He also went so far as to put his arm around Adder's back on the top of the chair. Doing things like that still made him a little nervous, but Jack had told himself to make little efforts every once in a while to touch Adder like this. It would help get Adder more and more used to him. Adder looked over at Jack to see what he wanted.

Jack whispered, "Hey man, you never wanted the pot that I brought in. But I got something different. I want to see if you want some tonight."

Jack stood up and grabbed the rolled-up towel off the desk. He unrolled it, and out of it he pulled a small bottle of Jack Daniels whiskey. This was some of Jack's favorite stuff. A bottle is hard to hide in prison, though, much harder than a few tiny joints.

The Jack Daniels was a score this time. And to go with the Jack Daniels, Jack got something he'd wanted to see again. Adder's eyes lit up and a huge smile spread across his face. That alone was worth the risk for Jack.

Jack opened it and said quietly, "C'mon, let's see if we can get drunk off this little bit."

He handed the bottle to Adder, who immediately tipped it up and chugged as hard as he could. Adder grimaced and almost choked as he tried to swallow. It dawned on Jack that this was probably the first drink of alcohol Adder had had in what was almost fifteen years. No wonder it burned.

Jack involuntarily said, "Fucker!"

Then more quietly, "I want some, too, you know! This shit's my favorite."

Adder brought the bottle down, but it was now a third empty. Adder groaned low from the scorch of the whiskey going down and wiped his arm across his mouth. Then he let out a groan from the joy of getting some alcohol in his system. Jack could smell the whiskey in the air on Adder's exhaled breath, and he eagerly anticipated his own taste of it. Adder handed the bottle to Jack, who tossed back a couple of his own gulps. It burned fiercely and then mellowed out, and Jack thought how good the whiskey tasted after way too long.

He sat down on the edge of the desk and put the bottle down next to him. Jack said, "Oh, I wish I could get this in here more than this one time. The joints are easy to hide, but I'd rather have this."

Adder took another swig on the bottle. He leaned back in his chair again and ran his hand over his chest and stretched some more. His eyes were closed as he let the Jack seep into his bloodstream.

"And to make matters worse, when we're done, I gotta get rid of the bottle."

Jack added, used to the one-sided conversations, "You know, I probably could have sold this bottle to someone here for a ton of scratch."

Jack took another big swig and scratched at his own chest a little bit.

"I could have kept this all to myself, too, ya know. But I decided to share it with my ol' roommate, Adder." He poked Adder in the middle of his chest with his finger to illustrate the point while he had another belt out of the bottle.

"Besides, if I drank it by myself, then that'd just make me an alcoholic. And I don't want that." He grinned cock-eyed at Adder, and Adder actually cracked a smile back at him this time.

Jack pointed at him and said, "Finally! See? I knew I'd get a little laugh out of you sooner or later. Damn, I wish I had my camera."

Jack shut up at this point, while he was ahead. He could feel the warmth from the whiskey spreading through him. They both took a few more turns drinking in silence.

Finally, Jack whispered to him, "You know, I don't know why you let me get away with punching you the other night. I haven't told anybody that I did that, mostly because no one would believe me. You're a hard one to figure out."

Adder looked at Jack, took another drink, then let out a small burp.

After a minute, Jack asked quietly and seriously, "Why don't you talk?"

The look in Adder's eyes got a little firmer.

"Shit, maybe you never could. I don't know. You're obviously not a mute."

Jack took another hit on the bottle and rubbed his hand absently across his bare chest again. Adder continued to stare directly at Jack's face, and unlike his early days at PattX, Adder was watching Jack very intently. Finally the lights on the tier went out and Jack and Adder were left in the dim lights coming from outside the cell. They could still see each other in the shadows, though.

They passed the bottle back and forth a few more times, and the bottle got down to the last swallow of Jack Daniels. Jack handed it to Adder, but Adder held it up and looked at it, then handed it back to Jack. He took it and held it out at Adder in a small, casual toast, then polished it off once and for all. Jack thought to himself that Adder giving him the last swallow was a perfect example of how Adder was actually a polite guy, respectful even.

Jack looked at the empty bottle in the dim light, snorted and said, "Last bit wasn't nothing but mostly a bunch of your nasty spit anyway."

Adder's eyes were still locked onto Jack, and hadn't drifted off of him for several minutes.

"Ok, I guess it'll be another year and a half before I get you to laugh again."

Jack and Adder wound up staring at each other in silence for another minute in the little bit of light coming in between the bars. Adder, in particular, watched Jack with a particular intensity.

Jack frowned at himself in the dark, then leaned forward a little bit and said in a dark whisper of need, "I want you to fuck me so bad right now."

Adder could hardly jump up out of the chair fast enough. Jack frantically tried to pull his boxer shorts off and almost fell over in the process, the booze having hit him harder than he realized. Adder got his own pants off and went to the sink to get the tube of lip balm. They had started using lip balm as a lube a while ago. Adder greased his dick up as fast as he could. Jack had bent over the desk and waited for his cellmate.

In a second, Adder came up behind Jack and pushed his way in. Adder was definitely on a roll this time, and got carried away very quickly. He grunted and got rougher than he ever had.

Jack genuinely wanted it this time, but even so, it was still a little too rough an attack for him, and one particularly painful punch caused Jack to look back at Adder and say, "Whoa, cowboy, slow down just a little there."

And Adder instantly did slow down. And then he stopped. Jack looked back over his shoulder to see what Adder was doing. In the dim light, Jack could see Adder just standing there and looking down at the floor.

Jack whispered, "You ok? I'm alright, you can keep going."

But Adder didn't. He pulled out and looked around the cell like something was wrong, like he wasn't sure where he was. Jack stood up and turned around. He asked, "You ok?"

Adder's gaze found Jack again but his expression was blank. In the dim light, it was hard to see if there was anything in particular in Adder's expression. Adder grabbed the bottle off the table and held it up for Jack to see. Then he punched Jack lightly in the chest with his balled up fist. Adder was telling Jack "thanks for the Jack Daniels."

Adder grabbed the towel and wiped himself off. Then he jumped silently up into his bunk, got under the blanket and faced towards the wall.

Jack just stood there naked and dumbfounded. What had just happened? Why did Adder stop? Did he do something wrong? Did he piss Adder off? Did something else happen that Jack had entirely missed? Had Adder decided that he wasn't a good fuck anymore?

The last thought actually cut Jack a little bit and made him feel a twinge of rejection. Jack thought it more likely that he had done something that made Adder mad. Was it because he asked Adder to slow down? Could that have been that big of a deal to Adder? Did that maybe make Adder feel a little rejected? How could it? Jack had actually told Adder to keep going after he stopped.

But then Jack thought it wasn't likely that Adder was mad at him, Adder had clearly thanked him for the Jack Daniels afterwards.

Jack eventually pulled his boxer shorts back on and got in his own bunk. He got mad at himself for feeling a little rejected. Being in close quarters with Adder for over a year, the sex, prison life, all of it, had conspired to push Jack too close to him. He had been so intent on getting closer to Adder for his own safety that he hadn't recognized that it had worked out too well. He wasn't in love with Adder, absolutely not; the guy was too ruthless and dangerous. And straight. And not really even Jack's type. And to top it off, the specter of what had happened with Stambeki, the betrayal of trust, reared its head. Getting close to people ended badly.

Day 520 – Friday, August 24th, 2001

Jack filled up his breakfast tray and walked out to a table. He pretty much took for granted how good the breakfasts were, but there was always lunch and dinner to remind him how bad it could be. He, along with everyone else, wished that Louis would one day get to take over the lunch/dinner shift.

He walked out into the chow hall and nodded at Hool, Turner, Bickers and Wilson, but walked on past them. Jack found an empty seat next to Adder and sat down with him. He had reached a point not too long ago where he occasionally skipped a meal with Hool and the others so he could instead sit with Adder, and there were always plenty of empty seats next to him. It raised some eyebrows the first time he had done it, but hardly anyone paid attention to this since they had seen Jack sitting out with Adder in the yard many times now. Wilson was glad that Jack was that safe and secure around Adder, but he still would resolutely stay as far away from him as possible.

They sat in silence as they ate. About halfway through the meal, a fight broke out between Fredo and Chica. Apparently, Fredo had made a disparaging comment about Chica's ability to please a man. Chica didn't approve and wanted to let Fredo know so, with his sharp fingernails. Jack watched the whole thing with mild interest; it was prison and fights happened occasionally. There was a lot of hooting and yelling from both the Kennel and the Brethren as the two went at it. Adder, exhibiting his usual amount of interest in these things, continued tucking into his toast and hash browns without glancing around to see who was involved, who was winning, or how close they were to him. The guards headed over to break up the fight and haul both of them off for a few days to remind them to play nice.

"It's nice to know that sometimes a fight can happen without me being in the middle of it," commented Jack, his mouth full of the institutional scrambled eggs that Louis managed to turn into something good by adding some cheese and onions and bell peppers. "Or you. The only difference is that when you're involved, they're over much more quickly."

Adder shot Jack a brief sideways glance.

Adder finished up all but a sausage link on his tray, and was about to get up and leave. Jack spotted it and said, "Hey, if you're not going to eat that, can I have it?"

Adder glanced down at it, then he picked up the sausage link, gave it a good, long lick, and put it on Jack's tray. Adder watched for Jack's reaction, but Jack saw an almost imperceptible trace of a smile on Adder's face. Adder was messing around with Jack, and Jack knew it.

Jack grumbled, "You son of a bitch," and bit into the sausage anyway. Adder walked on out and Jack stayed to finish his breakfast.

Jack was actually happy with how things had turned out so far. In a weird way, he almost felt like Adder had become a friend. Jack certainly felt comfortable around him, didn't fear him becoming suddenly or randomly violent with him anymore (although he had seen Adder do it to plenty of other people), and the sex had become pretty good now that Jack had a say in it. It was still one-sided sex, and Jack never held any illusion that Adder would be presenting his ass to Jack for his pleasure. Adder seemed to not mind the whole situation either. He had opened up enough with Jack to start subtly joking around with him, like he had with the sausage.

Drinking together with Adder that night definitely seemed to help. It was that same night when something happened to Adder while he was screwing Jack, and he had thought maybe Adder was done with him, or that maybe he had done something wrong. But the next day, Adder behaved towards Jack like nothing bad or strange had happened at all. He still wondered every once in a while what had gone through Adder's mind that night. He only could guess that Adder must have really appreciated the Jack Daniels because ever since then, he was much easier around Jack.

Right after that, however, and with Adder subtly opening up to him a little more, Jack had stopped trying to fool himself and he finally began to admit that he really had started to like Adder. It was mostly how he reacted to Adder's smile that made him face up to it. Jack would do almost anything to see Adder smile. He hadn't been in love very much, one time only, actually, but he was old enough and smart enough to recognize a crush when he saw it sitting around in a cell with him. And Jack had developed something of a crush on Adder.

He called a spade a spade, and didn't try to change it. Adder would be out of prison before too much longer. Jack would hopefully be out, too, sometime after that, and he could get on with his life. It was a one-sided and low-risk crush, so Jack just let it be without dwelling on it.

He had spent time wondering what Adder would actually do when he got out. Adder had been in prison for almost fifteen years, and the world was remarkably different than when he had gone in. As far as Jack knew, Adder had no money and no family. Adder had never worked at the prison, as he was considered too violent, so he had built up no money there. The tiny bit of money the correctional system would give him on his release would hardly buy a paper cup to piss in, so what would Adder do to survive outside? He wondered where Adder would go, and how would Adder handle people around him? He wouldn't be able to react violently to people around him on the outside the way he did at PattX. Jack sometimes wondered how Adder would react if he found him after they both got out. Jack thought about how maybe he could help Adder reorient himself some to life on the outside. Too much free time in prison meant too much time wondering about all kinds of things like this.

Somehow all these thoughts would get wound up in what Jack saw for himself once he got out of prison. Adder aside, Jack was having something of a crisis of identity. Ironic for someone that had stolen over fifty identities over the years to run cons under. He still hated insurance companies as much as ever, but what had happened with Stambeki and thoughts of how disappointed his father would have been hung over him and took the wind out of his criminally-talented sails. He wasn't quite sure how to make an honest living, though, either. He never had done it that way. He didn't know what to do. He didn't know.

He thought briefly again about Adder licking the sausage before giving it to him and laughed to himself. At least Adder had a sense of humor, even without ever saying a word.

~~~~~

Troy was wide-eyed and shouting at Jack, "We know you like his sausage, Carber, but none of us want to see you swallowing it in public!"

Jack ignored him and left the weight area. Even Hector and Ramon had noticed that Troy seemed more focused on Jack than anyone else in there, jeering at him from across the room. Jack knew he wasn't going to get anything done with Troy starting in on him, so he just left. Plus, looking at Troy's eyes, Jack was sure he was tweaked out on something, and it would be better just to avoid him.

Troy was always making some kind of remark at Jack, picking on him, trying to get Jack started. But today was worse than usual. He felt that Troy had never forgotten that he was interrupted before he could get what he wanted out of Jack that day in the library.

He went outside into the pound and was standing around talking to Hool and Bickers when he noticed that Troy had now come out into the yard, too. Jack started to feel like Troy was specifically chasing him.

He tried to stay in the conversation with Hool and Bickers, but he kept a close eye on Troy, who was edging nearer with Fredo at his side.

Hool and Bickers even noticed Troy casually moving closer and stopped talking.

Troy kept looking at Jack and started in on the taunting again. "Hey, Carber, I'm talkin' to you! Remember what I said about you and my property!"

And that comment set Jack boiling. Before he realized it, Jack had yelled back, "Look, if you don't want Fredo sucking my dick, you should take it up with him." Lots of the inmates around heard the comment and Jack knew instantly he'd have to pay for lobbing that particular barb Troy's way.

Both Fredo and Troy stopped dead in their tracks, their eyes flashing angrily. Fredo balled his fists up and clenched his teeth, and Troy's eyes got very narrow. Jack knew he had pissed both of them off with that comment. Fredo and Troy both started moving towards Jack a little more purposefully than they had before.

There were guards out in the yard keeping watch, but Fredo and Troy might get in a few good licks on him before the guards could get to them and break it up. Jack looked around and saw that Norrison was the closest one, but even he was way on the other side of the yard.

Jack started moving in that direction, passing near the door back inside the prison, and Fredo and Troy moved right with him, starting to circle around and cut him off before he got any closer to Norrison. Troy wasn't looking to trade barbs with Jack anymore; he wanted to hurt Jack.

Then several things happened very quickly. Fredo looked over at two of the Kennel guys near Norrison. He held up a fist in the air and grabbed his wrist with his other hand. The two Kennel dogs immediately ran after each other, past Norrison, and started fighting. In prison it's called chalking and it's done specifically to distract the guards from something else happening. Norrison immediately ran after them to break it up.

This gave Troy and Fredo a chance to get at him, and Jack started to back up away from the two of them quickly. He was about to run, but then he noticed Adder coming out of the prison into the yard. He was coming up lightning fast right behind Troy and Fredo.

In a split second, Adder had hit an incredibly vicious blow right to the base of Fredo's neck. Fredo never even knew he was in the crosshairs and crumpled to the prison yard dirt and lay unconscious.

Adder spun to do the same to Troy, but Troy already realized what was happening, managed to block the blow from Adder and kicked out with his leg right into Adder's abdomen. Adder stumbled back a few steps, but then ran forward and tackled Troy with his full weight. There was no way Troy could fight the full bulk of Adder plowing into him, and he fell over under Adder's bulk. Adder, now on top of him, started in with a series of brutal punches. Troy wasn't done yet, though, either, and he started punching back.

By this time, Norrison and the other guard, Harper, had realized what was going on and were calling for more guards and running over to Troy and Adder with Tasers already pulled out.

Troy got a foot free and pushed up into Adder's abdomen hard to get him off. Troy scrambled up to his feet and was about to kick Adder when he got hit by the Taser gun and fell back to the ground convulsing with the shock.

Jack was now only a few feet away and he saw Adder turn to see where the Taser had come from when he was hit with the other one. Adder jerked and fell forward onto the dirt a few feet away from Troy.

The instant Adder landed, something strange happened. Jack saw a tiny glint of light off from something flying off of Adder as he hit the dirt. It landed right next to Jack, about a foot away from where he was standing. Jack looked at Adder on the ground and saw something he had never seen before. He could see it clearly in Adder's eyes, as clear as a blue-sky day. It was so pronounced, he could see it even through the convulsions of the electricity passing through Adder. It was terror. Time stopped in that moment and Jack neither saw nor heard anything else. He saw the look of terror, and desperation, in Adder's eyes as they were locked right where the tiny glint of light had landed next to Jack.

And then Jack saw something else he'd never seen before. Adder started fighting against the Taser. The son-of-a-bitch actually managed to start crawling towards Jack. Norrison was yelling at Harper to turn the current up on Adder to control him and Harper was yelling back that it was maxed. Adder was actually fighting against the Taser and looked damn close to winning.

Jack took a small step to the left and stepped on whatever had landed there. He locked his eyes back on Adder, time still frozen, and

Adder's eyes flashed directly into Jack's the moment he saw Jack step on the thing that landed in the dirt. The pain that Jack saw in Adder when their eyes connected cut him down to the quick.

Time suddenly unfroze and Adder couldn't fight against the Taser any more, or lost the will, and lay on his stomach, twitching. But the look in Adder's eyes was already burned into Jack like a red-hot brand. Adder knew that Jack had whatever he had lost. Adder closed his eyes and gave up fighting.

Norrison yelled at Jack and some of the other inmates to back off. The others did back off, but Jack just squatted where he was. More guards came running and both Troy and Adder were handcuffed and hauled off. Marcus had come running out and was checking on Fredo who was still out cold.

The guards were so preoccupied with Troy and Adder that they didn't really notice or care that Jack hadn't backed away. While he squatted, Jack moved his left foot a little and discreetly felt around in the dirt without looking down. He finally felt a round piece of metal, which he picked up and palmed. He could feel that it was a ring, but he didn't look at it. Jewelry was absolutely not allowed at PattX, and if a guard saw him with it, it'd be gone instantly.

With the ring in his hand, Jack stood up and slowly backed away from the scene. A medical technician from the infirmary had shown up to check on Fredo and the guards were trying to decide if they needed a back brace and stretcher for Fredo or not.

Jack walked away from the scene. He worked his way back over to the door back inside and slipped in. Even back inside, he didn't dare look at what he had in his hand. He had a feeling it was more important than that kind of risk would allow.

Once back in his cell, Jack grabbed a book from the desk, then got on his bunk with it. He lay on his stomach with the open book so that it looked like he was reading in case someone walked by outside the cell.

Finally, with a little privacy, he could look at what Adder had lost. He looked closely at the ring, and what he saw made him feel like he had been hit by lightning.

It was a silver ring, with a serpentine design around the outside. But on the inside, there was a revelation. A thunderclap. An epiphany. There was an inscription which read, "William, I promise – Addy."

The realization almost blew Jack away. Adder was gay?! But even more, the ring itself... it was the key to Adder. The look in Adder's eyes when he knew he had lost the ring rose up in Jack's memory and scorched his mind's eye. Jack had thought Adder had nothing to tie him to anyone else or anything outside of the prison, but Adder did. He had this ring, this one tiny thing. And he had kept this ring an absolute secret from everyone else for almost fifteen years now. Everything about Adder was focused in this ring. Jack felt certain of it. It had to be this. Adder's isolation, the wall that separated him from everyone else, the hurt he feared, it all revolved around this ring. Adder had become almost a machine because what made him a person was all tied up in this small circle of metal, for *fifteen years* now. It all revolved around a person named William and a promise of Adder's.

But Adder had never had a visitor or any kind of communication from outside. Then the questions started popping up everywhere around Jack. Who was William? What was Adder's promise to him? If this was William's ring, why did Adder have it? Why had William not called or come to see Adder? Had William broken Adder's heart? Jesus, how did Adder hide this thing for fifteen years, including the body searches? Did he carry the ring with him everywhere or did he hide it somewhere in the cell most times?

Jack thought about the look in Adder's eyes when he realized he had lost the ring, how he had fought against the electricity running through his system trying to get to the it, almost overcoming it out of sheer desperation to get it back. That's how important it was to Adder.

A thought crept into Jack's mind, and it started making him nervous. Adder had gone through extraordinary measures to keep this ring an absolute secret every day for fifteen years. And now the biggest risk to this secret getting out was Jack. Jack had been in the wrong place at the wrong time today and saw something he shouldn't have ever seen. Now had the thing in his possession, even. Jack hoped, really hoped, that Adder trusted Jack enough to let this pass. But if Adder didn't trust Jack with this, he didn't feel like his safety would be as sure as it had been lately. Jack guessed he'd find out one way or the other in about seven days, maybe ten if Capt. Marcus was really put out by the whole melee today.

Sunday, July 28th, 1974

Mr. Buehner put his hand on Addison's knee. Addison listlessly pulled his leg away, recoiling in slow motion at his touch. Mr. Buehner smiled kindly and said, "That's right. That's right. That's how it should be."

Addison was fighting inside himself to pull it together. If he could shake the sluggishness off, he'd beat the shit out of this man. His head was slowly clearing, and he realized that this was the first time in, what, two weeks where the drugs were clearing and he wasn't restrained. Maybe it was a month? It was hard to tell how long it had been through the fog. It had been one or the other, drugged or tied down, every single moment since this person had taken him. Addison preferred the drugs. The bullshit that had happened when he had been clear-headed had been far worse.

Mr. Buehner sat with Addison on a bench in the parking lot of a cheap roadside motel just outside of Dublin. He looked over at Addison from behind his round, wire-rimmed glasses. His crooked, stained teeth beaming out at Addison. Mr. Buehner said in the raspy, whispering voice of his, "You should be so very happy, young Mr. Addison. You have been one of my greatest success stories. A true achievement. A testament to what Christian love and perseverance can achieve!"

The man paused to take in a long, rattling breath.

"You have sunk to the lowest level a human can sink, faced your demons there, and have now come out on the other side. It is all behind you now, Mr. Addison. You can rest. You have a lifetime of virtue, of love and honesty, of Christian sanctity ahead of you. The night is done, and the day has dawned. I am so pleased, so very pleased, that it was I that was allowed to lead you into the dawn."

The emphasis Mr. Buehner put on the phrase "so very pleased" made Addison's skin crawl. His mind was operating, but his body was still lethargic and uncoordinated.

"You are so lucky to have Mr. and Mrs. Tyler for your parents. To have parents that care this much for you, for your soul, and that have the resources to do something about this stain upon your heart is very rare. You are so loved, they could take advantage of this program to set you on the right path, the *only* path, before it was too late, before damnation and perversion was the only road left to you. Mr. Addison, you should fall at your parents' feet in fervent thanks when they arrive."

Addison thought about the dinner he had with his parents, the night Mr. Buehner took him away. A month earlier, they had found the magazine that Addison had hidden, the porno magazine with nothing but men in it, all doing things men were never supposed to do to one another. His mother had cried so much, and his father went completely berserk about what people would say when they found out his son was a queer. His father exploded in fury, raged and fumed for about two hours, and then went eerily silent. He said nothing else about it. He said virtually nothing at all to Addison after that, in fact. At the time, Addison thought it would blow over. But then came the dinner a few weeks later.

His mother had watched him very closely during that dinner. So closely that Addison wondered what was going on. Afterwards, he felt strange. Sleepy and slow and dazed. His mother put him on the sofa, and that's when this Mr. Buehner showed up and took him. And the horror began that very night after a long drive far away from his home.

Mr. Buehner looked out across the parking lot. "I know what would have happened. I know what lay down the road you were on, Mr. Addison. This tiny corrective action taken now is insignificant to the horror and pain you would experience if you remained a slave to the perverted flesh. You would have become a desiccated shell of a soul that even Jesus Christ would turn away from."

Mr. Buehner turned to Addison and let his eyes travel up and down his body, his gaze lingering here and there at certain points.

"But instead, you enter the... prime... stages of your manhood, strong and confident in the love of Christ and the love of your parents."

Mr. Buehner turned and put his hand on Addison's shoulder. Addison ripped away from his touch so violently and clumsily that he threw himself on the pavement at the foot of the bench. Addison looked directly at Mr. Buehner, fire and hatred burning in his eyes.

But Mr. Buehner just smiled widely at the reaction and sat up a little straighter. He knew the person casting the look at him was only a sixteen year old, but he was a six foot two, two hundred twenty pound sixteen year old. His voice shifted from the dreamy, philosophical timbre it had been to one more flat and matter of fact. He said, "I see you are fully back with me now. You should know that your parents will be here any minute. Any, ah, *flaw* this late in the therapy will have to be dealt with, at no additional charge to your parents. It will be a most intensive follow-up treatment, to begin when you are unsuspecting. So be careful about lashing out at the people that have only your purity at heart. It would be an unfortunate setback." The look on Mr. Buehner's face as he said this showed clearly that he wouldn't really consider it unfortunate from his point of view. Not in the least.

Addison had been ready to beat this man so that nothing was left but blood and pulp next to the bench, but he paused. This man knew what to say. The thought of being put back through any more of this made Addison wait. He looked at this man, surely the sickest, most perverted man ever to walk the earth. Addison spat at him, "You're a fucking monster!"

Mr. Buehner looked upward at the blue sky. He replied, distantly, "I am your savior."

Mr. Buehner looked back down at Addison, directly at his crotch. Addison got up off the pavement and sat down on the bench facing away from Mr. Buehner as much as he could.

The monster said, "You should also know that your parents have been fully briefed about the effects the reversion therapy typically has. They know that even when successful, those that go through it fight the idea of it and will say all sorts of lies, terrible and unfortunate lies, magnified by the drugs given to you to make you more receptive. They expect these lies from you, Mr. Addison, and know to ignore them. And of course, if they persist too much, it will be the thing that convinces them that additional therapy is needed."

Addison said nothing, but he could feel his eyes starting to fill up with water. This monster had him trapped. His parents had done this to him willingly; they had themselves administered the first round of drugs to him and handed him over to this demon with sallow skin and a hard dick. This man had fully prepped them to not believe anything he might claim about what happened. Again, the thought of having to go through any of this again would almost guarantee cooperation. Addison's mind played back for him briefly the image of Mr. Buehner stepping out of the motel bathroom, completely covered in skintight black fabric of some sort, head to toe, except for his pelvic area, which was completely naked. Addison himself was naked and his hands and feet had been tied down to the motel bed. What happened when Mr. Buehner had come over to the bed dressed like that made Addison shudder.

Addison felt Mr. Buehner's eyes boring into him from behind. Mr. Buehner said with the dreamy lilt returning, "You have been a remarkable subject, Mr. Addison. Additional therapy with you would not be... unwelcome."

Mr. Buehner started humming the tune to "Jesus Loves Me" softly to himself at this point. Addison just wished his parents would hurry up and get there and get him away from this place and this man as soon as possible. He wondered how many other boys this freak had done this to. Taken the parents money and repeatedly abused their children as "therapy." He knew he was still gay, no doubt about it. The therapy was a total sham. It was just the monstrosity of what happened to him and any others, and the threat that it would happen again, that kept them "straight" and kept the monster's secret safe. Addison felt so violated. His own parents had bought into this lie and handed him over to be this sick person's plaything for what felt like weeks unending.

A few moments later, a brand new Pontiac Bonneville came pulling into the parking lot, and Addison's parents got out.

His father, tall and dark haired, stared at Addison a moment with piercing and angry eyes, daring his son to still be queer and a waste of a lot of money. His mother timidly waited at her husband's heel until he went to speak to Mr. Buehner privately. She kept touching her hair nervously, and Addison assumed his father hadn't let her have a drink yet today. His mother walked over to Addison and seemed afraid to touch him. She finally did give Addison an uncomfortable hug and asked, "Honey, are you alright? Do you feel better?"

Addison didn't want to look at either of his parents any more than he did Mr. Buehner. He said, "I just want to leave."

Mr. Buehner and Addison's father walked over. Mr. Buehner went to put his hand on Addison's shoulder, and Addison violently yanked away from the man yet again. Addison's eyes would have burned a hole in the man's chest if they could.

Mr. Buehner smiled and looked at Mr. Tyler. He said to him, "It was a textbook case, Mr. Tyler. I think the reversion therapy went very well. The last of the sedative is wearing off of your son. He may be quiet and withdrawn the rest of today. This is normal."

Mr. Tyler said, "I'm glad we could nip this in the bud before it got out. It would have been disastrous. It's good to know there are people like you in the world that can help with these problems, Mr. Buehner. I hope we won't need to contact you again about Addison." Addison distinctly noticed his father looking directly at him on that last statement.

Mr. Tyler and Mr. Buehner shook hands, and then Mr. Tyler said, "Addison, son, let's go home. Go ahead and put your bags in the car."

Addison put his bags in the trunk of the car and they all got in. Addison sat in the back and wanted to shrink down as far as he could. He had been spitting mad when he was around Mr. Buehner, but now he just wanted to curl up into a tiny ball.

Mrs. Tyler turned enough so she could look at Addison in the back seat. She said, "Oh Addy! It'll be wonderful to have you home! The place has felt just empty without you!"

Addison sat in silence, brooding. How could his parents let this man do these things to him? Who were these people?

Addison's father kept glancing back at Addison in the rear-view mirror as they drove home. He finally asked, rather stonily, "Mr. Buehner assured me that the therapy worked well. Did it? Are you straight?"

Addison sat and didn't answer. He was drawn tight into his own world with everything else shut out.

Mr. Tyler looked back at Addison again in the mirror. He suddenly boomed, "Answer me!!"

Mrs. Tyler jumped in her seat and touched her hair again, unconsciously trying to fix an issue with it that didn't exist. She said softly, trying to calm her husband, "Oh, Blakely, you know Mr. Buehner said he might be like this. Let's talk once we get home, darling."

Mr. Tyler was red-faced from the frustration. He said angrily, "I think that if I spend ten thousand dollars to fix this problem, I deserve an answer to my question!!"

"Now honey, Mr. Buehner said it went very well. Once we get home and have had a chance to rest a moment, we can talk more then. I think Addison needs a little rest." She picked at her hair nervously several more times.

~~~~~

Addison stayed in his room once he got home. The whole thing made him so angry. He hated Mr. Buehner, but Addison knew he was stronger than the perverted things Mr. Buehner had done to him. He wasn't happy about the fact that his cherry had been busted by that freak, but in the end, he was a sick old man that had managed to fill too many parents' ears with lies. Addison was still gay and he knew it. Probably every poor boy that that man got his hands on stayed gay afterwards, they were just too scared to do anything that might bring the boogeyman back around. And so the parents got their money's worth, as far as they could tell. It worked on Addison.

But what hurt was his parents. They had let this man take him, drug him, spout bible verses, and do horrible things to him, all in the name of "reverting" him to a Godly, pure life. Had paid the man a lot of money to do it, in fact.

Addison had realized that his parents saw him as being a reflection of themselves years ago. Well, his father was that way, anyway. His mother was too cowed by his father and was too busy drinking to really put a stop to any of it. But Addison was just an accessory to his father, something to bolster his position in the community. He had first started to understand this when he was eleven and his father had signed him up for Little League. Addison had been excited at the thought of maybe getting to learn baseball from his father. But his father just hired someone to train with him twice a week. And worse, rather than put him on the team with several of his friends, he eventually found out his father put him on a different team just because the son of a prospective business partner was on it. Addison was just leverage in his father's eyes.

What they had allowed to happen to Addison over the last several weeks, though, was way beyond anything else. He had always been lonely and isolated in his own home, but it was far truer now than it ever was. His parents were supposed to love him. Was this what love really was? It wasn't the warm, secure feeling he thought it was supposed to be.

It was all because they had found that magazine that he had gotten his hands on. He had messed around a little bit with a couple of trampy girls at his school, but none of it had really been exciting. Not like he heard it would be. It was the magazine that made him realize. It was the men together on the glossy, fully-color pages that made him excited.

Addison felt lonely and confused and had no idea what to do or who to turn to.

Eventually, his mother called him down to dinner. He didn't want to go and have to look at his parents, either of them, but he did.

He sat at the large dining table with his parents and ate in silence, dreading when the subject would be pushed back out onto the richly polished mahogany table. His mother had obviously been drinking since the moment they got home. Addison picked at the roast beef and potatoes on his plate, but eventually the subject all came back up.

His father said through teeth that were almost clenched, "So I'm asking you again... patiently... did this treatment work?"

Addison couldn't sit quietly any more. "Well, it must have, dad. I didn't bring home any porno mags with me."

His father blew up, a vein in his forehead swelling up. "I will *not* allow you to treat this sarcastically! You will show me the respect I deserve! After everything I've given to you, the love I've shown you as a father, you will not answer me that way! No son of mine is going to turn *faggot*, you hear me?! It would make me the laughingstock of Macon! I didn't pay ten thousand dollars for this to not work!!!"

Addison himself was boiling. He felt red and hot at having been treated like an object by his father and by Mr. Buehner. He shrieked at his father, "You paid ten thousand dollars to have SOME PERVERT JACK OFF ON ME WHILE I WAS DRUGGED AND TIED NAKED TO A BED!"

His mother screamed and dropped her sterling silver fork loudly to her plate. She turned white and started touching her hair rapidly in different places. Mr. Tyler jumped up from his seat at the head of the table and pounded on it. He screamed, "YOU FILTHY LIAR! You want to make everyone else responsible for *your* shortcomings instead of taking responsibility for them yourself! Mr. Buehner said you'd throw out any kind of filth to shake our confidence in his treatment. He said you'd lie about the reversion methods. Mr. Buehner only helped you and this is how you respond! Myself, your mother, Mr. Buehner... we all just want to make you better and *this* is how you repay it!"

His father paused, his chest heaving. He pointed his fork at Addison and said, "And you watch your fuckin' mouth around your mother!"

Mr. Tyler sat back down and looked at his plate, still seething, but trying to regain his control.

Addison's mother stood up, still white, and said, "I'm going to go put this dish away. I don't think I'll be able to eat any more." She left to go into the kitchen. Addison and his father both knew she was going in there to start tossing back the first bottle of alcohol she could get her hands on.

Addison looked at his father through narrowed, angry eyes. He said in a soft, burning voice, "You don't know what that freak did to me, but I was there. I do."

Mr. Tyler took a bite of his roast beef defiantly and said through gritted teeth, "I don't care what he did to you, as long as he fixed you."

It felt like a brick wall slamming into Addison's head.

Whatever concept of what parents were supposed to be to their children was quashed by that. It was all fairy tales and pixie dust. It was all lies and no one cared that it was.

Addison got up from the table and fled upstairs to his room. He sat in his window and looked out across the manicured lawn and across the neighborhood of expensive homes. Addison was a big, strong man, even at just sixteen. But that statement had hurt. It hurt down to the very center of his bones. And something in Addison broke as a result. His father had shown his true colors in that one statement, and Addison wouldn't be the same. What had been sadness and disconnectedness with respect to his parents hardened, and turned into something else. Addison knew that as long as his father held the cards, he would have to keep himself in check. But over time, as Addison gained in independence, the tables would turn.

His father had won a battle. And ignited a war as a result.

Day 527 – Friday, August 31st, 2001

The waiting would be the worst part. Jack knew he would have to face Adder the instant he got out of Ad Seg, so he decided to stay put in their cell and wait for it. It had rained a lot the whole week, but today had been clear and hot. Most everyone had been antsy to get back outside a little bit. In the cell, though, Jack would have a little privacy to say what he wanted to say to Adder about this, even if the privacy to do this gave Adder an opportunity to beat the daylights out of him. Adder would get that opportunity no matter what, though, so Jack might as well face up to it.

He settled into the desk chair around 2 p.m. The guards would probably let Adder out sometime between then and 4 p.m.

A few days earlier, Jack had asked Norrison how Adder was doing in the tank. Norrison said Adder was wound up like he had never been before. The tank hardly ever bothered Adder since isolation was his modus operandi anyway. But Norrison said Adder was eating hardly at all and had been pacing around in the tank a lot. Jack knew the tell-tale signs of a caged animal and Adder would find him immediately after getting out of the hole, so Jack was just going to make it easy on him.

Wilson had certainly been happy to have a week of not having to worry about Adder or Troy. Norrison had told Jack that Fredo would probably have to wear a neck brace for a while until they could determine if the vertebrae would heal correctly or not.

Jack held the ring in his hand and flipped it over and over while he waited.

He wondered about Adder, William, and William's killers. What had led to it going down the way it did?

The day after Adder lost the ring, Jack went to the computer in the library and decided to try and see if he could maybe get a little more information. He finally had a real use for the personal information he had gotten from Jones, so he decided to see how far he could get. He had puttered around in the past, trying to guess account names for any of the guards, but never with any success. But this time he had lucked out; he had tried Jones' badge number. And Jones's password? His daughter's birthdate. People were so predictable.

Once in, Jack noticed he had access to prison records through an online system, so he checked on Adder to see what was there. As far as prison went, there was nothing in terms of visitors or calls except for two visits from a lawyer right after he had been sent away. But Jack noticed that it also had jail records prior to prison. The day of Adder's arrest in Macon, there were two visitors that came to see Adder in jail. One was a Blakely Tyler, who Jack assumed was Adder's father after seeing the prison records. And the other was none other than a William Samms.

Jack then started digging around on the web for something about a William Samms in Macon, Georgia. He finally ran across a story in the Macon Telegraph from November 26th, 1986. A person named William Samms had been found murdered execution style in his apartment after the police had gotten reports of gunshots there the afternoon before. It gave some information about the funeral up in Marietta, but that was it. William had been to see Adder in jail the same day he was killed, the day Adder had been arrested for shooting the security officer while trying to hold up a bank.

Jack had looked around some more to see if he could really find any other information on William Samms, but he was squeezing turnips at that point. There were no prison or jail records for a William Samms, and the one newspaper story was the only thing he had already found.

He spent several days after that spinning around the different scenarios that might answer the questions he was left with about this William person. Was William an accomplice of Adder's in addition to being involved with him? Did Adder have Samms killed because of something he knew? Had Samms betrayed Adder the same way that Chris Stambeki had betrayed Jack? Was William Samms' murder a warning to Adder to keep his own mouth shut while he was in jail? Is that why Adder had never spoken since? Was he afraid of retribution from people involved in his previous crimes?

The records he saw showed that Adder's arrest in Macon had involved some serious stuff. Adder had tried to knock over a bank, and wound up shooting a security guard in the process. He had fled with some money, carjacked someone right outside the bank without realizing there was a passenger still in it. He wrecked the car a few blocks later and the police caught him there.

Jack flipped over the ring in his hand a few more times, and then looked over at the desk. There were playing cards, a thing of Q-tips, an insulated coffee mug, and four or five tubes of lip balm which had never been used on lips. There was also a pile of magazines. And there was the paper airplane, and the most recent origami figures that Jack had made, a penguin and a camel. All of these things were Jack's, all of them. They told small tales about Jack, about the things that tied him to the world around him and the people in his life.

Not one thing on the desk belonged to Adder, though. Adder still essentially just had the volume of the encyclopedia in the desk, only now he was back on volume A. All Adder had was the ring. It was the one and only thing he was tied to.

Jack still didn't know the exact details of what happened with William Samms, but it plainly had had a profound impact on Adder. It had built a wall around Adder and stolen his soul for many, many years.

Jack held the ring and looked at it in the afternoon light coming in from the bank of frosted windows on the other side of the tier.

He had spent part of the week coming to grips with his feelings for Adder. While it had all been an idle crush, Jack didn't mind it. But with the ring, Jack realized there was now a potential there that had not been there before. The understanding that Adder was gay, along with the thought that maybe Adder had manipulated him back into sex had put Jack in a different frame of mind. So Jack had started getting himself under control and rooting out those feelings for Adder. He wasn't going to go through another Stambeki betrayal again.

He looked over at the origami camel. It had taken his father forever to teach Jack that one, but they did it over and over until Jack could do it right. Now, Jack could fold camels blindfolded and wearing gloves. He wished it all was as straightforward as his father had said it would be.

Jack's mind wandered back a few months to when there had been an origami stork on the desk, balanced on one leg. Adder was at the desk reading the encyclopedia and Jack was in his bunk. Adder finished reading and put the encyclopedia back in the drawer and closed it, which caused the stork to topple over. Adder had reached over and picked up the stork and set it back up the way Jack had left it. That memory had stuck with Jack for some reason.

His mind also drifted back to the very first day he arrived at PattX, how Adder had punched Jones in the eye right in front of him, then how Adder had knocked Jack out a few days later just because he wanted Jack's pillow. He raced forward and thought about the night they drank the Jack Daniels together and the beautiful smile on Adder's face. He knew he had gone beyond just trying to get Adder to not be violent a long time ago, and Jack felt pale at the thought of making the same mistakes over, and with the worst possible person. The same anguished, stupid mistakes that caused so much hurt and pain.

~~~~~

Jack looked up and saw Adder walking rapidly, almost jogging, back into the cell, a look of staunch determination on his face. It hit Jack immediately that Adder was definitely thinner than when he went into the hole, almost gaunt, and his face had a hollow look to it that had never been there before. Jack sat up in the chair as Adder came right up to him. Adder's lips were pressed shut and his eyes were looking directly into Jack's, a firm and fierce look. Adder held out his open palm to him, and Jack couldn't help but notice that Adder's big hand was shaking just a tiny bit. Jack reached out and put the ring back into Adder's open hand. Adder never took his eyes off of Jack's, save for a split-second glance down in the palm of his hand to make sure the ring really was there, and then he looked right back into Jack's eyes again with the same harsh face.

Adder closed his hand around the ring and continued to stare at Jack, his jaw set and mouth frowning. Jack was getting nervous because it was not a relieved or happy look in Adder's eyes. Adder's hands were clenched at his side.

Jack stared right back at Adder and said firmly, "One day." His voice had more conviction in it than he was feeling.

Adder's expression didn't change at all.

"I want one day."

Pause.

"And then you can do whatever you want. But I want one day to prove to you that nothing's changed."

Pause.

Jack felt himself start to sweat and thought he was going to lose his nerve, but he took a deep breath. Jack leaned forward slightly and said very softly, "You've got your ring back and your secret is safe. I've had it over seven days now, and no one knows. In one day, you'll see for yourself this is true. No one saw the ring but me. No one knows it exists but you and me. No one knows about any person named William." Jack forced himself to take the risk on his next statement. "No one knows you're gay."

Adder's expression still hadn't changed and his hands were still clenching and unclenching at his sides. His eyes hadn't moved from Jack's, hadn't even blinked, and Jack could feel his stare boring into him.

"I've worked hard to gain your trust and I'm not going to betray it here and now. I know that it would probably be more than my life to do that."

Jack wanted to say, "I care about you more than that," but he wasn't about to let himself get that carried away.

But he did say, very softly and while looking right back into Adder's eyes, "There is a person in there after all."

Adder looked at Jack with the same thin lips, then straightened up, turned around, and walked out of the cell.

Jack clenched his teeth together tightly and sat unhappily. He wished he had another bottle of Jack. He wished it were back to that night when he and Adder had drank together, getting drunk in a prison cell in the dark. He sighed. He wished... he wished clouds were made of cotton candy and raindrops were made of Tennessee whiskey, too.

Day 530 – Monday, September 3rd, 2001

Jack awoke with a start. It was still dark except for the lights in the tier coming in. He heard a sort of soft choking sound, right next to him. He looked over and saw Adder there, squatted down right next to him.

For a second, Jack didn't know what to think and didn't know what the sound had been. Then he heard it again and realized that it was Adder making the noise.

Adder, the inhuman machine, was right next to Jack and he was crying.

It tore into Jack to hear the sound. To know that Adder's hurt and pain had risen up so high that even he couldn't hold it anymore. To know that Adder couldn't carry it himself and needed another person to share it with. It made Jack want to do just about anything to make it better.

He turned over to face Adder and asked very softly, "Hey man, you ok?" Jack reached out and put his hand on Adder's shoulder.

Adder didn't respond and continued to sob softly.

Jack sat up in his bunk and leaned back against the concrete wall. He patted on his bunk and gently said, "C'mon, sit up here with me."

Adder stood up and sat on the bunk next to Jack. Adder crossed his legs and buried his face in his hands and continued to cry. Jack was amazed. This guy had seemed impervious to being hurt. Jack himself had belted him damn hard right in the chin and Adder had laughed about it a few seconds later. And now, here he was crying like a three year old that had lost his teddy bear.

Jack put his hand back up on Adder's bare shoulder. Adder leaned back up against the wall and tried to stop crying, but couldn't quite manage it. He grabbed Jack's hand and interlaced his fingers with Jack's and held onto him.

Somewhere, out in the tier, someone heard the crying and yelled, "Carber, shut the fuck up!" It sounded like Runnion.

Well, they had gotten the right cell. Jack smiled silently to himself. If only they knew who was actually crying this time. It amused him no end, and Jack was fine that they thought it was himself and not Adder.

Jack leaned over a little to Adder and whispered, "They think it's me, so you can let it all out if you want."

Adder continued to hold Jack's hand in both of his and continued to cry a little more, moving one hand away only long enough to wipe at his eyes some. Eventually it slowed, then stopped, and Jack could hear Adder's heavy, tired breaths. He may have cried it all out, but he made no immediate move from Jack's bunk.

Jack said, "It's ok. You've bottled it up for a long time. You've got the ring and it's still safe. I know the thought of losing it scared you, but it's ok."

Another sob or two escaped out of Adder, and he sniffed loudly to clear his nose.

Jack sat there with him, his hand still in Adder's. What had happened was a sea change from the last couple of days.

Adder had gotten the ring back from Jack, and seemed on the verge of unleashing his anger and fear on Jack, but he didn't. Instead, Adder had completely ignored him since that point, even avoiding him. It wasn't lost on Jack that there was hardly any difference between being ignored by Adder and being Adder's closest pal. To anyone watching, there was no real difference. But Jack could tell. Jack had gotten to know the tiniest manners and moods of Adder that told him these things that no one else would notice. And Jack knew when he was being shut out.

Deep down, Jack had felt a little disappointed that Adder was ignoring him, but he knew it was better for himself this way. He had assumed that it was because Adder was angry that someone had found out about the ring. Jack had not mentioned anything about it again to Adder after he gave it back. He absolutely had not said anything to Adder to let him know that he knew the little bit extra about William that he did. That would have instantly ruined the trust that Adder had in Jack, and it was already precarious. At least it was up until now.

But tonight whatever had been building up in Adder over the last few days couldn't be held back any more. Adder was upset and hurting. And he wanted and trusted Jack to be there for him. So Jack was there for him. Maybe Adder hadn't been really mad at Jack the last couple of days. Maybe he had just been getting past the fear of having lost the ring for good, or the fear of having the entire prison find out about his private pain. Maybe Adder was just coming to terms with the fact that he had found somebody in this God-forsaken place that he could trust a little bit after all.

Jack had his own fight going on inside himself, though. He had to keep his own feelings in check. He wasn't going to let his emotions get the better of him the way they had before. It wasn't an easy task, though. He wanted to hold Adder and lay there with him, and make Adder feel better. He wanted to wash away the years of isolation and silence, and help Adder to let go of the past, as vague as it was to Jack. But Jack had his own demons of the past standing in the way. He reminded himself that he still didn't know exactly what had happened between Adder and William. Hell, Jack wasn't even entirely sure why Adder was crying right now, other than guessing it was just the emotional release from having lost the ring, regaining it, and realizing the secret was still safe.

Adder had stopped crying and now sat next to him silently, holding onto his hand and rubbing on it slowly.

After another minute or two, Jack rubbed up and down on Adder's arm with his free hand and leaned over. He whispered to Adder, "You doing ok now?"

Adder reached out and gave Jack a couple of pats on the knee to say "thanks."

Jack shifted around a little so he could look at Adder more directly, at least for what that was worth in the dark. "I don't know the story behind the ring, but it's obvious it's at the core of you. I'm glad you see that you can trust me with this. Not to mention that it's nice not being killed to shut me up about it."

Jack saw Adder smile a little bit and heard him let out a tiny puff of a quiet laugh. It was the stuff that made Jack's heart skip a beat; the stuff he was supposed to avoid. He secretly wished Adder would touch him more.

Adder uncrossed his legs and sat forward a little bit on Jack's bunk. He turned and looked back at Jack.

Jack said quietly, "For what it's worth, I think everyone has a pain or hurt that they carry around with them."

Adder reached back and ruffled Jack's hair with a big hand, and ended by putting his hand on the side of Jack's head and holding it there for a second.

And with that, Adder got up and hoisted himself up onto his bunk without a sound. Jack sat for a few minutes, leaned up against the wall, until he could hear Adder's steady breathing. He finally got back under his own covers and fell asleep, too.

~~~~~

Jack woke up that morning, and Adder was already immersed in his routine. He was standing, feet together and legs locked, but bent totally over with his hands almost flat on the ground in front of his feet. He would then go through and flex each individual muscle possible. The next position would be the one where Adder balanced on his left foot, leaned way forward and stretched his other leg out behind him. Then again while balanced on his right foot.

Adder seemed to be past what had happened the night before. He hadn't looked over at Jack, but Jack knew that Adder knew he was awake. The guy almost had eyes in the back of his head.

Jack was a little past it, too. He had made up his mind that he had to put a little distance between him and Adder. He never expected that Adder was trying to do anything underhanded to take advantage of him. But then, he hadn't suspected Stambeki of doing that, either, until it was too late. Really, Jack didn't think that even Stambeki started out trying to con him. It had wound up being a set-up out of convenience. But in the end, the best grifts were those based around natural circumstances anyway. What hurt so bad was only partly the money that Stambeki and Kanya had stolen. What really hurt Jack was that if felt like a betrayal by his father. His dad had wanted Jack to have someone that made him happy, someone like Stambeki. His dad had wanted Jack to find love and be glad he had it. And look how *that* had turned out.

Jack didn't think Adder was trying to set him up. But that didn't mean that he wouldn't if the chance arose. Even if Adder was a pretty straight-up guy, which Jack did think he was, Adder was going to be gone who-knew-where in a few more months, and then eventually Jack would be gone too, starting his own life over. And on top of all that, Adder had never pushed for anything more with Jack than what they had going now, which could be probably best described as a sort-of one-way "friends with benefits."

During the morning count, Jack and Adder stood outside the cell, along with everyone else. Capt. Marcus was counting today. He had walked all the way down the upper tier counting. On his way back he yelled out, "Thirty-six," which was one less than it should be. But right as he got even to Jack, Marcus looked slightly over towards him and yelled, "And one cry-baby." The whole tier erupted in laughter.

Jack didn't even respond. Marcus was such an asshole. He was very glad, though, that obviously everyone thought it was him that had been crying.

At breakfast, Jack specifically didn't sit with Adder, even though he very much wanted to after last night. Instead, he sat at his usual spot with Hool and the others. Thankfully, Hool, Bickers, Hector and the others didn't bring up the crying from the night before. It really wasn't such an unusual thing. You'd wind up hearing someone that couldn't hardly take it any more start crying about every other week or so. And that was just the stuff you could actually hear.

After breakfast, Jack worked out with Hector and Ramon in the gym, and then made his way to the lounge. He found Wilson there and they started talking over a game of checkers.

Jack could see Wilson was holding back a question, and then it finally broke its reins. "I know you probably don't want to talk about it, but did Adder hurt you? Is that why I heard you last night?" asked Wilson.

"No," said Jack. "I just got a little stir crazy in the middle of the night. You know how you can suddenly just hate this place worse than anything and can't stand it anymore. I don't think Adder even woke up."

Wilson had a look on his face that told Jack he wasn't entirely convinced.

Jack said, "I know you want to think the worst of Adder, but he had nothing to do with what you heard last night." Jack thought what a huge lie that was. Then he added, "I keep trying to tell you he's not nearly as bad as you think. I've just taken some time and put some effort into getting to know him, and given him a chance to learn a little bit about me. Adder doesn't see me as someone that would, or could, threaten him, so he leaves me alone."

Wilson still seemed a little skeptical.

After another couple of plays in the checker game, Jack turned the tables. "What about you? Troy gets out of the hole, and that night you didn't eat anything and you had another cut on your face. What did Troy do to you?"

Wilson looked away from Jack and studied the board closely. He said, "Nothing really. He was just mad that he had been in Ad Seg for a week."

"And so it's your fault and that makes it ok to beat up on you," Jack said flatly.

Wilson didn't answer.

"You should see that Troy's worse than anyone here. Troy's a dick just for the sake of being a dick."

Wilson still didn't answer, but this time Jack could tell it was because he agreed with him.

Saturday, July 5th, 1986

Addison sat on a paint-flecked, wooden bench outside of Margot's Restaurant and waited, feeling the warm, humid night air. His legs fidgeted rapidly. He suddenly wondered if he should have worn a black shirt instead of the gray and white one, but then he decided he was just being nervous. He hoped William would show up soon. He found himself constantly glancing to the corner of the restaurant looking for William in case he had missed him pulling into the parking lot.

It would be their fifth date, if he didn't include the day they met when he accidentally drove over William's foot in a parking lot. Addison wasn't sure yet what it was that was different about William. He just was, and it made Addison nervous, and happy, and horny, and warm, and kind of light-headed all at the same time. He had been out with plenty of other guys, and had more than his fair share of one-night stands. But sooner or later, none of them had worked out the way he had wanted. They all just seemed interested in his body, or they got scared of him, or they just wanted to be around his family money. The last group always amused him since his father used the money to keep Adder on what little bit of a leash he could, but wouldn't actually give him hardly any of the money at all. Really, Addison wouldn't have cared a whit if his father never gave him another dime, but he always took it so his father would have the illusion that he still had some control over him.

Addison had always been something of a loner, more by circumstances than by choice. He just always seemed to never quite make a deep connection with anyone.

He had thought that was probably the main reason he liked William. Over the last several dates, William had already proven himself different. He and Addison hadn't slept with each other yet, despite Addison's very pushy attempts on each date. He wanted to badly – William had a slim body with wavy, light brown hair and a shy smile at first, but which really came out when Addison made him laugh. William had asked all kinds of questions about his life, a lot of which made Addison uncomfortable and that he had only responded to vaguely. William seemed to want to really get to know Addison rather than just screw and run. He felt like William was really interested in him, on a deeper level than anyone else. He had built up some high expectations that maybe William would be the one where he could have that connection that had always just evaded him in the past. And that kind of made him nervous. And excited.

A few minutes later, though, William appeared around the corner of the restaurant and came striding up. Addison wanted to jump up and kiss him right there, but held himself back since they were out in public. He slapped William on the shoulder and beamed at him, "Hey, William! You look great tonight!"

William smiled broadly and his eyes sparkled a little bit. He said, "Thanks! You do, too. You always do!" Addison caught William glance at the tip of the dagger tattoo peeking out from under his shirtsleeve. He had specifically worn that shirt since William had seemed interested in the tattoo when he first noticed it on their last date.

Addison said, "Do you think? I thought about a black shirt, but put the gray and white on instead. Should I have worn the black? Would the black have looked better? I shoulda worn the black."

William laughed and said, "You look fantastic the way you are. You could probably wear a paper bag and look great!"

Addison made a big point of opening the door for William as they stepped inside. After they were seated at a table, William started looking over the menu, but Addison kept looking over at William.

Without even glancing up, and with just a trace of a smile on his face, William said, "The menu's down on the table, Addison, and I'm not on it tonight!"

"You always know what I'm thinking," Addison said through a big grin. "But you can't fault me for tryin'!"

After the waiter took their orders and had brought them their drinks, Addison asked, "So when will you be ready for us to spend a little, uh, one on one time together? I'm antsy, I know, but I can't help it."

"When the time's right, we'll both know it."

Addison immediately said, "How about now? Is the time right, now?"

William laughed and said, "NO!"

"Oh, ok, just checkin'. You know, if the time comes right in the middle of our steaks, it'll be a little awkward, but just let me know and I can push everything off this table in about one second!"

William laughed and shook his head.

Addison got a little more serious and said, "I, uh... look, I don't want you to think that all I care about is gettin' in your pants. I like the fact that you want to take things slow, and I respect it. All kiddin' aside, I like you a lot. If you come over to my place with me after dinner, I promise to be an absolute gentleman. I just wish I didn't have to say goodbye right after dinner."

William said, "We'll see. Maybe. You know, Addison, I like you a lot, too. It's not been easy to say no to you. You *are* hot as hell, after all. But, I just want to make sure this is right. I don't want to screw this up by moving too fast. It would be easy to just go full speed ahead if I didn't really care about what happened down the road. But I do care, so I'm making myself go slow."

Addison appreciated what William was saying. William just had more willpower than Addison did, but he was glad someone did.

"I have to admit, when you took a look at my foot to make sure it wasn't really hurt, I never would have even thought for a moment you might be gay," said William. "You're an intimidating guy, but you know that. It wasn't until you paused a minute, trying to decide for yourself, still holding my foot, that I realized there might be something there. I'm glad you asked me to meet you for dinner that first time. Really, really glad!"

Addison smiled and said, "I'm glad I took the chance, too! I still feel awful for running over your foot. But I wouldn't have gotten you to go out with me if I hadn't!"

"You're sort of a strange guy, Addison. Your family's got plenty of money. You're a big, good-looking, incredibly masculine guy. And yet you have no ego at all. I thought it was cute how quiet you were on our first date. I was really expecting the usual tradeoff with a guy like you. Money and looks equals asshole personality. But you're not like that at all. The more I'm around you, the more I see how sweet you are inside."

Addison thought about some of the things he'd done in the past. He felt the need to be honest and said, "Well, maybe not as sweet as you think. I've done things I'm not proud of."

William got a curious look in his eye, "Oh, this must be some of that stuff that you keep being so evasive about. You're not a serial killer, are you?"

Addison laughed and said, "No!"

William said, "Ok, so how bad could you be?"

"I haven't... I, uh... My father and I just don't get along very well. I've been a little rebellious over the years."

"Well, maybe you've done some things to get under your father's skin. But I don't think those kinds of things are really you. I think the real you runs a little deeper than that. Underneath the bad behavior is a good, kind person," said William.

Addison couldn't say anything back. It meant so much to him to have someone say this. It was one of the nicest things anyone had ever said. He couldn't help himself; he reached across the table and gently stroked William's forearm with his finger.

William allowed the affectionate touch, but said, "You might want to be careful. This is still the south, and there's a redneck over at that table watching you do that."

Addison looked back over his shoulder and saw the white trash guy with a half-assed mustache and a "Smith & Wesson" cap on, glaring at him and William. Addison turned back with a chuckle and said, "That scrawny asshole? He can kiss my ass!"

But William seemed a little more concerned than Addison. "Well, maybe *you've* never been gay bashed before, and so you're not worried about it. It's no fun."

Addison was astounded. "You've been gay bashed? What happened?"

"It wasn't much, and I was lucky... luckier than a lot of gay guys. I was leaving a bar up in Atlanta, and this drunk guy started calling me a bunch of names... 'faggot cock-sucker' and things like that. I told him to fuck off and started to walk away, but he picked up a board from a trash pile and hit me with it once. Not bad, but I did get a lump on my head. I managed to run away before he could come after me again."

Addison felt terrible, "William, I'm so sorry! That shit infuriates me! I get so sick of people actin' like they can dictate everyone else's lives!"

William shrugged and seemed to want to change the subject. He nodded at Addison's arm and asked, "So the tattoo... is that one of those things you're not proud of? Did it piss your dad off?"

Addison smiled again and said, "I actually kind of like the tattoo. But it did piss my dad off, royally! It was a double-score as far as I'm concerned!"

"You're the only gay person I've ever met with a tattoo," admitted William.

William paused a second, pink creeping into his cheeks, and then decided to admit more. "I'm a little embarrassed by this, but I think it's hot. I think part of what I like about you is that you seem a little dangerous, but you're not. Not really. The bad boy image is a big turn-on for me."

Addison couldn't suppress a smile at this. He said dirtily, "Well, if you come over to my place after dinner, I'll show you my other tattoo."

William's eyes got big. "You've got more than one?!"

Addison smiled slyly, "Oh yeah, the other one's pretty big. I'll warn you, though, it kinda creeps some people out. I've had three guys walk out on me because it scared 'em."

William was definitely intrigued. He said, "Oh, come on! You're just saying that to get me back over to your place."

Addison leaned back in his chair and said smugly, "Well, there's only one way to find out for sure!!"

William didn't want to be suckered by this, but still looked curious at the same time. Addison could tell he was very tempted to get a look at this other tattoo now.

Their dinners arrived and right after the waiter left the table, Addison asked, "Ok, is it the right time yet? I'll shove all this food onto the floor if it is!" He winked at William, who shook his head and laughed.

As they dug into their dinners, William asked Addison just exactly how rebellious he had been against his father.

Addison wasn't ready to get into all the details; he was scared it would run William off. But he didn't want to lie either. The tattoos were the tamest skirmishes in the war with his father. He thought about the drugs he had done in college. He thought about dropping out of college just before he would have graduated and how angry his father had been. He thought about the drugs he had occasionally run since then, the trouble with Paulson, the robberies, and other things he had been doing to pay off Paulson and get him off his back. He was very afraid that William would drop him like a hot potato if he found out about all that. Addison wouldn't particularly blame him. He knew he'd have to own up to that stuff with William eventually, just not tonight.

Addison said, "Pretty bad. One of these days, soon, I promise I'll give you the details you want, but just not tonight. Just bear with me 'til then. It's all I ask."

William got quiet, then decided to approach it from a different angle. "Have you ever physically hurt someone? Intentionally?" asked William.

Addison said, "Well, I can hold my own in a fight. But I've never started one."

Something of a cloud washed over William's face at Addison's response. It was one thing to project a bad-boy image; it was another thing entirely to actually live the bad-boy reality. William was cluing in to the fact that bad-boy Addison was more than a hulking body and skin-deep tattoos. Addison could see the growing concern in William's face, so he leaned over the table some and said, "I won't lie to you. I have gotten into some fights before, and I've hurt a few people. But only because they were trying to seriously hurt me first. Now this next part is really important, and I take what I say right now more serious than anything I've just about ever said in my whole life – I would never, ever, under any circumstance, hurt *you*."

William wasn't quite sure which way to go. The thought that Addison might be a violent person did concern him, but he couldn't ignore the feeling, deep down, that Addison wasn't really like that, even if he could be on occasion. Addison's response defused the conflicting feelings some and put William a little more at ease. He said, "There's that rough-trade in you coming out again."

As they finished dinner, Addison said, "Please come over to my place for a while. I swear, no clothes will come off. We could watch a movie on TV and I could just hold you for a while. I just want to be with you."

William said, "I might consider it, if you'll show me your other tattoo."

Addison gave him a lecherous look and said, "Alright now, I'll show it to you, but clothes have to come off for that to happen!!"

William laughed and said, "If it can't be helped, it can't be helped!"

Addison was walking on air all of a sudden. He had cleaned up his apartment some just on the off chance that William might come over. Just knowing that he had more time this evening with William gave him the biggest thrill he had had in months. They walked out together and headed around back to the parking lot. As they got around the side, Addison took a chance and put his arm around William.

Right as they got around the back of the building, though, they heard a voice call out at them, "Goddamn faggots!"

William immediately said, "Oh, shit!"

Addison didn't say anything. He just stopped and looked down along the back of the building. The white trash guy from the restaurant was back there, smoking a joint next to a beat up truck. The guy walked a couple of steps towards them, pointed at them, and said, "You fucking queers think you can go pushing your faggot selves in everyone's faces! You oughta all be killed!"

William pulled on Addison, trying to go back around to the front of the restaurant. He said urgently, "Let's just run. We can go back around to the front and wait for him to leave."

Addison wasn't budging. He said with a smile, "Run? From this punk? You're kidding, right? Stay right here."

Addison started to walk towards the guy and William stood in place, calling after him, trying to get him to just walk away from this.

Addison said to the guy, "Did you just call me a faggot?"

The guy took a drag on his joint and sneered, "Hell no! I called you a goddamn faggot! You need to get yer pansy ass back to candy land, before I kick it back there!"

Addison actually laughed and looked around in disbelief. "Are you serious? This is a big joke, right? I'm about three times the size of you!"

Then Addison got very serious and got very close to the guy, towering over him. He said, calmly, "You have one chance to apologize to my friend for calling us ugly names, and for being a shit-for-brains dickwad. On your mark, get set, go!"

The guy looked at Addison like he was crazy. He chuckled a little bit, and then suddenly swung out hard and fast at Addison. William yelped, "Jesus!" but Addison was expecting it and jerked back so that the guy missed and lost his balance in the process. Addison lunged forward and grabbed the guy firmly by the throat with his large hand. He squeezed tightly. The guy's eyes bulged out and Addison pulled him closer to his face, practically lifting the guy off the ground.

191

The redneck started grabbing at Addison's arm, trying to get him to let go, but Addison ignored it. He snarled in the guy's face, "Last chance, asshole!"

Trying to free himself, the redneck scratched into Addison's arm and drew a little blood. That pissed Addison off. He held the guy by the throat with one hand and punched him hard in the face with his fist. Addison said, "Don't fucking scratch me, you sonofabitch! You do that again, and I swear to God you'll go home carryin' one of your eyeballs in your pocket! Now try again! *Apologize!*"

Addison let up on the guy's throat a little, but all he did was spit a "Fuck you!" at Addison.

Addison shrugged his shoulders and punched the guy in the face twice, even harder than the first time. Blood splattered out of the guy's nose this time. Addison threw him back and let him fall to the ground moaning.

Addison turned back around to William, who was still standing twenty feet away, white-faced and with his hand over his mouth in shock.

Addison smiled at him and finally William was able to move again. He yelled at him, "Holy fuck, Addison, you could have gotten seriously hurt!!"

Addison stopped and looked at William like he must have been watching some other fight. He said, "By that jerk? Not even close. He hits like a girl!"

Addison liked that. He turned back around to the guy still lying on the ground and yelled at him, "You hear that, dickhead? You hit like a fucking girl!"

He went to wipe the blood off of his hands on his jeans, and realized blood had spattered all over his shirt. He swore, "Dammit! All over my shirt!"

William still looked like he was in shock. Addison wanted to hug him to make him feel better, but couldn't do it with the guy's blood all over him. Instead, he got up close to William and looked him right in the eye. He said very seriously, "That asshole deserved it, and you know it. He'll think twice before trying to bash fags again."

William turned to go to the car, and said kind of jokingly, but kind of not, "Remind me to never piss you off."

Addison stopped him and said, "Whoa whoa whoa…" He got down on a knee in front of William and grabbed his hand gently. He said, "Listen to me. I mean this. I would *never* hit you! No matter what happens between us, you *never* have to worry about that happening to you. There are a lot of things in this world to worry about, but that ain't one of 'em."

William could see in his eyes how genuine Addison was being, and actually smiled at the comforting words.

They left William's car at the restaurant so they could ride together. On the way to Addison's, William asked, "What if you killed that guy?! He looked really hurt."

Addison said, "I just knocked him dizzy and gave him a bloody nose. He's fine. Believe me, I know when I've seriously hurt someone. I didn't even break his nose."

William was quiet, still trying to understand what he had just seen. He finally smiled and looked over at Addison. He said, "It's not often a gay guy gets to see a straight bashing!"

Addison just said, "Shithead swung first. You saw it."

~~~~~

At Addison's apartment, William waited on the sofa, trying to find something to watch on TV while Addison cleaned up the blood and changed his shirt.

When Addison came back into the den, he sat next to William and put his hand gently on the side of William's head. He said, "I'm sorry you had to see that tonight. I know you're not used to that kind of thing and it must have upset you."

William said, "I guess I had bought into the stereotype some myself because I never thought that a gay guy could kick someone's ass that, uh, effortlessly."

Addison laughed. "Oh, he was high and didn't know how to fight. I've gotten my ass handed to me a couple of times. I hope you don't ever see that. You wouldn't think so much of my abilities then."

William put his hand over on Addison's chest and felt around some. He said, "I have to admit. You really are a bad boy. It isn't just a façade. It's really sexy!"

Addison reached over, and put his thumb on William's chin. He leaned in and they started kissing. Addison didn't want to ever quit. He reached around and pulled William closer to him, making the kiss deeper and heavier.

A moment later, Addison pulled away and said, "I won't get carried away. I promised not to be pushy, and I'm not going to be pushy."

William looked at him like he was crazy, with lust in his eyes, and said, "Who said you could fucking stop?" He pushed Addison down onto the sofa and climbed up on top of him, kissing him hard. Their tongues felt all around. Their hands felt all around. Their bodies rubbed against each other.

But before it got too far, William slid down his body and laid his head on Addison's chest, feeling its rhythmic rise and fall with his breaths. His hand slowly slid down to Addison's crotch and felt his dick through his jeans. Addison didn't stop him, but he didn't push him to go farther either. Addison just ran his fingers through William's hair lightly and let him do whatever he wanted.

William looked up at Addison's face and said, "Let's go to your bedroom."

Addison gave him a squeeze and said, "Are you sure? You're not just getting carried away in the moment?"

William said, "No, I'm very sure. Now. Tonight. Right now is the right time." He very much appreciated the fact that Addison asked. He nodded at Addison, confirming again that the time was right.

Addison kissed the top of William's head and led him into the bedroom. They kissed and touched and took pieces of clothing off in between the kisses and touches.

When Addison finally pulled his pants down and stood back up, William saw the snake tattoo for the first time wrapped around his waist. He exclaimed, "Oh Jesus Christ! Look at that thing! Damn, you weren't kidding at all!"

Addison had forgotten all about it. He said, "Oh yeah! See? There is another tattoo. It doesn't freak you out, does it?"

William began to say something, but his mouth just dangled open for a moment. He finally recovered and said, "Wow! It is pretty extreme!" He reached out and touched it gingerly, right where the snake was biting its own tail under Addison's navel. "But after seeing you in action tonight, it's totally right for you. I can't imagine you without it." He stood up and pulled Addison's naked body against his own and grabbed his ass. "It's what makes you the hottest man in Macon!"

Addison was very relieved William wasn't turned off by it. Several guys had thought it was disgusting and left with hardly another word to him. He didn't think he could feel any happier about finding William, but he did.

Addison picked up a laughing William and threw him playfully on the bed. He got in with him and they explored each other from head to toe. Addison felt like stars were going off in his head every time William put his tongue on any part of his body. William was incredibly talented at finding sensitive spots on his body, and each one William found drove Addison crazier than the one before. William, for himself, was amazed at how the same person that had beaten the living daylights out of another person without hardly trying could be so gentle and loving with him. They both sensed that the match between them ran deeper than they had realized, and they both felt the joy of discovering it.

William moved around and made it clear that he wanted Addison to enter him, and Addison didn't have to be asked twice. Addison was so excited when he did enter William from behind that he got carried away, a little too carried away a little too quickly.

William looked back behind him and said, "Whoa there, cowboy! Take it a little easy and we can both enjoy this."

And it hit Addison. It hit him what was really happening. What William finally represented. Addison was mortified that he had gotten carried away and stopped his thrusting entirely. He was busy trying to fit in what he had just realized.

William laughed a little, looked back again and said, "You don't have to stop, either."

Addison came back to his senses. He began again, and he focused entirely on what would make William happy. And he did make William happy. He gave William the best night of lovemaking he had ever given anyone.

When they were done, Addison lay in his bed with William up against him, his head on Addison's chest. In the dark, Addison felt a couple of tears fall out of his eyes. He had found what he had been missing.

For the first time, he felt the connection with another person he had never felt before, not even his own parents. For the first time, he knew what it felt like to be a part of something larger than himself.

But deeper than any of that, William had given him a gift. The gift was that Addison's life could be different. Addison could have a life built around his and William's happiness, instead of his father's misery. William had shown Addison that he had a choice, and the realization was so fundamental that it changed Addison in that moment. That's what made William different from the others. It's what made Addison love William deeper and harder than he had ever loved anyone.

Addison rolled over onto his side and wrapped himself around William as much as he could, cradling him tightly to his body. He stroked William's hair and whispered into his ear, "I hope you're happy right where you are, because I'm never letting you go."

Day 567 – Wednesday, October 10th, 2001

Jack was just rounding the corner when he saw something that made him stop a second. He was walking from the weight area over to the TV lounge and caught a glimpse of Troy walking into the shower area, strutting like he owned the place. Same as always. Since it was just after lunch, he didn't think Troy was heading in there to actually take a shower. Jack decided to wait and see for a second.

Sure enough, a second later, Shimmey came out of the shower area and stationed himself where he could keep watch. Jack dropped back behind the corner where he wouldn't be seen. Troy was up to no good and probably had Wilson in the shower to beat up or rape. Jack decided this was a good chance to spoil Troy's party without a lot of risk – Shimmey hadn't seen him.

Jack went back the other way and found Norrison, who happened to be by the weight area.

He whispered to Norrison, "Look, you didn't hear it from me, but Troy just went into the shower area and Shimmey's hawking for him."

Norrison nodded that he heard Jack. They wouldn't be able to catch Troy actually doing anything since Shimmey was keeping watch, but at least they could interrupt it early before someone got too badly hurt. Jack was glad to do Wilson the favor.

Norrison called into his lapel radio to let them know they had a tip-off. Normally, Jack would worry about mouthing off to a guard like this since there was a big chance this information would find its way to Troy, which would be very bad. But Jack could trust Norrison to not let this slip, so he didn't worry about it. As Norrison was talking into his radio, Jack clutched his crotch and mouthed the words, "You owe me a blow-job" to him. Norrison flipped Jack off and smiled while he finished up on the radio.

Jack decided to waste some more time in the weight area to give the guards a chance to break up whatever was happening in the shower. He walked over to Dugger, who was curling dumbbells, and asked him if he wanted to play some one-on-one out on the basketball court later, and Dugger said he would.

As bad as the Kennel was, the Brethren, and even Quake himself, had always left Jack pretty much alone. Jack had always felt that Quake had something of a live-and-let-live philosophy, as long as Quake didn't want something you had. Maybe it was something in Quake's Creole background. Fortunately, Jack didn't have anything Quake wanted. Dugger, who was one of Quake's main men in the Brethren, had taken something of a liking to Jack, and that had gone a long way to keeping Jack relatively safe.

He spent a few more minutes bullshitting with Dugger, then finally decided that whatever the guards would do in the shower would be done at this point, so he said to him, "Alright, I'm gonna go on outside. Come on out later and we'll play some ball."

He started to leave, but yelled back at Dugger, "Hey, bring your ass because I'm gonna kick it."

Dugger shouted at him across the room, "Kiss it? Did you say kiss it? Nigger, I charge five dollars for that privilege!"

Jack laughed and walked on out.

As he walked by the shower area this time, he noticed that Shimmey was gone and no one seemed to be around, so he assumed the party was over.

The bright warmth of the autumn sun, which still felt like summer to Jack, hit him as he stepped outside into the pound. It was hot, but a lot less humid than it had been over the last few weeks. He glanced over at Adder's picnic table, which was empty. Adder had gotten himself thrown in Ad Seg again a week ago.

Jack had been right there when this one happened. Adder had been in the lounge area, almost dozing with his eyes closed in a chair and Jack, for whatever stupid reason that seemed like a good idea at the time, wanted to see if he could sneak up on him. He got within a few feet of Adder and the next thing he knew, Adder was up and had a big hand grabbing Jack by the neck and a fist pulled back. For the inmates that saw what was happening, they surely had to think Jack was a goner, but Jack could tell it was all put on. Adder's hand on his neck was loose and, despite the fist pulled back, he saw the look in Adder's eyes, and his eyes told the truth. The guy was just horsing around with Jack. Jack didn't even flinch he was so sure of it.

Before Jack could call Adder's bluff on smashing his nose out the back of his head, Adder let go entirely, spun around and kicked the knee in on a big, black guy named Ham that had come up too close behind him. Ham's knee made a sickening crunch sound and he went down with a scream like a little girl. Adder kneed him in the face, sending Ham onto his back. Adder was about to smash his foot into Ham's nuts, but Harper managed to shoot him with the Taser before he could do any more damage to the guy. Another couple of guards showed up, and they hauled Adder off to the hole for yet another week.

He may have gotten away with it that time, but Jack promised himself he'd never sneak up on Adder again. Even with Adder's preternatural sense about who was around him, the risk was too great.

Over on the far side of the basketball court, Jack saw Hool, Wilson and Turner standing around together, so he walked over to see them and spent a few minutes listening to Hool's bad, old jokes. Jack got the idea finally that they had been out there a while, Wilson included, so he didn't think it could have been Wilson in the shower area with Troy after all. And as glad as he was that it hadn't been him, he wondered who had been the unlucky person forced into the shower area with Troy this time.

~~~~~

After a little basketball with Dugger and after a shower together (where Dugger had repeatedly slapped his own ass and asked Jack if he was ready to plant his sweet, lily white lips on it), Jack walked back out to the yard to relax. On his way, he met up with Bickers, who now had a black, swollen eye that had not been like that at breakfast. He was headed to the commissary to get some ice to put on it. Jack was surprised as Bickers was usually really careful about his own safety and kept very aware of his surroundings.

Jack asked him, "That's new. You ok?"

"Fuckin' fine!" he grouched.

Jack would have bet a million dollars he knew where it came from. He asked him, "So who gave you the special present?"

Bickers looked around to make sure no one was close enough to listen and said, "That son-of-a-bitch Troy!"

"Ohhhh."

"Probably would have been much worse, except Jones came by right as Troy was just getting started. Troy was fuckin' pissed," said Bickers as he filled up a cup with ice.

"You've got me to thank for that," said Jack, proudly. "I saw Troy going in there and Shimmey keeping watch. I arranged for the party crasher."

"I owe you one, then. I'm probably not off the hook with Troy, though. Troy wasn't happy at all. But I can't think of a single person here that I'd like to stick it to more than Troy. Fucking redneck shithead!"

Bickers left Jack to go back to his cell to ice his eye down and Jack went on outside. Everyone eventually had their turn with Troy, and today it had been Bickers'.

Jack went out to Adder's picnic table and sat down for a while. It was probably about time for Adder to get out of the tank, and Jack thought that's probably why he had wound up there in Adder's usual outside spot. He hadn't quite figured out what to think of the past several weeks since Adder had broken down crying in the middle of the night.

Adder had seemed even closer to Jack after that night than ever before. Hell, he had cried like a baby on Jack's shoulder, so he *should* have felt closer. Adder smiled more at Jack than he ever had and seemed to watch Jack more than usual. The odd part was the sex. Adder had pretty much stopped asking for anything from Jack after that night. Jack knew he should be glad that even Adder was putting some distance there, but he couldn't help but feel a little disappointed. To make matters even more confusing, Jack had asked Adder if he wanted a blow-job at one point recently, and Adder let Jack go for it. But once Jack got the ball rolling, there didn't seem to be any enthusiasm on Adder's part. And then Adder had gotten thrown back in the hole for the last week.

Jack had always seemed to be able to read people pretty well, but he couldn't figure this one out.

He looked out past the fence at the trees in the distance and thought about how Adder never minded Jack sitting here, talking about whatever bullshit came to mind. He thought back over how he felt the first time he ever saw Adder smile, the night he punched him. He was so mad at Adder, and then Adder smiled and his anger had all melted away immediately. He couldn't quite figure out what drew him so much to Adder. The big guy wasn't his usual type – younger and blonder was more of Jack's type. But despite that, he was now more attracted to Adder than he had even been to Chris Stambeki. Adder was just very different deep inside than what the outside showed. Adder was a hurt and isolated man hiding deep inside a huge, dangerous criminal's body. Jack might even think of him as sensitive. It wasn't lost on Jack, either, that he definitely knew Adder, and even understood him, better than anybody else ever had in the last fifteen years. It made Jack oddly satisfied, and guarded about his feelings getting away from him, to know this.

It was the kind of thing Jack wished he could talk to his father about.

And then Jack remembered a thing his mother used to say on occasion. She would say that, "A person's actions talk more than his mouth." Adder could cry around Jack and then turn around and permanently disable people without breaking a sweat. Jack wondered if he was making it more complicated than he needed to.

~ ~ ~ ~ ~

Adder never showed up outside, so Jack went back to the cell a little early before dinnertime. He had started thinking about his mother more and wanted to be alone. He sat down in the chair in his cell, threw his feet up on the desk with a "thunk," and stared blankly at the desk as his mind wandered back over the things he remembered about his mother.

He had loved his mother, and her death had hit him very hard. He had only been nine when she died, and it seemed like a given that it would hit a nine-year-old hard. He remembered how the emphysema slowly weakened her until she couldn't get out of bed, without the strength to even gasp for the air she desperately needed. He remembered how his father struggled with her illness, trying to be there for her and for Jack, run the house, and keep a job to pay the insurance premiums to a company that in turn refused to pay the claims they were making. It was an awful time, and Jack had felt pretty separated from both of them, his mother because of her weakness and his father because he was so frantic trying to hold everything together. He felt like a burden on two people that already had far too much to bear as it was. His mother became racked with guilt because she had been a smoker, and the feelings of guilt just accelerated the disease, but Jack's dad never blamed her. Jack relived the painful memory of his mother trying to cry one night because of what her illness was putting her husband and Jack through, but not even being able to do that. The disease had mercilessly stolen even her ability to cry.

Jack missed his mother terribly, but after she had passed, his dad focused everything he had on Jack and tried to make up for what had happened, for lost time. Jack became much, much closer to his father as a result. All they had anymore was each other. They were left dirt poor because of all the bills, but they had each other, and Jack's dad made the most of every moment. He had seen how his father had been there for his mother in every possible way right up until the end. And then when she was gone, he was there for Jack. Even as a willful teenager, Jack knew he had a special gift in his father's love and never took it for granted. Watching his mother's slow, painful death had taught him to not take for granted the love given by another.

The memory of his mother was more distant than his father, but she had been a kind woman. Her dark hair and sparkling eyes were what Jack recalled with the most detail. She would tell the best jokes, even ones with dirty words in them occasionally, and then she'd laugh herself silly and tell Jack not to ever say that word. She and Jack's dad loved each other so much. He missed both of them more than he could stand sometimes.

Suddenly, Jack was pulled from his memories. He jerked and looked back over his shoulder because a strange sensation had crept up his spine. Adder was standing right behind him with his hand outstretched towards Jack, almost touching him. Adder froze for a second when Jack looked around, with an almost embarrassed expression on his face, but then he reached past Jack and stood the fallen origami camel back upright on the desk. Jack looked at it and realized it must have fallen over when he put his feet up on the desk.

Jack said, agitated, "Christ! Adder, you about scared me shitless!"

Then more calmly, but puzzled, "For a second, I thought you were going... It looked like you..." Jack stopped and repeated the word "don't" to himself in his mind. Then he said, "Well... never mind."

Adder squatted down next to Jack with his arm resting on the back of the desk chair, and looked steadily at Jack for a moment. He wasn't smiling, but he certainly wasn't angry or sad. Jack looked back, right into Adder's deep-set eyes, right into their sometimes-gray, sometimes-blue irises. Adder looked scruffy from not having shaved in a week. It felt odd that he could have ever really feared this person the way he had. But Jack knew that that was two other people a lifetime ago in a different place.

Adder broke the gaze and looked down at the floor for a moment. Then he glanced back up and gave Jack a couple of friendly smacks on the back. He stood up and went over to the sink to wash his face.

It all left a strange taste in Jack's mouth, even more pronounced after all the reminiscing he had done about his parents. He would have given absolutely anything to have Adder speak and just say what was going through his head.

Day 621 – Monday, December 3rd, 2001

Jack wrung his hands around and around until he finally had to grip them together hard just to get them to stop. With his hands under control, he had to start fighting his leg, which now wanted to start bouncing to pick up the slack that his stilled hands left behind. He didn't think he would be so nervous, but now that he was here, he realized he was counting on getting out sooner rather than later. He shifted in his chair again while the Parole Board members checked a few notes about his history at PattX and consulted among themselves.

He had been brought in today to face them to see if he would be released early or would have to wait longer, based on his "rehabilitation." Jack knew that the worst thing that would impact this decision would be the time he was thrown in the tank for getting into the fight with Devers. The board had already asked him many questions about changing his ways, what he would do if he got out, etc. Jack had good answers ready for all of those; con men always had good answers for these kinds of questions.

He also felt heartened by the fact that Norrison had been the one to take him to the hearing room in the administrative section of the prison. The board had asked Norrison about his direct experience with Jack, and he was able to answer that he had spent a lot of time around him, that he was one of the least troublesome inmates there, and one of the very few that he never worried about turning his back on. Norrison was now waiting quietly in a seat near the room's exit.

Finally, the board finished their discussions and they all faced back towards Jack. The man chairing the meeting was in his late forties, a little doughy, and had an ugly bald spot on the back of his head. He looked at Jack over his reading glasses and said, "Mr. Carber, thank you for meeting with us today. I think that based on your situation, and information on your history here at Patterson, we are going to assign you a release date of Monday, April 15th, 2002, with six months of probation following it. I must remind you, however, this is a conditional release date, and it can be changed or revoked at any time. Keep your nose clean, Mr. Carber, and you'll be out of here soon."

Jack was immediately relieved, and the nervous suspense that had been clenching him tightly finally relaxed. He stood up, smiled broadly, and nodded towards the board and said, "Thank you. Thank you very much." He turned to smile at Norrison, too, who had also stood up and was opening the door to lead Jack back to his tier.

As Jack was about to walk out, the chairman called after him, "Mr. Carber, I've got one other question for you, if you don't mind."

The good feeling inside Jack faltered a little bit, but he turned back and said, "Sure."

"You're currently cellmates with Addison Tyler, I believe?"

Jack wasn't quite sure where this was going to go. He answered, "Yes, sir."

"You're no doubt aware of how dangerous this inmate can be."

"Yes, sir."

"If it were up to us, we would prefer to keep him here longer and away from the general public, but since he will have served his full, unreduced sentence very soon, the matter is out of our hands."

Jack just waited.

"You, however, have now been his cellmate much longer than anyone else has managed. In fact, we hear that you have managed to get close to him in a way that no one else has done. Is this true?"

Jack said, "I can't speak for what anyone else's experiences have been with Adder, and I wouldn't say I'm close to him. But I have, over time, managed to find a certain balance in being around Adder."

"We are merely curious as to why and how you've managed to achieve this with Addison."

Jack wanted to say that it was really none of their business, but a bullshit answer would do just as well. He answered, "I think people have exaggerated how, uh, close I am to Adder. But the reason why I put the effort into this was simple self-preservation. I didn't want to get the crap beat out of me. The 'how' isn't really magic, either. Familiarity breeds a level of comfort. So rather than avoid Adder, I spent time near him, without getting close enough to be threatening. That's when I realized that Adder isn't really the random, unpredictable monster everyone thinks he is. He's actually very disciplined, and is happy to respect other people's boundaries, the way he expects his boundaries to be respected. Adder tends to actually gauge any kind of response to someone to the degree that they represent a threat to him. This being a prison, Adder is surrounded by dangerous people and responds to that. I just made an effort to make sure he didn't see me as a threat. Over time, he's come to see this and now I'm pretty safe around him. I think once Adder is out of prison, his violent behavior will drop to nothing because no one on the outside is really a threat to him and he knows this."

Jack knew this was a tailored version of the truth, along with a little speculation, but it would give the parole board something to chew on. Actually, he didn't think they'd even bother to chew on it. It wouldn't be what they wanted to hear, and so they'd dismiss it.

The chairman almost scoffed, "Huh! It's almost like you see Adder as an actual person."

That immediately, seriously pissed Jack off, even as he knew it would be the likely response. But he held his tongue and just smiled grimly at the chairman.

The chairman said, "Ok, thank you, Mr. Carber."

The chairman turned to the other board members and laughed a little bit as Norrison led Jack out of the room.

On the way back to the tier, Norrison asked Jack, "Do you really believe all that stuff you said about Adder?"

"Yeah, I do."

"Seems a little far-fetched to me."

Jack gave up. He didn't care if anyone else saw what he did. Everyone else had just tried to control Adder outright to bring him in line and had gotten nowhere. Jack just let Adder be himself and got to know him on his terms. And Jack's method was, after all, the one that had gotten somewhere with Adder.

Jack asked Norrison, "So what do you think Adder will do when he gets out?"

"He'll go right back to what got him in here to begin with. He's got no money saved up except the per diem the prison system pays him while he's here. He won't last a week or so on that. He has no other skills or people to help him outside. He's maxed out his sentence, so there'll be no probation to keep him in check. He'll probably start off mugging people since he can do that with his bare hands. Then he'll probably manage to get a gun at some point and it won't be long after that before he's back in here for the rest of his life. I just hope no one gets seriously hurt before he's thrown back in the system."

Jack didn't like to hear it, and it worried him, but Norrison had a few good points there. Adder didn't have a lot on the outside to help keep him out of prison. Jack just didn't want Adder to wind up right back inside.

~~~~~

Adder was sitting up on top of the picnic table with his arms around his knees and his chin resting on his arms. The collar on his coat was pulled up to help keep the cold air out a little bit. Jack walked over to the table, his breath fogging in front of him and the cold air stinging his eyes. It had rained the day before and a nasty cold front had moved through. Most of the other inmates had stayed inside, but a few were braving the weather in the yard. Jack took a swig of coffee out of the big insulated mug of his and sat down next to Adder.

"I just got done with my parole hearing a little while ago. Looks like I'll be getting out April 15th, as long as I don't go around on some murderous rampage before then."

Adder looked at him a little sideways, smiled some and nodded to let Jack know he was happy to hear it.

"And you're going to be getting out very soon yourself," said Jack. He wondered if he should broach the subject or not. He probably shouldn't, but he wanted to know. "Most people think you'll wind up right back in here pretty soon. They think you'll viciously attack the first little old lady that gets within five feet of you."

The corner of Adder's mouth pulled down grimly and he sighed softly.

"Yeah, I know that wouldn't happen, either."

Jack looked out past the fence at the trees beyond. He couldn't count the number of times now that he had sat there with Adder looking at those trees.

He changed the subject and said, "You know, I sit up here with you and look at those trees past the fence almost every day. I wish I could go walk around in them, see what's beyond them. Do you know what's over that way, past the trees? It almost drives me crazy sometimes."

Jack stared at the trees that had been just out of his reach for so long, like they were making fun of him, waiting for him to come closer so they could move farther. He could see them rustle in the chilly wind just a little.

"I've been thinking, myself," he said with a burdened exhale, changing the subject yet again. "I think I might be done with all the grifting. The more I think about my father, the more I know he wouldn't be proud of what I've done, even with all the reasons I had after his death and my mother's death. It's not what he would want for me. I know I should have a long time ago, but I think it's time I *listened* to him and let go of my own selfish anger."

Adder continued to look forward over his arms. Jack took another big sip out of his coffee mug. He had said it to another person, which meant it was going to be hard to weasel out of it now once he got out.

"Prison does do one thing it's supposed to... it gives you time to think about what you've done and how you wound up here."

Jack pulled his coat tighter around him to try to keep the cold out. His nose was freezing.

"I know you've thought about it for fifteen years now."

Jack rubbed his hand on his nose a little to try and warm it up.

"But you've done your time, and I hope you can let go of the past. I hope the past can let go of you. You've done your time, in both this prison, and the one you built for yourself. I doubt you're the same person that started this sentence, but the person that's here next to me now finishing it doesn't deserve it anymore. I hope that you can finish this sentence, get out, and be happy."

Jack thought, hoped, that maybe if Adder could get out and find a new life and be happy... maybe if that happened... then maybe that would mean one of them got past PattX. Adder had looked at Jack as he said these things, his eyes distant and as gray and cloudy as the skies overhead. Jack looked over at Adder and picked up the coffee mug. He said, "Here, have some coffee. You've got to be freezing out here."

Adder took the coffee mug and took several big gulps out of it, but continued to watch Jack out of the corner of his eye. He handed the coffee mug back to Jack, who took it and shook it a little and realized there was hardly anything left. He said, "How do I always wind up with the last little bit that's nothing but your slobber?" and tossed back the last bit of coffee.

Adder snorted and smiled again for Jack. Those smiles still sent electricity through him.

Jack stood up and said, "Ok, I'm freezing my nuts off. You can stay out here and let yours break off like icicles if you want." He headed across the yard towards the door back inside.

~~~~~

Right before lights out that evening, Adder had been reading in the chair, which he had turned to face towards Jack. Jack had been on his bunk reading *Lord of the Flies*, but he had noticed a couple of times that Adder was looking at him and not the encyclopedia volume he had open in his lap.

Jack put his book down on the bunk.

"One less day before you're out."

Adder nodded slightly.

"What are you going to do when you get out, Adder?"

Adder took a slow, deep breath. Jack watched his wide chest move up and down with the effort. Adder shrugged and put on a "wait and see" face.

Jack nodded this time. They both knew he would face a tough time outside.

"You gonna go back to your old tricks?"

Adder shook his head "no."

"No? Really?"

Adder paused for a moment, considering his answer. He reached down to his shoe and fished down into the side of it. He pulled out the ring and held it up for Jack to see. Jack didn't get it at first, then he remembered the inscription. He knew what the promise was now. The whole thing fit a little more. He had promised William to get out of the life of crime. And William had been killed. Adder probably never got a chance to give William the ring and that's why he still had it. Jack was really moved to know Adder was adamant about honoring this promise even after fifteen years. Adder was much more of a good person than anyone gave him credit for.

Jack nodded and said sadly, "You promised William. Even now, you're going to honor it. Is that it?"

Adder gave a wan smile and nodded "yes." And then Adder's eyes narrowed and his brow furrowed and he looked at the ring very intently. He studied it like it was suddenly talking to him. His eyes got slowly wider and his mouth dropped open just a little. He looked up at Jack, the revelation written on his face.

Jack was too wrapped up in his own thoughts to notice Adder, though. He looked off at the dark, frosted windows outside the tier and said, "That's good. You're a good person, Adder."

Adder looked at Jack and the amazement faded into a weak smile, touched with a little sadness.

Jack looked at his own hands and added quietly, "A better person than I am." He really meant it.

Jack yawned and stood up. He picked up the book off of his bunk. As he went to put it on the desk, he gave Adder a little swat on the back with it.

Jack took his shirt off and went over to the sink to brush his teeth. As he was finishing up, he saw Adder standing behind him in the mirror waiting to brush his own teeth. He turned around to get out of Adder's way, but Adder was looking right at Jack and not the sink.

Jack stood there for a second and Adder reached up, a little slowly and tentatively, and gently put his hand on the side of Jack's face. He smiled at Jack, a small, tender smile to say "thank you" for the things Jack had said.

Jack nodded once to acknowledge what Adder was saying. He wished Adder would hold his hand there. He wished there was more of this kind of touching.

But Adder did continue to hold his hand there, touching Jack. Jack suddenly had the image of Stambeki in his mind, touching his knee in the bar, then he recalled the sharp pain when he first realized Stambeki wasn't coming back for him. Jack's face flushed red and he took a step back from Adder. Adder's hand dropped as Jack's face was pulled away from it and Adder's face had the disappointment written on it. Adder's very large frame suddenly looked small.

Jack came back to himself a little bit and said, "I meant what I said, including the things out in the pound earlier today," and he gave Adder a pat in the middle of his chest.

Adder stood there and nodded weakly, then moved over to the sink to brush his teeth.

The lights went out as Adder was finishing up. Jack had already settled into his bunk at this point. When Adder finished, he stepped over to where Jack was. He stood next to Jack for a moment and Jack could see a little of the snake tattoo around Adder's waist in the dim light, and then he stepped up and lifted himself silently up into the top bunk.

Day 648 – Sunday, December 30th, 2001

Jack sat on the padded bench and curled the dumbbell in his right hand. He hadn't been doing a very good job with his morning working out. The others in the weight area were grunting and huffing and puffing like usual, but Jack didn't seem to be able to get into it.

He got up and put the dumbbell back on the stand. He moved over to the side and watched everyone else instead. He frowned slightly when his eyes eventually drifted over to Adder at the biggest punching bag, but wasn't surprised when they landed there. He was punching it hard and fast, with no gloves on. He'd throw in a kick every once in a while, plus the occasional spin.

Jack had been more and more distracted lately. Four days from now, Adder would be out. Gone. As odd as it was now to think it, he was going to miss Adder. A lot. He was having trouble concentrating on anything he was thinking about it so much.

Things between them were as they had been for a while now. Adder still didn't ask for any kind of sex any more, and as far as Jack knew, he wasn't going anywhere else to get it. Jack really didn't ask for it either given how weird and empty it was the last time. It had always been unilateral sex, but even that last time Adder didn't seem to get anything out of it, either.

Contrasting with his lack of sexual contact with Jack, though, Adder had been closer to Jack than ever. Jack hadn't had any fear of

Adder in so long, the days when he did have to be wary around him seemed like they belonged to someone else. Like they were someone else's problem. Jack would talk about anything and Adder seemed happy to listen. He seemed to smile at Jack so quickly and easily these days, and he seemed to keep a closer eye on Jack, too. Jack looked up again and, even now, Adder was glancing back over at him.

He wondered if he had handled it right. He had kept Adder at an arm's length and gotten all wrapped up in him at the same time. Was that the right thing to do? He didn't want to get hurt again, and Jack knew there was an infinite number of ways to get hurt. And only a tiny number of ways to find happiness.

Everything about this situation had hurt written all over it in multiple ways.

Jack realized he had been standing around in a daze and decided that he should just give up on the workout.

~~~~~

Right after lunch, Jack was about to go outside to the yard to see if he could push his way into a game of basketball. A game with some of the guys would force him to focus or get knocked flat on his ass. When he was almost outside, he heard Bickers call out his name behind him. Bickers caught up to Jack and asked him if he knew the priest that came on Sundays.

Jack said, "Yeah, I know who you're talking about."

"He just asked me if I knew who you were. He wants you to come see him. He says it's important."

Jack couldn't figure out what Father Anthony would have for him that was important, other than the same old itch deep inside that needed scratching.

He nodded to Bickers and headed back towards the lounge area. It was different, though, to have Father Anthony specifically request Jack. He had never done that before, and it made Jack a little curious. It had been months and months since he had bothered with Father Anthony at all. Since the time he had gotten the whiskey from him, as a matter of fact. He hadn't missed Father Anthony at all since then, and he didn't think the priest had missed him either. So much had changed in the meantime. The friendship he had developed with Adder, even without the sex, was far better than anything he ever got out of Father Anthony.

Maybe Father Anthony was finally going to loosen up some, though. Maybe the Father wanted to actually talk to Jack, really talk, for a change.

Jack didn't see Father Anthony in the lounge area, so he walked around to where the swing office was and saw the door open with Father Anthony inside. He knocked on the door and Father Anthony waved him on in.

Jack came into the office, and as Father Anthony went to close and lock the door, he said to him, "It's been too long, Jack. How are you doing?"

"I'm doing ok," said Jack with a nod. "I'm getting out April 15th."

Father Anthony smiled and said, "I heard that. I'm very glad. I had a feeling you would get out very early. I also know that Adder is getting out in a few days. I wanted you to come by so I could congratulate you on keeping Adder at bay. You've kept safe for almost your entire stay in a very dangerous place."

Father Anthony continued, "Once Adder is out, you'll have very little to worry about. The biggest danger you face will be gone, and then you can coast a little until you're released."

Jack thought it was ironic how much things had changed. The last person he wanted to keep at bay at this point was Adder, and he felt safer around him than anyone else in the prison.

Jack said, "Yeah, it won't be much longer now." Jack didn't think this was the only reason Father Anthony had asked for him, so he waited to see what else Father Anthony wanted.

There was a moment of awkward silence while Jack waited, but eventually Father Anthony lowered his voice conspiratorially. He said, "I know it's completely against the rules, but I thought we'd have a small celebration." As he said this, Father Anthony reached into his briefcase and pulled out a small bottle of Jack Daniels and two cups.

Jack was genuinely impressed. Father Anthony wanted to have a drink with him. Maybe Father Anthony really was about to loosen up some and move past the role-playing.

Father Anthony said, "I remembered that you liked Jack Daniels, so I thought it would be appropriate."

Jack's grin was genuine. "Well, you remembered exactly right! This is great!"

Father Anthony reached over to his briefcase again and pulled a tiny bottle from it. He put it next to his cup and looked at Jack.

Jack pointed at the tiny bottle and asked, "What's in there?"

Father Anthony said, "Oh, nothing."

Jack's heart sank. Whatever was in the bottle was the catch. Father Anthony was back to playing some game. He picked up the bottle and looked at it. It looked like a very small pill bottle, but it had a small amount of a powder in it. He opened it and smelled the contents. It didn't smell like anything. He tapped a tiny bit of the powder out onto his finger and looked at it. Jack thought he recognized the powder, having used it on people in the past. He tasted it, but it didn't taste like anything, either.

Jack looked at Father Anthony. "Did you bring roofies in here with you? Is that what this is?"

Father Anthony took the bottle out of Jack's hand and put it conspicuously right next to his own cup and moved Jack's cup father away.

Jack was starting to get the idea, but he was having a hard time believing it.

"I've got to step outside for just a moment. Will you go ahead and pour us a drink while I'm out?" Father Anthony stood up and stepped outside.

Jack was stunned. Given how Father Anthony ignored his question, Jack felt dead certain now that what was in the bottle was Rohypnol, and Father Anthony wanted Jack to drug his drink, and then rape him. He had hoped Father Anthony was getting past this, but he had just gotten worse. This was what Father Anthony really wanted to see Jack about today. A far more twisted version of the game they had played in the past.

Jack gaped at the little bottle in his hand. He felt very tired and very disappointed. He wasn't taking this charade any farther.

A few moments later, Father Anthony came back in the door, but his smile faded some when he saw that Jack was still staring at the small bottle of powder and that the cups were empty.

Jack was done with this whole thing.

"I'm not going to drug your drink or have sex with you."

"Of course not," said Father Anthony with an appropriately confused look. "I'm not sure what you're even talking about."

Jack rested his arms on the desk and leaned forward slightly. "Look, Father, I appreciate the things you've brought me in the past. It was a risk for you to bring those things in here, but it was always for harmless uses. But I'm not playing this game with you anymore."

Father Anthony started to look shocked, but Jack kept on before Father Anthony could start in.

"The truth is I've been willing to play this game, and I never would have actually hurt you. But if you were to try this stuff with most anyone else here, you could get seriously hurt. Getting it for real isn't anything like the fantasy fuck you look for here." Jack knew he should stop there, but he couldn't help himself. He pushed recklessly ahead. "You need to drop this mask and face up to what you are, man. If you'd just be honest with yourself, you could probably be a lot happier than what these bullshit games can bring you."

Father Anthony got a completely incredulous look on his face. "Are you implying that I'm gay? I'm a Catholic priest! It's completely against the teachings of the Catholic Church to be gay, completely incompatible with my responsibilities as a priest! I'm insulted you would even insinuate this!" Father Anthony started turning a little red, though, and Jack could see a few beads of sweat forming on his forehead.

Jack stood up and held the tiny bottle up. He said angrily, "You put a bottle of crushed up roofies in front of me and made it clear you wanted it to go in your drink. You *want* to be drugged and sexually assaulted! It's the entire reason you asked me to see you today! Drop the goddamn games for one fucking second!"

Father Anthony stood there, disbelieving, and obviously very uncomfortable with how this whole meeting was going. Father Anthony shifted nervously, unsure of what to do with himself. Jack was amazed at how far the father wanted to push this, to deny what he was doing.

After no response, Jack calmed back down and said, "You need help. You need help badly with this problem before you get yourself killed."

Father Anthony lashed back out at Jack. "I'm a Catholic priest! I would never do the sick things you say! You're a monster for even saying these things!" Father Anthony couldn't stand it anymore; he reached over with hands shaking and grabbed his briefcase. He didn't even look at Jack as he hurried out of the room.

Jack was left in the empty room with the roofies in his hand, seeing red at the door. He couldn't believe what had just happened, how completely adamant Father Anthony was at carrying on with the ridiculous charade. How completely unable he was to take the mask off, even for just a moment.

And as he sat thinking about this, a bottle of roofies in his hand and a bottle of Jack Daniels on the desk, he realized how much risk he putting himself in staying in the room with these items. If Father Anthony turned him in, he could get in a tremendous amount of trouble, not to mention a pushed out release date. He knew he needed to get the stuff out of the room before anyone came and saw him in there with it.

He had snuck stuff out before, and he could sneak it out again, but he needed to do it fast. He had his coat on since he was originally going to go outside, so he decided to sneak both things out in that.

First, he went to peek out the door to make sure the coast was clear and that Father Anthony wasn't hanging around outside. He didn't see anyone. Except Troy. The worst person he could possibly see right then immediately saw him look out the door. Jack's heart sank and he cursed under his breath.

Troy shoved his way into the office with Jack and said, "What are you hiding, Car..."

Jack had palmed the roofies in his hand, but Troy saw the Jack Daniels on the table and stopped in mid-sentence.

"Well, well, bitch! This is my lucky day!"

Troy turned to Jack and punched him hard in the stomach. Jack doubled over in pain, red stars shooting across his eyes. He almost dropped the bottle of Rohypnol, but just barely held onto it. Troy crossed to the door, closed it and locked it.

He had an evil grin on his face and said to Jack, "I was on my way somewhere else, but, sometimes, opportunities just fall in your lap. I'm either livin' my life very right, Carber, or you're livin' yours very wrong." The pleasure on Troy's face was like a ray of menacing sunshine.

Jack had managed to stand up straight again, but felt queasy from the punch and was fighting to get his breath back.

Troy asked, "How'd you get the JD, Carber? Did you get the preacher to mule for you? How did a worthless cunt like you manage that, huh?"

Troy sat casually on the edge of the desk. He opened the bottle of Jack and took a big swig out of it. Jack glared at him and wished he had spiked the Jack now with the Rohypnol.

Jack heaved, "You'd better clear out. Father Anthony's coming right back." It was a flimsy, desperate attempt to scare Troy away, but Jack would try anything right now.

Troy put the bottle down and moved past Jack to go see for himself, bumping into Jack as he went. Troy opened the door and said, "I doubt that faggot's coming back."

As soon as Troy turned to look out the door, Jack realized he had a brief moment of opportunity. He dumped the Rohypnol into the bottle of Jack, picked the bottle up, and swirled it around a little to dissolve the powder.

Troy closed and locked the door again, then turned back around to face him just as Jack lifted the bottle to his mouth and pretended to take a swig for himself.

Troy said, "It might not be so bad if he does come back. I could fuck the two of you together. Preacher man'd think it was the second coming!" Troy laughed heartily at his own pathetic joke.

But then he got serious again and watched Jack very intently. He took his shirt off, never taking his eyes off Jack. Jack knew the intent was to intimidate him, and it was unfortunately working. Jack looked at the weird tattoo on Troy's chest. Troy grabbed the bottle and took another swig out of it.

He asked Jack, "Carber, we got us some unfinished business. Are you going to make this easy or difficult? Difficult for you and fun for me, that is." He took another swig from the bottle and wiped his bare arm across his mouth.

Jack knew he needed to get Troy to drink as much as possible and buy some time for the drug to kick in. Jack cringed at the thought, but he knew he might have to give in to what Troy wanted to buy the time he needed. But he couldn't make it too easy, or Troy would get suspicious.

Jack said, "'Smatter, Troy? Is Fredo's dick too little for your skinny ass, so you want to try mine to see if it fits a little better?"

Troy leaped over at Jack and grabbed him by his shirt, almost lifting Jack off the ground. Troy was just a thin, wiry redneck, and yet was really strong for his size. Jack kind of dangled and felt incredibly stupid at being this helpless around a guy smaller than him.

"That's a sorry attempt at baiting me, Carber," Troy hissed at Jack. "I'm thinking this will be easier." He let go of Jack.

Jack asked, "Why do you even care? Wilson takes care of your needs!" Jack knew the answer to these questions; he just wanted to keep Troy talking if possible.

"It's not about my needs, Carber. It's about control. It's about power. Power over shits like you. I can do anything to your body that I want to, and you can't do anything to stop it. I want you to know that for a fact. I want to see that understanding in your eyes. I want that control over everyone. Today's your turn. You're just lucky the Jack Daniels has put me in a good mood."

Troy took another swallow out of the bottle. His other hand darted out and grabbed Jack's throat. Troy clenched down hard on Jack. Jack's eyes immediately started watering and he couldn't get a single breath through Troy's vise-like grip. Troy took another slow belt from the bottle while holding Jack like this.

Troy looked at Jack, who was grabbing at Troy's hands and trying to gasp for air. Troy asked, "Now, are you going to behave this time? If you bitch up quick enough and beg, you might not do too much time in the hospital afterwards."

Jack nodded after forcing the furious snarl off his face.

"Good. Show me what a good cocksucker you are. Lube me up, Carber."

Jack's throat was on fire, but he didn't think he should put up a fight any more. Troy leaned back against the desk while Jack knelt down on the floor. Jack had managed to avoid this for almost two years now, but at this point, he needed time more than he needed his pride. So Jack caved in and allowed Troy to shove himself into his mouth roughly. He went down on Troy for what seemed like forever, intentionally doing a bad job of it. Jack was glad to see that Troy had almost finished the bottle now. Troy groaned a little and just watched Jack from above.

Troy said, "I'm surprised Adder could train you this well with that tiny dick of his."

Troy handed Jack the last little bit of the Jack Daniels and said, "Here, I always buy a bitch a drink before I fuck her stupid."

Jack pretended to take a small sip from the bottle. He grimaced and rubbed his throat some, hoping Troy would understand why he didn't finish it.

Troy said, "Get back to work. I'll stretch your throat back out for you, punk." Troy polished off the last bit of the whiskey as Jack worked on him a little bit more.

Finally, Troy kneed Jack half-heartedly in the shoulder and told him to stand up.

Jack stood up and Troy told him to pull his pants down.

Jack said, his voice raspy, "Don't you want to cuddle? I heard you like to cuddle a lot."

Troy grabbed Jack's hair, spun him around and bent him over the desk, slamming him down hard. He told Jack to stay there and pull his pants down, or he'd never walk the same. Jack did as he was told this time, with no more smart-ass comments.

Troy leaned over Jack from behind, and Jack could smell the alcohol on his breath. "You've been a cock-suckin' thorn in my side from your first day. I'm sickh of that pung-ass attitude of yours. Gettin' all chummy with that retard, Adder. Time for you to show Troy the respect he deserves. Who's your bone now, Carber?"

Troy finished pulling his pants down and pushed in, cruelly hard, and Jack almost leapt out of his skin from the searing pain that shot through him. Troy started to pound on him violently and Jack's eyes watered from the punishment.

Troy leaned back over Jack and said, "See, if you juss give in and admit who's fuckin' who, this whole thing gets a lot easier. Tell me you like this. Tell me you wish I'd do it to you every day. Where's your snot-nose additude now, Garber?"

Troy's speech was slurring now. It was starting to kick in. Jack had just started to get used to what Troy was dishing out, too.

Jack said, "Oh, you're the top, all right. You've shown everybody at PattX who the top is, and you're it, Troy."

Then Jack added, "Oh wait! Except Adder! Adder would wipe the floor with your ass if you tried this with him. That's why you've never tried, huh? Too chickenshit for him, aren't you?"

Troy stopped and grabbed Jack by the hair and slammed his forehead down on the table, but it had a fraction of the force Troy probably wanted. The roofies were taking control very seriously now, but Troy still hadn't realized it yet. Troy started back up slamming his dick into Jack, but it had become a mechanical and lackluster effort.

Troy said, "That sonofabitch! I could kigg his mute ass any day!"

Then Troy slowed down his half-hearted punishment of Jack's ass. Then he stopped. He said, not really to Jack, but to himself, "But you know, there's a better chance. Sonofabitch's gettin' out in a few days. He's fuckin' nobody outside. I got *people* outside. I could have him sliced up for bar-b-que outside... outside." Troy was thinking out loud to himself, and with the drugs, he'd almost forgotten Jack was even there.

Jack's blood ran cold at what Troy was thinking about. Adder would be very vulnerable outside. Troy could arrange for any kind of revenge against him once he was out in a few days.

Troy totally stopped, no longer interested in Jack. "Iss perfeck. Thinks he's home free, an' he'll get it when... leas' 'shpects it." Troy stumbled back a little bit and put his hand on his forehead to try to clear his head.

Jack pulled his pants up and turned around to watch Troy. His head was spinning over what might happen to Adder. After spending all this time in prison. Holding onto his secret for dear life. The pain of his loss. But finally getting out and being ready to move past it, all to end because of Troy's petty grudges.

Troy was holding his head with both hands. He looked foggily at Jack and said indistinctly, "What'd you do?"

Troy leaned on the desk, breathing heavily as the drug pulled him farther and farther down.

Jack watched Troy. He knew Troy would follow through on this. He had absolutely no doubts on it. It would be Troy's chance to really hurt the one person at PattX he never managed to hurt before. Troy wouldn't pass that up, even if it meant he wouldn't be there in person to do it.

Jack's palms started to sweat thinking about it. It was just an idea in Troy's head right now. But Jack could stop it. He could end it right here and now, before it could become more than an idea. He looked at Troy still bent over the desk, breathing heavily with his pants still pulled down around his ankles, his dick hanging limp in front of him.

It would be a terrible step for Jack to take. While his mind was spinning, Troy lost his balance and muscle control, and he fell over on the floor behind the desk. His eyes stared up blankly and his mouth hung open a little. The drug had made his eyes glassy and his breaths had turned to shallow pants.

Jack trembled at the thought that was running through his mind.

He tried to think of his father instead, for comfort. He remembered what his father said to him. Jack had felt closer to his father at the moment he said it to him than any other point in time. It was what his father had said about finding love. And protecting it.

Did he love Adder? Jack knew that he did. He had known this a while. Did Adder love Jack? Jack wasn't sure about that. He wasn't sure it mattered. But the real question was, did he love Adder *enough* to do this? To protect him? Could he take this step for someone knowing he couldn't ever take it back?

Jack was surprised at how easy the answer was.

He looked at Troy on the floor with eyes still open. Troy's mouth was hanging open at a strange angle and a slight groan was coming out of it.

He couldn't believe what he was about to do. He hoped his father would forgive him. Jack was taking a leap into a void and he'd never be the same person after this.

He grabbed Troy's shirt and wiped down the desk and the bottle of Jack Daniels, and he pulled up Troy's pants.

Jack took the bottle of whiskey and was going to smash it on the floor but stopped. It would be so loud to do that. Someone was bound to hear it. He took Troy's shirt and wiped the bottle down again and wrapped it in the shirt. He took his own coat off and wrapped that around the bottle, too. He licked his lips and hoped the sound would be deadened enough. He hit the bottle on the concrete floor and felt it shatter within the jacket and shirt. It made more sound than he wanted, but it was done now.

He took the coat off and shook it out in the corner to make sure there were no glass shards in it. He then dumped the broken glass out of the shirt and on to the floor. He shook the shirt out, too.

Jack now looked back over at Troy, who was still lying there and staring straight up at the ceiling. His mouth was moving a little, like a gasping fish out of water, like he was trying to say something, but no sounds were coming out.

Jack used the shirt to pick up the neck of the bottle, which had a particularly sharp broken edge.

He held the bottle neck with the shirt and pressed it up against Troy's neck. He spread the shirt out some so the blood wouldn't spray. He looked at Troy's eyes again and almost had to stop. His heart was about to jump out of his chest it was beating so fast, and he felt freezing cold. Jack closed his eyes and thought about all the things Troy had done to Wilson, to Bickers, to Hool and Turner. The things he'd do to Adder if he just got the chance.

Jack kept the sharp edge of the bottle against Troy's neck and he closed his eyes, all the time knowing that the next time he opened them, he'd be a different person. And finally, before he lost his nerve and feeling like the bottle was really against his own neck and not Troy's, he pushed in and twisted as hard as he could, with all of his weight.

The sharp, broken bottle neck went in deep. He felt Troy's body tense up involuntarily and Troy made a horrifying gurgling noise. Jack's eyes filled with tears and he sobbed to himself, "Oh, *Jesus Christ*, what did I just do?!"

He opened his eyes. The shirt was soaking up blood rapidly and it was starting to spread across the floor. He let go of the bottle and moved away a little bit. Time moved in slow motion while Jack watched in horror at the only thing in the room that was moving – Troy's blood spreading slowly out from his body, a black red crawling across the cement floor. He looked at his hands and body to see if any blood had gotten on him, but he didn't see any.

The shirt over Troy was totally soaked and the pool was spreading faster. Jack wanted to burst out of the room and run away as fast as he could, to escape what he had done. But he had to make sure and he had to think.

He grabbed Troy's wrist and felt it. Jack could barely breathe and his lungs felt like they couldn't hold air anymore. He thought that this was never going to work. He'd be found out almost instantly and on death row within weeks. Jack felt Troy's pulse get very weak. And then, a moment later, it stopped entirely. Jack sobbed again. He was a cold-blooded murderer now.

The smell hit him at that moment. It was the smell of blood, of spilled and depleted life. The red pool steadily spread out around Troy, thick and viscous, staining the concrete floor. It emptied out of Troy, taking his life with it. Taking with it whatever vestige of humanity Jack had left in himself.

He wanted to go curl up in the corner, but he forced himself to pull his head out of the fog it had sunken into. He forced himself to think. He was about to let go of Troy's wrist, but instead he moved Troy's hand up to the rag and the bottle neck and wrapped Troy's hand around that for a second to get blood on it. Maybe he would get lucky and they would consider it a suicide.

Jack stood up and looked away from the body. He had to think about what else to do and then get out of there.

He took his shirt off and looked at it closely. There was no blood he could see, though. He rubbed the back of the shirt on his face and looked again. Still no blood, so his face was clean. He put his shirt back on.

He had already wiped down the desk, so he didn't have to worry about that. He turned to the door and used his coat to wipe down the door handle. Then he remembered the chair. He wiped down the back of the chair where he had grabbed it when he sat down. Jack put his coat back on and put the small bottle in the pocket. Then he realized he couldn't open the door without touching it again, so he took his coat back off.

He couldn't think of anything else he needed to do. He couldn't think of anything else he might have touched. He used the coat to open the door a tiny crack as he peeked outside. He didn't see anyone. He pushed the lock button so the door would lock behind him when he closed it and stepped outside. He pulled the door closed with his coat.

But just as he turned from the door and put the coat over his arm, he saw Bickers coming around the corner. He flushed red and felt his heart jump into his throat.

Bickers said, "Hey, what did the priest guy want?"

Jack almost couldn't speak. He'd already been caught and it would all fall apart fast. He coughed to force his voice to work. "Oh, nothing really. Just wanted to congratulate me on getting out in a few months."

Bickers nodded, then seemed to notice that Jack was a little flush. "Oh, ok. You feeling ok? You look a little white."

Jack's heart pounded some more and the blood drained from him. "Just feel a little queasy. I, uh, I think the fish we had for lunch was, uh, past its date."

Bickers seemed to buy this. He said, "Hell, we'd be lucky for it to actually be fish to begin with. Well go outside and get some fresh air. It'll make you feel better." Bickers walked on and Jack decided he did need to be out where other people could see him. He wanted to go back to his cell and collapse in the corner. He looked at his own hands and they were trembling. But he knew he needed other people to see him out and about.

Jack got out to the prison yard and decided that a little running would be the right thing to do. He could be alone, people would see him, and the physical effort would calm his body down. He went over to the prison wall and stretched a little bit, took a few deep breaths and started an easy jog, but it took a terrible effort to keep going. He wanted to just fall down, and he was still freezing cold, like it was all his own blood that had spread out across the office floor, but he kept himself going.

He tried hard to focus on everyday things around him. The fence, the prison wall, the basketball court. Anything to keep his mind off of what he had just done. But it didn't work very well. He saw Troy in the office leaning on the desk, then falling over behind it, eyes staring up vacantly, mouth gulping like a fish. He saw himself holding the sharp bottle up against Troy's neck and covering Troy with the shirt. He felt the bottle sinking deep into Troy's neck and the red stain spreading rapidly across the shirt, and then the puddle of it on the floor. He heard that awful gurgling noise. The last cry of Troy, probably doing anything to cry for help. He saw the blood running out, all around Troy.

Jack had to stop running. He bent over with his hands on his knees, and felt like he would vomit at any moment, like his body would try anything to purge what he had done, no matter how fruitless it would be. He didn't know if he could live with what he had become. As awful as Troy was, he had sliced into the guy's neck and let his life drain out onto the floor. Who was worse in the end, Troy or Jack?

He forced himself to think about Adder. Troy had put Jack in a position of choosing between him and Adder, and Jack had to choose. He told himself that he did what he did so Adder wouldn't face something worse when he wouldn't be prepared to handle it.

Jack forced himself to start running again. He was out of the office, but he wasn't out of trouble. Bickers had seen him there. How long would it take before the guards realized Troy was missing, or found his body? He knew that the longest it could possibly go would be up to the evening count. Surely the Kennel would notice Troy was gone before then, though. Would they go to the guards? Jack expected that Capt. Marcus would come running after him any minute, shoot him down with a Taser and tell Jack it was so obvious that he had done it. He looked over his shoulder at the main part of the yard, but it all looked the same. There was no commotion yet. When would it happen?

Jack kept running, a little harder now, like he could outrun it somehow. He still felt waves of panic, though, no matter how fast he ran. He tried to think about what else he needed to do to cover his tracks. If they came and asked him where he was during that time, what would he say? He needed to know of someplace away from the swing office, but that probably had no guards in it to catch the lie. Best would be no other inmates, either. But then it wouldn't be much of an alibi. He didn't know what would be the best answer. Then he wondered if they'd look for and find any kind of DNA. He knew he couldn't hide from the DNA, and he felt a little hopeless. Too much was out of his hands. He was going to get caught. But then, honestly, he felt like he deserved to.

A depression began to wash over him. Prison had turned him into a monster. Even on his most evil, malicious day ever on the outside, he would never have even vaguely considered doing something like he had done today.

Jack stopped to catch his breath. He had been around the yard probably nine or ten times now, and it was a good-sized yard. He was on the far side of it, away from everyone. He looked back over the yard and saw Wilson, Hool, Turner, Bickers, Hector and Ramon huddled in a group near the basketball court. He thought about the fact that Bickers didn't have much love for Troy, and Wilson would never get beat up again. If Jack was a monster, at least a little bit of good came out of it.

He finally looked over to the one spot he had forced his eyes to avoid. He looked around and saw Adder, sitting cross-legged on top of the picnic table, his coat pulled tight around him. Jack didn't know what he had with Adder, but that was the real reason he had done it. If it weren't for his concern for Adder. If it weren't for what he felt for Adder, he never would have been able to do it. That's what it came down to. Troy had put Jack in a position to choose between him and Adder. That's why it had been as easy as it was. Even if his choice had made him a murderer, he had chosen Adder. He might go crazy from it in the end, but he had done what he could to protect Adder. He remembered what his father had said about protecting love when you find it. All Jack had was Adder, and he didn't even know what that really meant or if it meant anything much to Adder, but it was all he had left.

Jack decided he had had enough. Thinking about Adder had made him feel a little better. He walked over to the table where Adder was sitting, stretched a little bit, then climbed up on top of the table and sat next to him. He wanted desperately to lean over and cry on Adder's shoulder, the way Adder had done in the middle of the night, but he couldn't. All Jack could do now was just wait for it to all fall apart. He looked out at the trees past the fence, time moving as slow as molasses. Jack only had a few days left with Adder, and now he would give anything to have more.

He looked over at his cellmate, who was watching him closely. Adder had a curious look on his face.

Jack looked away from Adder again and muttered, "I know I'm quiet. Not sure what to say today." He pulled his knees up and wrapped his arms around them. He wanted to be as small as possible. He wished he could just disappear, and it took all of his concentration to not start crying uncontrollably. He didn't look back over at Adder, even though he could feel the pressure of Adder's eyes still upon him.

He stayed like this for a long time, and Adder sat there with him. Adder normally would have maybe gone running a little bit himself, or jumped rope, or maybe would have done his meditation thing, but today he just sat with Jack. Jack wished he had spent more time with Adder than he had. He felt like he knew Adder better as a person than anyone else at PattX. He might have known more things about Wilson or Hool or Bickers, but he knew Adder as a person better than any of them.

Eventually, Jack glanced back over his shoulder and saw Capt. Marcus talking urgently into his radio. The whole thing was about to explode. Suddenly, Jack thought about the tiny bottle, the one that held the crushed up roofies. He panicked wondering if he had left it in the office or not. It would ruin any chance he had if he had left them in there. He felt down in his coat pocket and was relieved to know the bottle was still there. He needed to get rid of it, though. Jack decided to go back to his cell and wait for it to all happen. The bottle was tiny, so he could flush it down the toilet there.

He stood up, but his legs almost felt like they wouldn't support him. He looked over at Adder and nodded a good-bye, and began his walk back inside.

He had almost gotten all the way back to his cell when he heard someone running up behind him. He turned around and saw Bickers coming up to him.

"I don't know if you heard yet. They just found Troy dead."

Jack put on his best surprised face and said, "Are you shitting me? How'd it happen? Where'd they find him?"

Bickers said, "I don't know what happened, but they found his body in the swing office, locked inside."

"No shit! When did they find him?"

Bickers finished lighting up a cigarette while keeping a keen eye on Jack and said, "Just now. I was walking by and they made me go around. Jones told me what happened."

Jack wondered if Bickers was trying to see how he would react.

Jack just said, "Huh!"

Bickers watched Jack for a moment, then said calmly, "Troy was a filthy sonofabitch. Personally, I'm glad he's gone. The Kennel dogs will be the only ones that miss him. I hope it was painful, whatever happened to him. But he's hell's problem now."

Jack just nodded a little bit. He felt like he was shaking like a leaf. Could Bickers see that? Bickers still watched him very closely, directly in the eyes, and took a long draw on the cigarette.

Bickers said softly, with the cigarette hanging out of the corner of his mouth, "It's a shame you and I were in the library after lunch because maybe we could have had the honor of finishing the bastard off." Bickers' eyes didn't blink as he watched Jack. "And that's exactly what I'm going to tell the guards if they ask me." He gave Jack just a touch of a wry smile, and Jack didn't know what to do. Jack couldn't say anything, and no words would come out. Bickers just turned around and left, headed back towards the yard.

~~~~~

Jack got to his cell and he flushed the small bottle down the toilet. He collapsed on his bunk with his head in his hands. A little bit of the weight had lifted. He had one person on his side, and that person gave him an alibi. He felt like he didn't deserve anyone on his side, but Jack thanked God he did have this one.

He lay down on his bunk and faced the wall. He finally could be away from everyone. Whatever else happened now was mostly out of his control. He just had to focus on coming to grips with what he had done, so he just lay still, staring at the cinderblock-colored wall.

At some point, Jack rolled over and Adder was standing there, watching him. He blinked up at Adder and said, "Where'd you come from? I must have dozed off."

Jack wondered how long he actually had been out. He tried to act nonchalant. "Hey, is it time for dinner yet?"

Adder held up all ten fingers on both hands.

Jack said, "Ok, ten more minutes."

Jack felt like he needed to bring it up to Adder. Jack would have to talk and speculate about it just like everyone else was going to do.

"Did you hear about Troy?"

Adder nodded his head slowly.

"I wonder how it happened. Bickers told me they had just found him in the swing office, but he didn't know how it had happened."

Adder just shrugged his shoulders.

Jack rubbed his eyes. He wished he didn't know how it happened. He had made a life out of lying to others to gain their confidence, but this lie stung. Jack lay back down to wait for dinner. Adder stood and rubbed his mouth and chin thoughtfully for a minute before getting up on his own bunk. Jack looked up at the bottom of Adder's bed. He thought how Adder was right there, just a few feet away from him. Jack reached up towards the bottom of Adder's bunk, but couldn't quite reach it. *What is he thinking about right now,* Jack wondered.

A few minutes later, the alarm sounded and Adder jumped down, ready for dinner. Jack got up, too, and they headed off to the chow hall. Jack decided to sit with Adder, even though he knew everyone would be talking about what happened to Troy and he wanted to find out what people were saying.

He stuck close to Adder and they sat down together to eat. There was definitely a lot of talking and movement around the chow hall tonight that wasn't usually there. Adder ignored it as if nothing unusual had happened. Jack noticed that at the tables where the Kennel guys usually sat, people had shifted around a lot. There was a conspicuous, empty seat where Troy usually sat. Jack heard the gurgling sound in his head again and shuddered.

He finished quickly and idly picked at his food. He didn't have much of an appetite and was feeling nauseous even looking at it. Adder was almost done himself, but his tray was almost clean. He said to Adder, "I'm going to go see what I can find out about what happened." He got up to go sit at the table with Hool and the guys.

When he sat down, Jack said, "So, does anyone know yet what actually happened?"

Wilson seemed pretty quiet, but Hool spoke up. "Not much. Troy was found in the swing office, locked. His neck was sliced open."

Jack asked, "With what? Did someone get their hands on a knife in here?"

Hool said, "No. I heard it was a piece of glass."

Turner said, "It was a bottle. A broken bottle."

Hector jumped in now, "It's no easier to get a glass bottle in here than a knife."

Turner shrugged, "Someone did."

The conversation continued on for a while. The only thing everyone really agreed on was that most of the people at PattX would be good suspects; everyone hated Troy except the Kennel dogs. And Jack found out that there was already a power struggle within the Kennel between Fredo and Runnion to take it over. Jack wasn't surprised that they couldn't even remain united for a few days out of respect for Troy.

Jack did hear that someone else said that Troy might have committed suicide. That made Jack feel better. Hool said he thought Capt. Marcus wouldn't bother a whole lot investigating it. Getting rid of Troy was a favor someone did for Capt. Marcus as far as he was concerned.

~~~~~

Jack settled into his bunk in his cell. He didn't feel like reading, and it wasn't lights out yet, but he was ready to just sleep. He had already stripped to his boxers and lay back in his bunk. Adder was sitting near the desk reading, but facing towards Jack.

Jack closed his eyes. In his mind, he saw the bottle full of Jack Daniels. He saw Troy falling in slow motion off the desk, lying on the floor, his eyes straight up. Jack held the piece of glass in his hands and looked at Troy through it, the glass distorting his face. He took the glass shard and started ruthlessly stabbing into Troy's neck, over and over. Jack dropped the glass and looked at his hands and they were covered in Troy's blood. It was dripping off of his hands there was so much of it. He didn't know how it had happened. He looked at Troy, whose face was covered in blood. The eyes were still staring blankly upward. And then, the eyes darted over and looked directly at Jack. A hard, accusing look. Jack jerked up and yelped, "Shit!!"

He looked around, and realized where he was. He looked over and Adder was still sitting in the chair, giving him a concerned look. Jack realized he was breathing fast and sweating. He nodded at Adder and said, "I'm ok. One of those dreams where you're falling."

Jack didn't want to go back to sleep now. His mind kept dragging him back in time to the swing office. His mind wouldn't let it go and kept making Jack relive it.

He got up and drank a couple of handfuls of water from the sink. He splashed some on his face and wiped it off. He sat back down on his bunk and tried to decide if he should try and stay awake, or just fall back asleep and let his mind punish him. He ran both hands through his hair. He wasn't even sure what time it was. Time didn't seem to apply to today. He was glad it was almost over, though. If he could get through a million more days, then maybe he'd feel normal again.

He sat there for a few disjointed minutes. Adder got up and brushed his teeth and stripped down to his jock strap. As Adder was about to jump up on his bunk, Jack held up four fingers at Adder and said, "Four more to go."

Adder smiled at Jack and gave him a smack on the shoulder, then jumped up onto his bunk. Just as Adder had gotten settled in, the lights went out for the night. Jack almost panicked at this. He wanted it to stay light because his mind would play all kinds of tricks on him in the dark. He stood up and moved over to the cell door to be nearer to the lights outside in the tier. He looked out and wished there were people and lights all around again.

After a few minutes, he gave up and went to sit back down on his bunk. He got under the sheets, but tried to think of other things. He thought about how his whole life had led him to this place. He wished he was sixteen again and with his father, right before his father had gotten sick. It had been the best time of his life. None of this was what his father had wanted for him.

Adder rolled over in his bunk, his arm dangling down off the side of the mattress. Jack thought about how Adder had just smiled at him. Jack thought about how he would do anything for that smile. About what he *actually had done* for that smile, just today.

Jack had wanted to cry on Adder's shoulder earlier. Why had he held back from Adder all this time? Was the specter of Stambeki that bad? Was Chris Stambeki going to hold sway over him for the rest of his life? Jack's father had told him there was a million ways to get hurt. But Jack thought it was the one way you did get hurt that made you draw back afterwards. But his father's point had been to focus on the tiny chance you did have to be happy.

Jack looked up at Adder's hand hanging down. That was his tiny chance, that hand hanging down, and Jack's fear had let it dwindle down to just four days worth of a chance now. He had killed to protect this person, and yet still drew back from him in fear.

He had let his father down, all right, but it wasn't by killing to protect Adder. It was by keeping Adder at arm's length this whole time.

Jack reached up, but even still was a little afraid. Afraid of the millions of ways he could get hurt. But this time, he forced the fear aside as best he could and instead reached out for the one small chance he might have to be happier. He could reach it this time, though. His fingers reached up and touched Adder's fingers hanging down. Adder's hand flinched and reflexively jerked away. Then Adder reached back down and touched Jack's hand back. Adder's fingers laced together with Jack's and held them.

It was such a small thing, a tiny contact, but it made Jack feel better. For the first time that day, the world stopped spinning and lurching out from under him. He pulled his hand away and got up out of bed. He stood up next to Adder on his bunk. He reached over and put his hand on the side of Adder's head, the way Adder had done to him one time before. He wasn't sure if Adder would let him continue or not, but he decided he had to see. He stroked the side of Adder's face, his fingers slipping through Adder's short, faintly graying hair.

Adder's eyes were closed and he was content to let Jack do whatever he felt.

Before Jack realized it was happening, Adder had reached out and ran his own hand through Jack's hair. Jack moved closer and let his hand wander down over Adder's face. He touched his nose, then his chin, then lips. Adder put his hand behind Jack's neck and pulled him a little closer. Jack leaned in towards the man he had feared so terribly for so long, and their lips met.

And they kissed. Slowly, lightly, and gently. The rest of the world froze in place and time stood still for this kiss. Since Jack had been here, time had stood still in many cruel ways, but for this one thing, time stood still and just let paradise happen.

For the first time since Chris Stambeki, Jack kissed another person.

When they pulled out of the kiss, Jack could barely see Adder's eyes sparkling. Adder rubbed the back of Jack's head and grinned at him. He sat up and jumped out of his bunk, his 260-pound body as silent and limber as a ten-year-old gymnast. He stood with his back to the cell door, and Jack watched his big frame silhouetted against the lights from the tier. Jack reached out and touched Adder's chest with the back of his finger, running it up and down. Adder took Jack's hand in both of his and pulled Jack closer.

Adder moved both hands to either side of Jack's head and leaned in to kiss him again. Their lips met, warm and soft. And promising something more. Adder put both arms around Jack, pulling him into his bare chest. He wrapped Jack up in the kiss and the embrace, and Jack felt safe for the first time that day, completely surrounded by Adder. Jack was where he had really wanted to be for a long time. The kiss got deeper and deeper and he felt Adder's hands roaming all up and down his back. Jack himself was pulling Adder as tightly against him as he could. He didn't want to ever let go.

But Adder pulled back out of the kiss while keeping his arms around Jack. Jack could see the smile on Adder's face in the dim light. Adder squatted down slightly and grabbed Jack around his middle and lifted him up off the ground in a tight bear hug, the huge smile on his face bright enough to light up the whole tier. Adder reached his head up and kissed Jack again while holding him in the air. He set Jack back down on the ground, and Jack had to laugh himself at how he was being thrown around like a rag doll. Jack reached out and touched Adder's face again. He grabbed Adder's hand and held it up to his mouth and kissed it.

Adder spun Jack around so that he faced away, wrapped his arms around Jack's chest and pulled him back into himself. He rested his chin on Jack's shoulder and held Jack like this and swayed side to side a little. His hands ran up and down Jack's chest as his lips traced light paths along the side of Jack's neck.

Adder let go and motioned for Jack to lie down on the lower bunk. Jack did and Adder knelt down next to Jack. He started to kiss all over Jack's body – Jack's arms, then his chest, then his legs, and finally his face – touching each spot delicately. Adder got up, placed himself over Jack, and lay down on top of him and kissed him deep and richly, their tongues twining together, their breaths shared between them. Jack felt like it was magic to have the full, massive weight of Adder on top of him.

They spent the rest of the night kissing and holding each other. They both let the fear and pain that had held them back dissolve to nothing, and the fire that had been held back was finally let loose. They made love, but it wasn't anything like the one-sided, mechanical sex they had had in the past. It was shared equally and nothing between them was forbidden any more.

Day 650 – Tuesday, January 1st, 2002

Jack sat down and dug into his breakfast with Hool, Bickers and the others. Everyone still had Troy's death on the top of their minds and they all continued talking about it almost non-stop. The tense air in the chow hall had rapidly died down from what it was like two days ago. The frantic buzz had all but evaporated and things were already back to normal, except for the Kennel, which itself was now far more focused on the dynamics of the power struggle than on Troy's death.

Turner said, "The guards are questioning a lot of the inmates about it. Are they going to interview everyone?"

Bickers said, "They're just interviewing the ones that weren't visible when Asshole died. Marcus talked to me yesterday, but Jack and I were in the library when it happened."

"I heard that it was a bottle of Jack Daniels, and that Troy smelled like he had drunk the entire bottle," said Hool. "Maybe it was a suicide after all. Is Marcus going to have an autopsy done?"

Bickers laughed. "Sounds to me like more paperwork for Marcus!"

Jack asked, "Did they ever figure out where the bottle of Jack Daniels came from?"

Turner said, "Troy has been getting drugs and shit into this prison for a long time. Runnion or Fredo could have gotten that bottle in and set Troy up."

Starting the day before, Jack was glad to hear that the general consensus was that either Runnion or Fredo had betrayed Troy to take over the Kennel. The idea of a suicide was still floating around, but most people weren't buying that one. Not for Troy, anyway.

Jack watched Wilson, who had been very quiet since Troy's death. He had been nervous acting, too. As sad as it was, while Troy was around, no one bothered Wilson that much, except Troy. Wilson had to be afraid of what would happen now that he was up for grabs. Jack knew that as soon as either Fredo or Runnion took over the Kennel for good, Wilson would go to the winner. Neither of those two would be any better for Wilson than Troy, though.

Turner started wondering out loud if maybe one of the guards killed Troy, maybe even Marcus himself.

Jack was only halfway listening at this point. He glanced over at Adder, who was sitting alone and finishing the last few bites of his breakfast. Adder had the same amount of empty space around him, the same invisible wall, as usual. Jack wanted to hear the latest news and theories about Troy, so he had sat with Wilson and the others, but he wished he was sitting with Adder now.

He and Adder had had two nights together now. Really together. After lights out, the nights had been magic, and the prison, Troy, and the past all faded to nothing while he was with Adder. Given what Jack had done just a few days ago, they would have been nightmarish horrors for him had it not been for Adder. Adder gave him the comfort and security that he couldn't have gotten from anyone else. It made the last two days bearable.

Adder had made it clear, though, yesterday morning that they needed to keep things the same during the day. Jack didn't care at this point, and he would have happily let the rest of the prison know about his and Adder's relationship. Adder obviously didn't want that, though, and Jack obliged. Jack assumed that he had his reasons for this. Probably Adder just didn't want the whole prison to think he was gay all of a sudden with him being this close to getting out. But the thought that maybe it was because Adder knew this was just a disposable, last minute fling before he got out of prison crossed Jack's mind also, and it troubled him. The thought of the hurt like what happened with Stambeki was always in the very back of Jack's mind. He focused on how Adder was with him when they were in the cell at night, and this is what kept Jack believing that it was worth more than just four days of convenient affection to Adder. Adder was tender and caring, and seemed as starved for the true intimacy as Jack was. Adder seemed so happy to be there with Jack, to touch and hold and kiss him – as happy as Jack was to be with him.

It was for only four days, but Jack wanted to be the one other thing that Adder could hold onto, could connect with, other than the ring and his troubled past.

As they were getting up from breakfast, Jack got close to Wilson and asked, "You've been really quiet. You holding up ok?"

Wilson nodded weakly.

"I would think that maybe you would have been happier about not having to deal with Troy anymore."

Wilson glanced behind him and said nervously, "I'm fine. I'll be fine."

"Will you talk to me? Can we go to the lounge area for a few minutes? Will you talk to me there?" asked Jack.

Wilson reluctantly nodded again.

They got to the lounge area and Jack picked up a deck of cards. He started dealing out the cards for a few hands of poker.

Jack said to Wilson, "You don't actually miss Troy, do you?"

Wilson looked at his cards for a second, embarrassed at being read so easily. "I know it's fucked up, but I do. Not that he was good to me or that I even liked having him around me. It's just that I knew what I would get with Troy. And no one else would bother me out of fear of pissing him off. Except Adder that one time. I can't really do anything to protect myself here. Troy was bad, but if you're drowning at sea, you'll cling to any lifeboat you can get, and dealing with rotten treatment from one person instead of a whole prison full is a fair trade."

Jack really felt awful for Wilson. The poor guy was completely powerless and helpless. He knew Wilson had no idea about any steps to take to make things better for himself.

Jack dealt another hand of cards.

"What do you think will happen to you now that Troy is gone?" Jack knew the answer to his question, but he wanted to know how Wilson saw his own situation.

"I don't know. I guess either Runnion or Fredo will take over the Kennel, and I'll go to whoever wins."

Jack pulled another two cards off the stack for his hand. "Yeah, I think you're right." Actually, Jack knew it looked like that right now while Runnion and Fredo weren't thinking that much about Wilson. But their fight for control of the Kennel could easily wind up dragging Wilson into it, with Wilson being the pawn getting the worst of it in their power play. That could be worse than simply being on the sidelines until a winner was declared. Jack wouldn't say that to Wilson, though, since it would just worry him that much more.

Jack said, more softly, "Why is it that you feel like you can only sit back and wait for other people to decide what happens to you?"

Wilson just said, "Huh?"

"You could take a more active part in finding a new person to put you under their protection."

Wilson immediately said, "Shit! That would totally piss off Runnion and Fredo!" Jack easily saw in Wilson's eyes how much he didn't want to piss off either of those guys.

"Yeah, but the point is that if you find the right person, they'd be able to protect you from those two. You want to find someone that could protect you, but who wouldn't treat you quite as bad as Fredo or Runnion would."

Wilson seemed nervous about the idea. "But I... who? How would I... I don't know anyone like that."

Before Jack could lead Wilson to the right answer, Wilson piped up and asked, "Do you mean... are you... are you talking about *you?*" The hopeful look Wilson was giving Jack was heartbreaking, but Jack had to stop from laughing out loud.

Instead, he shook his head and said, "You and I both know there's no way I could do that for you." Jack added with a smile, "But thanks for the vote of confidence, even if it would get both of us killed pretty fast."

Jack had already thought about one person that would be a good first choice and he laid it out for Wilson. "Do you know Dugger at all?"

"Quake's guy? You're thinking I should move over to the Brethren? They'd kill me!"

"No, no. They wouldn't," insisted Jack. "They don't see you as an enemy. It seems kinda inhuman, but you're a piece of property they can steal away. You'd actually be something of a feather in their cap. You haven't been around Dugger at all, but you know I have. Dugger's a decent guy. If you keep him happy, he'd have no reason to wail on you the way Troy used to. And Dugger actually smiles. God knows he puts up with my smart-ass comments and knows they're just jokes. But with Dugger, you'd have all of the Brethren looking out for you. I'd say looking out for you like they do Chica, but everybody knows Chica doesn't need anybody's help."

Wilson sat and thought about it some. Jack had put the cards aside for now since they had stopped looking at them. Finally, Wilson asked, "Do you really think Dugger would treat me better than Fredo or Runnion would?"

"Fredo and Runnion have the same mean streaks in them that Troy had. They'll be just as bad as Troy... probably worse just to establish their leadership. I wouldn't cross Dugger, but if you do right by him, I really think he'd do right by you."

For the first time, Wilson started to consider that there might be the tiniest chance he could get out from under the Kennel dogs. "Do you think Dugger would?"

Jack said, "Let me talk to him today out in the yard. If this is going to happen, it needs to happen fast before Fredo and Runnion settle their own score and set their sights back on you."

Jack asked Wilson, "Would you be happy with Dugger? I know you don't know him that well, but I give you my word he'd be much better to you than Fredo or Runnion would be. I know it might be scary to make this kind of a jump, but I won't do it if you wouldn't be happy with it. So would you be happy with Dugger?"

Wilson lit up, hope in his eyes for one of the few times Jack had ever seen it there. "Jesus, Jack, yes! If you think you could make this work, then yes!"

~~~~~

Right after lunch, Jack made his way out to the yard. Dugger would be out there with several of the Brethren, maybe playing basketball.

Dugger was there, but was just watching some of the others out on the court today.

Jack went up to him and said, "Hey! I need to talk to you!"

Dugger nodded at Jack, his bald head shining in the daylight. "'sup?"

Jack looked around to make sure no one was close enough to listen, and to make sure no one was really watching that much. He didn't even see Wilson out there right now, which was best.

Jack said, "Hey, have you ever thought of having your own personal piece of ass? On a regular basis? I mean, you are Quake's right hand. Don't you think you deserve that?"

Dugger smiled very big, his white teeth gleaming in the winter sunlight. "Are you finally offering up that lily white ass of yours to me, Carber?"

Jack shook his head and scratched at his neck indifferently. "Well, as interesting as it might be to get fucked by the only black man in the state of Georgia with a two inch dick, I wasn't talking about me."

Dugger let out a huge laugh. "When did you start pimpin'?"

Jack got serious, "C'mon Dugger, I'm not kidding around. You know who I'm talking about."

"Did Wilson ask you to come ask me?"

"No, actually he didn't. Wilson's a little bit of a leaf in the wind. He was pretty much going to let everyone else decide how his ass got divided up. I thought you deserved this, certainly more than Fredo or Runnion."

Dugger said slowly, "What makes you think I couldn't just take him if I wanted him?"

Jack almost wanted to punch Dugger for playing this stupid ego game. "Well, of course you could if you wanted. But why do that when you and Wilson could easily come to a mutual agreement?"

Dugger was silent, thinking about it.

Jack tried again, "Look, Wilson's a good guy and he's been treated really bad. He'd be good for you and look after your needs. It can't be easy watching Quake get it whenever he wants with Chica, while you've got nothing. In return, Wilson just wants to be protected and to not be beat up for no reason by his bone. You've got way more honor than Troy ever did, and Wilson would be glad to have you."

Dugger looked off a little and continued to think, obviously intrigued at the thought of this happening voluntarily.

Jack tried to sweeten the deal. "Plus, how great would it be for the Brethren to snatch Wilson away from under Runnion and Fredo's noses while they're fighting each other?"

Dugger laughed again. "And what do *you* want out of this?"

Jack deadpanned, "You're going to let me pop that black cherry of yours. That is, if Chica hasn't gotten to it first."

Dugger smiled and shook his head.

"Seriously," said Jack, "I ask for nothing and you are not in my debt for making this easy for you. If I were to ask for anything, it would be to simply treat Wilson with a little dignity. He's gone a long time without."

"You've definitely got me considering it. But I'll need a little time to really think about it."

Jack cautioned Dugger, "You know that at some point very soon, Fredo and Runnion will turn their attention back on Wilson. You need to move very soon if you want this to go smooth."

Dugger said, "I'll take one hour to consider it."

"I'll be around," replied Jack.

Jack went to go sit on the picnic table to see what happened. He looked back and saw Dugger heading back into the prison. Dugger would never admit it to Jack, but he was going in to ask Quake about taking on Wilson. Dugger wouldn't be able to make that decision alone, but wouldn't ever admit that to Jack, either.

Jack wanted to go find Wilson to tell him where things stood, but there wasn't much to tell yet, so he decided to wait. Instead, he watched Adder jogging around the yard. Adder was a pretty good runner, which was a little unusual for someone his size. After he finished, Jack knew Adder would go in to shower. Jack was always a little jealous of the fact that Adder could go take a shower alone whenever he wanted without having to fear being ambushed. Well, if the story he had heard was right, Adder *had* been ambushed in the shower before, but he didn't let that scare him off from showering whenever he wanted. Jack wished he could go take a shower with Adder. To be with Adder, pressed up against him under the warm water, would be like a dream.

Jack waited there on the picnic table, but it hadn't been ten minutes before he heard Dugger calling him from behind. He stood up and met Dugger halfway.

Dugger waited till Jack got to him and said, "Quake wants to talk to you."

Jack hadn't expected this. Suddenly he realized that this whole thing could be taken as a slight towards Quake.

Jack asked, "Does he want to talk to me in a good way, or a bad way?"

Dugger said blankly, "I don't know. He didn't say. He's in the TV lounge."

Jack asked, "Did I fuck up?"

"You'll have to ask Quake."

Jack started to get nervous, but went in to see Quake. In the TV lounge, there was Quake and Chica, several other Brethren members, and a couple of other inmates.

As soon as Jack walked in, Quake said from the sofa he was sitting on, "I need everyone to leave the lounge now. Jelly, make sure we're alone."

They all grumbled some, but got up and left. Chica stayed behind.

Quake said, "Chica, I need for you to leave, too."

Chica got up and warned Quake, "You'd better not fuck this cracker while I'm outta the room." As he passed Jack, he ran his hand up Jack's chest seductively while giving him a warning glance before walking out.

Jack waited on Quake. Quake sat there for a moment, arms stretched wide across the back of the sofa he was on, and he studied Jack with dark eyes.

Finally, he said, "Why did you go to Dugger with this offer? Why did you not come to me with it first?"

Jack had frantically thought about that very question all the way in.

"I probably should have. But you have Chica. You're Quake, and if you had wanted Wilson, you would already have Wilson. It was an assumption on my part. Perhaps a bad one. I did not intend any disrespect."

Quake actually smiled and laughed a little.

"Carber, you play this game very well!"

Jack smiled nervously. He wasn't sure where he stood with Quake at this point, so chose to keep quiet.

Quake said, the Creole accent woven in his voice, "Don't worry. Don't worry. It doesn't bother me that you went right to Dugger. I wouldn't take Troy's leftovers anyway."

Quake laughed again and said, "Besides, no one is smart that gets on Chica's bad side."

Jack laughed at this. Quake was actually joking around with him now. He was beginning to feel like he was on much safer ground.

Quake continued, "I am curious about the fact that you are putting Dugger and Wilson together, but want nothing in return. What do you get out of this?"

Jack said, "You know I'm friends with Wilson and have been since my first day here. Wilson's a good guy, and will be faithful to the Brethren. I've watched too much of the bad treatment he got from Troy for all the loyalty he showed him. That's all Wilson wants, is to feel safe. As for Dugger, he's a good guy, too. He would appreciate what Wilson could do for him. And I think all of the Brethren would like the embarrassment this would cause to the Kennel. Everyone that deserves to win would win in this deal."

Quake considered this. He said, "You realize you put yourself in danger by setting this up, do you? It will perhaps get around that you made this happen. The Kennel dogs will hate you for shaming them."

Jack had thought about this, too. It was possible the Kennel would hear how this happened, but it wasn't a given. And he was always in some kind of danger around them anyway. What difference was a little more?

Jack said, "Yeah, well... I can take care of myself, I guess."

Quake sat for another minute looking at Jack. Finally he said, "I will let Dugger take Wilson, if it is what Dugger wants."

Jack was instantly relieved.

Quake then added, "You are right, too, by the way. Dugger is an honorable person and will treat Wilson far better than Troy, Fredo, or Runnion. I am fortunate to have him in the Brethren. I think that, too, you are an honorable person, Carber. This is why you and Dugger get along well."

Quake finished with, "You don't have too much longer here at PattX. The Brethren will stay quiet on your involvement in this. If your involvement in this does get around, stick close to the Brethren and we will help look out for you. On your way out, would you let the others know they can come back in? And one last thing, I will explain my decision to Dugger, not you."

Jack said, "Of course" and left. He was amazed. That couldn't have possibly gone better. He had really taken a liking to Quake. Dugger was waiting outside the TV lounge, along with a few others.

Jack said, "Quake said everyone can go back in now." To Dugger, he said, "He wants to talk to you now. I'll be out in the pound."

Jack went back out to the yard and waited. Hool, Bickers, Wilson and Turner were in a group. Wilson was watching Jack to see if he could tell what was happening, but Jack wanted to wait a little longer, until Dugger came back out.

He watched Adder still running laps around the yard. For two years, he had watched how Adder focused on his mind and body. He worked out, ran, meditated, and did his morning ritual. He read encyclopedias. Adder only allowed himself about one or two hours of television a week. He couldn't wait until after dinner when he could be alone with Adder, even if it meant another day with him was almost over. There would be only two more.

A few minutes later, Quake and some of the Brethren members came out into the yard and walked over to the basketball court. Dugger came out, too, but he walked over to where Jack was.

Dugger was smiling. He said to Jack, "We're good. Tell Wilson to meet me in the TV lounge in a few minutes." And Dugger went back inside with one of the other Brethren members.

There were a fair number of Kennel guys out in the yard, so Jack started to go back inside. Wilson was still watching him, and Jack jerked his head at Wilson to tell him to follow him.

Once inside, Wilson followed a few seconds later. Jack said, "It's done."

Wilson nodded, but seemed nervous.

Jack put his hand on Wilson's arm and said, "Don't be nervous. Dugger's good. And this whole thing was personally approved by Quake. You're in very good hands now. Dugger wants you to meet him in the TV lounge in about ten minutes."

After Wilson left to wait before going to see Dugger, Jack went back to his cell and got his coffee mug, filled it up at the commissary, and went back out to the prison yard. He sat up on the picnic table and looked out at the trees and the clear sky. He had done a very good deed today. Wilson was still a little scared, and the Kennel would definitely get red-hot over this insult for a while, but their ability to do anything would be disjointed and uncoordinated given their own infighting. Jack hoped the Brethren would do a good job of protecting Wilson. He'd hate for Wilson to get seriously hurt at this point after trying to do all this specifically to protect him. Jack also hoped that his involvement in this was kept quiet. He'd hate for his own butt to be seriously hurt, too. But overall, Jack felt very good about what he had done.

Adder came out of the building a few minutes later, freshly showered. He walked over and sat up on the picnic table with Jack. Adder looked over at him, and gave him a tiny smile and the slightest wink. Jack wanted so bad to scoot over closer to him, to touch their legs together, but he fought off the urge to do so. It had become almost impossible for Jack to keep his hands off of him.

He gave Adder the thirty minutes he would want to close his eyes and meditate. Jack drank some of his coffee to keep warm, then lay back on the table and looked up at the sky. There was no fence, no guards, and no prison wall this way. Just the limitless sky and silent clouds, setting a steady tick of time with their slide across the blue heavens. Time seemed slow in moments like this, but the reality was that they were always over way too soon. He wondered how things were going between Dugger and Wilson right then. He wondered what went through Adder's mind when he was meditating. He wondered what went through Adder's mind all the time, actually.

Jack was still nervous about what would happen as a result of what he did to Troy. He still felt like he'd be found out, even if the general murmurs were focused on Runnion and Fredo. The huge wave of emotion he felt after finally giving in to his feelings for Adder almost overshadowed his fear, but the dread was still there, lurking in the back of his head. He sat up and looked out past the fence at the trees in the distance. There they were, teasing him as always. They never got any closer and Jack couldn't get any nearer to them.

When Adder was done, Jack told him of what he had done for Wilson and Dugger. He was expecting a smile from Adder for the good thing he had done. But by the time he had explained it, Adder looked alarmed and worried.

Jack asked, "You seem upset by this. Did I do a bad thing? Are you mad at me?"

Adder shook his head no. Adder looked around, found a Kennel guy and looked very pointedly at him. Then he looked at Jack and made a slicing motion across his neck and then pointed at Jack. Adder pointed at himself and held up two fingers.

Jack said, "I know it would piss off the Kennel if they found out I did this. And I know you're here only two more days. You don't need to worry, though. The Brethren is going to keep very quiet about my involvement, and after you're gone, Quake promised to have the Brethren keep an eye on me."

Adder gave Jack a sideways, skeptical look.

Jack laughed and said, "I know they won't look out for me the way you will, but I'll be fine. Besides, I can take care of myself."

Adder's eyes got real big.

Jack said in mock irritation, "Kiss my ass! I can, too!"

Adder let it drop, but didn't seem comfortable with where the situation stood.

A few minutes later, Jack heard Norrison coming up behind them.

Norrison was yelling at them from about twenty feet away, "Hey, Adder, I'm coming up, but it's just to tell you something about your release."

Jack thought it was funny that the guards, including Norrison, preferred not to sneak up on Adder, even when it was good news.

Norrison reached them and Adder just ignored him. Norrison said, "Hey, Carber."

Jack greeted him with a "Norrison."

"Adder, you're out day after tomorrow. Please wait in your cell after lunch, and we'll come get you to take you out. We'll take you to one of the prison administrators who will cash you out for the balance of your prison per diem. They'll explain to you how to get back into town if no one's going to come get you. And they'll explain to you about the halfway house if you need somewhere to stay for a while when you get out. You don't have any probation to deal with, so they'll skip all that. And you don't have to stay at the halfway house if you don't want to. Any questions?"

Adder sat there silently.

"Imagine that," said Norrison.

Jack asked, "How's the thing with Troy going?"

Norrison moved a little over to Jack's side of the table so he could talk to him, or maybe just to get a little farther away from Adder. He said, "Marcus officially closed the investigation this morning. It was a suicide."

Jack felt a wave of relief. He didn't realize just how big the weight on his shoulders was until just now when it had been lifted off. He said, "Really? That was a pretty fast investigation."

Norrison obviously thought so, too. He looked around to make sure no one was listening. He looked uncomfortably at Adder, who wasn't paying any attention at all, but then decided he wasn't going to repeat anything anyway.

"Of course it was fast, and of course it wasn't an investigation. Capt. Marcus is just wrapping this up to be done with it. The room had been wiped down of all prints. If Troy had committed suicide, why would the room be wiped down? Capt. Marcus just wants to be done with this, and deeming it a suicide is the easiest way."

Norrison looked genuinely aggravated that Capt. Marcus hadn't done any real police work. "This is the wrong way to handle this," he said. "Someone killed Troy, and by letting this slide this time, it makes it easier for someone to decide to try again later. Troy was no Mother Teresa, but he still deserved to have his killer found."

"But it's not my decision, is it?" The irritation wasn't even thinly concealed in his voice. Norrison turned around and headed back towards the prison building.

~~~~~

Jack sat in the cell after dinner with Adder, waiting for lights out. Dinner had been quite a scene. When Wilson came in and sat at the table right next to Dugger, the whole chow hall became deadly silent. Marcus and Jones called into their lapel radios immediately to have some backup ready in case it turned into a full riot.

The Kennel tables did suddenly burst into a lot of yelling at the Brethren, and two of them even jumped at their table. They started fighting, but the guards ended that pretty quickly. Quake didn't seem too ruffled. Jack had watched Fredo and Runnion closely during this. They were obviously very angry about this, but they didn't dare join in. They just sat and stewed over Wilson. Neither of them could afford to be thrown into the tank right now if they were going to gain control of the Kennel. Right after the guards hauled off the ones that had been fighting, Fredo and Runnion both just got up and left. They gave Dugger and Wilson scathing looks on the way out. The whole chow hall buzzed after that.

Jack had tried to read something to pass the time before lights out, but it was impossible. Finding out that Troy's death was officially ruled a suicide, helping to put Wilson in a safer place, and knowing that he was about to be all over Adder made reading impossible.

Adder had been reading the encyclopedia, but Jack had noticed he wasn't turning pages at his usual rate. He knew Adder must be thinking about something. Adder eventually put the book up and stood up.

He made Jack stand up in front of his bunk.

Jack said, "What's up?"

Adder scratched his head for a second. He put his hands on both of Jack's shoulders and head-butted Jack. Not a real head-butt, but a fake one. Then Adder took his knee and pretended to knee Jack in the balls. And finally he took his hands, put them around Jack's throat and pretended to choke Jack.

Jack actually laughed. He asked him, "What the hell are you doing?"

Adder looked right into Jack's eyes, then got down on one knee in front of Jack and looked at the floor.

Jack said, "Oh!" because he understood what Adder was saying. Then he said "oh" again as it sank in.

Jack squatted down to be on the same level with Adder. He said, "Look, Adder, you don't have to apologize for those things. I know that if you could probably take them back, you would. It was scary early on, but things turned out good. I obviously don't hold any of that against you."

Jack stood back up and so did Adder. Adder did the pretend head-butt thing again and pointed at Jack, then at his own head.

Jack laughed again and said, "I'm not going to head-butt you. I'd probably just wind up knocking myself out cold in the process. You forget that I slugged you good that one night. Maybe we should call it even."

Adder smiled at this. All Jack could think was *would the fucking lights please go out?*

And then the smile faded from Jack's own face. He had an admission of his own to make. He'd be keeping something secret from Adder if he didn't confess.

He said, "Hey, Adder. Look, I have something of my own I need to get off my chest that affects you. It might affect how you feel about me. God Almighty, I hope it doesn't, but being honest with you is more important."

Adder was watching him very curiously.

Jack licked his lips nervously and said, "I know that William is William Samms. I know that he came to visit you the day you were arrested after the botched bank robbery. And I know that he was murdered later that day."

Adder's eyes got really big and he leaned forward a little bit, disbelieving that Jack knew all of this.

Jack quickly added, "But that's all I know. I don't know anything more about your relationship with William, other than what I might guess."

Adder's brow furrowed a little bit.

"When you lost the ring, I had a burning curiosity about William," admitted Jack. "I hacked into one of the guards' accounts on the PC in the library and found the record of William's visit to you in jail, and then found a newspaper story about his death that same day. That's all there was, though. I wasn't trying to be sneaky, and I wasn't trying to get the goods on you. I probably shouldn't have done it. I'm sorry I did it. I just didn't want to keep this from you."

The lights on the tier blinked out. Jack stood there waiting for some sort of reaction from Adder. Adder just stood for a moment, considering what Jack had just said.

Adder finally took a couple of steps over in the dim light to where Jack was and put both hands on his shoulders. Jack asked, "You're not going to head-butt me, are you?"

Adder smiled and pulled Jack into a gentle hug. He held Jack and kissed his forehead.

Jack put his arms around Adder and said, "I guess this means I'm ok."

Day 652 – Thursday, January 3rd, 2002

Jack woke with a start, but as soon as he moved, two thick arms pulled tightly around him, holding him close, reassuringly. Adder was sitting up in Jack's bunk, and Jack relaxed back against his chest again, cradled in his arms. They had stayed up all night trying to stretch time out as much as possible. Jack had fallen asleep at some point, and time had slipped away from him. Now it was gone before he realized he was losing it.

Jack could tell from the light coming in the windows across the tier that daylight was breaking, but it was still early. He pulled up against Adder's arms and whispered over his shoulder, "I'll get up so you can do your routine."

Adder held onto him tight, though. Jack looked back up at Adder's face only to see a serious expression as he shook his head "no" at Jack. This would be the last few moments of time that they would have to themselves. This would be the last chance they had to really say goodbye. Jack dreaded the fast approaching moment the cells would open for the morning count.

He sat up in his bunk and leaned against the cell wall. He put Adder's legs in his lap and ran his hands up and down them. Jack looked over at the snake tattoo wrapped around Adder's waist. He had gotten to know that tattoo so well over the last few days. He reached over and touched it and traced his finger along the snake.

They stayed like this as long as they could. Finally, Jack got off the bunk and knelt down next to Adder. He put his hand to the side of Adder's face and said, "You have no idea how much I'm going to miss you."

Adder stood up and pulled Jack to his feet. He pulled Jack into a kiss, probably the last one they would get to have. Jack felt Adder's mouth against his, felt his tongue and the unshaven roughness of his face against his own.

When the cell doors clanged open, Adder pulled away, and they parted for good.

Jack knew this moment would come, but he felt very empty inside anyway.

~ ~ ~ ~ ~

Upstairs, Jack loaded a pile of shirts into one of the washers and moved another load into a dryer. He wished he could have stayed with Adder throughout the entire morning. He had spent breakfast with him, but then he had to come work the laundry right after that.

He spent the whole morning thinking about Adder and how it would soon be all over. He thought about the new life that Adder was going to have to make for himself. He thought about the price he had paid to buy Adder's safety outside. Jack's father came to mind as well. Would his father have been happy to know what Jack had had with Adder, even if it was really only for a few days? Would his father have been disappointed in Jack to know he had held off as long as he did?

He also thought about some of the things that Norrison had said about how hard it would be for Adder on the outside. He thought about what a person in prison for fifteen years would have to face outside. He thought about how unused to everything Adder would be, having really only TV, newspapers, and magazines to expose you to the world. It must be scary, but Adder wasn't letting any of it show.

As he thought about Adder, Jack arrived at a decision.

He grabbed one of the laundry order pads that they used for the contract service that picked up the sheets and towels. He tore a page from it and wrote down a note for Adder.

It was a special note that he wrote, and he sighed heavily as he read it over when he was done. It was the final failure of the Jack that had come into the prison, but he didn't need any part of that Jack anymore. He looked over what he wrote one last time. It might help Adder some, or it might guarantee that he never saw Adder again, maybe both. No matter what, Jack felt like his father would have been proud.

He took the page and folded it, carefully and intricately. When he was done, Jack held up a perfect origami snake.

~~~~~

Jack and Adder both ate lunch in silence, Jack no longer sure what to say and everything he thought about saying seemed stupid and pointless. When they finished, Jack went back to the cell to wait with him. He had no idea exactly when the guards would come to release Adder, so he had no idea how much time they had left together.

He sat on his bunk, leaning against the wall, and Adder was in the desk chair facing towards him. After a moment, Jack got up and went over to Adder. He squatted down next to him and handed him the origami snake.

"It's a small gift. Kinda stupid, actually. It's just a snake. Just promise me two things, don't let anyone take this from you, and open it up only after you're totally out of this place. Will you promise me?"

Adder looked at Jack and nodded solemnly. He held the snake gently in his open palm, turning it over to study it.

Jack stood back up, glanced outside the cell, and leaned over and gave Adder a quick, stolen kiss on the forehead. He flopped back down on his bunk and they waited once again in silence.

Jack sat and watched Adder, and Adder sat and watched Jack. All they could have at this point was to be in the same room together, but that was good enough for the both of them.

~~~~~

Even with expecting them, Jack was startled when Capt. Marcus and Harper showed up to get Adder.

Marcus said in irritation, "Well, well, well. It's the moment none of us ever thought would arrive. In a little bit, Adder, you'll be the boil on the outside world's ass instead of mine."

Capt. Marcus glanced at Jack and said, "Is this all the going away party you could scrounge together, Adder? You'd think after fifteen years you would have made more friends."

"Ok then, no trouble now, Adder," said Capt. Marcus. " You realize you're getting out, so don't fuck it up and start being an issue here at the end. The Taser's charged up and ready to go and I got no qualms about using it. Now c'mon!"

Jack and Adder both stood up. But Adder, rather than go to the cell door to leave with Marcus and Harper, crossed the cell to the bunk. He grabbed one of the pillows off of his top bunk and threw it at Jack, who caught it against his chest. Jack clutched the pillow in surprise. Adder, facing towards Jack and away from the guards, gave a sly smile and winked at Jack. Then he turned to leave.

Jack grinned and said, "Oh, you're a funny guy, all right."

Adder was already outside the cell, following behind Capt. Marcus and Harper. At the very last second, just before he was beyond the cell, he glanced back one last time at Jack.

And then he was gone.

The mid-afternoon came to a screeching halt. Jack looked around the cell and thought to himself that he'd never have Adder sneaking up on him in here again. He hugged tightly the pillow Adder had thrown at him. The same pillow he had taken from Adder on his first day at PattX. All that was left was the pillow and the final breaths Adder had left behind in the cell.

Jack wanted to cry, and laugh some, and crawl into the corner, all at the same time. The difference between Adder being there with Jack and being gone was just a sliver of time, but it felt like a huge gulf. He already missed Adder, and it hurt, but he knew that what had happened between them had been a good thing, even if that was all there was. Jack was happy to have had the few days together at the end that they did get to share. He wished Adder all the luck in the world as he was now pushed out into it.

Tuesday, November 25th, 1986

Addison lay back on the bench in the jail cell. It had been two hours since it had all gone sour, but he was still pumped from the adrenaline. It had subsided some, but the rush was definitely still there. It felt like some of the old highs he used to get when he did coke. When he got out of here, it would be hard to not go right back to the same old tricks that put him in this cell today. He definitely would put it behind him, though, for Will. This was the last of these kinds of antics, no matter how exhilarating the danger was, or how much he was able to embarrass his father.

There would be a price to pay for everything that had happened today, though. Will would be furious, for one, mostly because he'd be so worried about Addison. He wouldn't be mad for long, though, when Addison gave him the ring to show him how serious he was. Maybe he'd do it in front of his father, if he could keep them in the room together at the same time. His father might just have a heart attack right there in front of the two of them. The other price was the guilt that he genuinely felt over the security guard. Shooting the old guy in the leg was totally unnecessary, but also totally an accident. The guard at the bank had pulled that gun out of the drawer after Addison had taken away the one he carried, and it took him by surprise. He hoped the guard would wind up being fine, and maybe have a cool story to tell his grandkids.

Addison smiled to himself at how ridiculously bad things had gone. Shooting the guard in the leg, losing most of the money he had stuffed in a bag on the way out, carjacking someone and finding out there was still another passenger in it as he drove off, and then crashing into a light pole when trying to avoid an oncoming police car. He had tried to tell the guy in the car not to worry, he was trying to get a couple of blocks away and then he'd be out of his hair, but the guy was white as a sheet and didn't seem to hear anything Addison had said to him.

He had a hard time feeling bad about how wrong things had gone. Even having had the strong feeling earlier to not hit the bank didn't bring him down. Before he went, he knew he shouldn't do it, really *knew*, but went ahead and robbed it anyway. It was all just a rush and he knew it would make his father lose sleep for weeks and weeks, and he'd still get off pretty lightly in the end.

Addison knew he'd have to get a little more time from Paulson to deliver the money he promised. Then he'd be out from under Paulson's thumb once and for all and he and Will could finally just go away to anywhere Will wanted and start over. A nice, quiet life... the way Will wanted to live it.

He took the ring out of his shoe and flipped it over in his hand. Addison was glad he had been able to hide it long enough so they didn't find it when the cops took all of his personal belongings from him during booking. He would do anything in the world for Will, but all Will wanted was for Addison to quit the crime, to stop trying to get back at his father, to finally focus on his own life and his own happiness. Will's insight was one of the things that Addison loved the most about him. He could cut through the bullshit and see things at the basic level. Addison had been committing crimes for years, knocking over convenience stores, stealing cars (including from his own father's dealerships), burglary, and others, but it wasn't until Will pointed it out to him that he realized that the only reason he did any of it was so that his father would be embarrassed and angry. Addison hadn't realized just how much he loved rubbing his father's face in his failure at producing a "good" son.

Will had freaked out some when he found out that the "coordinating deliveries" that Addison did for a living were transferring drugs and that "facilitating financial deals" meant robbing jewelry and convenience stores. They got into a pretty big fight over it and Will said Addison should never have kept that from him. Addison said he warned Will early on even if he didn't go into all the details. But Will already loved Addison at that point, and Addison reassured him that he had never hurt anyone doing it, and he'd never hurt Will, ever. Will was able to accept this. Will already knew that underneath it all, underneath the roughneck image and crimes and fighting and guns, Addison was a good-hearted person. Addison was just driven by the wrong motivations. Will knew he'd never meet anyone else like Addison, for sure. For his part, Addison knew for the first time that someone saw deeper into him than anyone else had, saw the person he really was, and was happy to have him for what he was. Will liked Addison for Addison, and not for some reflection of his own vanities. It was a watershed realization for Addison. The fact that Will still accepted him for who he was made him want to change. He would, in all ways, become the person Will saw deep inside him. And the best part was that the things that he'd change were only the irrelevant things, the things that already felt like weights around his neck anyway.

Finally, the thought that his life could be different, that there was someone he could really share it with, had taken hold of him and made him feel like he could fly. They knew that what they had together was bigger than the mess that this day had become, and that they would get past it.

And for Will, Addison was going to shift his life around entirely. He would live his life out of love for Will, and no longer out of anger at his father. He had to put some effort into getting Will to understand that he had a few outstanding commitments that he had to fulfill to some dangerous people, and then it would be done. He'd walk away from everything his life had been about with no regrets, all for Will.

And the ring was to show Will how serious he was about this. He had it inscribed with the words "William, I promise – Addy" on the inside as a permanent reminder. The outside of the ring had a serpentine design. Will had always been fascinated by the snake tattoo around Addison's waist, and the ring was a certain nod to that.

Addison's thoughts about all this were interrupted by the black guy in the holding cell with him. There was another white guy, too, but he looked scared to death and stayed huddled in the far corner. The black guy had come over to the bench Addison was stretched out on and said, "You need to sit your honky ass up so someone else can sit down."

Addison looked at him sideways. The black guy was looming over him, threateningly. Addison didn't threaten particularly easy, though, and he could fight when he needed to.

Addison said to the black guy, barely concerned, "Sit on the floor."

This made the guy mad. He scowled and said, "I wasn't *asking* you, asshole."

Addison remained laying in place obstinately. He looked right through the black guy, unconcerned, and said, "I don't give a shit."

The black guy pulled back and punched down at Addison's face hard. Addison expected it, however, and deflected it some with his arm. Instead of hitting Addison in the chin, though, the black guy's fist connected with Addison's lip and split it open.

Addison actually laughed a little, and jumped up. Suddenly, his full six foot five frame bore down on the black guy. Addison clumsily sandwiched the black guy between himself and the bars to the holding cell. What Addison lacked in grace he made up in sheer force. Before the black guy knew what was happening, Addison grabbed his throat and pulled back with his other arm and punched him in the forehead. The black guy's head snapped back and banged into the iron bar directly behind it. He sank down to the floor and made a vague "unnghhh..." sound. The black guy hadn't been knocked out, but Addison had knocked him silly.

He said, "You know where to find me if you want some more," and spat a mixture of spit and his own blood on the black guy's shirt. He sat back down on the bench and wiped some of the blood off his mouth and chin. His fist hurt like hell from where he had hit the guy.

The other guy tried to crawl even further into the far corner, white as a sheet. His mouth was hanging open slightly and he was making a strange little scared noise. Addison looked over at him, which caused the guy to flinch in fear and to try to get even farther away. Addison said, "Christ! What's your problem? *That* guy's the asshole!"

A few minutes later, a guard came to get Addison to go see his father. The guard asked him where the blood came from. Addison replied innocently that he had bitten his lip, he was so very afraid for his life in this place.

The guard took him to a small meeting room where his father was waiting, standing rigidly next to a table. His father was tall, too, but not as tall as Addison. He had neat, carefully cut, dark hair that had turned mostly gray at this point. He was trim and was wearing an expensive pinstripe suit.

Addison strode in, wiped some more blood off his mouth and sat down on the table. His lower face was smeared with it and it was drying onto his forearm, too, now. He said, "Hi, pops!" brightly. Addison loved making his father twist.

His father frowned as he stared at his son. The guard left, and Addison waited, giving his father time to get a good look at him and the blood all over his shirt and face.

His father finally said, in a burning whisper, "Christ, Addison, what the hell is wrong with you?! A bank robbery? Shooting a guard?"

Addison smiled and said, "Aww, pops, you know I didn't do any of that! It's all a misunderstandin'. I was raised too right to do that kind of stuff."

His father stood there a moment longer. Addison ate up every minute he could watch his father seethe like this. He knew his father would rant and rave a little bit, but in the end, he'd send his lawyers in to minimize this as much as possible. There were lots of things that Blakely Tyler loved more than Addison, and chief among those was his reputation among the people of Macon. His father would spend all sorts of money to protect his own reputation, which would force him to help Addison so it could all be swept under the rug. Addison was able to rub his father's nose in all sorts of things he had done knowing his father would never let it get out.

His father said, "I've stood by you through all of your terrible behavior. I've done everything a parent with resources could possibly do to help you become a respected member of this community, like me. But now you've sunk to a new low, even for you. And two days before Thanksgiving, too. You've ruined everyone's holiday. Your mother's heart is broken. She'll go to an early grave probably because of you."

Then his father spat at Addison, "I wish I wasn't your father!"

Addison wanted to laugh. His father had said that to try and hurt him. But he had wished for that very same thing as well, with all of his heart, for almost all of his life.

Addison opened his mouth to make a smart ass comment back, but the door opened again. The guard came back in and said, "This guy's here to see you, too."

William came into the room, looking very upset. Addison lit up and felt even happier as he exclaimed, "Will!!" The guard left and closed the door, and Addison rushed over and pushed William against the wall and started to kiss him deeply, right on the lips.

William pushed back on Addison and said, "What the hell?! You're getting blood all on me!"

Addison had forgotten about that. He said, "Ooh shit, I am! Sorry!" and stood back looking at Will, a big, dopey grin plastered on his face.

Addison's father looked absolutely disgusted – it was a well-practiced look for the man. It wasn't the first time he had seen this offensive display from Addison and William. Addison flaunted this in front of his father as often as he could. Especially with William. Especially another man. Addison's father spat, "Even in here, throwing that perverted, sick behavior around!"

Addison said, "Well, pops, I try to keep it in places like this, with no windows, so no one finds out your son is a faggot. Thank heaven for small favors, huh?"

William looked uncomfortably between the two men. He said, "I didn't realize your father was here. I should leave so you can talk to him."

Addison's father looked down his nose at him and said, "Don't bother. I was just leaving. I have no desire to be around... this." He gestured loosely at Addison and William to indicate his distaste.

"If it weren't for my position in this city, I'd not bother helping you at all," he said, fully focusing back on his son. "Don't say anything at all until the lawyers get here." And his father, clearly having had enough, turned and walked out the door.

Addison smiled now that he was able to focus entirely on William. He tried to pull William to him, but he was having none of it. He pushed back on Addison's shoulders like he often did and kept Addison at arm's length. He said, "Addy, are you ok? What happened to you? You're covered in blood!"

Addison laughed and said, "I'm fine! Just some punk in the holding cell asking for a little trouble."

William reached over to Addison's face to wipe away a little blood left behind. Addison grabbed William's hand and held it tenderly against his face. William said with a frantic, worried, and increasingly irritated voice, "Why the hell are you smiling? You're in a lot of trouble, with the police *and* with me!! It was on the news, Addy!! The news! The bank robbery, the guard, the carjacking!! You're in serious trouble this time!"

Addison sensed the change and turned more serious. It *was* way worse than the last time, but his father's lawyers were really good, and his father had pull with several judges in town. He said, "My dad's got really good lawyers. I'm not worried."

Will frowned and said, "They won't help you with me."

Addison turned very serious now. "Yeah, I know you're mad. You know I didn't mean for any of this to happen this way. I'm sorry, Willy! I really am. But I swear to you we're almost past all this. I promised you to get out of this life and I hold that promise sacred. Look!" Addison pulled the ring out of his pocket and gave it to Will.

"That's how serious I take this, Will. How serious I am about you!" Addison reached out and put his hand gently on the side of William's face, cradling his ear.

Will turned it over and over and looked at it. He read the inscription inside, and the irritation in his face softened some. But then his brow furrowed and he pushed Addison away again. He punched Addison in the shoulder as hard as he could, which wasn't very hard, and said, "You son of a bitch! Don't you give me something like this, promising to get out of crime, on the very same day I have to come see you in prison for a bank robbery and shooting someone!"

Will handed the ring back to Addison angrily.

Addison looked like a scolded child. "Will, please, I really mean this! Today just got a little out of hand. It'll all blow over soon. I want you to have this! It means a lot to me. Please?"

Will stood back from Addison and said, "Addy, I love you so much. But I'm not taking that ring until I really see you taking me, and us, a little more seriously. It's past time for you to grow up, Addison. You can't be frozen in time, digging your nails into your dad's skin all your life."

Addison's head hung. "I'm sorry. I know you don't like being around him."

"No! I don't like being around *you* when you're around him!" snapped Will. "You change! You're not the same person around him! I'm just something you use against your dad when we're both around!"

Addison's head dropped even farther. "No, Will! I love you! I really love you!" he said, trying to convince Will even as he knew Will was right.

Will said, his voice now touched with sadness, "Yeah, Addy, you do. But that doesn't mean you're not using me to get at your dad."

And with that, Will wheeled around and left. Addison stood there for a moment. That hadn't gone the way he wanted at all, and for the first time, he truly considered the day to be a disaster. He stared blankly at the ring still in his hand, but then he had to stuff it back into his pocket just as the guard came to take him back to the cell.

~~~~~

Later that evening, the guard came back to get Addison out of the holding cell again. He told Addison that his lawyers had arrived to meet with him. Addison hoped they'd have him out of there soon so he could go tell William once again how sorry he was, and that he did take their relationship seriously. Plus he was going to need to get a little more time from Paulson.

When the guard got him to the small meeting room, someone else was still in there and he couldn't find Addison's lawyers. The guard took him over to the processing area where there were several desks and policemen. He handcuffed Addison to a bench to wait for the room to open up and so he could go look for the lawyers.

Addison sat and waited, ignoring the TV up on the wall tuned to the news and the two or three other people that had been freshly arrested and were being processed at the desks. Addison still felt bad that Will was so concerned about what had happened. He regretted trying to hit the bank now. He should have just hit two or three convenience stores instead. He would have gotten the same amount of money and the risk would have been less. He should have listened to the voice that had told him not to do it.

But then something caught Addison's attention. He looked up at the TV and the newscast. They had mentioned an address that Addison recognized. Police had been called to the address because neighbors heard gunshots earlier that afternoon. When the police arrived, they found the resident, a victim of a home invasion, shot in the back of the head in the bedroom. The victim had been identified as William Samms, originally from Marietta, Georgia.

Addison's blood ran cold and he felt like the person on TV must have been speaking a different language. It sounded like William had been killed. It couldn't be. But it was William's address. Then the realization hit Addison. It was Paulson. Paulson had gotten tired of waiting for Addison to pay off what he owed. He had somehow found out about him and Will, and Will had become the punishment for screwing today up.

Addison sat handcuffed to the bench, his mouth hanging open in disbelief. The police and other people in the room moved around like nothing had happened. But for Addison, time had stopped right on the words from the TV, "identified as William Samms."

Addison thought, he was just here, standing right in front of me. He was fine then. But a few hours later he was dead, shot in the back of the head execution style. The shock froze Addison's heart. William hadn't taken the ring, and now he was dead. He was dead because of Addison's screw-up. Sweet, innocent, naïve, harmless, lovable William had been ruthlessly killed. The one and only thing in his life that brought him any happiness, that connected him to a better life, had had his head almost blown off. The only person that ever really cared about Addison.

Addison wished he had listened to that voice that told him not to hit the bank. He had felt dead certain he shouldn't attempt this particular hold-up and he had ignored the feeling. Addison whispered to himself as the breath drained out of him, "What have I done?"

And then he shut down. He withdrew into himself and shut the rest of the world out. Whatever happened outside of him didn't matter anymore. Paulson, the police, his father, the trouble he was in… nothing mattered at all. Those few words of his own guilt were the last ones that would escape his mouth.

Day 686 – Wednesday, February 6th, 2002

Jack sat on the picnic table and looked out past the fence at the barren trees in the distance. The sky was an even gray no matter where he looked. There was a sharp wind whipping around and changing directions randomly.

He looked at the trees and turned the broken bottle piece over and over in his hands where he held it down between his knees. He felt the sharp point and edge against his fingers. He felt empty inside, nothing at all, just hollowness and echoes and distance. He knew he should go inside and wash his hands off, but he didn't feel any rush to do this. He finally did pull his eyes away from the trees in the distance and looked at the piece of bottle. The bottle and his hands were covered in blood, already thick and sticky in the cold air.

He turned and looked back over his shoulder, across the prison yard, but there was no one else outside. It was only Jack and the whipping wind.

He looked down at the body lying next to him on the picnic table. The face was partially covered with a shirt soaked in blood. Blood had run off the body, dripped off the picnic table, and pooled on the cold dirt below. He reached over and lifted up the shirt by the corner and pulled it off the body. The person under the shirt was covered with a fine, fuzzy layer of frost, spreading over the cheeks and nose, the blue lips... even the eyelashes. Even the blood had crystallized into tiny scarlet flakes of ice on the face, neck and body. It was Jack's own body, his own empty and frozen eyes staring straight up, the side of his own neck all gashed in.

He looked away from the body and down at himself and realized he had no shirt on. He looked at his chest. On the right side was a gruesome tattoo of the skin pulled back and pinned in place, showing the grisly, bloody red muscle underneath. At that same moment, Jack's body next to him made a strange, choked, gurgling noise.

Jack bolted upright in the dark. He put his hand on the wall next to him to steady himself and felt the cold sweat all over him. His heart was pounding and he had to fight to slow his fast and shallow breathing down. He wiped his arm across his forehead and took slow, patient breaths. Out in the tier, only the sparse light of the middle of the night came into the cell from the walkways.

He had learned to hate this dream. When his mind was elsewhere, time would sneak him back to the murder and make him relive it. Worse, it would vary it in odd ways. It delighted in dragging Jack back to that particular, terrible moment. Why couldn't it take him back to any of the last four nights he had had with Adder? Why couldn't he relive those over and over? Why did it always pull him back to the murder?

Adder had kept these dreams away. Even immediately after the murder, when it was still fresh in his mind and he was terrified of what he had done and terrified of being caught, terrified of what he had turned into, he spent the nights with Adder and Adder had kept him firmly there with him so that the dreams didn't trouble him.

He pulled the covers back and swung off the top bunk, which squeaked as he did so. He stepped onto the lower bunk, then the ground below. How did Adder manage to get in and out of the top bunk every time without a sound? It squeaked every time Jack did it.

The guy in the lower bunk rolled over irritably and complained, "Jesus, Carber."

Jack walked over to the sink and said matter-of-factly, "Shut it, Wheezer."

He ran some water from the tap and splashed some on his face. He wiped it off with the towel, then dried the cold sweat off his chest and arms.

He pulled the chair from the desk up to the bars to the cell and sat down in it. Jack looked across the tier at the frosted windows, dark in the middle of the night.

Wheezer was obviously a light sleeper and woke up every time Jack got down from the bunk in the middle of the night, which was a lot more often than either of them wished. Wheezer might have otherwise been a bad inmate to piss off, but he had joined up in the Brethren pretty quickly after arriving at PattX a few weeks earlier. And that meant that he was told to leave Jack alone. So, he didn't have to worry about Wheezer.

Hooking Dugger up with Wilson had been the right thing to do. Dugger had treated Wilson well, and this opened Wilson's eyes up to just how bad Troy had been. Wilson, in return, would do anything to keep Dugger happy. Dugger had helped to ensure that the Brethren looked out for Jack.

When Wilson got snagged by Dugger right out from under the Kennel's nose, it had definitely brought things to a head between Fredo and Runnion. A lot of people got thrown in the tank for the fights that broke out, and finally Fredo managed to get Runnion in the wrong place at the wrong time. Runnion had just gotten out of the hospital two days ago and had lost the use of his left hand entirely. He had been in very bad shape when they rushed him out to an offsite hospital and Fredo had established his control of the Kennel.

The Brethren kept a very close eye on Wilson, and the Kennel made several attempts to get at him, but none worked.

Wheezer had wanted to know what it was that made Quake want to protect Jack's "saltine cracker ass." Jack had just said that it was between him and Quake.

Wilson was much happier, and told Jack over and over how much he owed him for helping him. It wasn't just setting him up with Dugger, it was everything Jack had done over the last couple of years.

Jack was glad it worked out well for Wilson. But in addition to that, Jack had found himself in a good place with Dugger and didn't have to go it totally solo at PattX as a result. The whole thing with Troy had evaporated, and was almost forgotten now among the guards and the inmates. The rest of Jack's time at PattX should be, for the most part, a breeze.

But Jack felt hollow and alone. He knew why, of course.

He missed Adder. He missed him every moment of every day. He missed sitting out on the picnic table with him. He missed the way Adder would tap him in the chest affectionately with his fist. He missed how, those last few nights, Adder would lie on top of him kissing him and biting at his neck, Adder's weight totally covering him and grinding against him. He missed the snake tattoo. He missed that devilish smile. Shit, how he missed that magnificent smile.

Jack could hear Wheezer breathing regularly and thought how he would just wake him up again when he went to get back up in his bunk.

He wondered where Adder was. Was he still in some halfway house? Had he found a place of his own? Had he just skipped out and gone as far away from here as he could, disappearing forever? Had he already moved on and started to forget Jack? Did he think of Jack very much? At all? Had he really stayed straight, or had he gone back to crime? Had he tried to get a job somewhere? What kind of job could Adder even get?

Jack leaned forward in the chair and grabbed the bars with both hands and rested his forehead on them. Outside the frosted windows across the tier, it was the middle of the night.

He wished he could sit outside and look at the stars. Jack wished that, wherever Adder was, he could be with him, and they could sit outside and look at the stars together.

Day 754 – Monday, April 15th, 2002

Jack fidgeted some and waited. He had waited for this for over two years now, so a few moments more weren't important, no matter how important they felt. He stood and waited at the last set of bars between him and his freedom, and as soon as the prison administrator reviewed the paperwork with the guard controlling the door, it would open. Norrison was with him, to escort him out of the front door of the prison. But despite that, Jack was nervous that something would be wrong at the last moment, that it would be all a mistake, and they'd haul him back inside for the last year of his sentence after all.

Despite his thoughts, he was nervous about getting out, too. He was as nervous now as when he first arrived at PattX. His hands were cold and clammy, but he waited patiently. He wanted to think that what made him nervous was simply that he had a life ahead of him to rebuild from scratch. Nervous that he had to build an *honest* life and that he wasn't sure how to do that.

But Jack wasn't really kidding himself. He knew that, in reality, what made him nervous was Adder. That's really what had turned his mouth into dry canvas, his tongue into burlap. He had hoped and fantasized since the day Adder got out that he would be waiting there for Jack on the day of his own release. He wanted it, and he was scared of what would happen to him if Adder wasn't there. And now he was at the moment of finding out if this was Stambeki all over again or not. Of course he was nervous.

The final set of bars clanged open and Norrison put his hand on Jack's shoulder amiably and led him through. He walked with Norrison up through the lobby area to the front door.

They stopped and Norrison clapped his hand on Jack's shoulder a couple of times. He said, "Take care, Jack. And good luck."

Jack nodded silently and pushed open the door and walked out.

He blinked in the bright sun and looked around. There was the front walkway that led over to a small visitor parking lot. There was a set of trim bushes surrounding a couple of flagpoles with flags for the U. S. and the state of Georgia. And it was obvious there was no Adder. Jack immediately felt a stabbing pang of disappointment.

He looked around again, just in case. But, no. No Adder.

There was still a chance, though. They had told Jack that if no one was picking him up, that he would need to walk to the road and wait for a bus to town across the street, and they gave him a voucher for it along with the cash out from his books for the work he had done in the laundry, plus the prison per diem. And there was a business card for his probation officer that he had to see once a week.

He started to walk down the prison drive towards the street, which was about two hundred yards away around a bend. In contrast to the trampled dirt that was the prison yard he had stalked for the last two years, the front drive of PattX was flanked by sprawling, green lawns and well-maintained landscaping. He pulled at the sleeve of his t-shirt, which was tighter on him in the arms and shoulders than the day he had been arrested.

He tried very hard to stop from getting his hopes up. He did what he could to quash the daydream of seeing Adder standing there, waiting for him. It was a stubborn daydream, though.

Instead, he tried to think of what he would need to do to eventually get a job, how long he'd have to stay in the halfway house, what kind of job he could get, where would he go after his probation finished, etc.

Adder kept creeping back into his mind, though. Was what happened the last four days with Adder just an illusion? Was it just a mirage that Jack saw, but not Adder? Was it all just as one-sided as everything between them before that, and Jack was only seeing what he wanted to see? He knew that maybe he had sabotaged his own chance of having Adder show up to meet him by giving him the note before he left. It was the perfect out for Adder if he wanted to skip town. But Jack also knew that if that's how it turned out, his life was completely reset back to a zero and he would have to start over from there. He would be at rock bottom and he could start climbing back up from there. Adder had just felt so completely, all-consumingly right that to have lost him forever would be a tough pain to heal. He thought about the snake on Adder's waist, biting its own tail. It was so easy to become your own worst enemy.

He glanced back at the prison as he walked along the drive. He could see the wing that he knew was his own on the left side. He could now see the other side of the frosted, barred windows that he spent two years looking at from the inside.

He stopped for a moment, his feet too heavy to move, and suddenly wondering if maybe the best thing that had ever happened to him was only his for four days, and was back behind him, behind those windows. How was he supposed to move forward with that thought in his head? How was he going to deal with it if that was the truth? That Stambekis were all he was ever going to have?

He eventually forced one foot in front of the other and got to the bend in the prison drive, and about another thirty yards beyond it was the road. There was a polite sign saying "Patterson Correctional Facility" on a low brick wall next to the entrance, and across the street from that was what looked like a cross between a junkyard and a car repair shop. Parked in front was a huge black pickup truck, splattered with mud and with dual snorkels rising up right behind the back corners of the cab. To the right of that was a dusty, worn-down gas station with some rough wooden benches that looked like they had last been painted twenty years ago. Next to the benches was a bus stop sign that leaned to one side. Jack could see an old, redneck man inside the gas station through the dirty windows. An older black lady with large hips was coming out of the gas station with a Coke can in her hands and started to amble her way across the street and up the prison drive, probably to see a family member.

Jack stared at the benches next to the bus-stop sign. They were empty.

And so Jack hit bottom. No one else was around. He stood dumbly at the end of the drive and looked at the vacant benches. He didn't really have the will to go sit on them. He really wanted to sit down on the side of the road where he was and never move again, stuck in limbo between prison and life outside, slowly decaying away to nothing. He had thought about what he would do if Adder wasn't there, but it still crushed him.

And in the back of his mind, he heard laughing. His chest closed in on him and he began to have trouble breathing because he heard Troy laughing at him. "You got nothing, Carber!" said the amused dead man's voice in his head. "Nothing and no one! All you got is me kicking you in the nuts, boy, and that's all you'll ever have." And with a mock sympathetic tone, it said, "Stop fighting it, Carber... just let it happen. You can't fight me, shithead!"

Jack stood without moving for a long moment, letting Troy twist the knife in him. He turned back, facing PattX. He could go back, bang on the door. Demand to be let back in. Admit to what he did to Troy. He could give up the rest of his life and... and... what? Let Troy win? He turned back to the street again. It didn't matter. Troy and Stambeki won, no matter if he went back to PattX or got on the bus.

The breeze kicked up some dust over at the repair place, which danced and swirled down the road away from Jack. He eventually forced his foot forward a step to make himself just go sit and wait on the bench.

Just as he did so, he looked up. A person wearing blue jeans, a white t-shirt, and a black baseball cap was coming around the corner of the gas station. He was looking down and wiping his wet hands on the front of his jeans. It was a big guy. The guy looked up and saw Jack on the other side of the road. He froze for one second, and then a huge smile broke through his black goatee. But Jack knew that smile anywhere. It was the sun breaking through the thick clouds of a thunderstorm for him. He felt like he had just been jolted back to life with a defibrillator.

Jack wanted to cry and laugh at the same time. He ran across the street to Adder, and Adder almost knocked him over running to meet him. Adder grabbed him in his arms and squeezed Jack like a boa constrictor, squeezing him for every ounce of his life. Jack wouldn't have traded the feeling for anything in the world.

He felt Adder's cheek against his, the black goatee now streaked with gray against his own face. Adder finally let go and held Jack at arm's length to look at him, then pulled him back and gave him a big smack of a kiss on the lips, then held Jack back again to make sure it was really him. Then he pulled Jack back into a softer, deeper kiss. Their mouths open wide and tongues trading places, Adder's arms wrapped around Jack's neck. And in the next instant, Adder had pulled his face back to lock his eyes with Jack's. Adder couldn't seem to decide between kissing Jack and looking at him to make sure he was really there.

Jack noticed that Adder's eyes were watering up just a little. Jack found his own eyes doing the same thing. He knew absolutely for sure that Adder was his this time. The ghost of Stambeki had been totally run off the instant Adder had come around the corner from the gas station bathroom. And Troy could rot in hell.

Adder pulled Jack back into another smothering, desperate hug, his face up against Jack's ear, tickling it. And then the one thing Jack hadn't even thought to consider happened. Something miraculous happened.

"Thank God you're alright!"

It was no more than a whisper in Jack's ear, but it felt like the entire planet had suddenly shifted off its axis.

Jack's entire body jerked and he did start crying this time.

He said through his choked tears, "Huh? Did... was that... did you just say something?"

Adder smiled and kissed him full on the lips again, then he put his whiskered mouth up to Jack's ear again. The words that came to Jack were soft and gentle, but they caused goosebumps to break out all over him. "I said, 'I love you more than anything in this world, Jack Carber!'"

Jack was struck totally dumb. For two years, he had not heard a single word of out Adder, and he knew that there hadn't been one for thirteen years even before that. To hear words from him now, suddenly, was transformational.

Adder said, "You ok?"

Jack still was finding it almost impossible to take in everything that had just happened. He couldn't contain it and felt like he was going to explode all over the side of the road.

Jack looked into Adder's eyes and could barely babble through his tears, "I'm... I... Jesus! Adder, I don't know what I would've done if you hadn't been here. I really..." But Jack broke up again and couldn't say anything else.

Adder pulled him back into his chest and rubbed his back and said, "Shhh... It's ok. I *am* here. And you're never gonna get rid of me ever again, even if it means I gotta lock you up just for myself."

Jack laughed at this despite all the emotions surging through him. He felt better after having heard Adder make a joke and laughing at it.

They sat down on the bench, and suddenly Jack had a million and one questions to ask him, but they were all tripping over one another and he couldn't pin one down long enough to actually ask it.

Jack finally asked the most obvious one, which wasn't even a question, "You're talking now."

"Yeah, it was time. I paid my fifteen years' dues to the state of Georgia for what I did, and fifteen years of my own punishment for what I let happen to Will. For a long time, I didn't think I'd ever really forgive myself, and maybe I won't ever really forgive myself. But somewhere along the way, I got me a reason to let go of the past." Adder had grabbed Jack's hand and was stroking the back of it gently. He said to him, "I thank God for you, Jack. I did my time, to society and to myself. It's time to move on."

It was so strange to hear Adder actually speak. Jack had never really even imagined what Adder's voice would be like, but now that he heard it, it wasn't quite what he was expecting. It was a little deeper, but shallower, too. Adder had a touch of a southern, country accent. It all made Jack think of the woods and crisp leaves and autumn evenings.

Adder asked him, "Are you ok? Did anyone inside hurt you after I left?"

"No. No. I was fine. Dugger and the Brethren kept an eye on me."

Adder looked down at Jack's hand in his, still worried and relieved at the same time. "I worried so much. After Will, to have somethin' happen to you…"

Jack said, "Well, I can take pretty good care of myself, you know. I'm not totally helpless."

Adder smirked and said sarcastically, "Uh-huh."

Jack laughed. "I can, too! I clocked you a good one that one night. Not many other people at PattX could have gotten away with that!"

"Well, you're right about that." The stupid grin never left Adder's face and he continued, "That night you decked me. I couldn't tell if you were the stupidest or bravest man in PattX."

Adder ran a hand through Jack's hair. "I went with bravest. I was so proud of you for that."

Jack looked down at Adder's hand and noticed the ring on his pinky. He said, "You don't have to hide it anymore."

"I don't have to hide it anymore," repeated Adder.

The bus pulled up, and they both got on it and sat near the back. There was only a handful of other people on it.

Jack asked, "Are you at the halfway house? Can we stay together there?"

"No, I've got a place for you and me. I don't know what I would have done without you, Jack. The note saved me. I only used a little of the money, but it kept me from being desperate after getting out."

Jack thought about the note he had given to Adder, folded up as a snake. The instructions for getting to the last bit of money Jack had in the hidden account. Jack had given Adder a passport to anywhere he wanted to go, to just take the money and run, but Adder had chosen to wait for Jack. He felt like it would have been worth ten times that amount of money to feel like he did right now.

Adder said gently, "I know why you gave me the money, knowing I could take it and disappear."

Jack didn't say anything. Adder ran his hand over Jack's head again. His eyes swept across Jack's face, studying him. He said, "I'm here, and you've got your answer. I'd be here even if it had been a million dollars."

Jack put his hand on Adder's leg and almost felt foolish for having doubted for a moment that he would be there waiting on him today. Adder was every bit as sharp as Jack had thought he was.

Adder grinned at Jack sideways and pulled at his t-shirt a little. "The t-shirt looks good on you," he said. "But I can't wait to get you back and take it off."

Jack started to ask other questions. About William. About Adder's crimes. About his parents. About all his time in prison. But Adder told Jack he'd rather wait until they got back to a more private place to get into those things.

So Jack told Adder about what happened with Runnion, and Fredo taking over the Kennel. About how much better off Wilson was with Dugger. About taking the top bunk and the motherfucker squeaking all the time.

And Adder told Jack about what he had been doing since he got out. The halfway house until he could find an apartment. Having to pay months' worth of rent in advance since he had no ID, no bank account, nothing.

The bus arrived in downtown Atlanta, and then another bus took them to the southside to where Adder had rented the apartment. By the time they got into Adder's apartment, Jack hardly even noticed what the place was like, other than it had a real bed in it. With a real mattress, and big enough for both him and Adder together. He was too busy taking Adder's shirt off and pulling at his pants to bother with irrelevant details.

As Jack was frantically trying to undress the both of them, Adder was trying to explain what he had to do to get the little bit of furniture that was in there, but Jack shoved him down onto the bed and said through a lopsided grin, "Christ, Adder, don't you ever fucking shut up?"

And Adder did shut up, and laughed. And Jack attacked him like a man just out of prison.

They spent several hours really saying hello to each other, and then they talked. Adder had bought a CD player for Jack as a present, and even a new Bonnie Raitt CD to play in it. Jack was amazed that Adder had remembered that detail. They played the CD and talked, and touched, and felt so glad to be together.

Jack found out everything about Adder. Adder's father, the perverse "conversion" therapy, his rebellion into crime, and William. Jack asked all about Adder's prison time, how he learned to fight the way he did, his choice to punish and isolate himself by never speaking, by never allowing himself to connect to anything or anyone. Adder explained everything to him. He learned about how Adder meditated every day, thinking about how his rebellion against his father had wound up costing him William, the best thing that ever happened to him. How he became his own worst enemy.

Adder said, "I spent years and years pulled so deeply into myself that it was like I was sleepwalking. Nothing seemed real except the pain. I picked almost every fight I could, hoping. I was hoping I'd pick the wrong fight and get put outta my misery. But it never happened, and the rage felt good, too, but it never lessened. Not until I found one guy that I finally felt like I could trust myself around again. That kinda made me want to." He ran his finger down the bridge of Jack's nose. "For the first time since I got put away, I had something other than rage and emptiness."

Jack talked about Father Anthony, and how that was how he got the pot and Jack Daniels. And for the first time, Jack told Adder the full story of how he met Stambeki, and how he had been betrayed so painfully. Adder finally understood why Jack seemed to care so much about him, but still kept him at an arm's distance until the last few days.

Jack told him, "I never did thank you for that day you attacked Troy and Fredo. I probably would have gotten seriously hurt if you hadn't jumped on them first."

"Really?" said Adder. "I wasn't sure why and it all happened fast, but I knew I needed to head them off hard. It was the right thing. I'm glad I did. I only had a strong feeling like that once before in my life, and I ignored it. I wasn't going to make that mistake again." Adder glanced down at the ring on his little finger.

At the end of letting it all out, Jack was sitting up in bed with Adder close up against him, Adder's arm over Jack's stomach. They had been quiet for a few minutes, finally having exhausted almost all of the past. The Bonnie Raitt CD had repeated back to the beginning and was playing again.

Jack knew it was time to give up his last secret.

"I, uh…" The words tried to catch in his throat like sandspurs. "It was me. I killed Troy." He looked down at his hands like he wasn't sure who they belonged to.

Adder was silent for a moment, but he didn't seem surprised. He eventually said, "I know. I knew it was you almost as soon as you had done it. I heard someone mention the day after it had happened that it was a broken Jack Daniels bottle, and I thought about how you acted the day it happened. I knew it was you."

Jack asked, "It doesn't bother you that I killed him in cold blood? It didn't bother you then?"

Adder rubbed around on Jack's stomach and said, "No, Jack. You're not a killer. I don't know why you went and did it, but I knew you probably had your reasons. And any reason good enough for you is good enough for me."

"It was for you. Troy wanted to get you. He couldn't get to you easily at PattX, so he was going to have people get you once you got out. I was there when he had the idea, and I had a chance to stop it before it got any further. I can't believe I did it, Adder. I feel like I crossed a line in my life that I can never cross back over. I believe Troy would have arranged to have you killed or seriously hurt. The guy had no human soul at all."

Adder sat in silence and considered this for a long while. He squeezed Jack a little harder and held onto him a little tighter.

Jack told him the full story of how it happened. But right when he got to the gurgling sound coming from Troy's throat, the panic rose in Jack. The memory of the murder rushed back on him and time wanted to pull him back to that moment yet again. His voice cracked, and the pain and fear of what he had done washed over him again and choked him. "Jesus, Adder, I'm not a murderer! I didn't want to kill him, but I did! I just wanted you to be safe! I killed another person in cold blood! What was I supposed to do? What am I going to do?!"

Adder sat up and pulled Jack to him, wrapping his arms around him. He said, "Shhh... shhh... It's ok, let it out. Just let it out. I won't let it drown you." He rocked him until the weight lifted off of Jack again.

Jack wiped his eyes and sniffed once. He said, "I'd do it again, though. I'd do anything to protect you."

Adder said, "You didn't do anything that shouldn't have been done long before. Even Marcus knew better than to waste his time investigating Troy's death."

Jack took Adder's hand and held it in his own. He looked at the ring on Adder's little finger, out in the open finally. Adder looked at it, too, and whispered to Jack, "You and Will were the only two people ever in my whole life that cared about me for myself. Even my own parents put me through hell to make me something other than what I was. And no one, not even Will, ever did things to protect me and look after me the way you have."

~~~~~

Both Jack and Adder eventually got hungry and Adder insisted that he take Jack out to get a steak on his first day free. Jack didn't care just as long as he was with Adder. Adder took him to a steak place he had found not too far away from the apartment. It wasn't a palace – the chairs were a little gimpy and the red-and-white checkered vinyl tablecloths had seen healthier days – but that just meant the food was good enough for the place to stay in business despite its shabbiness. There were all kinds of country junk on the walls, from lassos, to boots and spurs, to a huge set of mounted steer horns. There was a cross section of people in there eating, drinking and talking; some older people, several families, a table with men from an office with their khaki pants and polo shirts on.

Adder ordered himself and Jack a round of Jack Daniels, straight up. He held his glass up to Jack and said, "Here's to gettin' drunk with the people that matter."

The food was definitely much better than what PattX served for dinner. Jack was a little surprised at how comfortable he was back out in the free world. It was almost like he had never left.

Over their steaks, he asked Adder how the adjustment to outside life after fifteen years had been for him.

"I wasn't used to it, that's for sure. I felt lost and wasn't really sure what to do with myself. I'd been on such a routine in prison that I was lost without it on the outside. I had a hard time gettin' used to strange people being near me, things that would have made me bristle in prison, but I had to tolerate it here. I'm just now gettin' used to the idea that just because someone's walking up behind me doesn't mean I can haul off and pop the shit out of 'em. It's been tough. I've spent a lot of time alone in the apartment just to not have to deal with it. Plus, it was just lonely. I wanted to come see you, but I wouldn't risk what might happen to you if people found out you and I were close that way. I was already worried enough about you."

Adder placed his knife and fork back down and stared at his plate for a moment. He said to Jack, slowly and carefully, "I need to make sure of one thing. I know I'm done with my old ways, my bad ways. I need to know that you're done, too. It's important for you to be done, to never go back to that life. Things won't be right for you if you do go back to all that. Please, Jack... tell me you're done."

Jack could sense that the question was very serious for Adder. For the only time he could remember, he noticed Adder had turned a little pale and seemed to be nervous about how Jack would answer. Jack got the uncanny feeling that everything hung on his answer to Adder. But Jack was able to answer honestly, "I'm done. Absolutely. For you and for my father, I'm done. And you've got my word on that."

Jack could see the genuine relief in Adder's face at hearing the words coming out of his mouth. Adder said, "Well, that just leaves one other thing for us to figure out."

"What's that?"

"What to tell our grandkids," said Adder with a happy grin. "Telling them we first met when I raped you in prison might be kinda awkward."

Jack almost choked on his Jack Daniels, which made Adder laugh at him. It was a deep and full laugh, and his eyes sparkled at Jack.

Adder reached over the table and touched Jack's arm, stroking it without a thought. He said softly, "I owe you everything, you know. Even more than my life."

Jack could see the sincerity and devotion in Adder's blue eyes. Jack nodded his head and said, "Everything, big or small, that I did was worth it. Every chance I took, no matter how scared I was, was worth it. You were there waiting today, and that made all of it worth it."

~~~~~

Adder wanted to walk back to the apartment after dinner. It was a cool spring night with a little bit of a breeze. It was dark out and the sky was very clear. They passed a small park on the way back and Adder stopped.

"Show me a few stars," said Adder.

"Now?"

"Sure! Why not? We can do whatever we want now."

Jack looked up and realized that, for the first time in over two years, he was able to see the night sky. They went into the park and sat up on top of a picnic table in the far corner of the park, where it was darker. Jack put his arm around Adder's wide shoulders and said, "You don't know how many times at PattX I wished I could do this."

Jack showed Adder the Big Dipper and the North Star, the seven sisters of Pleiades, Leo, Bootsie the Flamingo, and some of the others he could see in the spring sky. They were all so huge and immense and complicated and hanging right there over them. It made the earth, all of its problems, all of its joys, all its betrayals and victories, all of the people on it, seem small and insignificant. Jack remembered the nights like this with his father, and felt the same awe and wonder at the night sky that he felt so many years ago. Jack was the one being shown the stars then, and now Jack could pass that moment on to someone else.

It was heaven for Jack. Just sitting there with Adder, the stars glittering overhead, the warmth of Adder's body next to his, was all he could ever hope for. He knew now what his dad had wanted for him, and he had gotten it. He wished his dad could be there with the two of them. Jack felt more at home than any time since his dad had passed away.

And for once, time took pity on Jack and slowed down. The stars in the sky moved imperceptibly slowly across the sky and Jack knew for one of the few times in his life what it was to be happy in the moment. It was all so huge and immense and complicated, and warm and complete and simple, and held in a single point in time. Jack and Adder sat outside, free men, and enjoyed the night, thankful for each other, thankful for clear spring nights, and thankful that time could slow down every once in a while.

Day 755 – Tuesday, April 16th, 2002 – Epilogue

Jack walked up and down among the grave markers. He idly looked at the names and dates on the stones, all with no meaning for Jack, but meaning for someone somewhere.

His thoughts naturally drifted back to memories of his parents. Of everything they had been through. Everything his father had sacrificed to protect Jack, to make sure Jack knew he was loved above and beyond anyone else. And like looking up at the stars the night before, this was also something he'd pass on to Adder, who had had only an all-too-brief experience with it. Now that they had a different kind of time together, Jack would make sure Adder felt that same love every day.

He spent ten or fifteen minutes wandering slowly. The sky was clearing up from the rain shower that had swung through earlier. The clouds were moving rapidly across the sky, and Jack could smell the dampness on the grass and on the marble and granite markers.

Eventually, he made his way back over to where he had started, but he didn't get too close. He could see Adder several rows over kneeling on the damp ground, his head bent low. The grave Adder knelt at was a little unkempt and forgotten looking. Jack wondered how long had it been since anyone had come to visit it.

He turned and walked back away a few feet to give Adder his space. This moment wasn't meant for Jack. It was between Adder and

William. Jack had been the one to suggest it, and he had remembered where William was buried from the story he had read online, but this time was for William and Adder, even after all the years that separated them.

He looked out across the cemetery and thought about his own parents again. Jack thought about the pain his father must have endured after losing mom. Some pains were razor sharp and as cold as ice, and a person would do almost anything to avoid them. And other pains were warm and deep, and a person would never regret them for even a moment. Jack knew both.

He heard the faintest sound behind him and felt Adder's arms wrap around him, Adder's chin coming to rest gently on his shoulder. Jack put his hands over Adder's and they stood still for a moment.

Adder said in Jack's ear, softly, "Thank you for this. I didn't realize how badly I needed to say goodbye to Will. I owed him this, even fifteen years late."

Jack turned and looked at him. His blue eyes were still a little red and damp. Jack looked at the little bit of gray at Adder's temples and sprinkled in his beard. For Adder, time had stopped for fifteen years, but now, finally, he was allowed to move on. Jack pounded his fist lightly on Adder's chest a couple of times.

He turned to start walking, but Adder grabbed his hand and stopped him.

Adder said, "Wait, Jack... before we leave." His eyes were threatening to water up again.

Jack stopped and Adder got down on both his knees in the wet grass in front of him. Adder removed the ring off of his little finger, and took Jack's hand and put it on his finger instead.

Jack started to resist and said, "Adder, this ring is William's. I'm not William."

But Adder held Jack's hand tight and kept the ring there. He said, "No, but I can't give you any more of me than this ring. This ring has held my soul for fifteen years. It's everything that I am, and it's yours."

Jack lifted his hand and looked at the ring on it. He touched his hand to Adder's face and Adder closed his eyes. Jack took Adder's hand and had him stand up.

Adder smiled at Jack and together they walked towards the cemetery fence and the trees on the other side.

~~~ The End ~~~

Falling Off The Face Of The Earth

After his big-shot life in New York tragically falls apart, James Montgomery returns to his small hometown in south Georgia a defeated and broken man. All he has left is his mother to help him heal and regain his confidence before he's ready to get back out and re-conquer the world.

But being big-city gay in a small southern town has its own challenges. In addition to coming to grips with what happened in New York, his hometown of Lawder throws its own curveballs at him. James is confronted with a bitter enemy from his school days, and frustratingly can't seem to avoid the guy. His mother suddenly wants to expand the family. The one guy James takes a liking to and starts dating has a lot of hang-ups about being gay. And he watches almost helplessly as a new young bully starts to repeat the kind of abuse he suffered during his own school days.

Here where he grew up, the one place he should feel safe, James feels maddeningly off-balance. He starts to think that maybe going home was a bad idea after all. Maybe he'd be better off moving on and really starting over, completely from scratch. Maybe he should walk away from Lawder, just like he walked away from his life in New York.

But maybe, if he'd give it a chance, he'd re-think everything he ever thought he wanted out of life. And maybe what he thought was important, isn't so important after all. Maybe he could have everything he never realized he wanted, if he just looked around himself for a moment.

Latakia

Matthew likes his life in Richmond. He has his friends and his softball and his volunteer work. And he has a very good-looking boyfriend, Brian, who he's been happily dating for over a year now. So what if his friends tend to question just how good his boyfriend is, and so what if Brian tends to have inexplicable mood swings. And so what if Brian seems to invite Matt's suspicions on occasion. If he just shows a little faith and trust, he'll appreciate what he has with Brian the way he should. Right?

But suddenly, Matt finds himself in a desperate life-or-death situation on a trip overseas, and he realizes just how much he misses home, and Brian. He's luckily rescued by a team of US Special Operations Forces, only to immediately find out they're a bunch of bigoted jerks. Worse, a quirk of his situation forces him to spend time with them that he'd rather not. And that's when he finds out that first impressions can be misleading. When called upon, he steps up when every fiber of his being tells him not to, and discovers something deep inside himself that he didn't realize was even there. And his life will never be the same. He finds that he can, after all, make some very overdue changes in his own life.

What Matt doesn't realize is that the bond of brotherhood runs both ways. And he winds up changing the lives of several of the men on that SpecOps team as much as they changed his.

All it takes is faith and trust.

The Sticks (A Short Story)

Percy's given up. He's given up and wants to be as far away as possible from the place that has been the source of his troubles all his life. But to his disappointment, he finds himself in the last place he expected. And a chance encounter with a redneck and a stubborn hound dog aren't helping, either. That is... until they do.

Invincibility can be found in the strangest places.

The Last Day Of Summer

Rett's done some running away in his life, from family and from boyfriends, and he's not above doing it again. His current boyfriend wants to take their relationship to the next level, which makes Rett hesitant and doubtful. Luckily, a job offer in a new town solves his problem for him, giving him the perfect excuse to run away yet again from the uncomfortable feeling of someone trying to get close to him, even if it means picking up after seven years of school and starting over.

Most guys would kill for his new job, and Rett's certainly desperate for the paycheck. But the irony of the new position isn't lost on him — he's never cared a whole lot for sports, and even far less about the world of professional sports, which is right where he's landed. Then he finds out he's not the only one that's new to pro sports, and he gets closer and closer to one of the players as they try to make sense of the whole crazy thing together. And things seem good!

But when his family, whom he had long since left behind, shows back up with a family crisis, his life starts to unwind and Rett allows everything around him to painfully self-destruct. It's only then that he realizes he's got to get back up, stand his ground, and teach himself the one thing he never truly learned growing up.

He's got to stop running away and finally learn what it really means to be a man.

Photo credit: C. J. Harris

About The Author

The author, when not writing, spends his time cleaning up litter along the shoulders of Highway 82 outside of Tuscaloosa, Alabama, per the court orders. Coincidentally, the author has some advice to give his readers. If you wind up selling pot, even just a little bit, to someone you don't realize is a superior court judge in Alabama, make sure you have some evidence HE approached YOU. Because, otherwise, you're going to get stuck with "consequences" and that asshole judge won't get anything.

If you so desire, you may contact JF Smith at:
jfsmithstories@gmail.com
www.facebook.com/jfsmithstories

Made in the USA
Lexington, KY
23 March 2014